CONVERSION

ALSO BY MITCHELL HOGAN

THE NECROMANCER'S KEY
Incursion
Corruption
Subversion

THE SORCERY ASCENDANT SEQUENCE
A Crucible of Souls
Blood of Innocents
A Shattered Empire
At the Sign of the Crow and Moon—novella
The Last Arrow—short story

THE INFERNAL GUARDIAN
Shadow of the Exile
Dawn of the Exile

THE TAINTED CABAL
Revenant Winds
Tower of the Forgotten—novella
A Goddess Scorned—novella

SCIENCE FICTION
Inquisitor

CONVERSION

THE NECROMANCER'S KEY: BOOK FOUR

MITCHELL HOGAN

CONVERSION

Published by Mitchell Hogan

Copyright © 2021 by Mitchell Hogan

First Printing, 2021

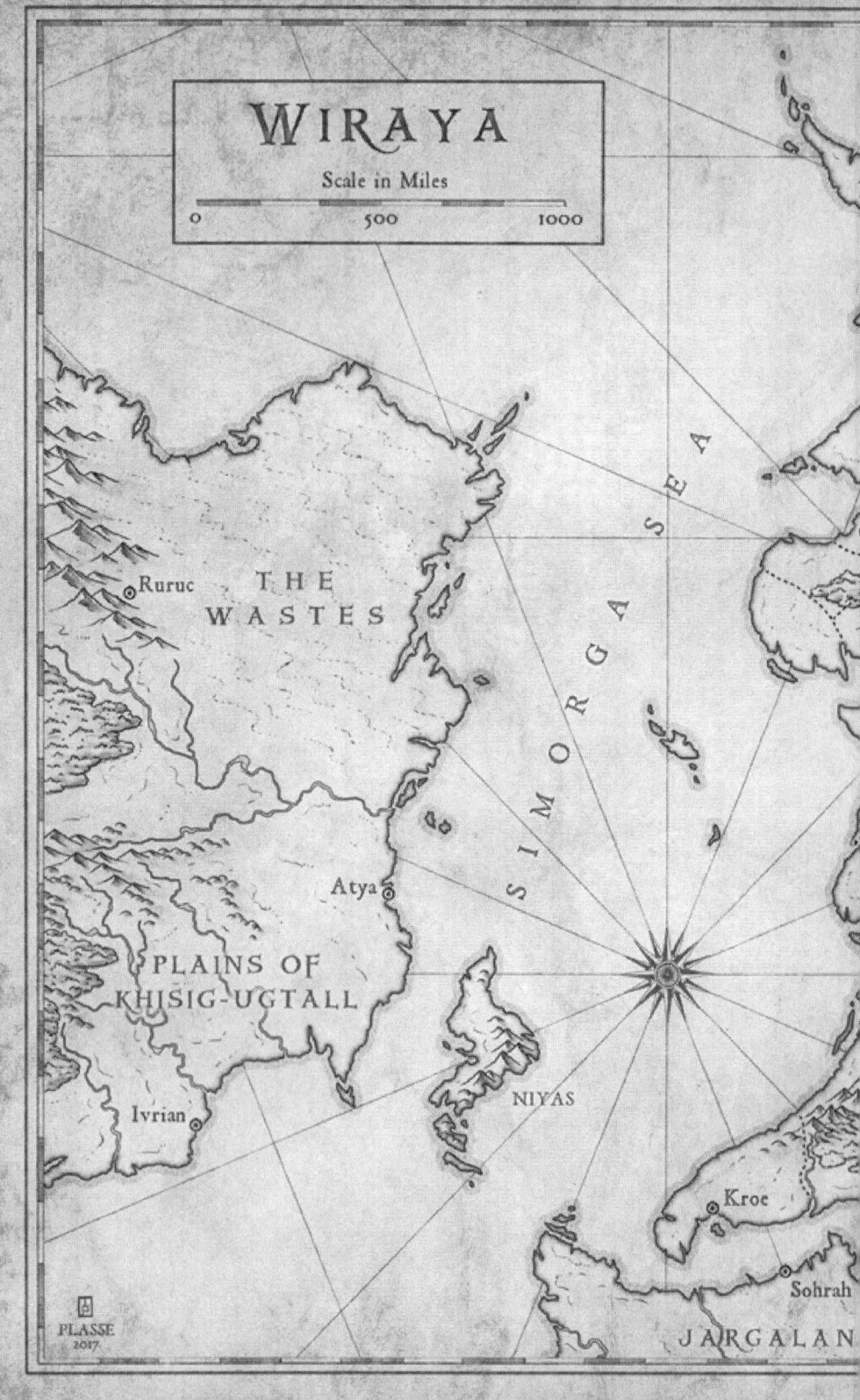

WHAT'S GONE BEFORE

NECROMANCY BEGAN ON THE island of Niyas, when the peoples of Wiraya were little more than savages roaming the wilderness. The dawn-and dusk-tides were already known, but Niyandrian sorcerers discovered the corrupted tidal forces absorbed into the earth. They grew obsessed with the earth-tide's promise of immortality and with the secrets of the dead.

When Queen Talia of Niyas sought to raise her people to eternal life, the powerful countries of the mainland conspired to put an end to her rule. Allied armies invaded Niyas. Battles were fought with steel and sorcery. Thousands died. Cities fell. And, at last, the mainland allies, led by the Order of Eternal Vigilance, prevailed. Queen Talia died when her capital, Naphor, fell, and Niyas was placed under mainland occupation.

But there were rumors of a child: the heir to Niyas, the daughter of Talia, the Necromancer Queen. In secret, a guardian was appointed to protect the heir.

BOOK ONE: INCURSION

Carred Selenas, Captain of the Last Cohort and Queen Talia's former lover, leads the resistance against the foreign invaders as they await the return of the Necromancer Queen and the reemergence of the Niyandrian people and culture. But it has been years since Talia died, and her people are losing heart. With one failure after another, Carred's resolve crumbles, but duty keeps her searching for the lost heir—the symbol all Niyandrians could rally behind and the key to Queen Talia's return from the dead.

Anskar DeVantte has been raised in the sacred disciplines of the Order of Eternal Vigilance, the military arm of the Church of Menselas, God of Five Aspects, his entire life. Born with the mark of sorcery and the ability to manipulate the dawn-tide, Anskar must endure the Order's brutal initiation trials if he is to become a consecrated knight. Against the Order's rules, he assists a Niyandrian postulant, Sareya, with the sword she is forging for the second trial, and they become lovers.

The blind sorcerer Luzius Landav arrives with his assistant, a dwarf woman named Malady. Landav brings the trainees crystal catalysts that will enable them to draw upon the dawn-tide for their protective sorceries. Landav senses Anskar also has a dusk-tide repository and, more disturbingly, can also store the dark-tide.

Using their catalysts, the trainee knights imbue the blades they forged during the trials with strengthening cants using the dawn-tide. Anskar names his sword *Amalantril* ("Moontouched") after Sareya's Niyandrian name.

Anskar, Orix, and Sareya are among the seven trainees to pass the trials and are raised to the interim rank of knight-liminal. The Seneschal, Vihtor Ulnar, declares he will take Anskar under his wing.

Anskar questions Vihtor about his past and his parents. The Seneschal is guarded and forbids him from asking again.

Landav and Malady implant the catalysts beneath the skin of the trainees. Anskar's body rejects the dark-threaded crystal, and he grows critically ill.

As Anskar recovers under the care of the priests of the Healer, a golden-eyed crow disturbs him in the middle of the night. Anskar enters a fugue-like state as he follows the crow through the wilderness to a Niyandrian ruin atop Hallow Hill. There, a wraithe—one of the ancient beings that haunt Wiraya—urges Anskar to enter the ruin, where he finds a statue of a woman carved from bone, upon her forearm a vambrace crafted from a peculiar silver alloy.

Carred Selenas receives word from her spies that one of the Order's newest knights, a woman named Sareya, could be the Niyandrian heir, and also that Hyle Pausus, the Grand Master of the Order of Eternal Vigilance, is on his way to Niyas from the mainland city of Sansor. She comes up with a plan to bloody the Order's nose and snatch Sareya away from them.

Carred and her rebels are attacked by Luzius Landav and Malady, and in the ensuing fight, Landav transports himself and Carred to a shadowy realm, where she meets a secret consortium who put pressure on Carred to disband her rebellion. She refuses and uses a ring Queen Talia gave her to break Landav's power and return to Wiraya. The rebels capture Landav, but Malady escapes. Carred cuts off the sorcerer's head.

Anskar approaches his namesake, the knight Eldrid DeVantte, to ask about his mother and father. Eldrid claims to know nothing except that he gave Anskar his surname at the request of Vihtor.

The trainees undertake their first mission, each mentored by a fully consecrated knight. To everyone's surprise, Vihtor announces he will join them. Ambushed by rebels, they lose almost half their number, including the trainee Petor.

As dusk approaches, they find a farm with a cottage to shelter in before dead-eyes attack in the night. Anskar hears a woman screaming inside the cottage. He and Vihtor investigate, only to find the cottage empty apart from the corpse of a woman recently killed.

After nightfall, dozens of sickly, spindly-limbed dead-eyes attack. Anskar uses dark-tide sorcery to hold up the ceiling, which bows under the weight of dead-eyes. Sareya uses dusk-tide sorcery to incinerate the rest of the dead-eyes with violet flames, and then, exhausted, she collapses.

Carred discovers that Niyandrians are being rounded up a few at a time and sold by the Order of Eternal Vigilance as slaves. After years of failures and self-doubt, she cannot stand by. She frees Niyandrian slaves from a warehouse and burns down the building.

Carred receives word that her rebels attacked a group of knights and their trainees from Branil's Burg, but were driven back by a young knight who bristled with sorcerous energy, aided by a young Niyandrian woman, Sareya. Carred speculates that, if Sareya is Queen Talia's daughter, the young knight may be the heir's guardian. Both must have been conditioned by the Order, unaware of who they really are.

After the knights' expedition returns to Branil's Burg with Petor's body, Anskar examines his vambrace using dark-tide power. He has a vision of a full suit of intricately forged plate armor and is inexplicably overcome with a burning need to possess the armor.

Luzius Landav's servant, Malady, turns up at the Burg, carrying Luzius's severed head in a sack. The decomposing head seems to speak to Anskar, who is horrified. Malady is revealed to be a demon, and tells the Grand Master that he was deceived by the new Niyandrian converts. Malady escapes, and, fearful of betrayal, Hyle Pausus orders the recently branded Niyandrians killed. Four of the Niyandrians, however, cannot be found.

The trainees are raised to the rank of knight-inferior. In another year, they will be expected to either take solemn vows or leave the Order and never return. To clear his head, Anskar rides from the Burg, intending to find some space. When he returns, he finds Naul's dead body, which speaks to him, telling him to help Sareya. Anskar finds Sareya bound and gagged, kneeling at the center of a circle formed from a golden chain. Within the circle stand four Niyandrians: the four escaped converts.

As Anskar fights two of the men, the dark-tide within him bursts its bindings. One Niyandrian's hand withers, and the second's face putrefies. The Niyandrian woman, a sorcerer, confronts Anskar, her dagger dazzling with silver fire. But she holds back and gasps with reverent awe: "*Melesh-Eloni!*"

Anskar escapes his kidnappers and causes the carriage to crash. The Niyandrian sorcerer begs Anskar to come with her, but knights of the Order arrive. Vihtor kills the sorcerer and is shocked to see that Anskar's eyes are now somehow cat's eyes, like those of a Niyandrian.

Back inside the Burg, Anskar is sure Vihtor knows more than he is revealing, but Hyle Pausus decides Anskar is a gifted knight-inferior and will take him to Sansor with his retinue. Vihtor doesn't voice an objection, and agrees that it could be dangerous for Anskar to remain in Niyas.

Anskar visits Sareya in the infirmary, where she tells him that *Melesh-Eloni* means "godling."

Anskar departs Branil's Burg by ship the next morning, consumed by questions that he feels he may never get answers to.

Carred and a small group of her followers watch the passage of the lone galleon as it heads out to sea.

One of the slaves Carred rescued, a young woman called Noni, is possessed by the spirit of Queen Talia and tells Carred that there is no daughter: the heir to Niyas is Talia's son, the knight-sorcerer Anskar DeVantte. Talia reveals that Carred is Anskar's guardian, and now is the time for her to step into that role.

Carred vows to bring Anskar back to Niyas so that the entire country will rally to her cause. Under Anskar's lead, the faithful will take back Niyas for Niyandrians. Queen Talia will return. And the dead will live forever.

BOOK TWO: CORRUPTION

Entrusted by Vihtor Ulnar to the protection of the knight Lanuc of Gessa, Anskar DeVantte sails on the *Exultant* across the waters of the Simorga Sea to Sansor. Anskar and Orix discover Niyandrian slaves chained in the bilge. The *Exultant* detours to the coastal city of Atya, where the Grand Master plans to sell the slaves.

That night, Orix is set upon and almost raped by one of the knights. Anskar uses dark-tide sorcery, which corrupts the knight's arm, and then Orix runs the man through with his sword. Instead of disciplining Anskar, the Grand Master tells Anskar that, if he plays his cards right, he should fit in well at the Mother House in Sansor.

Carred Selenas is visited by Queen Talia, who possesses Noni and speaks through her. Talia exhorts Carred, Anskar's guardian, to find him and keep him safe—Anskar is the key to returning Talia from the realm of the dead. She commands Carred to find the old Niyandrian sorcerer Maggow, and enlist the help of Malady the demon and the abyssal realms.

Maggow summons the demon Malady and binds her to his will. He also informs Carred that the *Exultant* is heading west, away from Sansor. Carred procures a ship and gives chase.

The *Exultant* arrives at Atya, where Anskar, Orix, and Lanuc go ashore for a few days to explore the city while the slaves are sold. They are approached by a woman named Blaice Rancey, who claims her business is ransacking ancient tombs and that she's an old friend of Lanuc's.

Blaice claims to have knowledge of a recently unearthed ancient ruin, and the Grand Master Hyle Pausus puts together an expedition to explore the ruin and claim its treasures for the Order. As they journey to the ruin, they are joined by Niklaus du Plessis, who claims to be the

Chosen Sword of the goddess Sylva Kalisia. Lanuc explains to Anskar that gifted knights and sorcerers, including Lanuc himself and now Anskar, are not only tolerated in secret but are called upon by the Grand Master to sacrifice their purity in the defense of the Order.

Blaice and Niklaus decipher the code that unlocks the entrance to the ruin and lead the group inside. They come to an inscribed brass circle set into the floor of a chamber—a portal. Anskar, at Hyle Pausus's urging, uses dark-tide sorcery to activate the portal, and the group are transferred to the fabled city of Yustanwyrd, buried underneath the ruins of the seven cities that succeeded it.

Carred crosses the Simorga Sea and lands near Atya, and then finds her way to a Traguh-raj tribe. The tribe's leader agrees to lead them to the unearthed ruin in pursuit of Anskar. Carred and her new companions capture Orix and Lanuc, who were left outside the ruin as guards.

Blaice leads Anskar and the rest of the group to a building atop a hill of granulated quartz, where they are attacked by eight statues holding black wavy blades. They resemble the ancient wraithe Anskar encountered atop Hallow Hill. There is also a massive reptile's head with jaws that open onto absolute blackness.

Anskar's vambrace grows warm and tugs him toward the lizard's maw with increasing urgency. Anskar passes between the statues, continues into the reptile's gaping mouth, and is pitched into the void.

Anskar finds himself confronted by a group of wraithes, who know that he is the child of the Necromancer Queen of Niyas. The ancient beings also reveal that Anskar's vambrace is a step on the path to godhood. They deny the existence of the portal stone Blaice and the Grand Master seek, and state that the members of the expedition have seen things they shouldn't have, before using sorcery to send him back to his companions.

Anskar rejoins his companions in a chamber littered with crystal boxes. From one container, Blaice and Niklaus remove a severed hand with an ebony ring.

Fearful of the wraithes' warning, the companions flee back to the entrance hall, only to find the eight statues are now living wraithes. In the ensuing fight several companions are killed, along with a wraithe. Hyle Pausus and Anskar are overwhelmed, but then Anskar's vambrace flares with brilliance, and he briefly finds himself in the realm of the dead. The shade of Queen Talia appears, with a golden-eyed crow perched on her shoulder. The Necromancer Queen says that the vambrace is not enough, and that there is much more to be done before Anskar comes for her. She sends him back to Wiraya.

Anskar, the Grand Master, Niklaus and Blaice flee, with the wraithes sending birds made of smoke to attack. Anskar's sword, *Amalantril*, is ineffective against the smoke birds, as are all their weapons. Only Niklaus's sword, which bears the image of his goddess, has any effect against the birds. Niklaus saves the Grand Master and tells him and Anskar to flee. As they do, Niklaus is smothered by hundreds of the birds and is lost.

Finally free of the disastrous ruin, Anskar, Blaice, Hyle and the rest of the survivors stumble back to their camp, only to find Orix and Lanuc tied with rope. Lanuc shouts at them to run, but before they can, Traguh-raj warriors cut off their escape. With them are Carred Selenas and the demon Malady.

To Anskar's dismay, Carred reveals to all that he is the son of Queen Talia. Anskar demands to know who his father is, but Carred is unable to answer.

Anskar is exhausted, his repositories depleted, and so is unable to muster a defense. When Carred agrees not to harm his companions, Anskar agrees to go with her. Carred takes Anskar back to Atya. When they near the wharves, Anskar draws on the dark-tide and shadow-steps away to where the *Exultant* is moored. As knights come to his aid, Malady pursues him through the shadows. The demon slaughters a few knights and is about to capture Anskar when the dawn-tide arrives. Anskar uses the dawn-tide power flooding his repository against Malady, and she flees. Carred, seemingly admitting defeat, departs on her own ship.

Safe aboard the *Exultant*, Anskar is heartened when Lanuc, Orix, Blaice, and the Grand Master return unharmed with the remaining knights. On the final night in Atya, Blaice seduces Anskar.

One night aboard ship while they're bound for Sansor, Queen Talia visits Anskar in his sleep and begins to teach him sorcery in a twilight dreamscape. The next day, Carred's ship attacks, and the knights and rebels fight with steel and sorcery. Amid the slaughter, and at the Grand Master's behest, Anskar uses dark-tide sorcery to turn the tide of the battle, killing the old Niyandrian sorcerer Maggow in the process. Unable to seize Anskar, Carred and Malady abduct Orix instead.

The *Exultant* finally arrives at Sansor, and Anskar and the knights find refuge at the Order's Mother House. Anskar makes the acquaintance of Gisela of Gessa, Lanuc's daughter, who is a priestess of the Five and a healer.

Carred is once again beaten down and depressed at another failure to secure Talia's heir. She briefly contemplates giving up, but instead goes against her better judgment and gives Malady a task: capture Anskar and the demon can go free.

Anskar wanders the Mother House and finds himself at a forge, where he meets Braga, a foul-mouthed blacksmith. He watches her working for a time, and despite her surliness, they strike up an unlikely friendship.

After Carred's failed attempt, Talia once again possesses Noni and speaks through her. Talia tells Carred to seek out the necromancer Tain and to use his knowledge to create a suit of Armor of Divinity as a fallback plan, in case Anskar fails to make his own.

The Grand Master Hyle Pausus summons Anskar and, in front of senior priests, urges Anskar to make peace with his burgeoning abilities and harness them for the good of the Order. Hyle Pausus sends Anskar for further training under the ancient Abbess at the Abbey of the Hooded One, in an attempt to cure him of his disillusionment with the Order of Eternal Vigilance.

Arriving at the Abbey, Anskar is given a cold welcome by the Abbess. He is confined to a cell and left to contemplate for long lengths of time, only broken by meals, prayer, and brief talks with the Abbess. Anskar's preconceptions about the Order and its morality are broken down little by little. The Abbess's talks are his only lifeline, and Anskar clings to them as if his sanity depends on it. They speak of demons and demon lore; Malady, Carred, and Niyas; Menselas; and balance, despair and death, as the Abbess challenges everything Anskar has grown to believe.

When the Abbess declares Anskar ready, he summons and binds the demon Malady to his will. Malady takes him briefly to the abyssal realms, then swiftly on to Carred before a winged demon can attack them. Malady reveals that knowing a demon's name grants a sorcerer power over that demon, and makes him a gift of the winged demon's name.

Anskar confronts Carred and Orix, who has been converted to the rebel's cause. Carred attempts to bring Anskar to her side, explaining the faults of the Order and the good Anskar could do if the Niyandrian people were liberated. Anskar rejects Carred, and Malady spirits him away, back to the abbey.

When they arrive, Malady tries to kill Anskar. Malady proves too powerful, until the Abbess arrives and slays her with sorcery. Afterwards, the Abbess, clothed in the illusion of Carred Selenas, forces Anskar to copulate with her, again and again, until he loses consciousness.

The next day, Anskar is summoned to see the Abbess, and still reeling and confused, he is taken to a vast chamber in which are gathered all of the priests and priestesses of the Hooded One. The Abbess reveals that she is a member of the Tainted Cabal, and that with Anskar joining their ranks, she believes they will be powerful enough to return the demon lord Nysrog to Wiraya.

Led by the Abbess, the congregation begins a ritual of summoning. Anskar is torn between extremes of savagery and terror. However, the demon lord Nysrog does not fully manifest and the summoning fails.

The Abbess is jubilant. She believes they only need to become a little stronger, and then, because of Anskar's abilities, Nysrog will once again walk upon the face of Wiraya.

Anskar comes to his senses and is horrified. He has to get away from the abbey before it is too late for him, and too late for the world. Swallowing his repugnance, he forces himself to go along with the Abbess and her deranged followers until an opportunity presents itself. As the Abbess and the priests begin an orgy, Queen Talia makes contact with Anskar, and he flees into the night.

Running for his life, Anskar is cornered by demons the Abbess has sent to capture or kill him. Unarmored and without a weapon, Anskar believes he is doomed, but Queen Talia shows him how to use the earth-tide, the power behind necromancy, to summon the dead spirit of a warrior and send it for help.

Anskar fends off one demon, using his vambrace to keep its fangs from his flesh. Help arrives in the form of Lanuc, Braga, and knights of the Order.

The Grand Master sends knights to the abbey, but they find the priests all dead, their veins turned black by some poison or sorcery. Of the Abbess there is no sign.

Once Anskar has recovered from his ordeals, he and the Grand Master walk the grounds outside the Mother House, discussing demons and the Tainted Cabal. The Grand Master's bodyguards are all slain by an assassin sent by the Abbess. The assassin incapacitates the Grand Master, and Anskar skewers the man with his sword *Amalantril*, only to find that there is no blood, and the assassin isn't slowed down by the wound.

Queen Talia tells Anskar to summon the dead using the earth-tide. Desperate, Anskar obeys and raises the Grand Master's dead guards. The assassin disposes of the animated corpses, but when Anskar scours him with dark-tide fire, the assassin is revealed as a demon.

Anskar recognizes it as the demon Malady pointed out to him in their brief sojourn in the abyssal realms. He halts the demon by uttering its name, then kills it.

The Grand Master declares that the Tainted Cabal have infiltrated the Order of Eternal Vigilance, and all must keep their eyes and ears open to detect the taint of corruption. Anskar is ordered to join Lanuc and a hundred knights on a mission to the Thousand Lakes kingdom, where they are to assist King Aelfyr, who is beset with problems from the Soreshi of the Ymaltian Mountains.

Breaking his promise to Talia, Anskar re-establishes the wards he had set against his mother, believing this new mission to be a manifestation of the mercy of Menselas and a way for him to atone for past sins and to give his life over to the providence of the Five. He feels free of Carred Selenas, free of the hold the Abbess had over him, and most of all he feels free of the specter of his mother.

BOOK THREE: SUBVERSION

Anskar DeVantte rides across Kaile, one knight among many among the Order's forces led by Lanuc of Gessa. Anskar vows never to use sorcery again, believing it is the source of all the ill luck that has befallen him and that it weakens his faith. Also afraid of his mother's influence, he blocks Queen Talia out.

As the forces journey toward the Kingdom of the Thousand Lakes to assist King Aelfyr, one of the Warrior's priests traveling with the knights takes an unhealthy interest in Anskar. Another priest of the Warrior, Josac, explains that the angry priest is Gann Harril, brother of Beof, whom Anskar severely injured during his trials and who had been sent away in disgrace. Anskar is warned that Gann wants revenge for what happened to his brother.

Carred Selenas continues her journey with the head of the necromancer Tain, along with Orix and Noni, in their search for the Armor of Divinity Tain claims to have created. Tain reveals that the helm that encases his head—all that remains of his Armor of Divinity—is the only thing keeping him alive.

Meanwhile, a woman driving a wagon approaches the Order's forces from behind: Braga the blacksmith, who tells Anskar she was urged to accompany the knights by a "ghost lady": Anskar's mother, Queen Talia.

The next day, Josac appears, bloodied and bruised. Gann, paranoid that Josac has sided with Anskar, attacks him with the Warrior's Fire, a divine ability gifted to priests by Menselas. Ashamed of his defeat, and telling Anskar he must fight Gann, Josac begins to teach Anskar how to use the Warrior's Fire. Anskar is hesitant, unable to embrace the Warrior's Fire until Josac demonstrates the power and beats him senseless.

Gisela of Gessa tends to Anskar's injuries and fully heals him. Although she is wary of what she has learned of Anskar from his confession, she agrees to attempt to teach him the way of vicarious suffering, a Healer's technique that involves taking the suffering of others upon oneself.

Anskar uses his newfound healing powers to take Josac's injuries upon himself, and the pain renders him unconscious. In the morning, Gisela relieves Anskar's pain by taking it upon herself, explaining that she has built a tolerance to suffering and will heal in a few hours. Having accepted at least this limited use of sorcery, Anskar embraces the dawn-tide as the sun rises.

When the Order's forces arrive at Kyuth, a coastal town in the north of

Kaile, they meet with Franklin Gore, mayor of Kyuth, and Brother Stevos, a priest of the Elder. Brother Stevos appears less devout than is usual for a priest, and is strangely accommodating to all of the other faiths, proclaiming it is no sin to worship with others for the sake of friendship.

Braga and Anskar strike up a friendship. When they are out one night, Anskar shows her his sorcerously imbued vambrace. Braga believes it is crafted of divine alloy, and that the only remaining knowledge regarding the metal is held in the scriptorium of King Aelfyr in the Thousand Lakes, and that the king's master blacksmith, Hrothyr, is the only person to have access.

That night, Gann makes his move and surprises Anskar with a vicious attack from behind. Fighting Gann off, Anskar taunts him in an attempt to enrage Gann beyond reason and give himself an edge. But immersed in the Warrior's Fire, Gann remains calm. After trading blows, Anskar desperately uses Menselas' gift of healing combined with the dawn-tide to snuff out the Warrior's Fire within Gann. The stolen fire is subsumed by Anskar, and he pounds Gann into a bloody mess. As Anskar lies insensate after the effects of the Warrior's Fire, Braga disposes of what's left of Gann along with Anskar's bloody clothes. When Anskar wakes, they agree not to admit to the killing. Anskar still feels a kernel of the Warrior's Fire within himself, now a part of him.

Lanuc tells Anskar and Gisela they must attend a ceremony worshiping the Lady Sylva Kalisia, at the behest of the mayor, Frankin Glore, and the priest of the Elder, Brother Stevos. Reluctantly, they agree, but as the ceremony progresses, both Anskar and Gisela feel more and more uneasy, believing that followers of Menselas should have nothing to do with heathen worship. Gisela eventually storms out, disgusted with her father's weakness. Anskar follows, telling Lanuc that he's already made too many compromises.

Carred's expedition arrives at an interconnected cairn of massive stones: the location of ancient suits of Armor of Divinity. Inside, they descend steps into a dark pit at Tain's urging. They investigate the tombs inside until they find a corpse clad in armor. But the armor is guarded by undead shades, a result of the necromancy used by Tain to murder the people who first helped him excavate the site. Taloc is killed by the shades, and Carred and the others only just escape. Tain urges them to continue to another location, where another suit of Armor of Divinity might be located.

Anskar and the force of Order knights continue their journey north. At Anskar's urging, Braga tries to remove the vambrace, but is unable to even scratch the metal with a hammer and chisel. They realize it will take great heat to work the metal, a heat that can be found in Hrothyr's forges in Wintotashum in the Kingdom of the Thousand Lakes.

Anskar tries to persuade Gisela to mend her relationship with her father, but Gisela is still angry with Lanuc for committing what she believes to be an abomination.

As soon as they arrive in the Kingdom of the Thousand Lakes, the knights are trailed by Soreshi scouts. The Soreshi grow bolder, and as the days pass, they no longer bother to hide their presence.

Meanwhile, the Tainted Cabalist Castellac furthers his plans among the Soreshi. For it is the Tainted Cabal who have deceived the Soreshi and caused them to attack the Kingdom of the Thousand Lakes. Castellac plans to break into the Scriptorium at the capital, Wintotashum, and steal the memory crystal of Morudjin, the priest of the Elder responsible for summoning the demon lord Nysrog into the world. The Cabal believes this will give them enough knowledge to return Nysrog to Wiraya.

The knights fight skirmishes with the Soreshi, who prove to be adept with sorcery. When the knights are almost overwhelmed, Anskar responds with potent cants of dawn- and dusk-tide. But the vitriolic gouts burn away all of his self-imposed bindings, and the dark-tide bursts forth, immolating the Soreshi around him. With dawn-, dusk-

, and dark-tide coursing through him, Anskar loses all restraint and revels in his power, ruthlessly slaughtering the Soreshi with sorcery.

The next day, the knights capture a Soreshi sorcerer named Zek, and Anskar stops them killing him out of revenge for the deaths the Soreshi caused. Over the next few days, Anskar and Zek talk about how sorcery works and how the tides interact. To the Soreshi, the dawn- and the dusk-tides are two ends of the same day. They have different applications, but neither is good or bad.

When the knights are attacked by mulag, supernatural creatures that travel with the mist, Zek saves Anskar by replenishing his dwindling dawn-tide repository, and the two become friends.

Arriving at Wintotashum, the Order knights are taken to greet King Aelfyr and a priest of Menselas named Brother Bonavir. King Aelfyr isn't impressed with the Order's small force of knights and makes his displeasure known. Aelfyr explains he plans to take the fight to the Soreshi, into the mountains.

King Aelfyr takes offense at Zek, a Soreshi, in their midst. He questions Zek, who reveals he believes an evil taint has corrupted many of the Soreshi. Aelfyr isn't convinced, but for the time being allows the Soreshi to remain with the knights.

Anskar and Zek talk more of sorcery, and Zek reveals that most Soreshi have braided their dusk- and dawn-tide repositories together seamlessly. As Anskar and Zek discuss religion and sorcery further, Anskar again becomes troubled with doubts about Menselas and the Order.

Queen Talia visits Braga and shows the blacksmith a full suit of armor, with Anskar wearing it. Braga believes Talia wants her to examine Anskar's vambrace and forge him a suit of armor using the same sorcerously imbued alloy. Brother Bonavir claims that Tain's notes are kept in the Scriptorium at Wintotashum.

Braga takes Anskar, Zek, and Bonavir to see Hrothyr, where they find out that Braga used to be married to him. Hrothyr admits he made the vambrace for Queen Talia, under duress. Hrothyr agrees to help them smelt the divine alloy required and to forge a full set of Divine Armor. Brother Bonavir says they will need the Ethereal Sorceress's aid in procuring the rare metals and minerals required, but her help will come at a price. Zek says he can steal the Necromancer Tain's notes from the Scriptorium using sorcery.

At another audience with King Aelfyr, Brother Bonavir talks up Anskar's sorcerous abilities, to Anskar's embarrassment. Aelfyr decides that Zek may be a spy and orders him imprisoned.

Anskar visits Zek in prison, and they further their friendship, discussing sorcery, Queen Talia, and the Armor of Divinity. Zek urges caution, as Anskar is in the dark regarding Talia's plans. Zek also teaches Anskar how to more effectively use the dusk-tide, and to crudely braid his dawn- and dusk-tide repositories. With Zek incarcerated, Anskar decides to break into the Scriptorium.

Queen Talia contacts Anskar, and he lowers his wards to speak with her. Talia approves of his plans and shows Anskar a way to break into the Scriptorium, using the same methods her spy Lengar previously used when he accessed Tain's notes for the knowledge that resulted in the creation of Anskar's vambrace. She also reveals that Lengar is still alive and might be of help.

But when Anskar breaks into Lengar's rooms, he finds the spy dead, killed by a man and a woman who are still there: Castellac and Haleki. The Tainted Cabal had come looking for a way to break into the Scriptorium in order to steal the memory crystal of Morudjin, the key to their summoning of Nysrog.

Castellac tries to persuade Anskar to join the Tainted Cabal, but Anskar refuses. At Talia's urging, Anskar uses the dark-tide to solidify shadow into lethal shards, and he shreds Haleki. Castellac shadow-steps away.

Able to break into the Scriptorium from Lengar's rooms, Anskar steals Tain's notebook. Brother Bonavir begins to copy the instructions for the creation of Armor of Divinity from the notebook. Next, they have to gather the rare ingredients.

Anskar visits Sheelahn the Ethereal Sorceress. She agrees to procure most of the ingredients required by Anskar except for the *nietan* horn, which Anskar must gather himself if he agrees to her contract: two unspecified services from Anskar sometime in the future. Reluctantly, Anskar agrees, and Sheelahn makes use of what she calls an *izindel* to transport Anskar to another of her depots close to where the *nietan* reside.

Carred and her group travel north to the Niyandrian coast at Tain's urging. The necromancer directs them to a shipwreck, where he claims a suit of Armor of Divinity is to be found. Carred has no idea how to retrieve the armor, until Queen Talia, through a possessed Noni, reinvigorates Carred's disused dawn-tide repository. Now able to use a cant to enable her to breathe underwater, Carred dives down to the shipwreck and takes the armor from an ancient skeleton.

Anskar steps out of Sheelahn's depot and finds himself somewhere under a blazing sun, with a dusty village nearby. A Traguh-raj woman arrives to greet him, Uraxa of the Agalot. Uraxa states that she is knowledgeable regarding the region and the *nietan*. They enter a crystal wasteland, all that remains of a once mighty city destroyed by sorcery in an ancient cataclysm. Uraxa takes Anskar to a crystal crevasse, wherein lies the *nietan*'s lair. After wandering through a warren of crystal passages, Anskar comes across a cavern with hundreds of smooth crystal eggs. The *nietan* appears, and Anskar is shocked that it looks like a small child with a crystal horn in the center of its forehead. In Anskar's mind, Talia urges him to kill the *nietan* and take the horn, but Anskar hesitates. He re-forms his wards and shuts his mother out of his mind.

The *nietan* transforms into a horned beast formed from compacted crystal. Rather than fight the creature, Anskar decides to leave it alive, and he retreats to safety. Believing he has failed, Anskar is relieved yet angry and disappointed that he will be unable to forge the Armor of Divinity.

Scurrying out of the lair, Anskar joins Uraxa. Holding her hand is the crystal child. The *nietan* offers its horn freely, and Anskar accepts. Translating for the *nietan*, Uraxa urges Anskar to cease following this path, and to remove the vambrace and cast it into the sea. Both Uraxa and the *nietan* weep tears for Anskar, for he is devoid of choice, swept along by his mother's plans.

Anskar returns to Wintotashum and the smithy, where Hrothyr says the rest of the ingredients needed for divine alloy have arrived by cart, courtesy of the Ethereal Sorceress. When Braga and Brother Bonavir arrive, Anskar implores them to remove the vambrace. Hrothyr attempts to, using pincers with tips made from divine alloy. Anskar's body convulses, and he passes out. When he wakes, the vambrace has been removed, and Gisela has been brought to heal him.

Anskar, Braga, and Brother Bonavir later discover that Hrothyr has been murdered. Hrothyr has a discolored forearm and they surmise he tried to put on the vambrace, which somehow killed him. They search for the vambrace, and when they find it, it leaps up and fastens itself to Anskar's arm. Bonavir reasons that only Anskar or Queen Talia can wear the vambrace, and anyone else who tries is rejected or killed. Using sorcery, Anskar returns Tain's notebook to the Scriptorium before anyone realizes it has gone missing.

Anskar joins the Order knights as they march against the Soreshi, reinforcing King Aelfyr's six hundred soldiers with their hundred. The Soreshi Zek accompanies them, although he is still guarded. On the way, they encounter many burned villages and corpses, along with signs of destructive dusk-tide sorcery, which Zek claims is considered an abomination by his people.

The King's forces take the fight to the Soreshi, and they attack an occupied town. The Soreshi sorcerers imbue their arrows with dusk-tide sorcery to penetrate the knights' arcane wards and their armor. As the Thousand Lakes soldiers hide behind a shield wall, Lanuc orders the knights to charge. Anskar unleashes the full potency of his braided repository, shielding the entire center of their line and allowing the knights to burst through the town's gates.

As the knights, Thousand Lakes soldiers, and Soreshi fight a bloody battle, Anskar comes face-to-face with a Soreshi sorcerer. Almost completely drained of the dawn-tide, Anskar attacks her with *Amalantril.* The woman blasts him off his feet, and the only thing that saves him is his ward sphere, which subsequently collapses under the strain. As the Soreshi sorcerer is about to finish Anskar off, he reaches for the dusk-tide, and his anger somehow also invokes the Warrior's Fire. He slaughters the Soreshi horde, blasting them into ash.

Anskar feels the tug of the dark-tide, and sees a man in black plate armor, who shadow-steps away. They now surmise the Tainted Cabal is behind the Soreshi insurgence.

The Armor of Divinity breastplate Carred retrieved from the shipwreck is damaged, but Tain uses the earth-tide to repair it, heating and shaping the metal. Tain uses Orix's essence to power his sorcery, as well as the iron and astrumium alloy in Orix's sword, destroying the blade. Orix almost dies in the process, and his face is warped, the features misplaced. Sick of Tain's deceptions and certain that he was deceiving her for his own ends, Carred yanks Tain's head from the Armor of Divinity helmet, and it crumbles into dust.

King Aelfyr and his forces celebrate the victory over the Soreshi with carousing and drunkenness. The Order knights and Anskar are subdued. In adherence to the strict ideals of the Order of Eternal Vigilance, they must remain sober and focused when on campaign.

Aelfyr has Zek locked in the town's dungeon as a precaution, and Anskar visits to keep him company and to continue learning all he can about the tides. Zek coaches Anskar on how to rebuild his crudely braided repositories to match his own: a latticework of gossamer strands of the dawn-tide interwoven in perfect balance with the dusk, each thrumming with a measured flow.

Later that night, Anskar joins Brother Bonavir and Braga at the town's smithy. Braga has been able to use the raw materials to forge three ingots of divine alloy. However, Braga says there's only enough *nietan* horn left for a few smaller pieces of armor. As they discuss the ingots and armor, the Tainted Cabalist Castellac appears. Castellac disintegrates Bonavir with sorcery. Anskar protects Braga with his arcane ward. Laughing, Castellac flees, but not before summoning a minor demon to attack Braga. Anskar's sorcery fizzles out, and in desperation he calls on Queen Talia for aid. But he is too late, and the demon grabs Braga and drags her into the shadows, where they disappear. Anskar snatches up the divine alloy ingots and pouch of powdered *nietan* horn, along with the copy of Tain's notes, and escapes the smithy.

With all of his confidants dead, Anskar confesses to Lanuc almost the entire story, and Lanuc informs King Aelfyr that the Tainted Cabalist Castellac was there and has killed Brother Bonavir and Braga. Learning from Anskar that Castellac wanted to break into the Scriptorium, King Aelfyr surmises he is after the memory crystal of Morudjin.

Queen Talia speaks to Anskar again, explaining that the vambrace was made for him alone and urging him to find another blacksmith to complete the Armor of Divinity. When Anskar balks, Talia says she can teach him how to raise Hrothyr from the dead to complete the work. Anskar is appalled, and he shuts her out again.

Angry and confused, Anskar seeks out Gisela in order to make his confession. She rejects him, and Anskar's anger grows. He is sick to death of being pulled between Menselas and his mother. He resolves to reject them both and pledge his allegiance to King Aelfyr in the morning.

Carred and the others arrive back at Naphor, the site of the old Niyandrian capital destroyed by Queen Talia. Orix despairs because of his disfigurement and has trouble eating and talking. Through her possession of Noni, Talia guides them to a ruined mansion and then explains that her ring, which Carred has carried with her all this time, is made from demonic void-steel. Talia says they need far more void-steel to complete the armor and that Carred must travel to the abyssal realms to procure more. Hidden in the vicinity of the ruined mansion is a portal chamber, and before Carred can object or agree, Talia sends her to the abyssal realm of Vulthanor to trade with the ruling lord.

Back in Wintotashum, King Aelfyr calls a full war council in order to drive the Soreshi out once and for all. Aelfyr reveals that the Tainted Cabal are behind the Soreshi and have insinuated themselves into the Ymaltian Mountains, taking over a long-abandoned Soreshi citadel. The previous night, the King reveals, the Scriptorium was entered and all the guards within slaughtered, mutilated, and defiled, and the memory crystal of Morudjin was taken.

Convinced that destroying the Tainted Cabal stronghold and retrieving the memory crystal is their only way of preventing a second demon war, King Aelfyr orders his army and the Order knights north to the Cabalist stronghold. Before they leave, they receive word that Gisela has been kidnapped by Castellac and will only be released if Anskar exchanges himself for her.

King Aelfyr forbids Anskar to go, but Anskar shadow-steps to escape the king's guards and breaks Zek out of prison to help him. They steal out of the city and ride in pursuit of Castellac's carriage.

Having been kept underground and unable to replenish his repositories, Zek partakes of the dusk-tide as night falls. To Anskar's astonishment, Zek's dawn-tide repository is also filled. Zek explains this is the benefit of a properly braided repository, and that the tides were never meant to be separated.

As Anskar and Zek approach the citadel gates, they are met by Castellac and a woman Anskar had hoped never to see again: the Abbess of the Abbey of the Hooded One, along with her son, Uspeth. Having no further need of Castellac, who is disfigured and broken from an attempt to summon a higher-order demon, the Abbess uses dark-tide to dissolve Castellac into a dark stain.

Anskar demands that they release Gisela now that he's here to give himself up. The Cabalists release Gisela, but she has been tormented and abused and driven insane. Gisela manages to mount a horse and ride to freedom with Zek.

Anskar is led deep into the citadel until they reach a summoning chamber with scores of dark-robed Cabalists painting symbols and polishing broad strips of brass riveted to the floor within a circle of quartz. The Abbess gives Anskar the memory crystal of Morudjin, and Anskar's mind is transported into Morudjin's memory of his disastrous summoning of Nysrog. When he returns, the Abbess and Uspeth are relieved Anskar's mind hasn't been damaged, and exultant with the knowledge he brings: that Morudjin's mistake was to try to coerce the demon lord with the dark-tide, which shattered Nysrog's mind into fragments.

Anskar refuses to participate further, so the Abbess uses sorcery to compel him. Anskar calls on his mother for aid, and Queen Talia answers with curses, saying that this is what they wanted all along: for Anskar to call on Talia's spirit in order to control her. After a sorcerous battle of resolve, the Abbess and Uspeth bind Talia to their will. Talia explains that they must use the earth-tide in order to complete their summoning of Nysrog.

Led by the Abbess and Uspeth, the Cabalists begin to summon the demon lord. As Nysrog begins to form, the Abbess forces Anskar to add his power to the summoning, and then commands Talia to use the earth-tide to reshape the demon lord. Nysrog's form begins to solidify, and the Cabalists rejoice, believing they are successful. But Talia has deceived them and was never bound to obey their will. The summoning deteriorates, and Nysrog's flesh slops in steaming puddles to the floor as he decomposes before their very eyes.

The Abbess is livid and tries to kill Anskar, but Nysrog recovers and destroys all of the Cabalists, then snatches up the Abbess in a clawed hand. Uspeth flees, shadow-stepping to safety, as Nysrog returns to the abyssal realms, taking the dying Abbess with him.

Anskar, exhausted from his use of the dark-tide, allows Talia to take the life force of the dead Cabalists and feed it to him. Anskar wonders how far he has fallen that he is willing to take for himself the very substance of these dying souls.

Anskar shadow-steps out of the citadel but is pursued by surviving Cabalist sorcerers and Soreshi. Under a terrible sorcerous assault, Anskar cedes control to Talia once more, and she uses earth-tide necromancy to summon a legion of skeletons from an old battle fought close by. Spent of all his sorcerous power and utterly exhausted, Anskar is carried by skeletons to safety while many more fight and delay the Cabalists and Soreshi.

But Uspeth has not fled, and finds Anskar in his exhausted state. Uspeth attacks Anskar, who unconsciously slings earth-tide power at him and uses the tide to create an arcane ward. Zek appears, having waited for Anskar once Gisela was safe. Anskar and Zek fight against Uspeth, the Cabalists, and Soreshi, holding them at bay with Anskar's earth-tide sorcery and Zek's braided repositories. But Zek is run through with Uspeth's sword and slain.

Anskar uses the dark-tide, but Uspeth's mastery is greater and the attack fails. In desperation, Anskar reaches for the earth-tide again. Uspeth has no counter, and the earth-tide corrupts his flesh, withering his limbs and rotting his body into a pool of pus.

But Anskar is sorely injured, and when Gisela attempts to heal him, she cannot. After being defiled by the Cabalists, she has lost Menselas' gift of healing. King Aelfyr arrives to mop up the remaining Cabalist and Soreshi forces.

King Aelfyr's army and the Order knights return to Wintotashum in triumph, the Soreshi insurgence quashed and the Tainted Cabal routed.

Anskar consoles Gisela, who believes her god has forsaken her.

Sareya, his ex-lover, arrives at Wintotashum. The Seneschal Vihtor Ulnar is dying, having been struck by a poisoned arrow. Vihtor has sent Sareya to bring Anskar back to Niyas before he dies.

ONE

CARRED SELENAS WAS A CHILD once more. Trees surrounded her. She was lost and crying for her mother. Wasn't it always the same?

She knew it was *the* dream again. Her adult self observed the scene from that liminal space between waking and sleeping, and she saw what her mother must have seen, watching from behind a tree.

Carred—four-year-old Carred—sniffed back tears as she noticed something at her feet. It hadn't been there before.

Stuffing leaked from blood-soaked cloth that had been ripped to shreds.

Little Nally, her ragdoll!

She turned in a trembling circle.

The sky between the overhanging branches shimmered red, then bronze, then faded away to black.

She was flat on her back now, and something hard was

pressing against the back of her head. She groaned and moved till the discomfort eased. Warmth penetrated her eyelids—they were closed. Sleepily, she traced the lines of old scars, relieved and a little sad she was no longer a child.

Carred cracked open one eye. Squeezed it shut against the glare. She tried again, blinking until she could see.

At first everything looked red, and she wiped her eyes in case blood had gotten into them. Had she fallen and gashed her head open? She felt her brow. Nothing. Not even a bump; only discomfort on the back of her head, from where it had lain on a rock.

As her vision cleared, she realized the red was the color of the sky, not anything wrong with her. And there were billowing clouds of yellow, green, and purple, swirling together in a poisonous brume.

She gasped, then clutched her chest and coughed. The air scorched her lungs and prickled her skin.

Was she still dreaming?

She groaned as she rolled to her knees. Bile burned her throat, and she turned her head and vomited.

Definitely not dreaming.

But where was she?

Nowhere on Niyas, that was certain.

The sun was twice its normal size, a ball of molten bronze. The ground shimmered like liquid, though it was as hard as diamond and abraded her knees. Standing stones with the pocked texture of sponges formed circles within circles around her, glittering with all the colors of the diseased sky. In the hazy distance were long, low mesas and pillars of porous rock so high they seemed to hold up the crimson sky.

Carred shook her head in disbelief. It felt as though her brain had been blown to pieces and fixed back together again, only jumbled up—like Orix's face.

Tain! Something she remembered.

The necromancer Tain had disfigured Orix's face using earth-tide sorcery. And she remembered ripping Tain's head from his helm and watching it disintegrate.

Then…

She spat to cleanse her mouth, and then untied the pouch hanging from her belt and opened it. The contents shimmered like… star-metal!

She'd been sent here to trade.

Sweet Theltek! Star-metal: the bane of demons.

Carred stood so fast she swooned and almost fell.

Where was the portal chamber—the eight-sided cubicle she'd entered? How was she going to get back to Wiraya?

"Talia!" she cried, trembling as she turned, like the girl lost in the woods.

No answer.

How could there be, without Noni? The Necromancer Queen spoke through Noni whenever she communicated with Carred from the realm of the dead.

She scanned the megaliths that surrounded her like ripples spreading across the surface of a lake—and she the pebble that had been dropped into the water. No answer there, at least nothing obvious.

She started towards the innermost ring of standing stones for a closer look. If there were no mechanism for the return journey… She didn't want to think about that. Talia knew what she was doing. She'd never abandon Carred. Well, probably never. It was more likely Talia didn't want her going back empty-handed.

You must go to my father. Trade with him, Noni had said in the

Necromancer Queen's voice.

Star-metal for void-steel. All that was needed to complete the Armor of Divinity.

Talia had seldom spoken of her father when she was alive, and never with affection. Was he Carred's only way out of here?

But what kind of father lived in the abyssal realms?

TWO

IT WAS RAINING WHEN ANSKAR DeVantte stepped out of the Ethereal Sorceress's depot—through the same blackwood doors by which he had entered mere minutes ago. The air was sticky, and lightning forked overhead. Thunder cracked so loud it made him duck. He turned around, intending to go back inside, but there was a man in the doorway. A man wearing a gray coat and blackwood mask.

"You startled me," he told the functionary.

The braids that bound the man's long, dark hair into slender ropes sparkled with reflected lightning despite the flash having already passed. It gave Anskar the impression that the braids had somehow absorbed the force of the lightning, the same way his repositories stored the tides of dusk and dawn.

Anskar froze for a moment, unable to look away from the mask. Empty eyes stared back at him.

"You have arrived at your destination," the functionary said.

"To re-enter the depot could incur another debt. Are you prepared to pay?"

Anskar looked away. "For the sake of a little rain and lightning? I don't think so. Tell Sheelahn I'll return soon to honor the debts I already owe her."

"Three," the functionary said. "The number of your debts is three."

"I know. I can count." Anskar hated the surliness in his voice.

He strode down the steps, away from the seamless bulk of the depot.

Lightning flashed again. Thunder boomed. His long hair already streaming wet, he hunched over against the downpour, pulling up the hood of his cloak as he ran for the shelter of an alley on the opposite side of the cobblestone street.

It had been bitterly cold when he had entered the Ethereal Sorceress's depot in Wintotashum. A fresh blanket of snow covered the city, and he had stopped to watch the eerie play of lights in the sky: swirls of green that came only rarely, he was told, beautiful and full of mystery.

But that tranquil memory seemed a lifetime ago, and King Aelfyr's capital city in the Thousand Lakes was suddenly half a world away, a journey that ordinarily would have taken weeks by land and sea. The calm and the white and the euphoria that infected Wintotashum after the King's great victory over the Soreshi and their Tainted Cabal masters had been replaced by the relentless drive of rain that pelted his cloak and left it sodden.

Because Anskar was no longer in Wintotashum.

He was in the port city of Dorinah.

Back home on the isle of Niyas.

"You came."

The effort of speaking caused Vihtor Ulnar, Seneschal of Branil's Burg, to hack and wheeze. He was lying beneath a stained, crumpled sheet atop the simple bed in his room. The wavering glow of a lantern on the nightstand etched his face in long shadows that made him seem already halfway to the realm of the dead. The stench coming off him was worse than a week-old corpse.

Yet Vihtor was still alive, kept that way, so the priest outside the door had told Anskar, by massive influxes of the dawn-tide administered by the healers. It wouldn't be enough. Anskar could sense the corruption that emanated from the Seneschal's wounded shoulder. It reminded him of the earth-tide. Three cones of incense burned on the windowsill, creating a fragrant haze in the room that did little to hide the stench.

"I came," Anskar said.

Vihtor beckoned him closer with a feeble wave of his hand, the skin of which had a greenish tinge. "Let me look at you in the light. You've grown into a fine man. Tall and strong."

Anskar resisted the urge to cover his nose and mouth against the stench as he crossed the room and set down the sack he'd brought with him from Wintotashum. Vihtor barely reacted when the contents clattered, and that was a relief because Anskar hadn't considered how he would explain bringing the components for the Armor of Divinity—a work of Niyandrian necromancy—inside the walls of an Order stronghold.

"Sit." Vihtor patted the bed.

Anskar perched on the edge of the mattress, Vihtor on his right, his sword *Amalantril* hanging from his left hip. He breathed as shallowly as he could through his barely open mouth. Already the sickening stench of Vihtor's wound and the strong incense were making his head spin.

"Sareya?" the Seneschal asked.

"Still in Wintotashum. She'll be returning by ship."

"Weeks away, then." Vihtor turned his head and coughed into his fist. "But she reached you with my message. That's good."

"She reached me," Anskar said. "Father."

Vihtor closed his eyes, and a shudder passed through his thin frame. He'd lost so much weight since Anskar had left for Sansor. "When did you work it out?"

"Later than I should have." About eighteen years later. It had all fallen into place recently. The favoritism Vihtor had shown him. Taking Anskar under his wing. Everything Vihtor had done to guide Anskar took on a new meaning now. He'd been an idiot not to see it sooner.

Vihtor's eyes glistened with moisture when he opened them. He winced and clutched at his shoulder, where blood and brown seepage stained his nightshirt. "I've heard of only a few methods of transport that could bring you all this way so quickly. All of them are dangerous, and their practitioners more so. What have you gotten yourself involved in, Anskar?"

"It was necessary." *Three debts that must be paid, when I have no idea how I'll repay even one.*

Anskar curbed his mounting impatience. He had so many questions to ask, but the time didn't feel right for any of them. *Why didn't you tell me I was your son? Why have you lied to me my entire life?* And what did it mean, if the Necromancer Queen of Niyas was his mother and his father a leader of the mainland army that had defeated her? How could this be? When had it happened? Some of those questions would have sounded like accusations if he'd asked them, and he wasn't altogether sure he wanted to hear the answers.

"They told you, I suppose, that I'm dying?" Vihtor said.

"Sareya told me."

Vihtor gave a thin smile. "She's changed a good deal since attaining the rank of knight-inferior."

She's come a long way in such a short space of time. Then again, we all have. "She said you'd entrusted her with the command of knights," Anskar said.

The thought chafed. Sareya had never taken the Order of Eternal Vigilance seriously. It wasn't surprising, considering how she'd come to be at Branil's Burg, and how Niyandrians like her were made to feel inferior.

"Just a handful of knights, and under supervision," Vihtor said. "You don't learn to lead except through leading. It won't be long before she's ready for solemn vows. Perhaps you'll take vows at the same time."

"And that wouldn't bother you?"

Vihtor had objected to their relationship before; he'd forbidden it.

"Whether it does or not, I won't live to see it. I should be dead already. I would have been had not the healers burned themselves out keeping me alive."

"Menselas is—"

"Merciful? So they keep telling me."

"It's the god's gift, not any power of theirs, that has kept you alive."

"They certainly seem to believe that."

"And you don't?"

Vihtor let out a sigh. "It wasn't an expression of faith—or lack of, Anskar. There's no need to worry on that account."

"I just thought—"

"You've heard, no doubt, that I was struck by a rebel arrow. It was during a tour of the strongholds under construction. Same thing that happened to us at Quolith."

Anskar nodded that he remembered.

"Outside the new burg at Kithos," Vihtor said, "we were attacked by Niyandrians. No more than a skirmish, really. They were lightly armed and mounted on coursers. Fast, and they fired bows from the saddle. Harrying us, nothing more. They fled the instant we counter-charged. Out of our force of sixty, I was the only one injured, if you can believe it."

"Was it an assassination attempt?"

"If so, I'd have to say they succeeded, wouldn't you? The arrow passed right through my ward sphere. I've never seen such a thing."

"Dusk-tide," Anskar said. "The Soreshi augmented their arrows with it in the Thousand Lakes."

"More than just the dusk-tide," Vihtor said, "if the healers are to be believed. Pity is, not one of them can tell me more, other than that they believe the arrow was cursed. Even the priests of the Elder are stumped as to what can be done about it."

Anskar almost said something then, about his mother's use of the earth-tide, but that would have opened up a whole other conversation, one he wasn't sure they had time for.

"Sareya told me the arrow was cursed," he said instead.

"A leftover from your mother's reign."

"Just like me."

"Oh, Anskar, son—"

"Don't call me that!"

"All right. I understand… You're not cursed. You are… Under Tion's direction, your training at the Burg… "

"You thought you could raise me as a mainlander and leave my Niyandrian heritage behind?"

"I couldn't kill you, Anskar. No matter the circumstances of your birth, I couldn't. And there were plenty who wanted me to."

"I'm not surprised."

"No one you know. Powerful people on the mainland. Don't worry, they think I did as they asked, which is why they no doubt left me to languish in this backwater. A leader of knights is meant to be an exemplar of the Church's faith, not a butcher of babies."

"But the Order continued to search for Queen Talia's heir... "

"Besides the powers that be on the mainland, and one or two others I trusted, no one knew we had Talia's child. The best way to protect you was to let them go on thinking the heir was still out there."

"So you let them abduct innocent Niyandrian girls instead? Girls like Sareya?"

"It would have happened anyway. What better way to disrupt Niyandrian society?"

"And they had no idea I was a boy."

"Your mother was clever, Anskar. Even her own people were looking for a girl. I saw no reason to disabuse them of the notion. All I wanted was to—"

The Seneschal winced and clutched his chest, not his injured shoulder, and his face contorted into a grimace of pain.

"Should I call the healers?" Anskar asked.

"No," Vihtor said through gritted teeth. "It's my catalyst." He opened the front of his nightshirt to reveal a mottled bruise over his sternum, threads of blackness spreading out from its center.

"By the Five," Anskar said. "What is this?"

"You're the one with the sorcerous abilities. You tell me."

Anskar shut his eyes and let his senses flow into his father. At first he felt only the remnants of the dawn-tide the healers had infused Vihtor with. But then he pushed deeper, and his senses recoiled. He gasped and his eyes snapped open.

"The crystal's been corrupted, and the dawn-tide essence within your repository is putrefying."

"An effect of the arrow, so the healers tell me," Vihtor said. "It has allegedly spread to my organs, my blood. Not a good way to die. But at least I got to see you again first."

Anskar hung his head. "Why...?"

"Why didn't I tell you who you were? I wanted to, Anskar, and never more than when you passed the trials. I wanted to so much, but—"

He broke into a fit of coughing that wouldn't stop.

The door opened, and a healer in a white robe stood there, silhouetted by the light from the corridor.

"Seneschal?" she asked. "Do you need more dawn-tide?"

She sounded hesitant. She was probably exhausted from what she'd already given him. To do what the healers had done to keep Vihtor alive must have taken unimaginable amounts of dawn-tide essence. Even when it was Menselas's gift worked through the healer, Anskar had felt for himself just how debilitating it could be.

Vihtor, still coughing, waved her away, and the woman backed out of the room and closed the door.

"Why?" Anskar asked. "Why couldn't you tell me?"

"The Order's rules, for one thing. You know how we must marry outside of the Order so that there is no favoritism? The same applies to our children. We aren't allowed to serve together. But in your case, I had no choice. I needed to keep you close. You saw what happened when those Niyandrian builders worked out who you were, Anskar. Carred Selenas and her rebels are fanatics. There's nothing they won't do in their search for the heir of Niyas."

"I met her, you know," Anskar said.

"Carred Selenas?" Vihtor tried to sit up but failed.

"She captured me herself this time."

"And you got away?"

"I'm here, aren't I?"

"What… What was she like?"

"Different than I'd been led to believe. What if we've misjudged her?"

"We haven't," Vihtor said. "Don't let her pull the wool over your eyes, Anskar. That woman is ruthless. Whatever she said to you, assume she was lying."

"At least she didn't want to kill me."

"Like the Consortium?"

"The what?"

Vihtor breathed out a long and rattling breath. "I must be dying to have let that slip. Forget you heard it. Really, forget."

"I fully accept Carred Selenas doesn't want you dead. What she has in mind for you is worse. She wants you to fulfill your mother's plans. Can't you see? That would have made us enemies, Anskar. Then I would have had no choice but to turn you in or kill you."

"Because Niyandrians are an evil that needs to be stamped out? And what about the Order of Eternal Vigilance? I've seen things since I've been away. Slaves sold in Atya. Sorcery that's meant to be forbidden. The Grand Master—"

"The Order is far from perfect," Vihtor said. "But its ideals are right and just, even if its adherents, even if the hierarchy, myself included, don't always live up to those ideals. I lied to you. All your life I've kept you from the truth of who you are. I believed—I still believe—I was doing the right thing, but I wish Menselas had shown me another way. Don't be too harsh on the Order, Anskar. It isn't entirely corrupt. It just needs good men and women to rise, and others will follow."

"I always thought that was you," Anskar said. "A good man. I idolized you."

Vihtor inhaled with a succession of gasps, then shuddered as he breathed out.

"I think I still do," Anskar said, "but I need to understand the choices you made."

"I know," Vihtor said. "Which is one of the reasons I sent for you."

"How did…" Anskar began, but he could find no tactful way of phrasing the question.

"How did your mother and I…?" A deep frown cut into Vihtor's forehead.

Rape!

Queen Talia's intrusion in Anskar's mind was so violent, he almost cried out.

The filthy bastard raped me!

Anskar strengthened his wards and instantly felt her absence. Whatever Vihtor had to say, he needed to hear this. His mother could give her version later.

"It wasn't something I chose," Vihtor said. "You must believe me."

"I imagine she'd say the same thing."

"Yes, I think she probably would." Vihtor's eyes widened. "She hasn't… I mean, Queen Talia was a necromancer… Has she contacted you? Does she…?"

"Does she speak to me from the realm of the dead?" Anskar fingered the vambrace that sat invisibly over the skin of his forearm. He shook his head and chuckled. "Is that even possible?"

Vihtor held his gaze for a long while. Anskar felt certain he'd given the game away when his cheek started to twitch, but then

Vihtor sighed and closed his eyes.

"I must sound crazy to you," the Seneschal said, "but with everything that's happened… the crow visiting your room, your fugue-state journey to Hallow Hill, the Niyandrian rebels who tried to kidnap you…"

"I don't think you're crazy to ask. It just sounds like the stories Tion used to read to me as a child. Morality tales, mostly. About the kinds of things that haunt the wilderness, and what they might do to a young boy foolish enough to leave the Burg."

"Ah, I may have encouraged him with that."

"An overprotective father?" Anskar asked. "Or the Seneschal making sure he didn't lose a valuable asset?"

"In the beginning, it was about ensuring you didn't fall into enemy hands. Later on, it was the former."

"How much later?"

Vihtor laid his hand atop Anskar's. "I told myself I didn't want to risk betraying who you were."

"Your son, you mean?"

"That would have involved fielding questions about the mother. Far better that you were an orphan. At first, I tried to pretend you didn't exist, that you were nothing to do with me."

Anskar withdrew his hand.

"And I was wrong," Vihtor said. "There are no excuses. I was weak. Did you know Tion once called me an immature prick because of it?"

"So Tion knew."

"He knew."

"All those years, and he never told me," Anskar said. "Actually, he lied when I asked him what he knew about my birth. Repeatedly."

"The responsibility is mine," Vihtor said.

"Really? And you take the blame for him running off with the widow Glaena too, do you?"

"That is disrespectful!" Vihtor tried to sit up again, but only managed to bring on a fresh coughing fit.

When it abated, Anskar said, "I'm sorry."

Vihtor's hand returned to pat Anskar's. It was speckled with blood from where he'd stifled his cough. "It's I who should be sorry. You're right to be angry, Anskar. Of course you're disappointed in me, but don't be too harsh on Tion. He never wanted the task of raising you, but he did his best all the same."

Anskar felt the sting of unshed tears. He nodded and smiled. "He did his best. My only disappointment with Tion was to discover that he's only human. You're not the only one who's an immature prick."

"That is no way to speak to your Seneschal!"

Anskar flinched, and Vihtor laughed and coughed at the same time.

"But it's how I want you to speak, for the time we have left, to your father."

Anskar gave a slow nod. "Was my mother really evil, or is that what the victors in war always say?"

"I have never believed, Anskar, that you are a reflection of your mother." All trace of humor had gone from Vihtor's manner. "You're innocent in all of this. You've shown yourself to be a gift of Menselas, not the curse I once treated you as. And so, what I have to say next applies to Queen Talia and not to you. You are correct: in war, each side always demonizes the other, but in your mother's case, I have my own personal testimony. Are you sure you want to hear this?"

Anskar squeezed Vihtor's hand and nodded.

"At the height of the war, Queen Talia came to me here at

Branil's Burg."

"How?" Anskar asked. "Was there a treaty?"

"She was a sorcerer, remember? A sorcerer without peer. Think about that. Why was Queen Talia so far in advance of every other sorcerer of her day? Why has there been no one past or present to rival her? Hard work and study? Certainly, those would have been factors. But what really set Queen Talia apart?"

Anskar shrugged. "Some Niyandrians are moontouched." Like Sareya. Moontouched was the meaning of *Amalantril*, the name she had suggested Anskar give his sword. "They have a natural affinity for the tides."

"For the dawn and the dusk," Vihtor said, "but not the dark. And while as a people, they're obsessed with the plight of the dead, there have only been a rare few necromancers among them, and none as accomplished as your mother."

Anskar looked up, half-expecting Vihtor to mention the earth-tide, the source of Queen Talia's power over the dead, but there was no indication the Seneschal knew about it. In that he wasn't alone. It wasn't exactly common knowledge that there were three tides, let alone four—even if the fourth was in reality a corruption of the other extant tides as they seeped into the earth.

"Tell me," he said. "What do you think the reason was?"

Vihtor stared at him so long, Anskar thought he wasn't going to answer. Finally, he said, "There was something about Queen Talia that made her seem more, or perhaps less, than others of her race. As with you, Anskar, I suspect your mother was not a pure-blood Niyandrian. When she came to me that night, she was more a goddess," Vihtor said. "Or a demon."

For a long while, the Seneschal was still, and Anskar feared that he was no longer breathing. He leaned closer to check and felt the slightest exhalation from his father's lips, cold and almost undetectable. Reaching out with his sorcerous senses, Anskar panicked. The last vestiges of the dawn-tide sustaining Vihtor had ebbed away.

He started to stand, intending to fetch a healer, but Vihtor's hand lashed out and grabbed his cloak.

"No," the Seneschal breathed. "No more healing. You are here now."

Vihtor managed a thin smile. He coughed weakly. "Give me a moment."

Anskar fought back tears as his father's eyes closed, and again he feared it was all over, that he would never hear what Vihtor had to say about the circumstances of his birth.

And then a thought occurred to Anskar: the arrow that had wounded Vihtor was believed to have been cursed, presumably with the sorcery that bubbled up from the core of the world: necromancy. He quickly unbound the wards that kept Queen Talia out, then called to her with his mind.

Heal him, Mother. Remove the curse.

Nothing. Not a whisper. Not even the sensation of her spirit sluicing through his marrow.

Heal him, please!

And still there was no answer.

Frantic now, he risked using his lips and whispered, "Mother?"

But Queen Talia was gone.

Vihtor opened his eyes at the sound of Anskar's voice. He gasped and shuddered, then let out a long, rattling sigh.

"It was at the height of the war," Vihtor said, his voice so frail that Anskar had to lean in to hear. "We had taken Dorinah after a long siege and a naval blockade. Our allies were landing all around the coast of Niyas. The Order of Eternal Vigilance was at the forefront of the invasion, as we were the only ones capable of defending against Niyandrian sorcery, and it was largely for that reason, I suspect, that I was given command of the allied forces.

"My room in the newly occupied Branil's Burg," Vihtor said, and now his words were mumbled and slurred, "was high up in the citadel. You know this, of course. I've kept the same room since. Yet one night, I was awoken by a cold wind coming through the open window despite the window having been closed before I went to bed."

His look said it all: Vihtor knew Anskar had experienced the same thing when the golden-eyed crow had come to his room.

"She was there, Anskar, silhouetted in the moonlight: my enemy, Queen Talia. My sword was beside the bed. I tried to reach it, but then she approached, and a silvery light bathed her skin."

Vihtor frowned and once more closed his eyes.

"Like a goddess, I tell you."

It reminded Anskar of the visits Niklaus du Plessis claimed to receive from the Lady Sylva Kalisia.

"You also said she was like a demon."

"Is there a third explanation? No? Then she must be one or the other. She came to my bed, Anskar, and I could do nothing to stop her. I didn't want to stop her. And after, when she left through the window and dissolved into the night sky, I felt cold and empty. I felt ashamed.

"I've carried that sense of shame and failure with me ever since, even after the fall of Naphor. I thought it had ended with the death of the Necromancer Queen, but then…"

"Did she tell you she was pregnant?" Anskar asked.

Vihtor's head lolled to one side—as much of a shake as he could manage. "You were supposed to be her big secret, her heir. I suspect she also viewed you as a weapon, but before you were old enough to be of use, the war was over."

"Then how?" Anskar asked. "How did you know about me? How did you find me?"

"After Naphor was destroyed," Vihtor said, "rumors circulated about Queen Talia having a daughter, though no one had known she was pregnant. You would know better than I: Is it possible to disguise such things with sorcery?"

Anskar shrugged. If it was, he didn't know how. Could any of the known tides alter one's physical appearance? Or had his mother's pregnancy bump been slight and easily disguised with the right clothing?

"She must have known the end was certain, "Vihtor said, "so she entrusted care of the child to a Niyandrian couple who kept a smallholding out in the country. I would never have found you, never even known you existed, were it not for a second visitor to my room."

"Let me guess," Anskar said. "A wraithe."

Vihtor nodded.

"Did my mother send it?"

"It didn't say, but I don't think so unless she's more devious than I thought. How would it benefit her to have you raised by her enemy?"

Anskar could think of plenty of reasons, not least of all the idea of the serpent's egg, safe within the enemy's walls, waiting to hatch. All those years learning the ways of the Order until his latent powers grew manifest with the fitting of his catalyst. That was when it had all started, when his life had gone so wrong.

"I grew angry when the wraithe told me Talia had been pregnant with my child. But it impressed upon me the need for haste—told me what might happen if the Niyandrians found you first, how you were the key to the Queen's promise to return from the dead.

"I rode alone from Branil's Burg, and when I came back, I had you in my arms. And I lied. I told the Order that your parents were mainlanders murdered by rebels still loyal to Queen Talia. Some thought they were knights, which is absurd, given our rule about spouses serving together. Others thought they were retainers traveling with the army. And I know you've heard the rumors of rape, given the color of your skin. Whatever they wanted to believe, so long as it wasn't the truth."

"And the couple who looked after me as a baby?"

"They didn't want to give you up. They were fanatical. They became rabid. The way they fought, it wouldn't surprise me to learn they were demons."

"Is that how you justified killing them?"

"They gave me no choice."

"You could have left me with them."

"The wraithe's warning…"

"How do you know it was telling the truth? Since all this began, I don't even know what truth is anymore."

"Then you must relearn," Vihtor said. "Menselas is truth. He is our guide, the teacher of our conscience."

"Maybe," Anskar muttered. Once he would have thought so, but now…

"What was that?"

Anskar refused to answer. Tension prickled between them before Vihtor let out a sigh that seemed to deflate him.

"What is that you brought with you?" the Seneschal asked, hand flopping over the edge of the bed, finger indicating the sack Anskar had left on the floor.

"Just a few things."

"What…" Vihtor coughed and tried again. "What kind of…"

"Just some gear I brought back from the Thousand Lakes."

"Show me."

Anskar lifted the sack onto the bed and opened it. He drew out the bag of powdered *nietan*'s horn, then one of the three ingots of divine alloy. His mind was racing with different explanations, but he also wondered how much Vihtor already knew.

This business with the Armor of Divinity had been niggling away at Anskar. Had he gone along with it for all the wrong reasons? For Brother Bonavir, for Braga and Hrothyr? Some misguided hope that he'd earn his mother's affection by carrying out her plans? He'd been a fool. He was no one's hatchling.

He opened his mouth to say as much, then shut it again.

Because Vihtor's head lolled to the side, his eyes open, staring, a line of drool trickling from the corner of his mouth.

Vihtor Ulnar, Seneschal of Branil's Burg, Anskar's father, was dead.

THREE

THE NEXT THREE DAYS IT rained so much the courtyards were flooded and the streets of Dorinah beyond the walls of Branil's Burg turned to rivers.

There was talk of leaving Vihtor's funeral until the new Seneschal arrived from Sansor, but Eldrid DeVantte said that was too long to wait, and many agreed with him. Vihtor had been Seneschal for almost two decades, and the grief at his passing ran deep among the knights.

Eldrid assumed temporary command, according to a document entrusted by Vihtor to the priests of the Mother in the event of his death. The healers added their voices to Eldrid's. Due to an effect of the cursed arrow, they said, the body had already started to decompose, and there was only so much that dawn-tide sorcery could do to manage the stench and the seepage.

The funerary pyre for Vihtor was a sullen affair. The entire garrison of Branil's Burg gathered in the drenched courtyard at the rear of the barbican, along with the postulant knights, the commanders of the outlying strongholds, and even a few Niyandrian dignitaries, who had long ago decided collaboration with Niyas's conquerors was easier than resistance.

A grim and ancient priest of the Elder led the prayers, and then plump Haldyca, the priestess of the Mother, set a torch to the pyre, weeping openly as one of her "children"—she called everyone her "child"—went home to the bosom of the Five.

And no one knew.

No one knew that Vihtor had been Anskar's father.

Anskar let his eyes rove over the men and women standing to attention around the blazing pyre, and he felt more alone than ever. Blosius—poor little rich boy Blosius, whom Anskar had beaten easily in the first trial what seemed a lifetime ago—met his gaze and wagged his fingers in greeting. Anskar couldn't meet his gaze and looked away.

There was a wake of sorts in the knights' refectory. Anskar stood by himself against a wall, picking up snatches of conversation from the packed tables. Many of the knights drank watered wine from goblets and assuaged their hunger with simple fare of bread, cheeses, and fruit. Anskar thought about watering his wine but decided against it. He needed a drink if he was to calm his nerves.

Sareya had apparently stopped at Sansor in Kaile on her voyage to the Kingdom of the Thousand Lakes. It seemed her message of Vihtor's imminent demise had been for Hyle Pausus's ears before anyone else's. So it hadn't been such a mad dash across hundreds of miles to ensure Anskar got to speak with his father before he died. There had been another, apparently more urgent, reason for her mission. Had Vihtor known about her detour to Sansor? Had he commanded it? What did that make Anskar—

yet again an afterthought?

The big question was, who would the Grand Master send to take command of Branil's Burg and become the next governor of Niyas? Speculation was rife, but whether Hyle Pausus would send a safe pair of hands, as Vihtor had been, or someone who would take a harsher line with the insurgent Niyandrians remained to be seen.

Eldrid DeVantte approached him, dressed in the Order's white cloak and a mirror-bright cuirass above a mail hauberk. At his hip was sheathed a broadsword, the hilt wrapped with golden wire, the scabbard studded with precious stones.

"Anskar, a word, if I may." The knight laid a hand on Anskar's shoulder and gripped it tightly. "Don't think for one moment that you're alone."

Anskar frowned as he searched out Eldrid's eyes. "You know?"

Eldrid glanced around to make sure no one was listening, then said in a low voice, "Your father was my friend, so, yes, I know."

"And my mother?"

Eldrid nodded gravely. "You are your own man, Anskar. Vihtor never tired of telling me that."

"You two spoke about me?"

"From time to time. When he needed to let things out. And never within Branil's Burg."

"Who else knows?"

"At Branil's Burg? No one, now that Tion's gone. But in Sansor…"

"The Grand Master," Anskar said.

"Has he asked anything of you, Anskar? Some special service?" Concern etched his face.

"I don't know if I'm supposed to say this…"

"Vihtor and I were like family. I guess that makes me a sort of uncle to you." Eldrid smiled. "More than that. I did let him give you my family name, after all."

"Are you saying I can trust you?"

"That's for you to decide."

Anskar watched him for any indication of mockery, any hint of deceit. Finally, he nodded. "When I left Sansor for the Thousand Lakes, it was with a special force led by Lanuc of Gessa. I was told each of us possessed special attributes."

"That's what Hyle Pausus asked of you? To use your talents in the service of the Order? Nothing else? I suppose that's a good thing."

"What else could he ask?"

"Nothing I'm aware of."

Now Anskar had the distinct impression Eldrid was lying, or at the very least being evasive.

"So you met Rindon, Naul, and Borik, did you?"

"You know them?"

"I've fought with them on occasion. Great men, all three of them. Proper heroes."

"Borik's dead," Anskar said. "The Sword of Supremacy shattered."

Eldrid closed his eyes and took in a long breath. "That's hard to hear. Were you there?"

"I saw him fall."

"Perhaps sometime you'll join me for a drink and tell me Borik's tale. I'd sooner hear an eyewitness account than the embellished nonsense of the bards. An eyewitness other than Rindon, that is, whose rendition would put even the bards to shame."

"I'd like that," Anskar said, "only, not right—"

"Later, I said. First, we have your father to grieve."

FOUR

IT WAS COLD IN THE citadel's front courtyard when the force Sareya had led to Wintotashum returned a few weeks later, but the skies were clear and the hard rains a distant memory. A single swallow arced and looped in perfectly clear skies, and Anskar wondered if it had lost its flock.

He stood in the second rank of knights-inferior, in between phalanxes of fully consecrated knights. The knights-postulant, both new recruits and those who had failed the trials on either the first or second attempt, formed ragged lines off to one side. Blosius was among them.

When he'd failed the first trial, Anskar having beaten him in the fight square, Blosius had been relieved. He was only at Branil's Burg because his wealthy father had insisted, but Blosius was honest enough to admit he was no fighter. He was just waiting for the day when he failed again, and the time after that, so he would be dismissed from the Order and free to pursue his real goals in life. Like his father, he intended to become a merchant.

The trouble was, Anskar wasn't sure Blosius would make it through another year and a half at Branil's Burg. The lad looked disheveled, his usually immaculate hair a tangled mess. His white cloak was stained and rumpled, his boots scuffed, and his eyes were permanently bloodshot. He'd been drinking, even so early in the morning; that much was clear. It looked to Anskar that the man probably did little else these days. Drinking outside of set times was prohibited, but Blosius's father sent him enough coin to get whatever he needed, and presumably enough to pay those charged with his care to bend the rules in his favor.

Among the group standing with Blosius, Anskar spotted the twins Clenna and her brother Rhett. Clenna, whom he had barely beaten in the finals of the first trial, saw him looking and nodded. It was the most respectful gesture he had ever seen from her. Niv was there, too, one of Sareya's Niyandrian girlfriends.

As the new arrivals marched through the barbican, Anskar picked out Sareya in her white cloak and glinting ringmail at the head of the twelve knights she'd been entrusted with. She had changed, that much was clear from the arrogant thrust to her chin, her expression aloof, maybe even disdainful. As her twelve formed a line facing the Burg's assembled garrison and postulants, Sareya continued on till she stood before Eldrid DeVantte. She gave a stiff salute, which Eldrid returned.

Then came a second, larger force of knights through the barbican, marching six abreast, immaculate in white and silver, all of them women. They must have been picked up in Sansor, Anskar reasoned, on the return voyage from Wintotashum. These knights parted down the middle into two columns, three abreast and six deep, and through the channel between them came the new Seneschal of Branil's Burg.

She was perhaps the tallest woman Anskar had ever seen, save perhaps for Ryala Mitredd, who had died below ground in the Lost City of Yustanwyrd. But whereas Ryala had been trim and muscular, etched with tattoos, the incoming Seneschal was rake-thin, her long, slender fingers almost skeletal. The skin of her face was stretched taut over her hollow cheeks, and she had a nose like a blade. Her hair was gray, cut severely short. Her one eye was glittery and hard, the other covered with a patch of white leather, the jagged edge of an old scar above and below. Her white cloak was trimmed with ermine and lined with crimson, and beneath it she wore a molded breastplate of steel, freshly scoured with sand and vinegar, judging by the way it shimmered and shined.

Anskar didn't miss the nervous looks that passed between the fully consecrated knights, and Eldrid DeVantte, normally relaxed and self-assured, noticeably stiffened.

"General Monash," Eldrid said, clicking his heels and giving an uncharacteristically awkward salute.

"You are relieved, Commander DeVantte," she replied without looking at him. "Our thanks for your service."

Eldrid hesitated for a moment, then stepped back into line.

General Monash placed a hand on Sareya's shoulder and let her good eye run over the assembled postulants and knights. Closer now, Anskar could see the eye was bloodshot, the iris a striking shade of violet. Sareya glanced at her, the merest trace of a smirk curling her lips before she resumed her look of haughty superiority, not meeting the gaze of anyone she knew.

"I am General Varensi Monash. Some of you have heard of me; some of you have served under me. Now you all do. From this point on, you will call me Seneschal."

She lingered over that last word, as if it left a bad taste in her mouth. Vihtor had described Niyas as a backwater. For a mainland general like Monash, that implied a demotion. Then again, she wasn't a young woman. Perhaps it was a step down before retirement.

"The Grand Master, in his wisdom, has sent me to you as a fixer. He believes a certain laxity has crept into the Order here on this benighted isle, a laxity that has for too long allowed the Order's enemies to go unchecked. That all changes today. You have been warned. Dismissed."

That was it? No word of condolence about Vihtor? No encouraging speech?

"Anskar DeVantte?" Monash said, her single eye roving the ranks.

Anskar's heart skipped a beat, but before he could raise his hand, Sareya pointed him out.

"A word, if that's not too much to ask."

Seneschal Varensi Monash didn't yet know her way around Branil's Burg, she said, so she had Sareya accompany her and Anskar to the Dodecagon. To Anskar's surprise, Sareya didn't leave.

Whether she knew it or not, the Seneschal seated herself upon the same carved blackwood throne Vihtor had sat upon during the first trial. It stood atop a half-dais in front of one of the Dodecagon's twelve walls, each of which had its own dais and throne.

Without waiting to be asked, Sareya seated herself on the adjacent throne.

Anskar remained standing on the mosaic floor, its blue and white tiles forming the picture of a grinning Death's head—not a tribute to the Hooded One aspect of the Five, who had formerly been known as Death, but a grim reminder of the ancient Niyandrians who had built Branil's Burg.

Rose-tinted sunlight came through the high glass ceiling, twelve lead-framed panels that converged in a point at the apex, which Anskar studiously ignored. When he had first entered the Dodecagon for the start of the trials, he had been shocked by the graphic images the stained glass portrayed: naked Niyandrians wearing skull masks, many coupling with each other or in lewd and erotic poses. Seneschal Monash, he noted, glanced up and then wrinkled her nose in distaste.

"I am sorry for your loss," she said.

"*My* loss?"

"Oh, I'm sure Vihtor Ulnar is grieved by all who served under him. A good man. An exemplary knight. At least on the surface. But you, Anskar—I have to believe his passing affects you more deeply, or am I wrong?"

Anskar glanced at Sareya, who remained stony-faced. Something was going on here, and he didn't like the way it made him feel.

"You look so guilty," Monash said. "But it is our belief that you did not know, at least not until—"

"Until Sareya came to Wintotashum with a message for me to return here," Anskar said. "But did you already know?" he asked Sareya directly. "Had you worked it out for yourself, or did Vihtor tell you? You said he trusted you now."

"As do I," Seneschal Monash said, casting a proud smile at Sareya. It could have been the smile of a mother, only Sareya was Niyandrian through and through, and Varensi Monash, whatever she was by descent, was anything but. Her violet eye marked her as something else, something exotic, perhaps Inkan-Andil. Maybe a touch of Soreshi?

"*Melesh-Eloni,*" Sareya said.

"What?" Anskar flinched as if she'd struck him.

"It's not just your father's identity that became clear to me," Sareya said. "Your mother's did too. And, do you know, I wasn't surprised. My only wonder is that I didn't work it out before. You came to me, remember? After the kidnappers left me for dead and took you instead. You came to the healers' infirmary while I was recovering and asked me what *Melesh-Eloni* meant."

"Godling," Seneschal Monash said. "Sareya told me all about it on the voyage here."

"You told her?" Anskar said. Sareya was supposed to be his friend. His confidante. They had slept together, told each other things they'd told no one else!

"And what it means to her people," the Seneschal said. "There are no secrets between us."

"But you barely know each other."

"It was a long voyage by sea," Sareya said. "You know this from your own journey north. Much can happen."

"Personally," Seneschal Monash said, "I find that the boredom of long voyages loosens tongues, and not always in a good way. Gossip and rumors proliferate under such conditions, but at other times, so does truth sharing and mutual self-knowledge. Part of the reason I was so successful as a general, so I am told: my knights knew me, and I knew them."

"What does that even mean?" Anskar said. "And if you were so successful, why were you sent here?"

"Don't be so insolent!" Sareya snapped.

Seneschal Monash held up a bony hand. "It's all right, Sareya. We'll allow him this one little outburst. He has been through a lot, lost so much. If it's a demotion that you think brought me here, then you are wrong. I volunteered for the post."

"You wanted to come to Niyas?"

"I wanted the challenge. Regrettably, our paths didn't cross during your brief stay in Sansor. I was away on other business, business that involved the Patriarch of the Church of the Five." She waved that off, as if it were not a big deal. "But when I returned and I was told of Vihtor Ulnar's sickness, and the Grand Master was taking counsel as to who would replace him, I proposed myself. You see, for years I'd been hearing reports about a lingering rebellion on Niyas, a rebellion that, had I been governor here, I would have swiftly put down."

"And that's what you intend to do now? You plan to go after Carred Selenas and her rebels?"

"You of all people should approve of that," Seneschal Monash said. "After all, they were the ones to kidnap you and kill friends of yours as well, so I'm told. Or have your feelings changed now that you know who you really are? Clearly they mean you no harm. I wish I could say the same for the mainland settlers and the knights left behind to keep them safe."

In truth, Anskar no longer knew what his feelings toward Carred Selenas and her rebellion were. It had once all seemed so simple, so black and white. Then he'd spent time with Carred. Whatever else she was—fanatical, desperate, delusional—she wasn't evil. But any softening of his heart toward her had been reversed when he found Orix in her bed.

"My feelings are unchanged. I'll be glad to see the rebellion put down."

Sareya look skeptical, her nose wrinkled and mouth twisted.

Monash merely smiled.

"Who else knows?" Anskar asked.

"That Vihtor was your father?" Monash said. "And therefore in breach of the Order's rules, raising you here in the Burg?"

"That Vihtor was my father isn't news that would trouble me if everyone knew. About my mother, I mean. I grew up with your taunts—remember, Sareya? You used to be quite the gossip."

"In the past," Monash said. "But thus far, Sareya has impressed me with her honesty, her transparency."

Anskar laughed at that. The culture of Niyas was steeped into her blood, wasn't it?

"I've changed, Anskar," Sareya said. "And yes, the Seneschal knows about what we did together."

"Not quite the perfect knight you would like us to believe, are you?" the Seneschal said.

"I've never claimed to be perfect," said Anskar. "I no longer even desire it."

"That, I'm afraid, is in your blood," the Seneschal said. "How could it be otherwise, with the Necromancer Queen of Niyas as your mother?"

"Yet Sareya used to speak so highly of her."

"Used to," Sareya said, and Monash nodded encouragingly. "Like what happened between us, that's all in the past now."

Anskar hung his head, and he shook with barely suppressed anger. "So what will you do with me?"

"So meek? So passive? So resigned?" the Seneschal said. "From what Sareya tells me about your—how many repositories did you say he had?"

"Odd," Sareya said. "Two of them are somehow melded together. There weren't like that before. And the third… it's grown so much deeper."

Anskar threw up an obscuring darkness around his repositories, and Sareya raised an eyebrow. He'd shut her out for now, but she seemed to be taking it as a challenge.

"If Sareya is correct," Monash said, "then I have to assume

it's not so much a case of what I aim to do with you as what you will permit me to do. Presumably you have the power to resist any attempts of mine to incarcerate you, and the Grand Master has spoken at length about powers of yours that he has personally observed."

"He wants to use me," Anskar said.

"I bet he does. You wouldn't be the only one, believe me. Think of it as an act of supreme service to the Five."

"To use forbidden sorcery?"

"You use it when it suits you," the Seneschal said. "Why not in the name of the greater good? But as to what the Grand Master does or doesn't want from you, that is of no matter right now. You have answered your father's summons, and in doing so have learned a little more about yourself.

"But tell me this, Anskar: Do you consider yourself the heir to Niyas? Is it your plan to hand yourself over to Carred Selenas and let her raise you to a nonexistent throne?"

"I've already told you what I think of her," Anskar said. "Like you, I want the rebellion put down."

"You're sure about that, are you?"

Of course he wasn't sure. He needed a clear head to think about all that had happened, all that was happening now. And he knew he was being an idiot over Orix. Menselas, he was acting as if he owned Carred Selenas, and she'd never expressed the slightest interest in him save as Talia's son and heir.

And then he recalled the sensation of making love to Carred, only to realize he'd been duped by the Abbess, that he'd sullied himself with a crone disguised by illusion. He winced as he fought down the urge to be sick.

"I can see that you're not sure," Monash said. "But we have a little time in which to work out the best course of action. Most likely, I will send you back to Sansor. I know Hyle Pausus. He is not the kind of man to discard an advantage. In the meantime, the fewer people who know about your true identity, the better. Last thing we need is an angry veteran exacting revenge for the atrocities your mother committed, or some traitor taking you to the rebels for a ransom."

"So what do I do now?" Anskar asked.

"Go on as normal," the Seneschal said, "until I meet with you again. I need some time to consider all the options. But do nothing you know you shouldn't, Anskar. Sareya's own abilities have grown much, she tells me, since you left Niyas for Wintotashum. She'll know if you use forbidden sorcery, and I have no doubt that she'd inform me. We'll be watching you, Anskar."

"There's no need, Seneschal," Anskar said. "Since Vihtor's… since my father's death, I've been doing a lot of thinking. You're right to be concerned about me, about my abilities. I'm concerned myself." Unconsciously he rubbed the vambrace beneath his sleeve. "And I've come to a decision."

"Denied," Monash said. "You may not leave the Order under any circumstances. Even if I thought that were a prudent thing to permit, the Grand Master would never agree to it, and I do so dislike seeing him upset."

"That's not what I meant," Anskar said. "Quite the opposite. Whatever it is I've inherited from my mother—my inclinations, my abilities—has sown only seeds of conflict. I was mentored by a priest of the Healer, Brother Tion. He wasn't a perfect man, but he filled my head and heart with ideals. Ideals I've failed to live up to, but ideals I still strive towards."

Sareya rolled her eyes, but the Seneschal leaned forward on her throne, her good eye glinting.

"I was undecided, but now, with what you've said and with

your coming to Branil's Burg, perhaps this is the best time. And so, with your permission, Seneschal"—and here he dropped to one knee—"I solemnly pledge before Menselas the God of Five Aspects never again to use sorcery. Of any kind."

Sareya laughed out loud, but Monash silenced her with a raised finger.

"The Grand Master will never permit that," she said, and there was genuine sorrow in her voice.

"But if my catalyst is removed…"

"No." The Seneschal stood. "Absolutely not. That's a direct order, Anskar."

"Because I'd no longer be useful?"

"Without your abilities, what are you but the focus of a condemned rebellion, the heir of an enemy queen? Go now, and do nothing foolish. And do not stray far."

"Am I a prisoner?"

"You have the freedom of the Burg."

But not outside it. Anskar turned on his heel and strode for the double doors he'd entered by.

"One last thing," Seneschal Monash said, and Anskar turned back to face her.

"The Grand Master asked me to remind you about a knight who died aboard the *Exultant* on your way to Sansor."

"Colvin," Anskar said. "He attacked Orix."

"You were defending your friend, I know. The Grand Master believes you. This Orix's blade took Colvin's life, but some kind of sorcery of yours ruined his arm first. There were witnesses. And while you may have had little choice, word spread to Colvin's father, Archduke Peleus of Laokeni in the Great Southern Mountains of Ealysia. Colvin's father is a powerful man, and a patron of the Order of Eternal Vigilance. I am instructed to inform you that

Archduke Peleus has taken out a blood feud against you and this Orix. The Grand Master has already tried to dissuade him, but under Kailean law, the archduke is within his rights."

"Blood feud?" Anskar approached the Seneschal's throne. "What does that mean?"

Monash shrugged. "Assassins, mostly. Sometimes sorcerers. His family against yours and Orix's. The archduke has a vast family and a good deal of power and influence. Orix?"

"He's from the Plains of Khisig-Ugtal."

"Oh. Then it doesn't bode well for him. And you, Anskar: we already know about you. You're an orphan now, if you were not effectively one before. Tread warily, and reconsider your oath not to use your sorcerous powers."

FIVE

I SHOULDN'T HAVE COME.

As if he'd had a choice. There was only one reason Vihtor, on his deathbed, would have summoned Anskar back from the Kingdom of Thousand Lakes, and nothing could have kept him away. Solving the first half of the riddle of his birth had driven him close to despair. To learn he was the son of the Necromancer Queen was hardly a source of comfort. But the second half—to realize that Vihtor was his father—had given birth to a stillborn hope. There were no dueling natures within Anskar, his father's light battling his mother's darkness. According to his own story, Vihtor had been used by Queen Talia, beguiled by sorcery to give her an heir.

And now Vihtor was gone.

The shadows on the wall of Anskar's room lengthened as the sunlight coming through the open window shifted. That was his only measure of time. He ignored the rumbling of his stomach, the dryness in his mouth. All he could do was lie atop his unmade bed, crushed between anger and despair.

I shouldn't have come.

At some point he must have fallen asleep, and when he woke, it was getting dark outside. The night was still, not even the slightest breeze.

He stood and looked out the window, and in his mind's eye he saw the golden-eyed crow that had led him to Hallow Hill. Its visit that night had been the first intrusion into his life by his dead mother. The crow had been crushed, but Queen Talia had returned by other means.

It was a shock to realize he longed for her. Better the Necromancer Queen's son than an orphan. He called to her with his mind, but she was nowhere to be found inside him. Had she really left him for good this time?

A part of him hoped so, but another part—growing since his meeting with the new Seneschal—was starting to wish that he had listened to her all along. After all, hadn't Queen Talia's shade saved him on any number of occasions? For her own reasons, maybe, but all the same…

What had Vihtor ever done for him, except pretend not to be his father?

And what had really happened eighteen years ago? Had Queen Talia really used sorcery to enter Vihtor's chamber at the Burg? Had she really surrounded herself with a glamor that made him powerless to resist her?

Or, as Queen Talia claimed, was Anskar the child of rape?

His eyes followed the movement of light atop the curtain walls that separated Branil's Burg from the streets of Dorinah—the lantern of a lone guard walking the battlements.

He stepped away from the window and began to pace the

room. The growing need for his mother was almost painful. Why now and not before? A lifetime with neither parent: he should be used to being alone. It made no sense, pining for the mother he had never known in life, the mother who had never nurtured, only used him. She was probably using him now, manipulating him through his feelings. Just because he couldn't locate her within him didn't mean she wasn't there.

"I'm sorry," he said through gritted teeth. "I was wrong to banish you. Mother?"

Silence.

"Talk to me. I promise I'll never shut you out again."

He waited with bated breath, but still no answer.

Because she's a liar! Anskar thought savagely. She wouldn't do this to him if she'd been telling the truth. How could he take the word of a necromancer over a knight of the Order of Eternal Vigilance?

And then he remembered his new resolve: the promise—or was it a threat?—he'd made to Seneschal Monash. He'd made up his mind, so why was he still going back and forth between his mother and father? Sorcery or knighthood? The will of the Necromancer Queen, or the will of Menselas?

His hand rested on his chest, above the catalyst embedded beneath the skin. Even if the Order refused to help him remove it, there had to be a way. And if that meant he was of no further use to the Grand Master or Monash, then so be it. Let them come for him and expose themselves for what they were. It wasn't his fault he was the son of the enemy queen. Had no one told them Menselas was supposed to be merciful?

He put on the padded gambeson he wore beneath his armor, and then the mail hauberk he'd made for the third trial. He buckled on his sword belt and made sure *Amalantril* was snug in the scabbard. His fingers spasmed where they touched the hilt, and Anskar withdrew them. Warily, he touched the hilt again, and while there was no discomfort this time, he could feel a faint vibration coming through the stingray skin he had wound around the handle for a more secure grip.

"What now?" he muttered. Some new interference of his mother's, or something else?

He drove his senses into the sword and felt only an answering pulse in the dark-tide: not so much in his repository but in his veins. As if the dark had exceeded its barriers. As if it had grown one with him, and by extension, the sword he'd so painstakingly made.

Fretful, he grabbed his white cloak from its hook on the inside of the door, then on second thought, dropped it to the floor. It would make him stand out where he was going, and that much easier to find.

He tied his coin pouch to his belt, then took the sack that contained the three ingots of divine alloy and the powdered *nietan* horn from under the bed, looped it by its string over his shoulder, returned to the open window, and sought out the shadows atop the curtain walls.

One more use of the dark-tide and then no more, he told himself.

Well, two uses: to the parapet of the curtain wall, and then a second step beyond, into Dorinah.

With a final look around his room, in case he had forgotten anything, Anskar gazed out of the window and then poured himself into the dark.

He stepped out of the shadows and made his way toward the alchemical lights of the main street.

There were still people out and about, despite the sun having set more than an hour ago. Most were nipping in and out of the stores that were still open, and others were starting to congregate at the eatery tables that spilled out onto the street.

Anskar's stomach rumbled at the smell of the food. He was starving from not having eaten all day, but he'd not come here to eat.

He waved down a passing two-wheeler trap and told the driver to take him west, to the old city, where the Niyandrians who hadn't fled Dorinah during the invasion had been forced to live after their homes were occupied by mainlanders.

Once they left the main street, the only light was from the warm glow bleeding through the shutters of the houses they passed, snatches of moonlight, and the swinging lantern that hung from a pole beside the driver's bench. Once or twice people moved from the shadow of porches to approach the trap, their hands held out pleadingly, but the driver swore at them and whipped the horse to greater speed.

For a while they bumped and clattered over cobbled streets, but eventually came to roads of hard-packed mud, pitted and cracked from the recent rains.

"What business you got in the old city?" the driver asked. He was a dusky mainlander who sounded decidedly uncomfortable about where they were going.

"I'm looking for someone."

"Oh? Who's that, then? Maybe I know them."

Anskar didn't elaborate on his answer. The less anyone knew, the better.

The driver sniffed, snapped the reins, and started to whistle to himself.

They crossed a stone bridge that spanned a canal. The air stank of brine and seaweed, and in the scant light coming from the trap's lantern, Anskar could see scum on the surface of the water. There was a broken cart just visible at the foot of the canal, either the result of an accident or someone had simply wanted to get rid of it.

On the far side of the bridge, the city changed drastically. Flames burning in metal drums cast flickering shadows and a good deal more light than the poorly maintained alchemical lights of the eastern quarter. The buildings were much older here, built from solid blocks of dressed stone, though in many cases the roofs had decayed and been replaced with thatch. Those in better repair had pitched roofs, tiled red, and they reminded Anskar of some of the older buildings he'd seen in Wintotashum.

"Where d'you want to get out?" the driver called over his shoulder. He had stopped whistling now they were passing through the Niyandrian quarter.

"A tavern?" Anskar called back. As good a place as any to start his search.

The driver gave him a pitying look and shook his head. He had no doubt thought Anskar was down on his luck, with a need for beer and cheap Niyandrian whores. Better that than the truth: that he was a runaway knight of the Order of Eternal Vigilance in search of a sorcerer skilled enough to remove his catalyst.

They stuck to a brick-paved street with wide gutters on either side. Presumably the old city had once had functioning sewers, but now the gutters oozed sludge and were teeming with rats.

"That do you?" the driver asked, pulling up outside a rickety wooden structure built atop an older stone foundation. There were patrons seated on the sprawling wraparound porch, drinking and eating in small groups, talking and laughing. All Niyandrians. A crude sign had been nailed to the gable that showed a skeleton with blazing green eyes raising a mug with a head of froth. Beneath the image were two words in Niyandrian. Despite his rapid learning of the spoken language of Niyas, Anskar had never studied the peculiar script they wrote with, so he had no idea what the two words said.

"Thank you," he said, as he paid the driver and stepped down to the street.

He felt exposed and out of his element when the driver pulled away, and he lingered outside the tavern until the clatter of the trap's wheels was no more than a distant echo. He felt the eyes of several patrons studying him, not with hostility, more curiosity. He nodded to acknowledge them, and they nodded back before resuming their conversations.

Steeling himself, Anskar climbed the three wooden steps to the porch and pushed open the door.

The place was heaving with Niyandrians and filled with pungent cravv smoke, a narcotic herb. A trio of musicians played jaunty reels and jigs with a fiddle, a lute, and a hand drum. A space had been cleared on the floor, where a group of Niyandrians were dancing in time with the music. Others were seated at the long bar, watching while they cradled their drinks. Still more sat at tables closer to the hearth, sharing food from baskets and eating with their fingers.

Dozens of eyes tracked Anskar's progress to the bar. He heard muttered remarks about his armor and the color of his skin: red to a mainlander, but pale to a full-blooded Niyandrian.

The atmosphere was charged with the seepage from dozens of dawn-tide repositories and laced with the threat of the dusk. If he had wanted just any old sorcerer, he could have simply taken his pick; but for the delicate operation he had in mind, he needed someone exceptional, and someone with the same experience with crystal catalysts that the blind sorcerer Luzius Landav had possessed. Anskar had no idea if Niyandrians even used catalysts, if they even needed them. He knew Sareya and the other Niyandrian girls at the Burg had been fitted with catalysts the same as his, but was that the norm among their people?

The bartender, a grotesquely fat woman with several chins, affected a tight smile as he approached. "You lost?" she said in broken Nan-Rhouric.

"I'm thirsty," Anskar replied in Niyandrian, and the fat woman's eyes widened. He saw her noticing his own cat's eyes, and she gave the merest shrug of acceptance. "And I'm hungry," he added.

"We all eat the same here," she said. "None of that fancy menu business the mainlanders use. Ain't the call for it, or the coin."

Anskar glanced at the tables, where people were tucking into baskets of seared meat, pinkish crawfish, and the diced tentacles of some kind of blue and purple striped octopus.

"Caught in the inlets," the bartender said. "Save for the rats, that is."

"That's rat meat?" Anskar tried not to grimace as he recalled the rodents gamboling in the muck-filled gutters.

"I'm joking. It's chicken. Least they tell me it is."

Anskar ordered himself a basket of food and a mug of Niyandrian black beer, then found himself a corner table where he could feel the warmth coming off the hearth.

The beer was bitter and burned his throat, as if it were laced with hot pepper or some other spice. He took a second sip and found he quite liked it. By the time his food came, he was feeling more relaxed.

"Another beer, *sanos*?" the serving girl asked. *Sanos* was Niyandrian for "lord," a title of respect between strangers.

"Please," Anskar said, then looked up as he felt the girl linger.

She was lithe and lean, dressed in a simple black tunic that set off her crimson skin. She wore no shoes on her feet. Her dark hair was pulled back into a long ponytail that left her sharp, intelligent face fully exposed. Anskar caught himself staring at her striking beauty, and she looked away, embarrassed.

"Forgive me," he said. "I…"

"Don't be sorry," she said, meeting his gaze now. Anskar saw the slight frown as she registered his cat's eyes. "I'm pleased you like what you see. It is I who should apologize for my bashfulness. I'm not used to being noticed by mainlanders."

"I'm half Niyandrian," Anskar said. There, he'd admitted it— as much to himself as to her. He'd spent a lifetime denying it, but here, in this tavern, amid the music and the smoke and the laughter, he almost felt proud of his mixed blood.

Then he saw that the serving girl's eyes had widened, as if she expected an answer to a question she had not asked, at least not with words. He saw the promise in her slightly parted lips, and she glanced subtly up at the ceiling, where Anskar assumed there were rooms upstairs.

And he was tempted. Sorely tempted. But he'd come to the old town on another matter, and it was early days still; the Church's morality hadn't yet released its grip on him. And so he pretended he hadn't picked up the signs, and the girl flounced off to the bar to fetch him another beer.

Anskar considered the fare in the basket the girl had left on the table and decided to taste the chicken. He popped a strip into his mouth, chewed, and spat out the chewy, gristly meat. It probably was rat after all. The crawfish tasted faintly of mold and sewage, so he pushed that to one side of the basket. Which left only the red and purple diced octopus tentacles. They were surprisingly good: succulent and almost sweet. He chewed ravenously until they were gone, and as he cast about for sight of the serving girl, both to see where she had gotten to with his beer and to order another basket of food—without the rat meat and the crawfish—an idea occurred to him.

Anskar surreptitiously sent out feelers of sorcerous awareness, knowing this might be one of the very last times he was able to do such a thing. He split the questing strands into dozens of separate threads and sent them to probe the repositories of the patrons around the tavern. Far better than asking around; this way he could see for himself who might be up to the task.

The music died, and along with it the hubbub of the tavern.

The trio of musicians were staring at Anskar. The patrons glared too, and several of them had risen and were exchanging hushed words.

Anskar swallowed and tried to shrink back in his chair. At the same time, he doused his sorcerous senses, but if anything, that merely drove the tension in the room up a notch.

He started as a woman plonked herself down in the chair opposite. "Looking for something?" she asked in a bright, almost chirping voice.

There was a heartbeat's silence, and then the music struck up again and the patrons resumed their conversations, though one or two people still cast suspicious looks Anskar's way.

She was young, and she was tall, and she was lean and well-muscled. High cheekbones, a shock of midnight hair that fell to her narrow waist, and breasts barely covered by strips of silk. Her appearance was just a little too enticing. Like Vihtor's description of Queen Talia the night she came to visit him, it could only be the result of a sorcerous glamor.

Before he could stop himself, Anskar sent out a thread of awareness to probe the woman's repository, but it was like running into a wall.

She smiled, then helped herself to a strip of rat flesh from his basket. He couldn't take his eyes from her glistening, red lips as she chewed, and then she picked a stringy bit of meat from her teeth and flicked it to the floor.

"Well?" she said, teasing him with a smile.

"I'm looking for a sorcerer."

She made an expansive gesture. "Take your pick. We're all sorcerers here. It's in the blood. You have the blood. I can see by your eyes. War bastard? Half-breed? Child of rape?"

Anskar pushed his chair back and stood to leave.

"I'm sorry," the woman said. "That was insensitive."

She didn't seem sorry. She seemed amused as she helped herself to a piece of crawfish and wrinkled her face at the taste. "Not fresh caught," she said, spitting the rank meat out into the basket. "Oh, I'm sorry, were you planning to eat more of that?"

Anskar raised his hands and grimaced, and she laughed.

"What kind of sorcerer are you looking for?" she asked.

Anskar reseated himself. "A powerful one."

"I like power."

"I have coin," Anskar said.

"I like coin, too."

Anskar reached for his coin purse.

"Not in here," she said as she leaned across the table and grabbed his wrist. She smelled of musk and something sweet, and Anskar felt the bloom of arousal. She released his wrist and settled back into her chair.

The serving girl chose that moment to return, and with a

scowl she slammed a mug down in front of Anskar, spilling beer, before stalking off to the bar.

"I need the help of a sorcerer," Anskar said, "to remove this."

He pulled open the top of his shirt to reveal the scar where his catalyst had been fitted. There were thready black lines over the site, which he'd not noticed before.

"I can see why," the woman said.

"Can you help me?"

"No, but I know someone who can. How much coin do you have? Because it's going to cost a fair bit. Added to which is the small matter of my fee for connecting you."

SIX

THE NIYANDRIAN WOMAN—SHE HADN'T told Anskar her name, and he hadn't given his—led him along a series of alleyways lit only by the two moons and a scattering of stars. Once or twice they startled people sleeping in doorways. The entire area was teeming with rats, which must have pleased the tavern's chef.

She brought him at last to the banks of the canal, where the stench of algae and pitching tar was overpowering. There were lanterns lit upon the few barges moored along the canal walls, and by their scant light, Anskar noticed that the woman had changed her clothes, though there had been no opportunity for her to do so. Back at the tavern, she had been wearing a flimsy gown of silk that left more exposed than it covered, but now she was dressed in a padded leather jerkin and black pants with knee-length boots. There was a belt around her waist, from which hung a sheathed dagger. Anskar tensed. He'd been careless to follow this stranger out here alone.

"How did you do that?" he asked. "Change like that?"

"Just shut up and follow." All business now. No more flirting. No alluring charm to bring his guard down.

They followed the wharf until they came to a ramshackle hut of rotting planks of wood nailed together, with a roof of moldering thatch. There were wicker fish traps above the water line by the hut, and gutted eels hung from a drying rack outside.

"There you go," the woman said. "That'll be five copper pennies. Or the old copper queens, if you have them, though they're scarce these days, as the Order's replacing them."

Anskar started to unfasten his purse, not bothering to waste his breath objecting to the price.

"It's dark inside," he said as he rummaged about for the coins. There were no windows, but he would have expected light to bleed through the cracks between the planks.

"Don't worry, he's home," the woman said. "He's always home."

"Aren't you going to introduce us?"

"You speak Niyandrian well enough. And introductions aren't free. Just trying to save you some coin."

He paid her the five pennies, and she left without another word.

Anskar stood alone in the dark and the stench, listening to the water lapping against the barges. This whole situation screamed *trap* to him, yet he couldn't bring himself to leave. Instead, he sent his sorcerous senses within the hut… and they whiplashed back into him. Light exploded behind his eyes, and he crumpled to the ground.

Anskar grunted and shook his head to clear it. Groggily, he sat up.

A shadow loomed over him.

"A braided repository." It was a man's voice, thin and rasping, the words Niyandrian. "The dawn balanced by the dusk. Huh. And something else... Who's been consorting with demons? Who's been consorting with the dead?"

Emerald light flared on the man's palm, casting his face in eerie shadow. He was shorter than Anskar had first thought, and dressed in a frayed black robe that looked as though it had been woven from spiderwebs and ash. He had the red skin of a Niyandrian, though it had grayed in patches, which was common with age. He was extremely old: limbs knotted with arthritis, wrinkled face, twisted spine. His nose resembled a beak, and twin tufts of hair stuck up from his otherwise bald head like horns.

"You came to see me?"

Anskar stood. "I think so."

"Who told you I was here?"

"A woman. She didn't tell me her name."

"A woman, was it?" The man stepped forward and sniffed at Anskar, then fixed him with a stare. The old man's eyes were yellowed with jaundice.

"I met her in a tavern," Anskar said.

"Isn't that always the way? And what do you want from me?"

Anskar opened his shirt, and the old man peered intently at the discoloration above the site of his catalyst.

He shook his head, chuckling to himself. "So crude, so inefficient, and certainly not intended for whatever you've been up to. What are you called?"

"My name is Anskar. Anskar DeVantte."

"As Niyandrian a name as Hyle Pausus."

Anskar frowned. He'd not worn his white cloak, so why the

mention of the Grand Master?

"Your blood is at war with itself," the old man said. "Mixed blood will often do that. Especially such a mix."

"I'm half Niyandrian."

"You might believe that. Half mainlander, perhaps, but Niyandrian? It's a very dilute half. Perhaps a quarter?"

"What else?" Anskar asked. "And how do you know?"

"Is that what you came to see me about?" the old man asked. "Then I must disappoint you. I see impressions, broad brushstrokes. Your Niyandrian parent was not a full-blood. More than that, I can't say."

"My mother…" Anskar started. Queen Talia was of mixed race? "Are you saying my mother was part mainlander?"

"I'm not."

"Then… what?"

The old man shrugged. "All I've seen, I've told you." He turned towards the shack.

"That's not why I came to see you," Anskar said quickly. "I want you to remove my catalyst."

The old man turned back, the emerald light on his palm splashing over the entrance to the hut. The door was open.

"Then you'd better come inside."

It was damp inside, from where the recent heavy rains had presumably flooded the hut and soaked into the boards. The thatch ceiling sagged and was thick with mildew. Patches of black mold crept down from the top of the walls. There was an overpowering smell of pepper and loam and urine. Flies flitted about the interior. Anskar's skin itched, and he flicked a black speck from his arm—a flea. Cockroaches scuttled about the base of the walls, and in one corner there was a lice-infested sheepskin, which the old man must have used for a bed.

Anskar started to back out of the hut. The removal of a catalyst was going to involve cutting him open, and for such a procedure—he had learned as much from Brother Tion—the environment needed to be clean. Before he reached the door, a wave of dizziness washed over him. The old man caught him by the arm and guided him over to the sheepskin on the floor. Was it the stench? The mold? Or had the old man done something to him?

Anskar tried to protest as the old man lowered him onto the sheepskin, but no words would come. Cold seeped into his limbs, and they felt too heavy to move.

The old man's face appeared above him, yellow eyes flashing with fervor, lips parted in a hungry leer. Anskar reached for his braided repository, but it felt as though it were submerged in a stagnant pond. The more he tried to access it, the more nauseous he became. He turned to the dark-tide, but it slid over and around his senses.

The old man held up a rusty knife. Anskar struggled to move, but he had as much control over his body as he did his repositories. The old man winked and smiled.

And the knife came down.

Anskar screamed as the rusty blade plunged into his chest. He wanted to writhe and thrash, to kick out at the old man sawing through his skin, but still he couldn't move. Blood sprayed. Hot wetness splashed his skin. And the pain! When would it stop? Menselas, the pain!

The old man set aside the knife and reached into Anskar's chest wound with a filthy hand. Anskar felt a pressure above his sternum; then, with a cry of triumph, the old man withdrew his hand. In his fist he clutched the crystal catalyst.

"Here," the old man said, shoving a dirty rag over the wound still pumping blood in Anskar's chest. "Press down hard."

Instantly, the paralysis left Anskar's limbs. Shaking with shock, and in excruciating pain, he pressed down on the rag.

The old man turned away from him and removed a loose floorboard, then two more. He reached into the hole he had opened up and pulled out a large wooden box, which rattled and chinked as he moved it. From the box the old man took a glass jar, unscrewed the lid, and dropped the catalyst inside. He held it up to his eyes, chuckling and muttering, then returned the jar to the box.

"Selling that will keep me in food for a good few years," the old man said, "and this, a year more." He cut the coin purse from Anskar's belt and jangled it in front of him.

A terrible chill entered Anskar's bones. He began to buck and spasm.

"It'll pass," the old man said. "Or it won't. You'll either live or you'll die, but remember this: the decision to have the catalyst removed was yours, not mine."

Anskar stiffened as a crushing pain entered his chest, radiating throughout his entire body. Cold sweat drenched his skin. His face contorted in a grimace.

And darkness fell.

SEVEN

ANSKAR THRASHED ABOUT BLINDLY IN night-black waters. Stinking sludge entered his mouth and nose, filling his lungs. His chest was a searing agony.

Menselas! Please, Menselas!

He felt pressure on his sternum.

Warmth seeped into his skin, his muscles, his bones.

Anskar gasped, and his eyes snapped open. He coughed, and corruption spewed from his lungs.

He was lying on his back, but someone rolled him onto his side. He could feel the clinging weight of his sodden clothes.

Again a pressure on his chest, gentler this time. A hand, he realized, the palm pressed against his wound. Heat suffused his skin, and he felt muscle fibers knit. He coughed up more water and bile, then managed to raise his head.

"He dumped you in the canal," Sareya said.

She was kneeling beside him, one hand directing the healing

flow of the dawn-tide—a feat that was supposed to be a divine gift, granted to the elite among the healers by Menselas. But then, Sareya had always been extraordinary when it came to sorcery. She was moontouched.

Her white robe stood out like a beacon amid the grime of the wharf. Her black hair was severely tied back, and when Anskar met her eyes, they narrowed in disapproval.

"That's a lie!" came the response in Niyandrian.

Anskar sought out the old man and found him held tight by two knights—women who had come to Branil's Burg with Seneschal Monash.

There were six more female knights standing in a defensive half circle around Anskar and Sareya.

Sareya delivered a curt nod, and one of the knights plunged her sword into the old man's belly.

His yellow eyes widened in horror at the blood drenching the front of his black robe, then he shrieked as the knight twisted her sword and his guts spilled to the wharf.

Sorcery erupted from the old man's well, a noxious mixture of undifferentiated tides.

Sareya leaped to her feet and directed a surge of her own sorcery at him. Dusk-tide coalesced around the old man in a sphere, and it looked at first as though he had warded himself, but then the sphere turned to fire, and the old man screamed. Skin melted like wax. Flesh sloughed away, and bones charred black clattered to the ground. The old man's skull bounced as it hit the wharf, rolled, and then made a splash as it fell into the water.

"There was no need to kill him!" Anskar said, as he rolled to his knees and stood.

"Wrong," Sareya said. "There was every need. An attack on one of our knights is an attack on the Order of Eternal Vigilance."

"What's happened to you?" Anskar asked. Her only answer was a raised eyebrow that somehow conveyed a warning. "And how did you find me?" *And where's my sack of void-steel ingots?* He cast his gaze around, searching for signs of his sack of void-steel ingots and *nietan* horn, but it was nowhere to be seen.

"Did you really believe I wouldn't feel your use of the dark-tide to leave the citadel? Or were you too stupid to consider that? My sorcerous powers have grown rapidly, Anskar, more so since my arrival in Sansor, when I was granted permission to fully explore who I really am."

"By the Grand Master?" Had Hyle Pausus seen her potential and recruited her to his cause, the same as he had Anskar? It made sense.

"A great man," Sareya said.

"Did you… I was carrying a sack of belongings. Did you find it?"

Sareya frowned, then shook her head. "No. Perhaps it's at the bottom of the canal—where I was tempted to leave you."

Anskar noticed then. "Your nails… You used to paint them with the Niyandrian symbol for 'Blackwing.'" Queen Talia's soul name.

"I was mistaken about the *Necromancer Queen*," Sareya said, emphasizing the title, as if to show she'd made up her mind whose side she was on now. She stepped closer to Anskar and lowered her voice. "Maybe you should start painting your nails. After all, she's your mother."

"So you've forgiven the Order for snatching you from your family? I thought you wanted to see Niyas restored to Niyandrians."

There was a brief hesitation before Sareya answered. "I've grown up. You have to face reality sometime. Childish fantasies and fairytales have no place in my life anymore."

She nodded, and two of the women knights grabbed Anskar by the arms.

"What are you doing?" Anskar demanded.

"Seneschal Monash gave you the freedom of Branil's Burg, not Dorinah. And your request to have your catalyst removed was denied. You're coming with us."

"As a prisoner?" Anskar said. "I don't think so."

He reached inside for his braided repository, but he almost didn't find it. It was a flaccid ruin, like a collapsed lung, as if it had been somehow punctured by the removal of his catalyst. He tried to summon power from it anyway, but all he got for his efforts was a feeble eruption of sparking motes and a slap around the head from one of the knights holding him.

Angry, he searched for the burning seed close to his heart—the Warrior's Fire he'd stolen from Josac—only to find it a desiccated husk.

Desperate now, he grasped at the dark-tide.

But it was gone.

The realization struck Anskar like a bolt of lightning. His knees buckled, and he would have fallen but for the knights holding him up.

Gone.

No more yawning pit of blackness that threatened to swallow him up. Nothing but an unbearable feeling of emptiness.

And then he found it.

No longer a reservoir of shadow, a bottomless well of inky essence, the dark-tide had shifted within him. It had dispersed. It flowed through his veins, intermingled with his blood. It permeated every muscle, every organ, every pore of his skin. Not a repository anymore, it was a part of him. Not a new part, either: it felt old and familiar, the way it should have been. The way he had been born.

And there was something else too: a putrid ooze that he felt as a weight in his guts.

The earth-tide that gushed up from the core of the world.

He sought out Sareya's eyes as if she could explain what had happened to him.

The only answer she gave him was a cold stare, then she strode ahead, the two knights dragging him along in her wake.

It was as though the removal of the catalyst had been like the destruction of a dam. A dam that had held back the blossoming of who he really was, the inheritance he had received. The catalyst had awakened the latencies within, then acted to constrain them.

With nothing to lose, he clutched at the vileness in his guts, followed its putrid trail through his feet and below ground.

Sareya flashed him a look over her shoulder. Emerald light effused from her eyes as she spoke a cant.

And Anskar passed out.

EIGHT

"YOU'RE MAD OR AN IDIOT, Carred Selenas," she told herself. "Oh, sure, I'll go to the abyssal realms. Anything you say, Your Majesty. Trade star-metal for void-steel? Not a problem."

Only it was becoming one.

By Theltek's multiple bladders, she was thirsty, and she still had no idea which way to go.

The stone circle she walked around looked as though it had been built by giants. Each megalith was over twelve feet tall and must have weighed tons. They were misshapen pillars of rock with the texture of coral, and they glittered with mineral deposits of every conceivable color.

But if the standing stones provided the key to getting her home once her task here was finished, they betrayed no clue as to what it was. No inscriptions, no anomalies, nothing. They were just stones, as far as Carred could see. Lots of massive stones. Someone had gone to a lot of trouble arranging them like this.

The next concentric circle of megaliths, though large enough to contain the first, was no different, nor the one after that.

She'd sweated so much from the heat of the bronze sun she felt desiccated. And the blasted sun hadn't even moved, by her reckoning. Ever since she'd arrived in this gods-forsaken place, it had remained directly overhead, scorching in its heat. It might even have been mocking her. Maybe it didn't move—not at all.

She remembered Talia telling her once, as they lay in bed together, that time flowed at a different rate in the abyssal realms. Perhaps it didn't flow at all. She wished she'd pressed Talia for clarification now, but at the time the abyssal realms was a sore subject for the Queen. She was obsessed with the place, or rather paranoid about it—one of the reasons she'd needed Carred in her bed: in case the demons came for her. The other was the unnatural chill that only body warmth could chase away.

But how long had Carred been walking among the stones? It felt like hours. She wouldn't have been surprised to learn it was days. How much time had passed back on Wiraya? Seconds, minutes, weeks, months, years? And did it matter to Talia how long this took? After all, time was surely meaningless in the realm of the dead.

Squinting against the sun's glare, Carred moved outward from one stone circle to the next, as if she were following the course of a petrified ripple in a fossilized ocean. No matter how far she walked, the mesas in the distance never seemed to get any closer, and the standing stones continued in ever-widening circles. The sun remained stationary overhead, leaving her with no measure of time, but it felt as though she had been walking for hours. Her legs were numb, her feet blistered and stinging.

She stopped in the scant shade of a megalith and leaned her back against it, then quickly pushed away when a shock ran up her spine. She hesitated, then touched her palm to the stone. The surface was frigid despite the heat of the day, and she felt a steady pulse, as if the megalith were alive.

A screech ripped through the air, causing Carred to jump. She stepped back from the stone, frantically glancing around. There was nothing there. She raised her eyes to the red sky, but other than the bronze sun and the billowing, multihued clouds, it was empty.

A second screech answered, this time farther away. There followed another, quieter, more distant. For a brief moment, her head buzzed with a cacophony of calls and replies, as if thousands of invisible birds flocked overhead.

And then it all went still.

Carred continued to turn slowly, heart thudding in her chest as she strained to listen. In her anxiety, the megaliths in front reminded her of battlements, and she found herself hunkering down behind one and peeking out from the side.

After an age of waiting, she started to relax. Not daring to touch the stone, she seated herself cross-legged in the long shadow it cast. She kneaded her aching thighs, then grew aware once more of the dryness of her mouth and throat.

Right on cue, her stomach started to rumble.

Damn Talia. She'd not given Carred time to consider what she was getting into. There had been no planning, no thought of bringing something to eat and drink. An oversight? Or had Talia expected her to complete her mission and return in next to no time? The way things were going, that didn't seem very likely.

Forcing herself back to her feet, Carred decided to press on. Food she could go without—she'd done so before for days, when she'd run away from home as a child, and later when hiding out in the wilderness with the agents of the Order of Eternal

Vigilance hunting her. But water… If they even had such a thing in the abyssal realms, she needed to find it, and find it fast.

Weary beyond belief, she staggered between the rings of stones, the bronze sun throbbing directly overhead. Something flittered in her peripheral vision. She turned, but either she wasn't quick enough, or there was nothing there.

On she went, dragging her feet. Her lungs burned with each intake of breath, and her eyes were stinging and dry.

She glimpsed something dangling from the top of a megalith—a tiny leg made of stuffed cloth, a white woolen shoe with one lace undone.

Nally?

Carred picked up her pace, but when she reached the stone, the ragdoll had gone. She blinked to make sure, cursed herself for the hundredth time for coming here, then stumbled on her way again.

Shapes were moving among the standing stones now: ghosts from her past, misty and indistinct. Taloc glared as she passed, arms folded across his chest. Jayda swayed as if she were upon the deck of her ship, oily black tears streaking her cheeks. She saw Kovin, bare-assed and running after something—she could guess what. Then a woman, denser, more solid than the others, stepped into her path and embraced her.

"Marith!" Carred gasped. "Thank Theltek! Marith!"

But Marith's arms passed through her, and in the next instant she was gone.

Carred pitched to her knees and sobbed. Not for long. She didn't have long. Her choices were simple: keep going, or die.

When she stood and got underway again, she was convinced the standing stones had shifted position. She eyed them warily for the longest time, then decided, as with the phantoms she'd seen, that it was an effect of dehydration or the poisonous air.

The megaliths no longer seemed like defensive battlements. They began to resemble malformed giants, crudely carved from stone, moving to hem her in. When she stared at them, they remained still, but when she blinked... Had they moved? A little to the left? A fraction to the right?

As she passed into the gap between two megaliths, she banged her face into hard rock and fell on her backside, clutching her nose. How was that possible? Had the megalith moved to intercept her?

The screeching started again, closer this time.

She could feel the pulse in her neck as she stood and brushed herself down. Gingerly, she touched her nose to make sure it wasn't broken. Flashes of light drew her eyes. Filaments of lightning, fine as a silkworm's thread, leaped from stone to stone.

She turned to take it all in.

She was within what looked like a gigantic spider's web of stone and light, and she was the fly. Only for a moment, and then the lightning was gone.

The scrunch of gravel caused her to turn just as a slender man stepped from behind a megalith, eyes like blazing sapphires. His skin was perfectly white and resembled alabaster, his hair a writhing nest of golden serpents. He had long, elegant limbs and golden fingernails. He was naked save for a loincloth and a leather harness about his shoulders and waist, from which hung half a dozen silver knives.

Carred's hand went to her sword, and the man responded with a cock of his head and a snaggletoothed smile. Confidence drained from her, and she relinquished her grip on the hilt as she backed away.

Screeches swirled around her, gathering in strength. In the

distance now, there were dark specks in the sky, wheeling and banking.

The man said something in a language she didn't understand, his voice chiming like crystal bells. His fingers danced over the blades in his harness. He spoke again, a musical cadence to his tone, a hint of breaking glass.

Carred glanced over her shoulder as she backed towards the gap between two standing stones, and she gasped as they slid together, cutting off her retreat. Around her, the circle she was within closed up like a noose, stones clacking together as they touched.

She turned back to the man.

He took his time coming towards her, nimble, graceful as a dancer. He raised a hand, shadows spilling from the fingertips and weaving a net of inky vapor in the air. With a disdainful flick of his wrist, the man flung the shadow web over her. She tried to duck aside, but she was cold and trembling and terribly weak. The net dropped over her, and where it touched, her skin prickled and tingled. The gaseous mesh molded itself to her form, encasing her like a second skin. She shivered and trembled, unable to move as the man crossed the last few feet to stand in front of her.

One of his hands went to his crotch, where he was hard beneath his loincloth. A cruel grin contorted his face, and he sprayed spittle as he spoke once more, his voice no longer chiming and musical; it was more of a growl.

Heat radiated through Carred's belly, bloomed between her legs. The man's tongue darted between his teeth, black and veined. He made a clutching motion with his hand, and Carred moaned, as if he'd drawn the sound out of her.

Above, the sky was filled with winged shapes, growing larger as they approached. The screeching was so loud, it pounded against her skull.

The man glanced up and roared with the force of a thunderclap, and the winged shapes scattered, then came to roost atop the closed wall of megaliths that surrounded Carred: scrawny, human-like things with feathered wings and scaly, gray skin. They watched her with black eyes. Several of them opened mouths bristling with needle-sharp teeth.

The man with the alabaster skin turned his sapphire eyes once more upon her. He closed his hand around her throat as he leaned in to lick her face. The shadow web holding her dissolved as he pressed his hardness against her.

Carred turned her face aside, and the man sank sharp teeth into her neck—just a little. Enough to taste her blood. The watchers atop the megaliths fluttered their wings and let out a chorus of squawks.

The man ground himself against her and then suddenly recoiled, as if burned. A knife seemed to appear in his hand, he had drawn it so quickly. He jabbed its slender blade towards the pouch hanging from Carred's belt. Jabbed again, and barked something at her.

Watching his eyes for permission, Carred untied the pouch and loosened the drawstring. The man took a step back, then indicated with the knife that she should show him what was inside.

Carred reached into the pouch and took out a pinch of glittery powder, smiling to show that it was all right. The man edged closer for a better look, and she flicked it in his face.

Star-metal.

He howled and flung himself back, clutching his face. Steam plumed between his fingers as he writhed and thrashed. He pitched to his back, wailing in agony as the flesh of his hands sloughed away, and beneath their bony remains, a black and glistening skull began to dissolve.

Crack followed crack all around her as the stone circle opened up. The winged demons atop the megaliths rose into the air on snapping wings, then with ravenous shrieks, they swooped down towards the dying man, rending and ripping. The sound put the fear of Theltek in her, and Carred had no intention of stopping to watch.

With the pouch of star-metal clutched in her hand, she was already running.

NINE

WHAT DID IT MEAN? WHAT had he become? The flooding
of his entire body with the dark-tide, its intermingling with his
blood, consumed Anskar's sleeping mind. He dreamed as well,
though all he retained were alternating impressions of horror
and hope.

He awoke back at Branil's Burg. He knew before he opened his
eyes that he was in the infirmary. Despite the healers' best efforts
to disguise it with bunches of dried lavender that hung from
the ceiling beams and incense burning in censers, the infirmary
stank almost as bad as the canal, as if all the bodily waste spilled
here over the years had soaked into the stone and the woodwork.

Gone was the excruciating pain in his chest, replaced by an
infuriating itch and a tightness that tugged at his skin. He threw
off the sheets covering him so that he could see, but the wound
had been packed and dressed, and a bandage had been wound
around his chest.

"Ah, the sleeper awakes."

A white-robed priest of the Healer approached along the gangway between the rows of beds, most of which were empty. The priest had a long, severe face, with hollow cheeks and red-rimmed eyes. A curling tuft of gray beard adorned his chin, but other than that he had no facial hair, and there was no hair at all on his head.

Anskar remembered the priest from when Brother Tion had been his mentor. On the few occasions Tion had been otherwise engaged—and Anskar could now guess why—Brother Mizral had stood in. Mizral had been a horrible confessor, sneering at every minor transgression that Anskar had recounted. Mizral gave the impression that everyone else was an abominable sinner, but that he was above such failings. By the good grace of Menselas, of course.

"Don't fiddle with the bandages," Mizral said. "Last thing you want's another infection. The first was bad enough. Whatever were you doing, allowing a savage to cut you open with a rusty knife? In a hovel, no less, or so they tell me. Are you a complete imbecile?"

"I had no choice," Anskar said, meaning that the old Niyandrian man had given him none.

"Nonsense," Mizral said. "No one made you sneak out of the Burg at night. No one forced you to go down to a squalid Niyandrian quarter. No one made you hand over a purse of coins."

"Actually, they did," Anskar said. "The old man took it from me."

"Are you answering me back, Anskar DeVantte? I do hope not. You already have enough sin heaped up on your plate. More than enough. Now, I've dealt with the infection caused by foulness entering your wound from without, but alas, there was little I could do about the foulness that came from within."

"What's that supposed to mean?" Anskar asked.

"There was a taint around the site of your catalyst. The crystal must have been severely corrupted." Mizral sniffed and shook his head. "Catalyst crystals have a specific function, and they're attuned only to the tides of dusk and dawn. Yours, I would wager, was used in other ways. You've only yourself to blame. Abuse, I call it. Self-abuse. The sort of thing that will make you blind, and then how will you find your way to the Five's eternal embrace? Whatever would Brother Tion think? On second thought, forget I asked that. Mend your ways, Anskar. Mark my words. *Mend* your ways."

"This taint," Anskar said. "Does it linger? What will it do to me?"

"Oh, you'll recover, given time. And prayer. And piety. And chastity. And if you stop doing whatever caused it in the first place. You'll experience a good degree of weakness, and probably a good few runs to the latrine, but now that the contaminant has been removed, you should recover."

"You mean my catalyst? Did Sareya retrieve it?"

"She did, and it's been hidden away for safekeeping."

Anskar shut his eyes and dropped his head back against the pillow. "I won't have it back."

Brother Mizral ignored that. "You're lucky to be alive. If Sareya had not put you to sleep when she did, the consequences of having your catalyst ripped from your chest, and your repositories ruptured in the process, would have had even more dire consequences.

"Now I must inform the Seneschal that you're awake. In the meantime, I'll send my auxiliary to give you a bed bath.

Seneschal Monash has a delicate nose, and she cannot bear the slightest hint of corruption—physical or moral. You should strive to be more like her."

Brother Mizral strode away down the infirmary, and a few minutes later Anskar heard the approach of the auxiliary who'd come to bathe him.

"Hello, Anskar," a familiar voice said.

With a combination of shock and confusion, he saw Blosius standing over the bed with a stack of towels cradled in his arms.

Anskar was too weak to protest as Blosius set about washing and drying him atop the bed. The young man did his best, but he was even more awkward with nursing care than he'd been in the fight square. Something else he wasn't cut out to do. When he'd finished, and Anskar had muttered his thanks, Blosius hesitated at the foot of the bed.

"Aren't you going to ask why I'm here?"

"Seneschal Monash?" Anskar guessed.

Blosius's face reddened, and he scuttled around the side of the bed so that he could lean in and whisper. "She expelled me from the postulancy. Said I was an incurable drunkard and a useless waste of space, more suited to knitting than fighting."

Anskar almost laughed. The Seneschal was right, although there were gentler ways of bringing Blosius to that realization for himself. Anskar had known Blosius was not cut out to be a knight from the start, and their fight during the first trial had only confirmed the fact. But it was the Order's rule that postulants who failed could have a second chance, and even a third. The official reason was that you learned more from your defeats than your victories, which sounded a lot like, "Losers make wiser and better knights in the long-term." The idea was nonsense to Anskar: lose in the real world, and you were neither wiser nor better, you were dead.

"I don't understand," Anskar said. "If Monash kicked you out, why are you still at the Burg? And why in Menselas' name are you assisting the healers?"

Blosius looked close to tears. "Because I begged her to let me stay. My father will kill me if I go home a failure. Worse, he'll disinherit me."

"Does he still send you an allowance?"

"Yes. But not for much longer, if word reaches him about what's happened. I'm surprised it hasn't already. I wouldn't put it past him to take back the coin I saved out of my allowance in the vault that used to be the Hooded One's chapel."

"So you saved some coins rather than spent it all? I guess that's something."

"Oh, I spend it well enough," Blosius said. "On wine and spirits, mostly. But my allowance is considerable. Father wanted to create the right impression. I've saved a good deal."

"And it's all here, in the vault?"

Blosius gave him a sly look. "A small fraction. You see, I thought something like this might happen one day, so I deposited the bulk of my savings in a Niyandrian-owned bank in Dorinah."

"Then why not leave?" Anskar asked. "You're no healer's auxiliary, and you're certainly not going to make it as a knight."

Blosius looked about to protest, but Anskar forestalled him.

"That wasn't meant to be a put-down. We all have different strengths and abilities."

"Some of us do," Blosius said dejectedly.

"You've already demonstrated one: having the foresight to

move your wealth before your father or the Order can take it from you. That was well done."

Blosius beamed at that. "Yes, I suppose it was."

"You intend to punish me?" Anskar asked when Seneschal Monash came to see him in the infirmary. He was still in bed, for he lacked the strength to walk farther than the latrine block.

"I intend to follow procedure," the Seneschal said. "You disobeyed a direct order to remain within the grounds of Branil's Burg, and you did so a second time when you had your catalyst removed—a catalyst, I might add, that was fitted at considerable cost to the Order of Eternal Vigilance. Not against your will, I might add. You entered the trials. And you consented to the fitting of the catalyst."

"I'll reimburse the Order," Anskar said.

"With what?"

"The coin the old Niyandrian stole from me. I assume Sareya retrieved it."

"She did, and it has already been added to the Burg's coffers. But such a paltry amount, were it still yours, would not even begin to compensate the Order for the cost of the catalyst. I fear the cost is beyond you."

"Are you saying the Order's knights owe a debt they'll never be able to pay?"

"What I am saying is that you are bought and paid for." The Seneschal's narrowed eyes dared him to challenge her.

"I just want to be a knight," Anskar said. "Nothing more, nothing less."

"A childish ideal," Monash retorted. She looked around to

ensure they weren't being overheard. "Do you really think that's what the Order is all about? Men and women warriors with the disadvantage of holy rules? Five aspects, Anskar. Menselas is a god of five aspects; not one, not two. No one said it was easy to be a consecrated knight. Menselas only knows how hard it's been for me—I would venture to say for all of us. Why should you be any different? Because the all-pious Vihtor Ulnar was your father? Because the Necromancer Queen was your mother?"

If she'd slapped him, it would have stung less.

"So what happens next?" Anskar asked.

Monash drew in a sharp breath. "I've made arrangements for you to return to Sansor, where I have no doubt the Grand Master will deal with you as you deserve. Don't look so worried. Hyle Pausus is not a reckless man given to wasting resources."

"He'll force me to use sorcery!" Anskar protested. "He'll insist upon restoring my catalyst."

"That, too, is my assumption," the Seneschal said, "and I mean to save him the bother. There is a competent sorcerer I trust on the mainland, in Kroe—a far shorter journey by sea than Sansor. I took the liberty of sending for her when Sareya first brought you back. We're expecting her to arrive in the next week or so."

The healers removed the bandages from Anskar's chest to reveal a thick, angry scar. The surrounding skin retained some purplish bruising and black veins from the catalyst's corruption. He was still frail, but Blosius started to mobilize him with short walks to the latrines and back, always supporting him under the arm. Even such a short walk brought Anskar out in a sweat, and he would often sleep straight after.

While he slept, his dreams were filled with rot, plague, and the dead. Some of those dead he knew: Ryala Mitredd, Naul, even Gann, whose pieced-up corpse somehow still managed to snarl and curse at him. He often woke screaming, and then curses came from the other patients in the dormitory.

After, he would lie awake, and the dead would now walk the infirmary: ghosts of patients who had died there, he assumed, for many were horribly injured or diseased, their bodies swathed in bandages. He watched them throughout the dark hours, and sometimes they would watch him too. A few of them even spoke, threatening what they would do to him if ever he tried to control them. He wondered at first why they should fear that, but it should have been obvious. The vile essence that had started in his guts was now a constant trickle from the ground up. While the dark-tide flowed within as naturally as his blood, the earth-tide oozed like putrid sludge.

One night, as the ghosts processed through the infirmary, the dark-tide pulsing in his veins, the earth-tide swilling in his guts, Anskar tossed and turned on his bed. He wished he'd never gone into the Niyandrian quarter. Wished he'd never asked the old man to remove his catalyst.

And it was then that Queen Talia came back to him.

You're beyond a catalyst now.

And just like that, his mother was back.

Anskar instantly tried to shut her out, but his braided repository was a shrunken ruin, and he couldn't draw more than a wispy thread of essence from it, which immediately dissolved into nothing.

Queen Talia laughed—not a mocking laugh; it was good-natured, almost affectionate.

There were many things I had to do to keep you from the eyes of the world, Anskar. *The first was to spread the rumor that you were a daughter, not a son.*

"And many Niyandrian girls were taken from their families as a result," Anskar muttered under his breath, in case the other patients should hear and think he was mad.

What was innate to you, I separated out and hid in the depths of your being. You were not supposed to discover the dark-tide within you, but it seems the fitting of your catalyst, the blossoming of your dawn- and dusk-tide repositories, shed a light into the darkness I placed so far beneath them.

"You have that kind of power?"

I did once, Queen Talia said. *Maybe I will again. But sorcery is seldom as predictable as we would like. During the removal of your catalyst, the vast well into which I had stored your affinity for the dark-tide was ruptured.*

"I feel it, even now," Anskar said, "in my blood."

It has come home to roost, Queen Talia said. *And perhaps the time for that is right. We shall no doubt see.*

"And the earth-tide?"

That power I feared had not passed to you, but after the fitting of your catalyst...

"I began to hear the dead speak."

A minor effect, but yes. When I worked my necromancy through you during the ritual to summon Nysrog, and later when you lay helpless outside the Tainted Cabal's citadel, I began to suspect. As with the dark-tide, I think the catalyst was holding you back, but now that it is gone... You have such potential for necromancy, Anskar. You could be great.

"Great like you? Maybe I don't want to be. And I certainly don't want to be a necromancer. I wanted to be free of all sorcery, not just the dawn- and the dusk-tides. It was a mistake having my catalyst removed. It's only made things worse."

Foolish child. You were meant to be hidden at the heart of the Order of Eternal Vigilance, not indoctrinated to the point of stupidity. I never for once considered that you might grow up believing their hypocrisy. Sorcery is natural to us, Anskar. Literally, it is in your blood. Menselas is no more than a lie perpetuated to control the weak of mind.

"My father didn't think so."

Your father was the biggest hypocrite of them all!

"He was a good man."

He was a rapist and a murderer of nations. If I come across his shade in the realm of the dead, I'll annihilate it for all the things he's done!

"Get out!" Anskar yelled, and this time patients roused from their beds to stare at him. "Leave and never come back!"

Oh, I'm going nowhere, you pathetic, impotent boy. You really think you can shut me out with the earth-tide? With the dark? They are the waters in which I gave birth to you.

"Get out!" Anskar screamed again.

And then hands were restraining him on the bed. A woman, voice tight with shock, said, "He's possessed. Menselas preserve us, he's possessed."

"Anskar?" a man said. "Anskar, it's me, Brother Mizral."

"Get her out of me!" Anskar cried. He thrashed and writhed on the bed, then tasted blood from where he'd bitten his tongue.

"Get Seneschal Monash!" Mizral said.

Warmth suffused Anskar's skin from where the priest of the Healer touched him, and he drifted slowly to sleep.

TEN

ANSKAR'S HEAD BOBBED AS BLOSIUS pushed him along the corridor in a wheeled wooden chair.

He was only dimly aware of his surroundings, having not yet fully recovered from the sorcerous sleep Brother Mizral had used to relieve his distress—a use of the dawn-tide that Anskar hadn't previously considered. A bit too late to worry about that now, considering the withered state of his braided repository. Although that could all change, if the Seneschal had her way and he was sent back to Sansor with a new catalyst embedded beneath the skin of his chest.

Anskar had heard little of the conversations that ensued when the Seneschal arrived at his infirmary bed, but he'd heard enough. Brother Mizral had told her that Anskar was begging for the spirit that possessed him to be exorcized. "Queen Talia of Niyas?" the Seneschal asked. Mizral must have nodded, because the Seneschal had given her permission for the exorcism to go ahead. Indeed, she had insisted upon it.

Blosius wheeled him into a gloomy chapel, its interior dimly lit by tall white candles on iron stands shaped like intertwining serpents. The air was thick with incense, which collected beneath the vaulted ceiling. Underneath the smell of the incense, Anskar detected dankness and mold, and he could see heavy tangles of cobwebs hanging from the ceiling beams.

On a plinth at the center of the chapel was a large pitcher, and around it stood three priests of the Elder, their faces etched with shadow. They looked for all intents and purposes like neglected statues: two women, both robed in gray, and one frail old man in a moth-eaten overcoat with only a single brass button remaining, and even that was hanging from a thread.

The man had been present at the pre-trials banquet—if that was what it could be called, considering the scant fare that had been served to the postulants while the consecrated knights ate and drank their fill. Anskar dimly recollected the old man's speech—something about yearling lambs that had been totally incomprehensible.

Blosius steered the wheeled chair close to the plinth, only stopping when one of the gray-robed women, her face and hair equally gray, held up a staying hand.

Seneschal Monash entered the chapel, Sareya at her side, and Brother Mizral and two other priests of the Healer following close behind.

Blosius patted Anskar on the shoulder. "Don't worry, old friend, it's going to be all right."

How would he know? Presumably he'd never gone through a ritual exorcism himself. Blosius's mother was back home on the mainland in some vast manor house, not in the realm of the dead. A living, breathing person, not an undying spirit sluicing through his marrow.

The only surprise to Anskar was that they had come to this dark and dusty place rather than the Healer's chapel. He'd never before set foot in the Elder's chapel, and it wasn't at all as he would have expected. The overwhelming impression was of emptiness and decay, whereas, he supposed, he would have expected floor-to-ceiling bookshelves and all manner of exotic exhibits. But then, the priests of the Elder he had met were fiercely competitive about their hard-earned knowledge. Perhaps the only way they could come together without arguing was in a place as nondescript as this.

The atmosphere in the chapel reminded him of the Abbey of the Hooded One, where he'd witnessed an attempt by the Tainted Cabal to summon Nysrog. That memory alone made him try to stand, but he couldn't move. Leather restraints secured his arms and legs to the wheeled chair. He struggled against them and threw his weight back, causing the chair to rear.

"It's all right," Blosius said, preventing him from tipping over backwards. "Everything's going to be all right."

"Be still, Anskar," Mizral snapped. "After all, you asked for this. Your mother's influence has been subverting you all along. If only Vihtor had been more alert to the threat and done something about it."

"Please, Seneschal," Anskar said, "don't send me back to Sansor."

Monash sighed. She might have been acting, but Anskar thought she looked genuinely saddened by the prospect. "I'm sorry, but it's out of my hands."

Sareya smiled reassuringly. "We're not defined by where we come from. I know that now. Soon you'll be free of your past, and everything that has been holding you back."

Anskar studied her through narrowed eyes. He wanted to believe her. Wanted to believe the Seneschal too. It partially made sense to him, that all his troubles had started with the fitting of the catalyst and, soon after, his mother's appearance in his life.

"You still want us to proceed?" the old man asked in his rasping voice.

"Of course, Brother Olaf," Monash said.

Brother Olaf lifted the pitcher from the plinth in trembling hands, while the two women priests began a sonorous chant in ancient Skanuric.

"Do you renounce the gods of Niyas?" Brother Olaf asked. "Theltek of the Thousand Eyes, Suten the Sly, Cataban Cat's Claw, Neruba Nightshade, Warlag of the Woods, Phayon—"

"I don't know them," Anskar said.

Brother Olaf sighed at the interruption.

"Can't you just lump them all together?" Monash asked.

"If you insist, Seneschal. Well, Anskar DeVantte, do you renounce them? All of them?"

"Yes," Anskar said. "I renounce them." He wished he could see Sareya's reaction, but she had moved behind him with the Seneschal, Brother Mizral, and the healers. Blosius squeezed his shoulder in encouragement.

Anskar started as Brother Olaf poured icy water over his head. It ran down his face and soaked into his shirt.

"Do you renounce the heathen culture of Niyas?"

"I do."

He shivered this time as the priest tipped more water over his head, and his teeth chattered. The incantations of the two old women grew louder, their voices shrill and piercing. A corona of the dawn-tide manifested around their heads, and when Anskar raised his eyes to Brother Olaf, he had to blink against the glare. The old man's face was suffused with golden light.

"Do you renounce all influence from the realm of the dead?"

"I do."

More water. He shuddered.

And then he felt his mother's presence. She started to squirm within his marrow.

"Do you renounce your mother, Queen Talia of Niyas?"

The seething within his marrow stopped, as if Queen Talia were holding her breath. It was enough to make Anskar hesitate.

"Do you renounce—?"

"I do!" Anskar cried. "Get her out of me!"

Brother Olaf's face blazed with the brightness of the sun, causing Anskar to shut his eyes.

"So be it!" the old man cried, and he joined his voice to the voices of the priestesses, weaving different words of Skanuric in between their steady cant, counterpointing, harmonizing, elevating the chant to a chord, a song, a symphony of the dawn-tide that swept through Anskar's mind and echoed around his skull. Its vibrations rattled his bones, pounded his flesh. He felt the words as fire, as blasts of lightning, as barbs of steel. And then an excoriating heat burned through his veins and his marrow. The last thing he heard was Queen Talia wailing in the distance, her cries growing farther and farther away, until, finally, they were gone.

Anskar hung suspended in some featureless limbo, aware of nothing save the cold hardness of the vambrace on his forearm. It was an anchor for him, a focal point that tugged him back to the world.

And when he opened his eyes to see the three priests of the Elder staring at him, expectation in their eyes, their skin back to its dull, lifeless gray, he knew at once he was free.

Queen Talia had gone.

"Did it work?" Monash asked.

Brother Olaf gave a weary smile. "See for yourself, Seneschal."

Monash, with Sareya trailing her like a shadow, came to stand in front of Anskar's chair. She frowned and glanced at Sareya, who gave a tentative smile as she nodded.

"There's no trace of the Necromancer Queen," Sareya said, then she narrowed her eyes.

Had she sensed it? Had she seen that the earth-tide still pooled in his guts, and the dark-tide mingled with his blood?

But when Anskar tried to grasp the dark-tide within him, it was like water dripping between his fingers. Without the yawning reservoir of darkness deep within his being, he could find no way to grasp the power, nor mold it to his will.

That was just as he wanted it.

And the earth-tide? The feel of it within him made his stomach clench and bile rise to his throat. Perhaps with his mother gone back to the realm of the dead, the earth-tide would drain away. And if it didn't, he would simply ignore it.

"You are free," the Seneschal said, and Anskar wept with relief. "But it changes nothing. You will have a new catalyst fitted within the week—one that will inhibit your powers until the Grand Master decides otherwise. And then you will return to Sansor."

ELEVEN

MARITH PELHUR WAS A CHANGED woman. She knew that, and the knowledge grated, but what could she do about it? And besides, had she actually changed, or had she merely accepted what she had always been? A sorcerer of rare talent. One of the moontouched.

Jared, her husband, had always warned her about delving too deep into the mysteries of the tides. Like all Niyandrians who embraced their innate gifts, Jared had been proficient with the dawn- and a good deal of the dusk-, but further than that he would not go, and he didn't think she should either. Yet maybe if either of them had gone further, Jared wouldn't have died during the war, when pestilence swept the isle in the wake of so much bloodshed; when corpses had been piled high, dumped in mass graves, or left floating in lakes and rivers, polluting the waters. But she had honored Jared's wishes when he'd been alive, and even after she had burned his body on a pyre of her own making.

Jared had been foolish to forsake so large a part of what it meant to be a Niyandrian, but he was hardly alone in that. Practice of sorcery had been on the decline at the time of the war, when there had been a general malaise, a misplaced belief that Queen Talia's power would keep the people of the isle safe and provide for all their needs. More likely, Queen Talia had wanted them to believe that so there would be fewer challenges to her authority in later years, should she achieve her goal of being Queen—Empress, even!—forever. The practice of sorcery had waned even more in the years since. Carred was a prime example of that.

But Marith had been a fool too; a fool to listen to her husband. If she hadn't listened, she would have been prepared when their daughter—all she had left in the world after Jared's death—caught the rot. If she hadn't been a fool, Kyra might still be alive.

Even after Kyra's death, she had honored Jared's wishes. She'd buried what she was along with her daughter. She'd denied what she had inherited from her grandmother, and she had embraced mediocrity. Marith Pelhur, a smallholder! She was supposed to be one of the moontouched, not a breeder of goats and cattle.

But then Carred had stayed with her that last time. Then the assassins had come.

Jared would understand. And even if he didn't, Marith wasn't going to neglect the advantages Theltek had granted her any longer, not if she had the chance to make a difference, not if her abilities might keep Carred, or even herself, alive during the coming conflict.

Because a conflict was coming, she was certain of it. She'd woken every night for weeks with a feeling of impending doom. A message from Theltek? A sickness of the mind? She had no way of telling, but she was taking no more chances. This time, she would be prepared.

She took one of the iron rods she'd had the blacksmith in Brittling Down, the nearest village, prepare and placed it on the workbench in the basement. On a shelf above stood the statue of Theltek she'd inherited from her grandmother, the last moontouched in their family line, and a woman who had embraced her gifts and earned the fear and respect of the entire district the family had always lived in. Theltek, depicted in bronze, with six eyes, six arms, and four legs—the best the sculptor could do to suggest a thousand or more of each. Theltek, whom Marith had kept locked in a box in her storage shed until the day Carred had fled and Marith had called down sorcerous fire on those who came to kill her.

She was still bitter. Every time she thought about what had happened, her fingertips burned with the need to unleash fire, and a gaping hole of emptiness opened up inside her.

Carred.

Marith had tried reaching out to her with her mind. She'd done it before, but only over short distances. When she failed, she'd tried something she had found in her grandmother's book of calculations, and she'd employed a bowl filled with water in order to scry far and wide for Carred.

She had seen many things, things that had made her laugh or fear to go out after dark. She'd seen things that would have made another woman blush. But she had not seen Carred anywhere on Niyas. And when she had extended her scrying, she realized that Carred was nowhere in the whole of Wiraya.

Nor was she dead, Marith was certain of that. Call if a gut feeling, call it a connection at the deepest level, but she knew. Of course, if she'd been a necromancer, she might have confirmed her feeling by communing with the realm of the dead.

But if she was right about Carred not being on Wiraya, yet still alive, that left only a few options, and none of them good. When Marith had tried to scry in the abyssal realms, the water had turned to blood.

She might have misread the sign, but she didn't think so. The same intuition that told her Carred was alive told her that she very soon might not be. She'd not stopped trembling since. She couldn't take another loss. Sweet Theltek, not Carred as well? *Damn you, Marith, you weren't supposed to get this close to anyone again. You swore an oath!*

She and Carred had seen each other only rarely, but each time they were together, it felt as though they had never been apart. Carred had a lover in almost every town; Marith knew that. They both used to joke about it, and while she was all right with it—and used to claim that she was indifferent—more sober times had made her honest enough to admit that it did bother her, that if she could, she'd have Carred here, alone, all to herself.

She shook her head as she placed a hand at each end of the rod and reached inside for the dusk-tide bubbling over in its repository. She had to stop fantasizing about long, warm evenings, sipping wine and making love. Such times might never come again. But if there was any hope, then she needed to work, and study, then work some more.

The demons, after all, weren't likely to give Carred back if Marith asked them nicely.

Shutting her eyes so she could focus, she teased the dusk-tide's vitriol from its repository, let the arcane power surge through her veins, and then drove it with the force of her will into the rod, all the while containing it, corralling it with the cants of restriction she'd learned from her grandmother's book of calculations, which the old woman had painstakingly written out by hand in the hope that her granddaughter might one day make use of the knowledge. Well, now that day had come.

The rod glowed red, then white, then an unearthly kind of blue. Its ends where she touched it grew blisteringly hot, then instantly chilled. As the last of the blue glow faded away, leaving the rod gray iron once more, Marith stepped back and nodded her thanks to Theltek.

She was about to pick up the rod and place it with the others she had prepared—weapons of sorcerous destruction even a non-sorcerer could wield, albeit for just one devastating blast—when she reeled, covering her ears with her palms against the clash and rumble and roar in her skull.

She lowered herself onto a stool, holding her head. Already the noise was abating, but as it did she could distinguish voices, snatches of speech. She picked up the odd word in Nan-Rhouric, a language she had no patience for, but Carred had insisted on teaching her the little she knew in case it might one day prove necessary.

Most of the meaning of the words she heard was lost on her. There were several voices—men and women. They seemed to be arguing in cold, businesslike tones. What stood out were "trade," "shipping," and "markets farther afield, and I don't just mean Niyas." Objections started at that last, anger, accusations, and curses. But they all stopped when a voice like wind chimes cut across them with such force, such finality, that Marith feared her skull might shatter. She couldn't understand the language, but its unnatural cadences and guttural consonants made her wonder if it was Nazgrese, the demon tongue.

After that, Marith experienced a silence so absolute she thought she'd been deafened. But then she could hear the mice pattering around the basement, and the occasional squeak.

She rose from her stool and turned to face the statue of Theltek on his shelf. Was this a new gift the god had granted her? A talent for eavesdropping, for hearing things from afar? Her grandmother had claimed such a power, but if that was what it was, Marith had no idea how it could work to her advantage. She'd had no control over it. The voices had just come, and then gone as quickly.

"What was that, Theltek, my lord?" she asked the statue. "Who were they?"

The statue stared back at her with six eyes made from specks of sapphire. *Wait and see,* it seemed to say to her. *Wait and see.*

Theltek of the Thousand Eyes was the most common title of the god. Of the Thousand Arms, the Thousand Hearts, the Thousand…

"Am I to be one of your thousand ears, O Theltek?" she asked.

She had the distinct impression that, somewhere, wherever the gods were supposed to reside, one of the thousand mouths of Theltek was smiling.

TWELVE

AFTER THE EXORCISM RITUAL, BROTHER Mizral insisted that Anskar be returned to the infirmary, where he could continue his recovery. Seneschal Monash agreed.

Anskar was still weak from the removal of his catalyst, though the veins of corruption beneath his skin were abating. He was worried at first that he would plunge into a state of depression and feel that he'd made a terrible mistake. Instead, he felt freer than he'd ever felt in his life.

It wasn't as though he wasn't used to being alone. Growing up, he'd been told he was an orphan, and when he'd finally discovered who his parents were, he mostly felt betrayed. Vihtor had lied to him, or at least omitted the truth; and Queen Talia had sought to control him from beyond the grave.

Well, now she was back where she belonged and Vihtor dead, and Anskar was truly his own man for the first time, with no one weaving the threads of his life.

Except for the Order of Eternal Vigilance.

Seneschal Monash, Grand Master Hyle Pausus, and even Sareya represented the greatest threats to his newfound freedom.

And so late the following morning, when Blosius was about to finish his shift, Anskar asked for his help.

"Your situation's not much different to mine," Anskar said. "Neither of us gets to choose where we go in life. Perhaps we can help each other."

"How?"

"You have money on the outside," Anskar said, "and I have contacts."

Blosius frowned, giving Anskar a dubious look. "What contacts?"

"Someone who could help us get away from here. Far away."

"And then what?"

"You said you had a lot of money. You can use it to decide your own fate."

Blosius frowned again, but then he smiled as if it were a brilliant idea that had never before occurred to him. "Slip away without permission? Defy the Seneschal? Defy my father?"

Anskar smiled, though it felt more like a grimace. "Be your own man; do whatever you want without others dictating what you can and can't do, and who you are. Here's what I want you to do. And trust me. Things will work out fine for both of us."

The passageways were deserted in the middle of the night, the only sound the creak of the wheeled chair as Blosius pushed Anskar away from the infirmary. It was dark, but not too dark to see. Spears of red and white moonlight beaming through the clerestory windows beneath the ceiling left dappled patches on the walls. Out of curiosity, Anskar tried to create a glowing sphere of the dawn-tide upon his palm, but all he got for his efforts was a pain in the head and a wave of nausea.

He turned his senses to the ruin of his braided repository, but he could perceive nothing now. Either the repository had withered away to nothing, or—and he immediately realized this second option was true—his sorcerous senses had started to atrophy. At least, those that pertained to the dawn- and dusk-tide. He could still feel the steady prickle of the dark-tide in his veins, and the slither of the earth-tide in his guts. It was no comfort. It just implied that those tides were more a part of him than the other two had ever been.

"Left here," he said, retracing the route he'd taken that first time he left the Burg, under the glamor of the golden-eyed crow.

"I'm not so sure about this," Blosius said. His resolve had been trickling away since they left the infirmary. "Perhaps I should appeal to the Seneschal. Maybe if I stopped drinking and practiced harder…"

"You're a skillful enough swordsman, Blosius," Anskar said, "but we both know you're no fighter. Even if Monash gave you another chance, you'd still fail in the fight square."

"You don't know that."

"But you do," Anskar said. "And that's what matters."

They came at last to a narrow wooden door, and as Blosius had arranged, it stood slightly ajar. They abandoned the wheeled chair in the corridor, and Blosius helped Anskar to stand, then supported him as they went outside. Anskar's breathing became labored, and his legs felt so heavy he had to shuffle across the grass to the shadow of the curtain wall.

Above them, it was dark atop the battlements, save for the

feeble glow of a hooded lantern to the north. Keeping close to the base of the wall, they made their way to the trade gate that led to Dorinah.

A shadow detached itself from the wall and approached them.

"Is it open?" Blosius asked.

"I said it would be, didn't I?"

Anskar recognized the voice, and then he saw it was Farin Glay, one of the older postulants, who had failed in the trials for the last two years. Farin was on his last attempt, and everyone knew he was going to fail again, which meant expulsion from the Order. He was a sullen lad, too prone to violent outbursts, and he drank even more heavily than Blosius. Indeed, Farin was the one to introduce Blosius to alcohol after Anskar had defeated him in the fight square.

"And the carriage?" Blosius asked.

"What's up? Don't you trust me?"

"Of course I—"

"Coin. Now." Farin held out his hand, and Blosius passed him a single coin—a gold crown, which was more than most laborers on the mainland earned in a year.

Blosius helped Anskar through the gate and out into the streets of Dorinah. The bulk of a trap stood out from the darkness across the road, its single horse patiently waiting. The driver's eyes flashed in the light of an alchemical globe hanging from a rod beside his bench.

"You agreed to pay Farin a gold crown?" Anskar asked as they crossed the road to the trap.

"Enough for him to leave the Order and set up shop as a locksmith," Blosius said. "That was his father's trade in Caronath, till the Order's recruiters came calling and his parents decided they had too many mouths to feed. Farin's one of twelve kids, and the only one with a discernible god's mark."

"Or mark of sorcery," Anskar said, for he was more and more convinced they were one and the same thing.

Blosius helped Anskar into the trap and climbed up beside him.

"Where to?" the driver asked, his voice laced with suspicion. He gave the alchemical globe a shake, and the light it emitted grew steadily brighter.

Blosius leaned forward and handed the man a coin—Anskar couldn't tell if it was silver or gold in the moonlight. "For your silence on the matter." When the man didn't respond, Blosius handed him another coin.

"I ain't never clapped eyes on the pair of you," the driver said.

Blosius sat back with a satisfied sigh. "Well, Anskar?" he said. "Where do you want to go?"

"To the depot of the Ethereal Sorceress," Anskar told the driver.

And Blosius looked at him in horror.

THIRTEEN

ANSKAR STILL HAD NO IDEA where he wanted the Ethereal
Sorceress to send him when the trap pulled up outside the looming
edifice of her depot. Maybe he should go back to Wintotashum
and pledge allegiance to King Aelfyr. After all, there had been no
love lost between the King and his allies of the Order of Eternal
Vigilance. But would Aelfyr welcome him back now that his
catalyst had been removed? It was a bitter taste of reality, to
realize his worth was dependent upon his power as a sorcerer.
Maybe he could return to Atya, perhaps find employment with
Blaice Rancey and make his fortune raiding the ancient ruins.
Or maybe not, considering most of Blaice's accomplices never
survived her expeditions. Certainly he couldn't return to Sansor.
East of the mainland, then: Mazin or Nagorn City, or one of the
other cities in the wilds like Caronath. Or farther still: the lands
across the Trackless Ocean.

Anskar rubbed his tired eyes and tried to throw off the weariness that had seeped into his bones. It was useless fantasizing about where he would end up. First he had to recover. And besides, Sheelahn might have ideas of her own. After all, he did owe her three debts, and if she agreed to transport him somewhere else, that tally would only rise.

"I don't know about this," Blosius said as the trap rattled away, leaving them standing at the foot of the steps that climbed to the depot. "I've heard she's some kind of demon, or at least a powerful sorceress from another realm."

"If she was a demon, do you think the Order would tolerate her here?"

There were no alchemical globes in this part of the city, yet the building stood out in stark relief, limned by a shimmering glow as ephemeral as moonlight.

There was a fierce clash and clatter from one of the shadowed alleys opposite.

"What was that?" Blosius asked, eyes wide. He was close to panic.

"I'm not sure," Anskar said, taking advantage of the noise. "But I don't think we should wait around to find out. Come on—whatever it was won't approach the depot."

Not judging by the way the place made him feel. It might have just been his imagination, or some lingering superstition, but he could have sworn there were invisible eyes watching him, and he had the uncanny suspicion that every word he and Blosius uttered was heard and noted within.

He struggled for breath, and his heart was a ragged patter in his chest as Blosius helped him to the top of the steps, where the iron-banded blackwood door was already creaking open.

The same polished-blackwood-masked functionary who had been there before—he felt certain it was the same man he'd seen in Kaile as well, and Wintotashum—stood in the entranceway, his thick, dark-gray-coated form backlit by the stark glow from within. When Anskar shrugged free of Blosius's arm, the man cocked his masked face to look at him with glittery black eyes.

"Is Sheelahn…" Anskar started, then licked his lips. "Is the Ethereal Sorceress…?"

"You are expected," the functionary said. There might have been a hint of disapproval in his usually flat tone. "You, however," he said to Blosius, "are not."

Blosius cast a look behind at the darkened street. "Perhaps whatever we heard has gone," he said. "It was probably in any—"

"No, you're staying with me."

Blosius sighed with relief.

"Will that be all right?" Anskar asked.

The functionary's dark eyes narrowed to slits, and he cocked his head, as if listening. Finally he said, "Your request has been granted. Come."

As the man led the way across the glossy checkered floor of white and green marble, Anskar was surprised to see that he was limping, dragging one leg that looked twisted to an impossible degree. The man's coat, usually so immaculate, had several rents in the back, through which skin like melted wax bubbled and blistered.

"What happened to you?" Anskar asked, huffing and puffing and clutching his chest as he struggled to keep up.

The man stopped walking and studied him for a long while before answering. "My service has been deemed unsatisfactory, and now it draws to an end."

"Unsatisfactory?"

"Insufficient for the full payment of my debt."

Anskar glanced at Blosius.

"We should leave," Blosius mouthed, but Anskar ignored him, and they pressed on.

No iron cage to take them down into the foundations of the depot this time. The Ethereal Sorceress was waiting for them through one of the many blackwood doors that led off the entrance hall.

It was a strange chamber the functionary ushered them into before giving a stiff bow and backing out, closing the door behind him. There were arched entrances opposite and to each side. The ceiling was domed and fluted with cut stone that gave the impression of ribs. It had more the feel of a crypt or a sacred chapel than anything else.

The Ethereal Sorceress, if indeed it was her, was without her mask and robes. She was stick-thin, and wore only a simple tunic, her feet bare, her exposed arms wrapped with coiling tattoos that gave off a faint violet glow. She had no eyes, just empty sockets, and her mouth was glistening, moist, almost sensual; but that was the only feature that could have been described as attractive to Anskar. She was flat-chested like a boy, and her facial structure was too angular, as if a gossamer layer of dusky skin had been stretched taut over razor-sharp bones. It gave the impression she had a skull like a faceted diamond. She appeared serene, perfectly still, as she sat cross-legged on a large cushion, a single crystal on the floor in front of her, a shifting, sparkling filament at its heart. Anskar could feel the charged atmosphere within the chamber even without his senses.

"Sheelahn?" he asked hesitantly, afraid that he was disturbing something extremely important, though there was no one else in the room.

"Not at this moment," she said in a tinkling voice, higher and brighter than her usual lilting tone. "At this instant, I am Haeth

Ho'akopeth."

"Sheelahn isn't here?" Anskar asked.

"She is and she is not. But you are here, Anskar DeVantte, albeit a truncated version of your former self. Your catalyst has been removed, and you are closed off from the dawn- and the dusk-tides."

She turned her empty eye sockets on him, as if she could see deep inside him. Anskar felt the expectation that he should explain himself, but he didn't want to risk saying the wrong thing. He was sure she was judging him, and that, in some indiscernible way, she disapproved.

Finally, Haeth Ho'akopeth said, "And you have brought someone to see me. A gift, or repayment of one of your debts? There are three still as yet unpaid."

"This is Blosius," Anskar said. "A friend."

Blosius nodded enthusiastically, cheeks blushing with evident pride. He looked about to thank Anskar, as if no one had acknowledged him as a friend before.

"You smell of wealth," Haeth Ho'akopeth said. "From Kaile, if I am not very much mistaken. A merchant family."

"How do you know all this?" Blosius asked.

Haeth Ho'akopeth ignored the question and instead asked Anskar, "What brings you to my depot this time, *Melesh-Eloni*?"

"You know?"

"If I did not, would I have used the title?"

"But how do you know?"

As with Blosius, she didn't answer the question. "You seek another favor," she said instead. It was not a question.

"Just one more," Anskar said, "and then I will begin to make my payments."

"No."

"No?"

"Your stock has gone down considerably. And not just because the removal of your catalyst has destroyed your ability with the dawn and the dusk. You have changed, *Melesh-Eloni*. The catalyst renders latencies manifest, but it was also a dam holding your true nature back."

"What do you know of my true nature?"

Haeth Ho'akopeth made a sudden clutching motion that caused Blosius to scurry back. Anskar lacked the energy. "You may still serve some purpose. I may yet have a task for you."

"I'm still weak," Anskar said. "I need more time to recover."

Haeth Ho'akopeth appraised him with her empty eye sockets. "You may return when you are recovered."

"But I need to get away from Dorinah. As far away as possible."

"And when you have recovered, perhaps you will. Farther, perhaps, than you think. But you have not answered my earlier question: Is your friend Blosius a gift, or repayment of one of your debts?"

"He's neither," Anskar said. "I shouldn't have brought him here."

"You bear the pious taint of the Order of Eternal Vigilance, Blosius," Haeth Ho'akopeth said, "and yet…"

"They want to expel me," Blosius said. "But for now I'm just an auxiliary for the healers. I don't blame them. I don't think I'm cut out to be a knight."

"You are an astute judge," Haeth Ho'akopeth said. "No, you are not. Yet you do not intend to return to your family in Kaile. Why?"

"They will not endure the shame my failure in the Order brings upon them. My father will disinherit me."

"You don't know that," Anskar said.

"Trust me, I do. You have no idea what he's like, Anskar."

"But you have plans, yes?" Haeth Ho'akopeth said. "You and Anskar DeVantte have plans for a new life?"

Anskar didn't. He'd not seen beyond this moment. He'd not anticipated the Ethereal Sorceress's refusal to aid him this time. If, indeed, Haeth Ho'akopeth was the Ethereal Sorceress. And if she was, what did it mean that she'd given him a different name this time? Sheelahn, she'd told him, was for those free of superstition. It had implied if not friendship, then at least an equal business relationship.

"I…" Blosius said, glancing at Anskar for support that was not there. "I don't know. Maybe I should return to the healers. They'll forgive me, won't they?"

"Come," Haeth Ho'akopeth said, standing with effortless grace and starting toward the arched entrance opposite the door they had come in by. "I have a proposition for you."

"Anskar?" Blosius asked.

Anskar frowned at Haeth Ho'akopeth. He didn't like the sound of this.

"I shall consider this introduction payment for one of your debts, Anskar DeVantte," Haeth Ho'akopeth said. "But know this: two yet remain. Return when you are feeling stronger."

He nodded. "Blosius?"

"If you think it will help…"

That depended on what she wanted from him. Part of Anskar felt responsible for bringing Blosius here and wanted them both to leave right away. But it was a small part. Something else that had changed within him—or had he always been this way? Did he even care about what Blosius might be getting into? Should he?

"Here," Blosius said, handing Anskar his coin pouch. "There's more in the bank for when I need it."

"You don't need to do this," Anskar said.

"Yes," Blosius said. "I do. It's not just being a knight I'm not cut out for. I make a lousy healer's helper. It can't hurt to hear what she's proposing." He started across the floor after Haeth Ho'akopeth, who stepped so lightly in front of him she almost seemed to glide.

"I'll pay you back," Anskar said.

Blosius gave him a feeble smile over his shoulder, and then followed Haeth Ho'akopeth out through the arch.

The blackwood door opened behind Anskar, and the functionary stood there, lopsided due to his injured leg.

"So," the masked man said, "it is concluded."

"What is?" Anskar asked. "You mean one of my debts is paid?"

The functionary shook his head. "I was speaking of myself."

FOURTEEN

THE FUNCTIONARY SLAMMED THE BLACKWOOD door behind Anskar, leaving him alone at the top of the depot's granite steps. The street opposite seemed to seethe with darkness, and a light drizzle was falling.

The functionary had unsettled him. Not only was the man injured, but there had been a tension about him, bordering on impatience. It felt to Anskar like resentment. Or anger. Or despair.

Or perhaps it was just Anskar's own feelings reflected back at him. He'd been counting on Sheelahn's help and hadn't even considered the possibility that she might refuse. What in Menselas's name was he going to do now? Not go back to Branil's Burg, that was for sure. It was likely Monash would lock him up before fitting him with a new catalyst and sending him back to Sansor.

He stared bleakly into the gloom of the street, reluctant to leave the relative safety of the depot.

The dark shivered in the mouth of an alley—movement, possibly a rat or a small dog. He felt certain there would be people lurking in the shadows, waiting for easy prey. It didn't matter how much he told himself he was being ridiculous, that even the most desperate rogue wouldn't stand about in the cold and the rain on the off-chance that some innocent victim would be out for a stroll at this time of night.

He felt once more the prickling of the dark-tide in his veins, but he had already failed to find a way to access it without the deep well that had once contained it. As for the earth-tide, he didn't want to feel its sickly sludge ever again. He only wished its presence within him could have been exorcized along with his mother, and that the dark-tide could have been taken from him too.

All he wanted, he tried to convince himself, was to be a knight. Nothing else. Not a sorcerer, not a tool of the Grand Master. And most certainly not a necromancer like Queen Talia. Just a knight, pure and simple, skilled with the sword and bound by codes of honor.

And he wept then, as he stood with his back to the depot's door. He was overcome with the feeling that he had made a terrible mistake, that he had misunderstood the Order and the compromises it needed to make in the world, that he should never have sought out the old Niyandrian man who'd removed his catalyst. Things were better before. He'd been a fool. And now he had nowhere to go.

Then maybe he should go back. That was what Vihtor would have wanted. But how could he when Monash was insistent upon a new catalyst?

He'd sooner be dead.

And so he left the safety of the depot and headed down the night-blackened road, guided only by the frail glow of alchemical globes. If they hadn't begun their hunt for him already, the Order knights were bound to discover he was missing in the morning, and then they would come.

Always moving away from the walls of Branil's Burg, Anskar had no destination in mind; at least, none he was conscious of, and eventually he found himself once more in the old city, among the Niyandrians.

There were one or two stores open, and Anskar wondered at the kind of business they might conduct at so late an hour. There were people on the streets, too, walking briskly or gathered in twos and threes at the corners. He tensed whenever they noticed him, but mostly they just watched as he passed, then resumed their conversations in Niyandrian.

Uncertainty checked him when he happened upon a tavern, the mournful lament of a fiddle coming through the open door. His last visit to a tavern hadn't exactly ended well. In the end, it was the promise of warmth that won out.

Inside, he was greeted by looks of surprise and suspicion from the half dozen people, not seated at the round wooden tables but lounging on four couches that had been dragged close to the crackling fire in the hearth. They were Niyandrians, dressed in patched, frayed clothing. Each held a long-stemmed glass that contained some kind of purplish drink, which had left its stain on their lips.

A woman with matted gray hair stood and set down her glass on a low table before she approached him.

"You lost?" she asked in passable Nan-Rhouric.

Anskar shook his head. "Are you open?"

"No one's serving beer at the bar, if that's what you're after. Just a gathering of friends. Only chance some of us get to really… talk."

"I see," Anskar said. "Then I'm sorry to have disturbed you."

"You don't look like a typical mainlander," the woman said, noticing his eyes, "though you sure sound like one."

"I'm Niyandrian," Anskar said in that tongue.

Her own cat's eyes widened, and she turned her head to the other five Niyandrians watching from the couches by the fire. She switched to Niyandrian herself. "You hear that? Says he's Niyandrian."

"One of his parents was, perhaps," a thick-set man said, "but not the other."

The woman raised a quizzical eyebrow at Anskar.

"My mother," he said.

"And your father? What are you, twenty?"

"Eighteen."

"A war baby?"

When he didn't reply, the woman must have assumed that he was. "Poor lad," she said, lightly touching his cheek. "Bet you'd like to find the bastard that did that to your ma."

"Did what?"

"Put you in her. You ain't the only one, son. But look at you: mail and a sword! You seem to be doing all right for yourself. You a sell-sword?"

Anskar was glad that he'd not worn his white Order cloak. But then he noticed a shrewd look enter the woman's eyes. She was appraising his worth. They all were.

"I just..." Anskar hesitated, then manufactured a sheepish smile. He hated that the lies came so freely now. "I go where there's work."

"Where you staying?"

"In town."

"Like that, is it? I guess you can never be too careful. You have coin?" She eyed the bulging pouch Blosius had given him.

"A few coppers," Anskar said.

"A few, eh? Three will buy you a drink—the same as we're all drinking. Sit up, Golvis, you lazy bastard," she said, leading Anskar toward one of the couches. "Make space for another."

Anskar sat, stiff and awkward, beside a broad-shouldered man with a perfectly bald head. He fumbled around inside his pouch for three coppers, but all the coins were either gold or silver. The Niyandrians watched him in silence. Finally, he withdrew a single silver talent and offered it to the woman.

"A few coppers, you say?"

Anskar swallowed, but then she let out a shrill, guffawing laugh, and her companions—four men and a woman—joined in, bursting the bubble of tension. After that, they resumed their chatter.

They spoke mainly of trivial things, grumbling about their partners back home, the inflated prices of grain coming in from outside the city, the fact that non-Niyandrians were starting to buy up the dilapidated properties on the edge of the district, with a plan to renovating them.

"Isn't that a good thing?" Anskar asked. "If the buildings were rundown?"

"What do you suppose will happen once they've gotten them all fixed up and looking lovely?" the woman who had first greeted him asked.

"More mainlanders will move into the area," a young man with long black hair answered for Anskar. "Prices will go up, and people like us will be forced to live in smaller and smaller parts of the city, till at last they squeeze us out."

"And that's what they want?" Anskar asked. "To drive Niyandrians out of Dorinah?"

"Not as stupid as you look, are you?" another man said, his face scarred by some old pox. His tawny eyes narrowed, as if he hadn't yet come to trust Anskar's presence here.

"You must be new in Dorinah," the other woman said. She was young—certainly no more than twenty—and a little on the plump side, which struck Anskar as unusual. Most of the Niyandrians he'd seen were either rake thin or lean and muscular. But then he noticed the swell of her belly, and she smiled as she noticed him noticing.

"Yes, I'm new here," Anskar lied again. He saw no benefit to telling them that he had grown up here, behind the looming walls of Branil's Burg. "Just passing through."

"Course you are," the pox-faced man said, then took a slurp of his purplish drink. "Just passing through on your way to where, though? There's nothing beyond Dorinah except the sea. Or did you come in by ship… from the mainland, perhaps?"

"Oh, I forgot your drink," the older woman said, standing from her couch to pour Anskar a measure from a carafe into a long-stemmed glass. "Taste it. See what you think."

Aware that the pox-faced man was still watching him, waiting for his answer, Anskar sipped the purple drink. He frowned at first, trying to work out what it could be. It was warm and viscous, and had the tang of strong spices; but underlying that was something salty and metallic—and there was a hint of lemons.

"It's… interesting," Anskar said.

"You could say that," the young man agreed.

"What is it?"

"An ancient Niyandrian delicacy," the older woman said. "Consider yourself among the privileged few. It's not everywhere that sells it."

Everyone chuckled at that; everyone save the pox-faced man,

who was still waiting for his answer.

"What brings me to Dorinah?" Anskar said, stalling for time. He considered coming clean and telling them that he had escaped from the Order of Eternal Vigilance, but how would they react to that? And the last thing he needed was rumors circulating about a runaway knight in the Niyandrian district. Business with the Ethereal Sorceress? Likely they saw Sheelahn's depot as another example of mainland business interests. Had the Ethereal Sorceress been in Dorinah before the invasion?

On a sudden inspiration, he said, "I'm looking for Carred Selenas." And maybe that was true. He hadn't seriously considered it until now, but perhaps he should seek out Carred Selenas and her rebels, and deliver the warning to Orix about Archduke Peleus, whose son Colvin they had killed aboard ship. Orix needed to know about the blood feud they were both caught up in. Anskar at least owed him that.

And now everyone's eyes were on him, and it grew once more deathly quiet.

At length, it was the pox-faced man who spoke. "Who's that, then?"

"Carred Selenas," Anskar repeated.

"Never heard of her," the man said. "Anyone know where this young man can find a… what did you say her name was again?"

Anskar licked his lips.

"Who is she?" the pregnant woman asked, glancing at the older woman. "A friend of yours? A relative?"

Anskar lowered his voice. "The leader of the Niyandrian rebels."

"So, you're looking for trouble, are you?" the pox-faced man said. "Well, you've come to the wrong place. We're all law-abiding subjects here." He downed the rest of his drink and wiped the purple stain from his lips with the back of his hand. "I'm off."

"The night be a friend to you, Dargul," the pregnant woman said.

"Be safe," each of the others said in turn, but then Dargul was off out the open door and into the street.

"Did I say something to offend him?" Anskar asked.

The older woman grimaced and then shook her head. "I don't think so. Not really. He's not been himself lately. He's probably just tired. I know I am." She stretched and yawned, though it seemed to Anskar a fake yawn.

"I should probably get going too," Anskar said.

"We all should," the older woman said, "once we've finished our drinks."

Anskar stood. "Forgive me if I leave mine. It's very good, but…"

"No need to explain," the older woman said. "You tried it, that's the main thing. It's not to everyone's taste. Well, thank you for your company tonight. You never did tell us your name."

"Nor me yours," Anskar observed.

"How rude of me. Maybe next time. Next time, we'll all tell him our names, won't we?"

"Next time," they all agreed.

"Good night," Anskar said, and then he headed for the door as quickly as he could without seeming impolite, or scared. Even the cold dark of the streets was suddenly preferable.

There was a scuff of movement from his right as he stepped out of the door. Anskar blurted a cant, but his sorcery failed: dawn-tide shield was useless now. He turned, but too late. Something struck him on the head, and he fell.

FIFTEEN

CARRED'S THROAT WAS FULL OF sand. She was no longer sweating, as the bronze sun had sucked all the moisture out of her, and she knew enough to realize that was a bad thing. The pouch of star-metal shavings hanging from her belt was an anchor slowing her down. She should untie it, leave it behind. Without it, she'd be lighter than air and could simply float away. But that was what it wanted her to do, wasn't it? The yawning sun hungered for her. As it throbbed in her vision, she could feel it pulling her towards it, tugging on the strings of her life.

"Carred?"

She awoke on a big bed beneath heavy covers, warm but not hot. Cool liquid touched her lips, trickled down her throat. Mistberry wine, and a good one at that. A hand supported the back of her head. She focused on the fingers holding the stem of the glass—manicured fingers, slender and crimson.

Her heart clenched, and she shut her eyes against the illusion.

"It's quite real, my love," a familiar voice said, and Carred groaned because she knew what she heard couldn't be true. "I'm quite real."

She heard Marith set the wineglass down on the nightstand. Felt her weight on the bed. There was a breath of chill air as Marith slipped beneath the covers, naked. They both were. "No," Carred uttered. "Not real. Get up. Keep moving."

Marith's fingers brushed her belly, the inside of her thigh. Her lips touched Carred's, her breath sweet from the wine.

"Open your eyes, my love," Marith said. "Tell me I'm not real again. I like it when you do."

Carred almost laughed. It was the sort of thing Marith would have said. And her touch… the hand that traced the contours of her breasts… it felt like Marith.

She screwed her eyes shut even tighter.

"Please don't do that," Marith said. "You're grimacing, Carred. Don't you want me anymore?"

Yes, I want you! Carred's thoughts cried. *The real you, not this.*

But she couldn't stop herself from gasping when Marith touched her now. Her lips parted in invitation, and Marith's tongue darted between them. Carred's hips lifted as she ground herself against her lover's hand. Marith was on top of her now, pinning her with her weight.

"Look at me, Carred. I need you to know this is real."

Carred opened her eyes, and they instantly filled with tears. "Marith? But how?"

"You saw what I did when the assassins came for you."

"I saw you were a powerful sorcerer."

"And you never suspected, did you?"

"But you're not this powerful. You can't rescue me from the abyssal realms…"

Marith nipped at the side of her neck as she murmured, "Far be it from me to boast…"

Carred pushed on Marith's hips and rolled out from beneath her. "You're not that powerful. No one is."

"Perhaps you're right." Marith sat propped against the headboard and picked up the wineglass for a sip. "So, you're still in the abyssal realms and the black sun is leaching the life out of you. I'm an illusion, a trick of your mind, the thing you most long for?"

Carred sat up too, her only answer the narrowing of her eyes.

"You used to tell me how afraid you were of dying alone."

She looked Marith in the eye. She *had* told her that. All she saw was her own face reflected back at her.

"Well, you're not alone," Marith said, offering her the glass. "I may not have the power to transport you back through the veil, but I can bring you comfort as you pass from life."

"You're all heart," Carred said. She upended the glass and finished the contents, her thirst not entirely forgotten. And now she thought about it, it lingered at the back of her mind.

"Are you traveling in the spirit?" she asked. "Is that even possible?"

Marith raised an eyebrow.

"Or am I imagining you?"

"Does it matter which?" Marith said, resting her head on Carred's shoulder. She went to stroke Carred's breast, but Carred caught hold of her wrist.

"Don't."

"No comfort at the last? Oh, Carred, I'd never forgive myself if you died in despair."

"Sooner that than this."

The bedroom flickered. Behind the walls—beyond? beneath?—

she glimpsed barren rock and bruised skies.

"It could all end for you with a kiss," Marith said. "More than a kiss, if you prefer."

With a surge of anger, Carred grabbed her by the throat. Marith grunted, then growled, then started to choke. Her limbs thrashed as Carred forced her back down to the bed.

They were on rocky ground now, Carred clothed once more, Marith coarse-skinned and pallid. Yellow eyes bulged from their sockets as Carred throttled her. Claws raked at the backs of her hands. Thorny flesh cut into her, but still she squeezed.

Then suddenly she was squeezing air.

She knelt on the hard ground, panting, heart thudding in her chest. She got one leg beneath her, then the other, swaying as she stood. Her vision blurred. The world around her spun.

And she glimpsed the silhouette of something round, hovering above the closest mesa.

Watching.

Waiting.

SIXTEEN

"HE AIN'T DEAD." AN OLD woman's voice. She'd spoken in Niyandrian.

"He's a big bastard, it'd take more than a tap to the head to send him through the veil. Anyway, even if he were dead, it's not permanent to your kind, is it?" —Another woman.

"There you go again, showing your ignorance," the old woman retorted. "And it ain't like you're no spring chicken, girl. Wisdom's meant to increase with each passing decade, so long as there's something between your ears for it to cling to."

Anskar could smell the old woman's stale breath now as it tickled his face. His head felt as though it had been crushed in a vise, his brain hammered into pulp. He'd lost consciousness a few times lately, and he was heartily sick of it. This time, he probably had a concussion.

"What's the point of a necromancer who can't raise the dead?" the other woman said. "Queen Talia could have done it."

"Huh," the old woman said. "Shambling dead with no brains, so I heard—you'd have fitted in well with them. But I ain't no Necromancer Queen with ideas of becoming a god. Raising corpses is an ideal few of us ever achieve, and I reckon Theltek likes it that way."

Anskar coughed, then tasted bile. He groaned and tried to open his eyes, but the light was blinding.

"Anskar?" A man's voice this time. Slurred, and yet...

"Orix?" he croaked weakly.

Shutting his eyes against the glare, he tried to push himself up on one elbow. A mountain dropped on his skull, and he fell back into a pit of blackness.

Anskar dreamed of Carred Selenas. Not the real Carred Selenas, who was scarred and lacked two fingertips, but the illusion created by the Abbess of the Hooded One: firm, naked, her crimson skin glistening with sweat as she groaned and gasped above him. He cried out her name, gripped her hips, raised his hands to her breasts—but they were flaccid, no more than creased folds of skin. He looked up into the Abbess's ancient face, saw again the rotten stumps of her teeth, her rheumy eyes. She cackled as she ground herself against him. A string of drool dangled from her lips; it broke free to spatter his face as she cried out in ecstasy.

Anskar woke and gasped in air.

He opened his eyes, and still the light was blinding. He shut them again, and his head started to pound.

Footsteps approached, accompanied by a whiff of mutton. He risked opening his eyes a crack, and they slowly adjusted to the glare. And then he realized there was no glare, just a dusky half-light, and the wavering glow of a candle's flame on the canvas ceiling. He was in a tent.

A wrinkled face peered down at him, and he almost screamed. But it wasn't the Abbess. She had died. He'd been there and seen for himself.

"I'll tell her you're awake," the old woman said. She was Niyandrian, her red skin dull and in patches almost as gray as the hair that hung over her face, matted and unbound.

She shuffled out of sight, and Anskar lay back on the hard ground, only a damp, stinking blanket beneath him. He remembered hearing Orix's voice at some point between the last time he'd awakened and his nightmare. Orix had sounded different: garbled and slurred. The result of drinking too much, or something else?

He heard the rustle of the tent flap opening, then a shadow fell over him. The canvas wall opposite was bathed with moonlight from outside, an interweaving of red and silver. And there, backlit by the glow, stood a woman.

His heart raced. Urgent need flooded his veins. Was this how Niklaus du Plessis felt in his longing for his goddess, Sylva Kalisia? Curse the Abbess for what she'd done to him! The after-effects of her twisted sorcery on his mind lingered like a taint.

"Carred?" he said, cursing the tightness in his voice. An image popped into his head of her with Orix, and for a second he could have killed his friend.

"*Melesh-Eloni*," she said, cat's eyes glinting in the candlelight.

She took a step toward him, resolving out of the silhouette that had defined her, with a smile that might have been relief, might have been triumph on her lips.

But it wasn't Carred Selenas. And then he remembered the

old woman and another talking before he'd passed out again.

"Who are you?" he asked.

The woman's eyes betrayed her surprise that he spoke in fluent Niyandrian. She was older than Carred Selenas, taller, her graying hair cut short. She wore a plain tunic that left her muscular arms exposed, and her feet were bare.

She looked down at him and raised an eyebrow. Anskar suddenly became aware that he was naked. He pulled the sheet out from under him and covered himself.

"My name is Vilintia Yoenth. How are you feeling?"

"Like a mountain fell on my head."

"Dargul must have hit you too hard, but he's not to be blamed. He did what he was supposed to do."

"He was supposed to kidnap me? But how did he know who I was?"

She made a yapping gesture with her hand.

"I talk too much?" Anskar said.

"Sometimes it is better to be more reserved in conversation. Carred has her people everywhere, and she's told them what to look for and what to do if they find you."

"Is this Dargul still here?" Anskar asked.

"Why? Do you want revenge? Or are you going to thank him for taking you where you wanted to go?"

"He could have just shown me the way," Anskar said.

"And risked an Order spy discovering where our camp is? I don't think so. Dargul did the right thing. And no, he's not still here. He's gone back to Dorinah."

Anskar sat up, holding the sheet to him. At a loss for words, he gazed about the gloomy interior until his eyes alighted upon a neatly folded pile.

"Your clothes have been washed," Vilintia said. "I thought

you might prefer them without the shit and the blood."

"Thank you."

"Don't thank me. Thank Eadgith. I merely ordered it done."

"Eadgith?"

"The crone."

Anskar searched out his armor and sword, stashed in a corner of the tent.

"I was going to have the mail sanded and oiled," Vilintia said, "the sword cleaned and sharpened, only there was no need. You take good care of them, don't you?"

He opened his mouth to reply, but she talked right over him.

"Of course you do. No doubt the result of hard-earned discipline in the Order of Eternal Vigilance. Such a good little knight. Nothing at all to do with sorcery."

"They're enhanced with astrumium," Anskar said. "And sorcerous cants."

"No, really. I would never have guessed."

"What's this about?"

"It's about you, whatever else? You made enquiries in a Niyandrian tavern. I trust you got what you asked for?"

"I wanted Carred Selenas."

"As I'm sure she wants you. Regrettably, our esteemed leader is no longer with us."

"She's dead?"

Vilintia shrugged. "Been gone for weeks. I'm starting to consider her missing. It's possible she's dead. Likely, even."

"And you're one of her rebels?"

"*Her* rebels? And there was me thinking we were fighting for Niyas. But yes, I am with the rebellion. I would have thought that was obvious. While she went off at your mother's behest, Carred left me in charge."

Anskar stood, still covering himself, and went to retrieve his clothes.

"I can look away if you like," Vilintia said.

"Please."

Anskar dropped the sheet and started to dress. As he pulled on his pants, he cast a look over his shoulder, only to find she was still watching him.

"I'm starting to see what Carred sees in you. No wonder she went to such lengths to find you."

Shrugging into his shirt, Anskar said, "What are you talking about?"

"Of course, Carred sees something in all manner of people. Tall, short, fat, thin… it doesn't matter to her. Niyandrian or mainlander, man or woman. She can never get enough. Just ask your friend Orix."

Anskar tried his best to look nonchalant, but he was seething inside. "Sounds to me that you don't like her very much."

"Maybe I have reason not to."

"Oh?"

She looked away, and he didn't miss the clenching of her fists—an action he knew only too well. "I lost someone."

"And you blame Carred?"

She turned back to face him, her expression stoic save for the slight rise of an eyebrow—nothing suggestive about it this time. "Knowing her, she'd try to shift the blame onto your mother, say that duty gave her no choice. Our Carred's always been the Queen's loyal servant. She'd leap into sharp-tooth-infested waters, if Queen Talia required her to. In fact, if the accounts I've been told of her recent exploits are to be believed, that's exactly what she did do. You may find this hard to believe, but I'm not the only one to be aggrieved by our erstwhile leader's actions."

"My mother?"

"That wasn't who I meant, but you make a good point. All those years of failure, you'd think the Queen would have given up on Carred by now and found someone else to do the job. But I was thinking of Orix."

"What's she done to him?" Other than give him what he wanted.

"Directly, nothing. Personally, I find the change in him somewhat amusing."

"I assume by change you mean Orix has abandoned the Order and joined the rebellion? I can't say I'm surprised."

"That isn't what I mean. Then there's the other matter: how Carred led the poor boy on, then quickly grew tired of him. Be wary when you speak with him. He blames you for that."

"Me? How—?"

"Jealousy. He believes Carred has eyes for you, which tells me he's more perceptive than his dumb appearance would have us believe. And like all Carred's victims, he thinks she can do no wrong. If only he were nicer to her, more complimentary… If only he'd not said this to her, and instead had said that… You know how men are—most never grow up. As if any action of his could change what Carred is."

"Why are you trying to turn me against her?" Anskar asked. It was bad enough there being factions in the Order, but here as well? Divisions in the rebellion would make Seneschal Monash's task that much easier.

"So, you admit you're *for* her, even though she had you kidnapped? You're just part of a strategy to Carred, one that was devised by your… Oh, don't tell me you're soft on her? For Theltek's sake, Anskar, she slept with your mother!"

"Soft? On Carred Selenas?" He grimaced as he tried to shut

out the images from his dream that condemned him as a liar. "She's covered with scars. And so what if she slept with my mother? She's old enough to *be* my—"

He stopped as Vilintia opened the collar of her tunic to reveal the puckered lines of a scar. Her lips parted, and she smiled, almost bashfully. "This is just the top of it. It's a long and jagged scar. Shall I tell you how far down it goes?"

Anskar swallowed.

"And—or perhaps you've not noticed?—like Carred, I am also close to your mother's age. I know I don't look it. I train, Anskar. Every day. I train really, really hard. I sweat buckets, so I prefer to exercise naked. You should see how my skin glistens and glows. I'd say, then, I look half my age."

He turned away to retrieve his sword belt and fasten it around his waist, then stopped as he felt her hand on his shoulder.

"Eadgith, the old woman who was tending you, says there is no dawn- or dusk-tide within you any longer." She guided him to look at her then slipped a finger inside the front of his shirt to trace the ridges of the scar over his sternum. "What happened to you? What have you done?"

Her musky scent filled his nostrils, and when she brought her face close to his and repeated in a whisper, "What have you done?", he didn't pull away.

The tent flap parted and Orix bustled inside, his face lost in the shadows of a hood.

With him was a young Niyandrian woman, skinny as a spear haft, and filthy with it. Her hair was knotted and tangled, her clothes soiled and frayed. She faced him squarely, hands on hips, her flat chest thrust towards him. But it was her eyes that demanded his attention: they reminded him of a frosted lake, and though they were aimed right at him, their focus seemed someplace else—within her head, most likely.

"So, you're awake," Orix said, his Nan-Rhouric slurred, each word malformed.

"Orix…"

"I thought we were friends."

Orix's speech was so awkward, it took a moment for Anskar to understand what he'd said. "We *are* friends."

"Then why didn't you stay when you had the chance?"

"I couldn't. Not then. So much has happened since, Orix. The Order… I'm not going back."

"You removed your catalyst," Orix said. "All that ability, and you threw it away. You're a fool."

"Show him what happened to you," Vilintia said in Niyandrian. When Orix didn't respond, she repeated the command slowly and in an overly loud voice.

Orix's hands went to the sides of his hood. The young woman with him said, "No, you don't…" but her Nan-Rhouric wasn't up to the task, so she switched to Niyandrian. "You don't have to, Orix," she said, waving her hands and shaking her head to make sure he got her meaning.

In Nan-Rhouric, Orix said, "Yes, I do. It's important he sees."

Orix pulled down his hood, and Anskar just stood and stared.

At first he could make no sense of what his eyes were showing him. He blinked, but still Orix's face screamed wrongness at him. It was a jumbled mess, the mouth in the middle of his forehead, the eyes on the chin. No wonder he couldn't speak clearly. He was a freak. A monster.

"This is how she left him," Vilintia said. "Your precious Carred Selenas. Once she grows tired of you, she ceases to care."

"What did she say?" Orix asked Anskar in Nan-Rhouric.

Anskar ignored the question and countered with one of his own.

"Is Carred Selenas to blame for this?"

"In a way," Orix said.

"What does that mean—in a way?"

When Orix seemed incapable of a reply, Anskar switched to Niyandrian and asked Vilintia: "What happened to him?"

"The necromancer Tain did it," the young woman answered for her. "But Carred—"

"Tain?" Anskar frowned at Orix. "*The* Tain? How is that even possible?"

"I carried him for a while," Orix said. "He was a head, nothing more. A speaking head."

"And this head did this to you? How?"

"Tain called it the earth-tide," Orix said.

"The earth-tide is for necromancy, not…" He gestured lamely at Orix's misshapen face. "Not this."

Vilintia looked between the two of them, struggling to follow the conversation. Apparently she'd understood enough. "Ask Eadgith."

"Noni doesn't care what I look like," Orix said, clutching the young woman's hand. "I don't think she even sees there's anything wrong."

It was a wonder she could see at all.

"What's up with her eyes?" Anskar asked.

"Your mother's to thank for that," Orix said. "She used Noni, spoke through her from the realm of the dead."

Anskar nodded slowly. "I'm sorry. I know what that's like."

"I don't think you do," Orix said. "Same as I don't think you have any idea what Carred Selenas is really like."

"I've a feeling you're going to tell me."

"I don't need to. You saw what it was like between me and Carred. Of course you saw. That's why you wouldn't join us.

Admit it: you were jealous."

"Hardly."

"What you say of Carred?" Noni said in stilted Nan-Rhouric. "That you… how you say? Like better than we have got."

"No," Orix said in Niyandrian, then gave up and switched back to Nan-Rhouric. "Of course not." He fumbled for what to say next, and even looked at Anskar for help. In the end he employed hand signals: *You have my heart,* he seemed to say. "Not Carred."

Noni smiled, though her eyes didn't concur. They remained glazed and inscrutable.

"Are you saying things were fine," Anskar said, "until… your face?"

"What do you think?"

"So she's a disloyal lover, yes? And Vilintia here blames Carred for… for what, exactly?"

"Taloc," Orix said. "His name was Taloc."

At the sound of the name, Vilintia said, "What are you saying? I'm the leader now. You will speak only Niyandrian."

"Think about it," Orix said, still using Nan-Rhouric. "If she rejected me because of this…" He jabbed a finger at his mangled face.

"Niyandrian!" Vilintia said.

"Best thing…" Orix started. He'd clearly made an attempt at learning the language, but it was painful to listen to. "Best…"

"The best thing you can do, Anskar," Noni said, "is leave. Return to Branil's Burg. Beg the white cloaks to take you back."

"Orix…" Anskar said, then to Vilintia: "Can I say one last thing to him in Nan-Rhouric?"

"Just one."

He glared at Noni, then appealed to Orix. "Stop this, please.

You're not thinking right. I understand why, with what's happened—"

"You understand nothing!"

"Enough, fat man," Vilintia said.

Orix might not have understood the words, but he understood the tone. He threw up his arms in exasperation, then paced about the tent, stopping only to pick up an earthenware bowl from a low table and sniff the contents. He grimaced and was about to set the bowl down again, when the old woman returned.

"Who said you could touch that?" Eadgith said.

Orix almost dropped the bowl as he put it down. Blood spilled from it onto the table.

Eadgith scowled at Noni and Orix, then Vilintia. "This is too much too soon, all of you here like this. He's still recovering."

"Then they can leave," Vilintia said, moving to the tent flap and holding it open for Orix and Noni.

"Wait," Anskar said, and Orix turned round. Anskar averted his gaze from the aberration of Orix's face. "Perhaps I can fix what's happened to you. I've used the earth-tide. Given time, perhaps—"

"Why would I need you to fix my face, when I've got Noni?"

"She can use the earth-tide?"

"Not yet, but she's sworn that she will. Whatever it takes."

Hand in hand, Orix and Noni stepped outside, and Vilintia let the door-flap fall closed behind them.

"That girl's seething with resentment," Vilintia said, "and I can't say I blame her. Until she and Orix returned from their mission with Carred, I thought Noni was one of the dead-walkers the necromancers are always trying to create, but that's because of what your mother did to her. And as for Orix's face… you have to think he has a point. Carred couldn't get enough of him before they left. She's such a bitch."

"Tell me about Taloc," Anskar said.

"Taloc?" Vilintia frowned. Her mouth twitched—almost into a smile. Then she swallowed thickly. "Carred should have told me herself what happened to him. It's a leader's responsibility."

"Perhaps she couldn't come."

"Believe that if you want, but I say she lacked the guts, or the compassion. He was… to me… Why bother? You're the *Melesh-Eloni*, above such mundane things as love. You wouldn't understand."

Vilintia held the tent flap open and hesitated at the entrance.

"Orix's face…" she said to Eadgith. "Explain to His Divinity here what the earth-tide can do. Other than mess with the dead, that is." And then she was gone.

SEVENTEEN

"SIT DOWN," EADGITH SAID.

Anskar looked around. "On the ground?"

"Where else? You see a comfy chair here? Of course the ground."

Anskar lowered himself to the tent's grimy ground sheet, and Eadgith passed him the steaming bowl in her hands.

"Drink."

"What is it?"

"Bat's piss, what do you think?"

Anskar frowned at the thick, greenish liquid in the bowl, then gave it a tentative sniff. It smelled of mint and sage and other things he didn't recognize.

Eadgith made a clucking noise with her tongue. "You really think I'd give you piss to drink? That there's a tisane. It'll pick you up."

Anskar tried to pass the bowl back to her. "I think I'll be all right, thank you."

"I didn't make it for the fun of it. Drink, I tell you."

He raised the bowl to his lips, wincing as he sipped. His eyes widened at Eadgith. The drink was sweet and salty at the same time, spiced and slightly meaty.

"What's in it?" he said, eagerly gulping from the bowl.

"Who knows?" she said, then tapped the side of her nose. "Who knows? But it'll put some life back into you, this one. Give you more energy, and kill any lingering pain. I've been spooning you a different remedy since they brought you in. Something stronger. I expect you'd still be out cold otherwise, maybe never come to."

"Dargul hit me that hard?" Anskar said, finishing off the dregs and handing Eadgith the bowl back. "He could have killed me."

"Dargul's an over-zealous idiot. Told him so myself, which is why he didn't stay long at camp."

"Thank you," Anskar said, "for the drink."

"You won't be thanking me when you have to run for the shit-pit."

Anskar swallowed. "And thank you for washing my clothes."

"Someone had to do it, and it weren't going to be Vilintia, the mood she's in."

"She said Carred Selenas left her in charge."

"Nothing wrong with your hearing, then. Guess Dargul didn't do no permanent harm."

"Vilintia wanted you to tell me about the earth-tide."

Eadgith looked as though she were chewing gristle, then spat a wad of phlegm into the bowl Anskar had just drunk from.

"Please tell me that wasn't one of the ingredients…"

"So what if it was? Main thing is, it works, don't it? Go on, admit it: you're feeling better."

Anskar blinked several times and rubbed the back of his head.

"Numb," he said.

"Better than broke," Eadgith said. "Like it was when Dargul brought you in. Without the other remedy I've been giving you, your skull would have stayed split, and them brains of yours, such as they are, would've coming seeping out. You'd have been as much use as that dumb Traguh-raj friend of yours, assuming you're still friends."

"His face," Anskar said, suddenly serious. "Orix told me the Necromancer Tain did that to his face."

Eadgith nodded sagely. "With the earth-tide."

"How, though?" Anskar said. "The little I know about the earth-tide is that it's for necromancy."

"And you'd be right. Did your mother tell you that?"

"She showed me," Anskar said. "Her… spirit?"

"I know what she is, so don't go pussyfooting around me. But spirits don't come back from the realm of the dead unless they know what they're about. I might do it, and maybe you might, but most folk…"

"You're a necromancer?"

"The earth-tide bubbles up my ass," she said. "A stinking sludge that oozes through my guts."

Anskar nodded. "I've felt something similar. Not my… not my backside. It starts as a tingle in my feet."

"With the right focus, the right preparation," Eadgith said, "I can hear the dead speak, and I can talk back to them."

"I've heard them speak, too," Anskar said. "But what do you mean by preparation?"

"I'm still talking!" Eadgith said. "I've put the life back in a swatted fly, made roaches squashed underfoot start to crawl. I even once made a dead mouse breathe. But I never made no people come back to life, even a poor semblance of life. That takes a necromancer of rare talent. A necromancer like Tain or your mother."

"I still don't understand what Tain did to Orix's face," Anskar said. "How can the earth-tide move his eyes and mouth around?"

"The one that taught me reckoned the earth-tide was a shaping tide."

Anskar opened his mouth to ask a question.

"I'm still speaking!" Eadgith said. "Theltek's fungus-riddled toenails, don't they teach you manners in that Order of yours? The earth-tide is the dusk- and the dawn- tainted by their journey through layers of earth and rock and shit and piss and all the leavings of animals, folks, and dead insects. It's the stagnant soup of the dusk and the dawn. It's corruption, poison, the warping of the true tides. How much more than that my old teacher knew, I never did find out. I was impatient to raise the dead, see. My fellah, Junin, had been cut down in a skirmish in the build up to the siege of Naphor. I wanted him back. Love'll make you impatient like that. Love's the great squanderer of opportunities."

"And did you bring him back?"

"Ain't you been listening? I never managed to raise no people, I said. Just flies and roaches, and that mouse I told you about."

"What happened?"

"With Junin? His butchered corpse just lay there, as stubborn in death as he'd been in life, refusing to do as I bade him. Three days I tried." She hawked and spat into the bowl again. "Screamed my voice hoarse with cants and pleas and barbarous words. But he didn't listen, see. My Junin never did listen. I cut myself and let the blood drip on him. Even touched myself for him—he used to like that. I grew sick on the earth-tide fouling up my veins, but I didn't give up. I went on and on. I'd still be there, bleeding and shrieking like a wounded dead-eye, if my teacher hadn't found me and put a stop to it."

"What happened then?"

"I killed the scrawny fucker—excuse my Skanuric."

"You murdered your teacher?"

"No one saw, and I'd appreciate it if you didn't go blabbing about it to all and sundry. Still, it was a waste of bleeding time. It didn't bring Junin back, and it left me floundering in the dark as far as the earth-tide's concerned."

"Couldn't your teacher have raised Junin?"

"He never offered, so I assume not, unless he was a smarter bastard than I took him for. Nah, the skinny little rotter never even offered."

"But you saw him use the earth-tide for shaping?"

"Not saw; just heard him boast about it. He claimed that was the main use of the earth-tide: to reshape stuff—rocks and wood, glass and metal. Animals too, he used to say. He liked to joke about making new breeds of dogs in next to no time. I thought he was an idiot like all the other idiots. All I wanted was to be able to bring my Junin back. The origins of the spirit are in the flesh, my teacher used to say, just to annoy me. Death changes the nature of their mutual attraction. Alter the corpse, and the spirit returns… if you know what you're doing. So, the two powers of the earth-tide are in truth one. 'The secret to raising is in the shaping,' he said like a taunt. 'What secret?' I asked. 'Show me!' But he wouldn't. Knowledge has to be earned, he liked to say. Idiot."

"Orix said Noni was going to fix his face," Anskar said.

"She's sweet on him, though Theltek knows why. I reckon they're two of a kind, both victims of some other bastard's lust for power. Tain didn't just twist your friend's face, he used Orix to power the sorcery that did it. Wasted away in front of her eyes, Noni said. You ever see what happens to the conduits we use for earth-tide sorcery?"

Anskar shook his head.

"Course, in your case, your mother likely used you as a conduit, same as Tain did Orix; only Queen Talia's a sorcerer of a different caliber. She'd be more efficient with her use of the tides, more measured."

"I felt drained after…" Anskar said, then stopped at the glare he received from Eadgith. "My mistake, please continue."

"Two of a kind, I was saying. Poor Noni was worn by your mother like a garment, then cast off when she was of no more use. Only thing is, Queen Talia left her taint in the girl. I suspect some residue of knowledge, too. Possession is a two-way street. The dead speak through the living, but often they leave snippets of themselves behind in the host. So, yes, maybe Noni could fix Orix's face, but not without my help."

"But I thought you couldn't—"

"I can show her how to access the earth-tide. More than that, she'll have to work out for herself. If she's lucky, and your mother really did leave her imprint in the girl's mind, she might intuit what to do. Poor girl's mad from being possessed and mad from being in love. And the way Vilintia tells it, she was a cowpat short of a dung pile before she got herself involved with Carred Selenas."

"You think Carred's to blame?"

"Don't go putting words in my mouth. You ask me, Carred Selenas is just doing what she thinks is the right thing to do: her duty. The real instigator's your mother. I'm not saying that's a bad thing. A powerful sorcerer, a great queen… who else is going to free us from mainland tyranny? You? Carred thinks so. Me? I'd say you don't know your ass from your head. I'd say you still got ideas of being a knight."

"I don't. Why did I have my catalyst removed, then?"

"You'd be better off asking yourself the same question."

Anskar had done little else, but verbalizing his fumbled answers could only help bring clarity. "Because I wanted to reject sorcery?"

"Why?"

"To avoid the temptation of using it?"

"Why?"

"Because I don't want to be like her."

"Who?"

"My mother! I don't want to end up like her."

The tip of Eadgith's nose almost touched her chin as she smiled. "Only you got rid of two tides, but not all three."

"Four," Anskar corrected. "And now two remain."

"Oh?" Eadgith said, narrowing her eyes. And again: "Oh."

"All I have," Anskar said, "came from my mother."

"Not all," Eadgith said. "Unless you was virgin-born."

"I meant my sorcerous abilities."

"Hmm. So, by removing your catalyst, you shut off your access to two tides and left yourself with the tides of death and demons. Not a bright move. I thought you were supposed to serve a god of balance. Though I always wondered how you could have five faces in balance. Surely it should have been four, or six."

"I made a mistake," Anskar said. "I didn't want to be of any use to the Order... To the Grand Master. But the new Seneschal threatened to restore my catalyst and send me to Sansor."

"So you ran away. Well, good for you that Dargul hit you over the head and brought you here. Carred will know what to do with you when she gets back. If she gets back. In the meantime, perhaps you should look at what you've got."

"I don't understand."

"I know nothing about the dark-tide, thank Theltek, but I'll gladly teach you what I know about the earth-tide."

"What do you want in return?"

"Want? I'm not the Ethereal Sorceress. Want! You're the *Melesh-Eloni*. Maybe I'll teach you because that's what my queen would want. I'm loyal to your mother. I'm Niyandrian, after all."

"The healers at Branil's Burg… I asked them to drive my mother's spirit out."

Eadgith cackled as if this were the funniest thing in the world. "She'll not have gone far. Lock the door, and the burglar comes in through a window."

"But I don't want her inside of me."

"Nor should you. Learn what I have to teach you, then perhaps you can speak with her again, on your terms this time."

"Maybe," Anskar said.

"But not before you're fully recovered."

Eadgith swilled the spittle in her bowl and added to it a pinch of white powder from a drawstring pouch at her waist.

"What is that?" Anskar asked.

"Powdered rat's skull."

She took a vial from her pocket and poured out the clumping contents. "And this is pig's blood." Eadgith took a stick from the table top and began to stir. "Works better with sheep's blood, but I could only get pig." She glanced at him. "Works even better with the blood of mainland scum, but, as with the sheep, there was none ready to hand. I thought about using Orix's blood, but I don't dislike you that much."

Anskar grimaced. "That's what you've been giving me to drink?" He was no stranger to blood, but the thought of drinking it made his stomach queasy.

"Daubing it on your lips. Like I said, the earth-tide flows best through a conduit. You have to experiment to find the right medium. Use none, and the tide'll use you. That's what was making you tired and sick before. That's what almost killed Orix."

Anskar became aware of a mephitic stench as Eadgith stirred the concoction in the bowl. At first he wondered if the old woman had broken wind, but then he realized the smell wasn't quite real, and it was coming up through the ground.

"Your feet tingling yet?" Eadgith asked. "Because my ass is. Here, get this down you." She offered him the bowl.

"But I just drank—"

"That was for the pain and to put a spring in your step. This'll aid your healing."

"My skull? You said, without the drink, my skull would have still been split open? Then you *do* know how to shape with the earth-tide."

"All I know is how to put the tide in you. After that, I let it do its work. It quickens the process of healing: knits bones back together, seals cuts, stems bleeding. But change the nature of a thing using the earth-tide? That's something I ain't managed. Theltek gave me common sense, wide hips, and tits a man could get lost between, but when it came to the earth-tide, all he had left for me was scraps."

Anskar leaned forward and touched his lips to the blood and powdered skull in the bowl. Instantly, his guts rebelled. It reminded him of the concoction in the long-stemmed glass he'd drunk from at the tavern in Dorinah.

"Drink," Eadgith said, holding the bowl to his lips.

Anskar pulled away, but the old woman grabbed a fistful of his hair and pulled his head toward the bowl. She was far stronger than she looked. Unnaturally strong.

"Drink!"

And Anskar drank.

EIGHTEEN

AS SHE'D SAID IT WOULD, the blood and bone in Eadgith's drink acted as a conduit for the earth-tide. That much Anskar felt as he gagged and half-choked on the salty, viscous fluid. She made him drink the entire bowl, saying it would be good for him, and then she left him alone in the tent, groaning and clutching his belly.

He could feel the earth-tide strongly then, a weight within his stomach that seeped slowly into his veins. A ballast that dragged him down to sleep, a sleep in which he sank deeper and deeper into the ground.

At first he thrashed about in his nightmare, fearing he had been buried alive, but even with dirt and soil clogging his mouth and nose, he could breathe easily. And then he realized he didn't even need to breathe.

Down and down he sank, packed earth and bedrock parting like water to admit him. He heard the rush of the wind high above him, smelled the freshness of the dawn-tide, felt it alter as it struck the earth and began to follow him beneath, through layers of soil and the desiccated husks of insects, through graves and barrows and blood-drenched battlefields. Felt it turn brackish and sour from filtering through death and disease, felt it turn to putrid sludge. And he was adrift now in a sea of that vile sludge, an underground reservoir of foulness that bubbled and steamed and stank.

But then the soft glow of daylight bled through his closed eyelids, and he heard someone enter the tent. He assumed it was Eadgith, come to check on him, but when he opened his eyes, he saw Vilintia Yoenth staring down at him.

"Any news of Carred?" Anskar asked blearily. His head ached, pounding with each beat of his heart.

"A thousand and one questions you could have asked me," Vilintia said, "and that's the best you could come up with? As I told you, she's gone. Been gone for longer than any of us expected. She'll come back, or she won't. In the meantime, you have me."

"Have you spoken with Orix?"

"What would I say to him? He speaks hardly any Niyandrian, and he's not a quick learner."

"And you don't speak Nan-Rhouric."

"Why would I want to? Niyas is for Niyandrians, Anskar. I'd have thought your mother would have taught you that."

"Now you sound like Carred."

"And that's a good thing, is it? As I said before, this is our rebellion—the whole of Niyas's—not just hers. If she comes back, good. If not... well, she did her best, but it's not as if she's won us a good number of victories. We'll go on. We'll prevail. And your mother will return."

Anskar stood. Vilintia was between him and the tent entrance.

"Am I your prisoner?"

"You came looking for us, remember? Or is there something personal between you and Carred?"

"That's ridiculous," Anskar said, though his cheeks burned. "I don't know what I wanted, only that I couldn't go back to Branil's Burg and the Order."

"So you say. What is it you want now, Anskar DeVantte?"

"Right now? To patch things up with Orix."

"If I were you, I'd give him more time. Let his anger burn out."

"I didn't do that to him. It's Tain he should be angry with."

"Having your face jumbled up like that, it's bound to make you unreasonable. As I said, give it time. And tread warily around Noni. I used to think she was just a simpleton—Carred used to make me mother her, if you can believe it. But she's changed. Eadgith says it's on account of being possessed by your mother, but I'm not so sure. She has the feel of the moontouched, though her repositories are hardly remarkable."

"I felt the same. I thought she was crazy. If she is, I'm sorry for that."

"You're sorry? You take the blame for your mother's actions?"

"No, of course not. But I..."

"It feels as though you're being blamed? I'm not surprised, with how Orix spoke to you, and then Noni. My advice: stay away from them. The *Melesh-Eloni* has more important things to worry about. Anyway, how are you feeling now? Eadgith says you drank a whole potion." She screwed up her nose. "Rather you than me."

"She didn't exactly give me much choice," Anskar said. "The pounding in my head has passed, but I still feel weak. Not from Dargul's blow, though."

"From the removal of your catalyst?" Vilintia asked. "Why exactly did you want it removed? Have you turned your back on the Order of Eternal Vigilance… for good?"

Anskar shrugged. He saw no reason not to tell her, so he gave a stiff nod.

"Why?"

"My reasons are my own," he said.

Anskar went on to recount his summons from Wintotashum and how Vihtor had died. But before he could get to the part about making his request to the new Seneschal that the catalyst be removed and her refusal, not to mention the old Niyandrian man doing the job instead, badly, with a rusted knife, Anskar stopped speaking and frowned at Vilintia.

"What?" she said. "What is it?"

"Shouldn't you be elated or something? I just told you Vihtor Ulnar is dead. You succeeded."

"Why would I care? Vihtor Ulnar meant nothing to me, save that he was the face of my enemy. We got lucky. What more is there to say? One of our scouts recognized him and took a chance. It paid off."

"The priests of the Healer said the arrow was cursed," Anskar said.

"You'd have to ask Carred about that, or better still, your mother. But so what if it was? It got the job done, didn't it?"

"It was dishonorable."

"You think there was honor in what the mainlanders did when they invaded Niyas?"

"They had good reason." At least, that was how Tion had explained it. Queen Talia's empire of evil, spreading its tentacles beyond Niyas; it had to be stopped.

"No, Anskar, they did not. They had *their* reasons. It isn't the same thing. Still defending the Order of Eternal Vigilance? I assumed your decision to have your catalyst removed meant you'd seen them for what they truly are."

"You thought I'd come to my senses?" Anskar said. "You thought I went to that tavern to seek out the rebellion, to join myself to your cause?"

"Isn't that what happened? It was the impression you gave Dargul."

"I didn't know what else to do!"

Vilintia flinched at the violence of his outburst. Anskar was shaking, doing his best to contain his anger and not lash out. He wanted to punch something.

And then he remembered one of the reasons he had come here.

"Orix is in danger. He and I both are."

Vilintia shrugged. "Tell me something I don't know. We're all in danger, all the time."

"Go ahead, why don't you?" said someone. "Let yourself into my tent, Vilintia. Never mind me!"

Anskar gasped, and Vilintia whirled around to face the entrance. There stood Eadgith, a freshly mixed bowl of blood and bone in her hands.

"We needed to talk," Vilintia said.

"And now he needs to drink."

Anskar's guts rebelled at the thought, but he didn't dare argue.

"You take such good care of him," Vilintia told Eadgith as she headed for the tent flap. "Carred will be pleased."

"Vilintia," Anskar said, "when Eadgith is finished with me, please send Orix to see me—ask Noni to explain. I wasn't joking about the danger he and I face."

"Will it affect the rest of us?"

"I hope not. I don't think so."

Vilintia nodded that she would and then stepped outside.

"Here," Eadgith said, passing him the bowl. "Drink up."

NINETEEN

ANSKAR WAS FEELING A GOOD deal better after the last dose of Eadgith's drink. His guts had still roiled as the viscous fluid drained down his throat, but this time he'd felt the earth-tide that infused the blood and bone was stronger than before.

And not just within the vile brew, either: even now, the essence from the world's core that his mother used for her necromantic cants rose through the ground, through the filthy blanket upon which he once again lay, and seeped into his skin. It was as if the imbibed pig's blood and powdered rat's skull drew it to him, dredged the earth-tide up from its deep reservoir in the bowels of Wiraya.

But would Menselas curse him for partaking of such sorcery? Anskar wondered. He didn't even know if the earth-tide was forbidden by the Church of the Five, because no one had ever mentioned it, either when he was growing up or during his training. More so even than the dark-tide, this sorcery of the dead, this "shaping" sorcery, was shrouded in mystery.

Anskar turned his attention to the dark-tide essence permeating his veins and marrow. This, at least, he was more familiar with. It disturbed him that he felt so strongly the call of the dark-tide. He'd made up his mind, hadn't he? The removal of his catalyst was a statement: he was a knight, not a sorcerer. But Seneschal Monash had made it impossible for him to return to Branil's Burg, and here, among Niyandrians and with Eadgith's potions filling him with the earth-tide... his resistance was crumbling. The urge to reconnect with the dark-tide inside him was an itch he had to scratch.

Whereas before it had collected in a reservoir set beneath his dawn and dusk-tide repositories, now the dark-tide coursed throughout his entire being, its ebb and flow echoing the beat of his heart. It wasn't easily detectable at first—he really had to focus in order to perceive its subtle motions—but once he had the knack, he could not only see the tidal essence with his mind's eye as millions upon millions of black particles dispersed throughout his body, but he could hear its crackling rustle inside his skull, smell its sulfurous scent, and he became convinced he could taste charcoal on his tongue.

He sat up and started to draw all those inner senses together until his grasp on the darkness within was once more almost tangible, as it had been with the well of blackness at his core. He found that if he focused on all of those senses, they merged into one, until he could no longer differentiate between smell and taste and sight and sound. Once he had achieved that unified grasp of the dark-tide, he tried to will the black particles within to shift, to flow, to stream toward his open palm.

A numbing, prickling sensation crept along his arm, and he felt the coarse scouring of his veins. But then a wisp of shadow appeared on his palm, and with an act of imagination and will, he made it flicker and sway and dance.

"What are you doing?"

Anskar looked up, and the wavering shadow on his palm vanished. "Orix, you startled me."

He tried to keep his expression neutral. Orix had come without a hood this time. The eyes on his chin blinked repeatedly, as if he were trying hard to focus, and there were food stains at the corner of the mouth set into his forehead.

"You had your catalyst removed," Orix said, holding the tent flap open and lingering in the entrance. "So, what was that you were doing?"

"Nothing useful," Anskar said, feigning disappointment. "A false hope. I can no longer do what I once could. Both the dawn- and dusk-tides are lost to me."

But he was excited about the progress he'd just made with the unfettered dark-tide. He had wanted to rid himself of all sorcery, wanted to become a pure knight; but somehow, knowing this power within him was not the effect of an implanted crystal grown by mainland sorcerers gave him the sense that this was *his* power, not something imposed from without. Yes, he'd inherited it from his mother, but so what? He'd gotten the red tinge to his skin from her too, and the Five only knew what else. Menselas couldn't blame him for that. You didn't sin by what you were, only what you did. The more he thought about it, the more he realized the Church was wrong about the tides. The Soreshi, Zek, had been right. Poor Zek, who had died, run through with a sword when Anskar had tried to rescue Gisela.

"No longer special, then," Orix said. "Carred will be disappointed." It was disconcerting, watching his misplaced lips forming words.

"Will she?" For some reason that troubled him, and the realization it did was also confusing.

"Do you think you're more to her than a tool to be used?" Orix said. "She was searching for you out of obedience to your mother, nothing more."

"You're quite the expert on Carred Selenas, aren't you?" Anskar said.

Orix let the tent flap fall into place behind him as he stepped fully inside. "Vilintia said you wanted to see me."

Anskar stood, relieved that he didn't sway from weakness. Eadgith's brew was nothing short of miraculous. But had it merely speeded the repair of fractured bone, or had the earth-tide flowing through the drink somehow reshaped his skull?

He tried to meet Orix's eyes, but Orix looked away and folded his arms across his chest.

"Friends shouldn't fall out over trifles," Anskar said.

"You're the one who refused to stay and join us."

"And now you don't want me to?"

"You made your choice," Orix said. "You did whatever you wanted, like you always do."

Anskar bristled at that. "Like I always do? What are you talking about?"

"You've changed, Anskar." And now Orix did meet Anskar's eyes—with a glare that almost looked comical.

"No," Anskar said. "You're the one who's changed, and I think we both know why. Be honest, Orix—you're the one Carred was using. She didn't ditch you because of what happened to your face; she was already tired of you."

"That's tripe," Orix said. "You know nothing. You weren't there." His cheeks flushed, and his hands balled into fists.

Once, Anskar might have been intimidated, but Orix had

lost a lot of weight, as if he'd not eaten in weeks, or as if his insides were being destroyed by the rot. Likely it was the result of Tain using Orix to power the very sorcery that mangled his face. Tidal essence wasn't just stored in repositories; every living thing absorbed it to a greater or lesser degree, in their tissues, their bones, their blood—especially the earth-tide.

"You're being a child," Anskar said. "Be thankful for what you and Carred shared, and move on."

Orix took a step toward him, and inadvertently, Anskar stepped back.

"If it's a fight you want…" Anskar said. He knew he was faster than Orix and way more skilled.

But then Orix's shoulders slumped, and an unreadable expression came over his face—unreadable largely because the position of his eyes and mouth made no sense.

"No, I don't want to fight you," Orix said. "Not today. Yesterday, though, I was this close. This close!"

"Brave man," Anskar said. "Yesterday I was barely conscious."

"That would have improved the odds in my favor. Don't the Warrior's priests say you should seek every advantage?" It was hard to tell, with his mouth where it was, but Orix might even have smiled. "And, in case you've not noticed, I have moved on. I'm with Noni now."

"And how's that working out?"

Orix shook his head. "She is… not easy. But Noni's been through a lot."

"At the hands of my mother."

"That's not the only reason, but it's the worst. When Carred found Noni, she was being kept in a cage, ready to be sold in the slave markets in Atya. And to be honest, I don't think she was right in the head before that. She's angry with Carred for…" He raised his hands to his face. "For what Tain did to me, and for discarding me the way she did."

"I got the impression she was angry with me, too," Anskar said, "and I've only just met her."

"The sins of the mother…"

"I can understand that."

"And my issue with you… you're right. I was jealous. I thought Carred only slept with me because she couldn't have you. After Malady brought you through that portal, Carred was cold with me for days. I don't think she ever truly liked me. Carred has needs. She has an emptiness inside her that craves to be filled. For a while, I helped meet those needs. Noni says I should think of it this way: if Carred used me, maybe I used her too. But understanding what happened and coming to terms with it are two different things."

"Thank you," Anskar said.

"For what?"

"For your honesty. It can't have been easy."

Orix shrugged. "Like you said, friends shouldn't fall out over trifles. Menselas, what was I thinking? Other than the… you know… Carred was so boring. All she ever talked about was—"

"The rebellion?" Anskar suggested.

"Try again."

"Queen Talia?"

"You," Orix said. "Anskar this, Anskar that. You'd think I'd not spent years training with you and living at the Burg together with you. 'I know,' I used to tell her. 'Can we talk about something else?' But she's obsessed. That's maybe why I reacted to you the way I did. I'm sick to death of hearing about you. How you are crucial to the rebellion. How you're destined to be the focal point of resistance against the mainlanders. How you'll bring down the Order of Eternal Vigilance. How you'll be the instrument of the return of the queen."

"Even if I wanted to, how am I supposed to achieve all that?" Anskar asked. He suspected that all he was destined to do was bring Talia back to life somehow, and then his role would be done. She would be the one to destroy the Order and liberate Niyas.

"I don't think she has a clue. All she knows is that you're Queen Talia's son—something she hadn't foreseen. Like everyone else, she'd thought Talia had a daughter. But now she knows who you are, and now that you're here… Why *are* you here, exactly?"

"To warn you." A half-truth seemed better than no truth at all.

The eyes on Orix's chin widened at that, and he uncrossed his arms.

"Remember that knight aboard the *Exultant*? Colvin, the one we killed?"

"We had no choice," Orix said. "And the Grand Master didn't take the matter further."

Anskar shrugged. There had been a choice. By the time Orix's blade pierced Colvin's spine, the other knights in the dormitory had been about to intervene, and Anskar had already mangled Colvin's hand with dark-tide sorcery. Not exactly self-defense.

"Has the Grand Master changed his mind?" Orix asked.

"Not as far as I know. This is about Colvin's family. His father is Archduke Peleus of Laokeni in the Great Southern Mountains of Ealysia."

"So? My father's Ufrix Mendav of the slum-town Skitch in the Plains of Khisig-Ugtall."

Anskar chuckled, but this was too serious for humor. "He's a very rich man, and a dangerous enemy, or so I'm told."

"He's also a very long way away," Orix said.

"The archduke has initiated a blood feud. He has decreed that you and I shall die."

"How do you know this?"

"The new Seneschal at Branil's Burg told me," Anskar said. "Varensi Monash."

"So the Order knows, and the Order does nothing?"

"I spoke with Blosius about it," Anskar said. "He suspects the archduke is a major donor to the Church. I think we need to take the threat seriously, Orix. A man with wealth like that has a long reach. Maybe he can find us, even here… wherever here is."

"You've not been outside the tent yet?"

Anskar shook his head.

"We're three days' ride from Dorinah."

"Three days?" Anskar was shocked that he had been brought so far yet had no knowledge of it. He needed to get back to Dorinah and find his sack of void-steel ingots and *nietan* horn. But perhaps they'd be safer at the bottom of the canal than in his possession.

"Dargul hit you hard. You'd probably be dead or an imbecile by now, if not for Eadgith. I don't like the look—or the smell—of what she does, but it bloody well works."

"So, where are we exactly?" Anskar asked.

"One of Carred's forest hideaways. She has them all over Niyas. There are more than a hundred rebels with us here."

"I hope that's enough, if Archduke Peleus catches up with us," Anskar said.

"So you're going to stay this time?"

"I haven't thought that far ahead. I just wanted to warn you."

Orix's eyes glistened with moisture. He went to wipe them, but they weren't where he expected them to be. He sighed, a heavy sigh that made Anskar wonder how he kept going, how what Tain had done to him hadn't driven him completely insane.

"Thank you for that," Orix said. "And… and I'm sorry for how I've behaved."

"You've already apologized," Anskar said. "Once is enough for me. We're friends, aren't we?"

"Friends," Orix agreed. "But what I still don't understand is why you wanted your catalyst removed."

"I'm starting to wonder the same thing myself."

"And you disobeyed the new Seneschal. Does that mean you can't go back?"

"To the Burg? If I do, they'll force me to accept a new catalyst, then they'll send me back to Sansor. The Grand Master has need of people with my sort of abilities."

"And you're not just talking about the dawn-tide," Orix said. "So Carred is right: the Order of Eternal Vigilance is just a big, shameless lie. They and the other mainlanders were the aggressors, not Queen Talia."

"I don't know," Anskar said. "The information just keeps coming, too fast for me to handle. And there's still so much I don't understand."

"So you'll stay awhile?" Orix said. "Learn what you can?"

"From Carred?"

"If she ever comes back. She left us near Naphor. At a mansion that belonged to Queen Talia's father. Your grandfather."

"Really? Why? What was there?"

Orix shrugged. "She collected something from the mansion, then Noni—she was possessed by your mother at the time—took us to some kind of folly in the wilds. Carred opened it with a ring and stepped inside. It was a portal, the way I understood it."

"A portal to where?"

"To the abyssal realms. Don't ask me why she had to go there. Something to do with Armor of Divinity."

"Carred is seeking the Armor of Divinity?"

"She already has one."

"She what?" How? Why? After all the time and effort he'd spent gathering the ingredients for and forging divine alloy! Anskar had the unpleasant feeling Talia had multiple irons in the fire, and he was just one of them.

"That's why we went looking for the Necromancer Tain, curse his severed head. He took us to where he'd found his own Armor of Divinity."

"But I thought... I've seen his notebook. Didn't he make the armor himself?"

"I think he just adapted it. But he didn't get it quite right, which is why he's just a head—or at least he was. Tain's gone now. There's apparently a missing ingredient."

"Other than astrumium?"

"Oh, we got the astrumium. Took it from my sword. The armor's stowed at that mansion I told you about, but it's not ready to use."

"Can you find the mansion?"

"Maybe. But we should wait till Carred gets back."

"If Carred gets back," Anskar said. "I wonder what she's looking for in the abyssal realms."

"Some kind of steel, I think."

"Orix?"— Noni's voice from outside the tent.

"I should go," Orix said. "She's still angry with you."

"And now she'll be angry with you for talking to me?"

"Not for long. I think she's in love with me."

Anskar smiled. "And you?"

Orix somehow managed to look bashful, despite his mangled face.

"Good for you," Anskar said. "She's very pretty." He didn't

know what else to say. That seemed more appropriate than saying she resembled an unwashed lunatic or an insane witch.

"Stay away from her, Anskar."

"I didn't mean it like that."

"Please," Orix said. "Carred I could forgive, but Noni… What we have is special."

Anskar gripped his friend by the shoulder. "Trust me, Orix, you've absolutely nothing to worry about. Besides, I'm done with—"

"Spare me," Orix said. "Only yesterday you were done with sorcery and wanting to be a pure and holy knight."

"It's complicated," Anskar said. "But you've no need to worry about Noni. Or Carred, for that matter. There was never any need for you to worry on that score."

It was hard to gauge from his misplaced eyes whether Orix believed him.

But then again, it was hard to know whether Anskar believed himself.

TWENTY

"THE MINES OUTSIDE SANSOR ARE no longer profitable," a man said. He spoke in Nan-Rhouric. Always the voices spoke in Nan-Rhouric, and Marith understood every word of it. Which was odd. Carred hadn't taught her that well. And Carred's own Nan-Rhouric wasn't exactly what you'd call fluent.

"Furlough the workers?" a woman suggested.

"An accident, I think," the man said.

"Leave it to me." This last voice was strangely accented, with the slightest lisp, and it had an old man's rasp.

"You have people in the vicinity?" the woman asked.

"I have people everywhere."

Marith had the sense he might have silently added, "And you'd do well to remember that."

She woke with the voices still echoing about her skull and the rough woven woolen blanket scratching her skin. She reached about for the glass of water she'd left on the nightstand, and found to her relief it was last night's mistberry wine.

Theltek, what time was it? Outside it was still dark.

She'd been drinking herself to sleep for days. It was the only thing to shut the voices up. Maybe she was developing a tolerance and needed to up her alcohol intake?

Why did the voices always come at night? Maybe it was daytime where these meetings took place? Or maybe tiredness made her more receptive. Then again, maybe it was the wine, contrary to her beliefs. She'd give it up, just in case.

She finished the glass—honey-sweet and smooth, it left a tingle on the tongue.

Well, best not be too hasty.

She lay back down, but she knew she'd not sleep now. She fretted for a while, shifting her head this way and that on the pillow. If Carred were here, she could think of something to do that would help her sleep.

The air in the bedroom felt stifling. No matter how deeply she breathed, Marith couldn't fill her lungs.

In the end, she gave up trying to sleep and rolled out of bed. The floor was cold on her bare feet, but she couldn't remember where she'd put her slippers.

She was heading to the kitchen for another bottle of mistberry wine when white light smacked her in the face, as if she'd walked into a wall.

She stood stock-still at the heart of a circle of standing stones. There were ever widening rings of megaliths rippling out into the distance. She caught a flash of red sky and a bronze sun, and she could hear someone panting, gasping for breath…

Carred?

Marith hit the floor face-first.

When she came to, there was warm wetness between her legs. Her whole body ached as if it had been through a mangler. She wiped drool from the corner of her mouth and rolled to her knees. She threw out a hand to steady herself and touched water. Piss, she corrected, as she brought her fingers to her nose.

Something was happening to her. Something she couldn't even begin to understand.

But whatever it was, she wanted more of it.

Because it had connected her to Carred.

As she washed and dressed, giving up on sleep for the night, she heard more snatches of conversation, this time hushed, secretive: two people talking on one side, two or three more on another. Plots and plans was the gist of it. Knives in the back or knives in the front? Decisions, decisions. She heard snippets of deals within deals, the kind of mutual back-scratching she'd always despised—at least in business. As she came away from the bathroom, one thing stood out clearly in her mind: none of what she'd heard was good for Niyas.

With a steaming mug of tea in hand, Marith went out onto the porch to wait for the dawn. A gray bar already limned the horizon, and the black sky was starting to relent. She sat on her rocker and gazed up at the gibbous moon. She fancied she could feel its wan light flooding her veins, in a similar way to the tides of dusk and dawn. Reflected light, she'd been told by her grandma years ago. The light of the sun. Of course, it could have just been the anticipation of the dawn-tide that she felt.

She'd always wanted Carred to experience the oncoming tides with her, out of doors, naked, which was when it felt best; but Carred had always turned bashful. She claimed she'd never wanted to develop her natural abilities, but Marith knew otherwise.

Carred was still scarred from her childhood. She'd told Marith about her mother abandoning her in the woods, her father's drunken rages, and Marith suspected that wasn't the half of it. If they could only spend more time together, Marith could help Carred to heal, and once she grew to accept who she was—who she really was, not just the unwanted brat of some vile bloody bastards—then she'd accept the tides, and they would embrace them together.

"Where are you, love?" she asked the face of the moon.

The knotting of her stomach told her she already knew. The red sky, the bronze sun above the circle of stones had given it away, confirming her initial intuition.

Marith had heard of mad sorcerers transporting themselves to the abyssal realms, but she'd heard nothing of them coming back.

She worried as she waited, watching the sky turn gray, rocking on her chair and sipping her tea. Waited till the first gash of red split the horizon. Then she set down her mug and stood, stripping off her nightgown as she walked from the porch.

And opened her arms to the gathering wind.

TWENTY-ONE

ANSKAR EMERGED FROM THE TENT to clear skies. There were dozens of tents dotted around the clearing, surrounded by a deep, dense forest. The air was brisk and refreshing, and the sound of birdsong filled the air. Acorns littered the ground, and high up in the trees, leaves rustled as squirrels raced along the long limbs.

He could make out wooden shelters in amongst the trees, and there were Niyandrians lazing in the entrances of tents, standing about talking or skinning rabbits and squirrels they must have caught during the early hours. Not a few of them glanced his way as he left the tent.

Someone called out Eadgith's name, and the old woman swore from within a nearby tent, then bustled out of the opening. She spat and wiped her mouth with the back of her hand.

"What is it now?" she snarled. "Can't you people even wipe your asses without my help?"

The woman who had called her pointed at Anskar.

"Oh, the prodigal son rises," Eadgith said. "And about time, too. Anyone would think you'd had your spleen removed with a rusty knife."

Anskar laughed dutifully as Eadgith shuffled over to him and proceeded to check his eyes, his ears, his throat.

"What is it?" he asked. "What are you looking for?"

"One of them, are you? A know-it-all patient."

"No, I just—"

"Hello?" Eadgith said. "What's this, then?"

She gripped his wrist, frowning as her fingers met the metal of the vambrace. She took hold of his other wrist, and this time Anskar felt the crawl and prickle of tiny insects on his skin. After a few moments, the old woman released him.

"Fine," she said. "You'll be all right. Just don't go doing anything else stupid, because I'm clean out of rat skulls, and I can't be bothered to hunt for more. Just kidding, love. There's always bones of one kind or another to be found. Piralka's gift we call it, the constant supply of the dead."

"Piralka?"

"The god of rot and decay."

"A Niyandrian god?"

"Course she's a Niyandrian god. Do you think I'd waste my time with them mainland frauds, like Sylva Kalisia and Jocal the Fecund? And don't go telling me there's only one god and that it's yours, the so-called god of balance. Menselas! God of Five Aspects, my tits. God of five assholes, more likely, the amount of shit he talks, from what I've seen of your scriptures."

Shocked, Anskar made to protest as his mouth dropped open.

"What, you think I ain't read the holy books of the Five? Gives me something to do when I sit at the cesspit, and something to wipe with after."

Anskar should have been outraged, should have condemned such blatant blasphemy, but instead he found himself half-chuckling, and then Eadgith was laughing along with him, and she clapped him on the back.

"Don't tell anyone I said so, love," she said, "but you're all right. Well, half of you is, at any rate."

"Did you know my mother?" Anskar asked.

"Aye," Eadgith said, suddenly deadly serious. "I knew her."

She turned abruptly away and cried out, "Vilintia, you dozy cow, the idiot's awake!" She turned back to Anskar. "Next time you want a catalyst removed, you come see me. Rusty knife, my nipples! Ah, here she is."

Vilintia came out of the trees, unstringing a hunting bow as she approached. The quiver slung over her shoulder was still packed with goose-fletched arrows.

"Hunting?" Anskar asked.

"He's a sharp one," Eadgith said as she acknowledged Vilintia with a wave and shuffled away to her tent. "No surprise there, I suppose, if he's the all-holy *Melesh-Eloni*."

"Seems like we're always hunting," Vilintia said. "When we're not foraging. All these mouths to feed, and we can't keep going down into the towns for supplies. The fewer people who know we're here, the better."

"Orix said you have more than a hundred people here."

"A hundred and thirteen," Vilintia said. "Fourteen, if we count you."

"And are you counting me?" Anskar asked. "Or am I free to go?"

"Is that what you want?" Vilintia said. "I thought you wanted to see Carred."

"Not much chance of that if she's gone to the abyssal realm."

"We'll see," Vilintia said. "But whatever you want to speak

with her about, you can say to me."

"I wanted to warn Orix about the blood feud, that's all."

"Yes, Noni told me about that. You think this Archduke Peleus will come against the two of you here in Niyas?"

"The new Seneschal thought so."

"Varensi Monash," Vilintia said, frowning. "What's she like?"

"She seems hard," Anskar said. "Experienced and dangerous. She used to be a general on the mainland. Some sort of fixer for the Order."

"I know the type," Vilintia said. "So, what will it be, I wonder? A renewal of the Order's attempts to flush us out of the hill country and the forests? Or will she go even further? The mainland rulers see us as less than beasts, or didn't you know that? Carred always used to say their ultimate aim was to rid Niyas of our presence so they could annex the isle to their stinking empire. Vihtor Ulnar was a formidable foe during the war, and as governor he was firm and relentless in the expansion of mainland rule, but I never got the impression that he would have gone so far."

"He wouldn't have," Anskar said. But how did he know? How much did he really know about the man who had only recently owned up to being his father? Had he been a just governor? An honorable knight? Or had he been, as Queen Talia said, a liar and a rapist? With a sinking feeling in the pit of his stomach, Anskar realized that he'd probably never know.

Vilintia frowned, but then suddenly shook herself and forced a smile. "Come, Anskar," she said, "let me show you where we are."

"You're not afraid I might escape and lead the Order here?"

"You won't do that," she said confidently.

Vilintia led him away from the camp and into the trees. A couple of Niyandrians tried to call her back for a word, but she dismissed them with a wave and a promise to speak with them later.

Just beyond the main camp, an old woman was sitting cross-legged and bent over beneath a tree, gray hair covering her head and face. She was uttering strange, nonsensical words and trying to make them rhyme. As they passed, she straightened up and swept the hair from her eyes, and Anskar saw that she was not old at all: it was Noni. Her hair was so caked with dust and detritus that it appeared gray. She'd been rake-thin before, but now she was almost skeletal, her skin pale and flakey. Her cat's eyes were almost pure white, and when she turned them on Anskar, she seemed to look right through him.

"*Melesh*," Noni said in a child's voice. "*Melesh-Eloni*, boney, crony, a prince all alone-y."

"Morning, Noni," Vilintia said, but the young woman merely dipped her head again, buried it in her lap, and continued to mutter rhymes.

"Is she mad?" Anskar asked as they continued past.

"Wouldn't you be, if you'd been through what she's been through? Of course, it could have something to do with all the mushrooms she's been finding in the woods."

Vilintia brought him to the edge of the escarpment the forest covered, from where they looked down the stepped scarp face to another stretch of woodland. A brook wound its way between the trees below, its waters glimmering in the morning sun.

"I thought you might want to bathe," Vilintia said.

"Do I smell that bad?"

"I'm not going to answer that."

"Shall I meet you back at the camp?" Anskar asked.

"I'll wait for you here. Don't worry, I won't look."

"That's what you said before."

"Then it will be different this time."

At the bottom, by the bank of the brook, Anskar glanced up before removing his clothes and stepping into the shallow stream. Vilintia was no longer visible to him.

The water was so cold he gasped when he entered it. It only came up to his knees, but as he grew accustomed to the temperature, he slowly lowered himself until he could sit and splash his torso and face, and then he lay back and looked up into the sunlit skies, and he felt oddly at peace.

There were threats everywhere: Seneschal Monash, Sareya, the Grand Master, Archduke Peleus... And things still didn't feel right between him and Orix despite their talk. But he felt at peace here and now, in the water, among the Niyandrian rebels who were the sworn enemy of the Order of Eternal Vigilance that had raised him.

But then the thought occurred to him: perhaps this was what his mother had intended for him all along—to reject his catalyst and the Order and to find his way to Carred Selenas and the Niyandrian resistance. The priests of the Healer might have exorcized Queen Talia, but did that make any difference to her scheming?

He was startled by the splash of a fish and sat up in the water. The memory of Zek catching fish with a modified use of the dusk-tide sprang unbidden to mind, and Anskar smiled before he almost wept at the sense of loss that swept through him. Too many people had died in the short time since he had first set foot outside Branil's Burg: Zek, Braga, Hrothyr, Brother Bonavir... Naul, who had been murdered when Carred's agents came to kidnap Sareya; Josac the priest of the Warrior; Borik, whose massive sword had shattered when he needed it most. And now Vihtor was dead as well. They were all dying, all the people he knew. Was that his destiny? To outlive all his friends, each successive year adding to the void of loneliness? The words of Noni's song repeated in his mind: *Melesh-Eloni, boney, crony, a prince all alone-y.*

He was being morbid, he realized. And not everyone was dead. There was still Orix, despite how much their friendship had cooled. There was Sareya, cooler still, and Lanuc, Gisela, Rindon, and Nul.

He thrust his face into the clear water and scattered half a dozen silvery fish. He recalled that Vilintia had been out hunting with a bow, and grew excited to employ Zek's method to provide the camp with fresh fish. But the instant the thought occurred, he realized he would be wasting his time. He touched his four fingertips and thumb to his chest, where he felt the scar from the removal of his catalyst.

Anskar climbed out of the water and lay in the grass till the sun dried him. He dressed, then climbed back to the top of the escarpment, where Vilintia was waiting for him, staring out across the weald below to where thin plumes of gray smoke were winding their way into the sky.

"Life goes on," she said whimsically.

"You're thinking of Taloc?"

She shot him a glare so fierce that he looked away. "I was thinking of that," she said, pointing.

"What is it?" Anskar said, squinting but seeing nothing save for forest and smoke.

"Tanturn," she said. "A village hidden by the trees, as yet untouched by the mainland invaders. All over Niyas, small pockets of our culture remain, but for how long?"

"Do you go there for supplies?" he asked.

"Rarely. Only when hunting is poor or we need horseshoes or fledging for arrows. Geban down in the village is a master fletcher, and he makes his own ash shafts, too. And we won't stay here forever. We've been here a month or so already, and that's probably too long. Last thing I want is for the Order to track us to Tanturn and find what they've been missing all this time. As things stand, the consensus is that we give Carred a little longer. Besides," she said, holding up a squirrel she must have shot while he was bathing, "who needs to buy supplies when we have bows and arrows and a forest full of game?"

TWENTY-TWO

ANSKAR HAD THE SENSE HE was being watched. By Vilintia herself, for the most part, but he didn't miss the surreptitious glances from several of the men and women who took it in shifts to patrol the camp and the surrounding woodland.

Orix kept out of his way, and the few times Anskar saw him, he was with Noni. If the two of them were ever speaking when Anskar came along, they ceased the moment they saw him. Noni would scowl and clutch Orix's arm protectively. As for Orix, it was hard to know what he was looking at and what he was thinking.

Eadgith had surrendered her tent to Anskar and started moving her few possessions into a larger tent shared by some of the other women. The old woman told him that she had taken Noni under her wing and was going to guide her in the way of the earth-tide.

So, Noni still intended to fix Orix's face. Anskar shook his head. He could have learned to do the same thing, and faster, he was convinced. And perhaps he still would do it, and prove to Orix that they were still friends, although how Noni would react to that wasn't a comforting thought.

"It can't be easy training Noni," he told Eadgith as she collected the last of her things from his tent.

"Why's that, then?"

"She seems…"

"Crazy? Perhaps she is. Nevertheless, the moon's either touched her or come real close. That girl has talent, but it's raw as a weeping leg ulcer. And as for madness, they say Theltek herself has a thousand warring minds, and a thousand competing thoughts in each."

"I thought Theltek was a man…"

"And a woman. And everything in between. They say Theltek has a thousand genders."

"That's absurd," Anskar said.

"Is it? And you know that how? It's no more absurd than her having a thousand eyes, a thousand ears, a thousand—"

"I get the point," Anskar said. "And it still sounds absurd. All of it."

"As absurd as a god of five aspects?"

Anskar gave a sullen grunt, but he had to admit she'd won that particular argument.

"Ask yourself," Eadgith said, "ain't it possible Noni's made after Theltek's image, and that there are many Nonis inside the one?"

"Huh," Anskar said. "Are you sure you're not confusing Theltek with Menselas? More likely her condition was caused by the trauma of being enslaved."

Eadgith spat. She did that a lot, he noticed. "What are you now, a poxy priest of the Elder with pretensions to knowledge of the mind? I tell you, the girl was that way long before the mainland bastards and the traitorous Niyandrians who helped them came along. She was born hearing the voices of one world while living in another."

"You mean the realm of the dead?" Anskar asked.

"Among others. The girl's empty-headed, a vacuum waiting to be filled. Makes her easy prey, if you ask me."

"For my mother?"

"That ain't what I meant. The rightful ruler of Niyas don't prey on her own, just grants them opportunities to serve her. No, I meant wraithes, for one thing. Demons for another. But she'll be all right now she's with me. I don't have no patience for demons." She shot Anskar a stern look and spat again. "And wraithes... they should have left this world long ago, but still they linger like an eternal fart from one of the many asses of Theltek."

That evening, Anskar ate a supper of boiled tubers, acorns, and leaves in the big tent Eadgith now shared with two other women, Jaeloi and Kentha. To his discomfort, Noni was also there. Outside, at fires around the camp, the rest of the rebels were roasting squirrel meat, which smelled good compared to the fare Anskar had been given.

"You don't like squirrel?" he asked Eadgith, and Noni giggled.

"I don't eat any flesh just to fill my stomach," Eadgith said. "There's power in flesh and bone, more even in blood—you've felt that now after drinking my potions. If I take aught from the dead, it's for a purpose; but as for food, this is all I need." She crammed a mushy piece of wild parsnip into her mouth and chewed noisily, as if the sound could somehow convince Anskar that it tasted good.

"And you, Noni?" Anskar asked. "Do you only eat plants too?"

"He's angry with you," she said, locking eyes with him, hers white save for the slitted pupil.

"Orix? Still? I thought we'd made up."

Eadgith stiffened and slowed her chewing as she watched Noni through squinted eyes.

"Colvin," Noni said.

A chill crept up Anskar's spine.

"He's here now," Noni said, "reaching for you with the hand he says you mangled."

Anskar set down his bowl, the food in his mouth suddenly tasteless and dry.

Jaeloi and Kentha watched him intently, faces turned from crimson to pink. He'd seen Sareya's do the same back at Branil's Burg whenever she was frightened.

"He blames you both," Noni said. "You and Orix. He'll not harm Orix. I won't let him. But you…"

"He's here with us now? Not in the realm of the dead?"

"Can't you feel his frigid fingers on your throat?"

"You're making it up to frighten me," Anskar said. "There are no fingers." Even so, he touched his throat just to be sure. "And I'd know if the dead were here. You're not the only one who can speak with them."

"Colvin is both here and there," Noni said, "but more there than here, else you would be dead—his threat, not mine."

"Can he hear me?" Anskar asked.

"He hears only me," Noni replied.

"Then tell him this for me: he got what he deserved. Ask him, Noni. Ask him what it was he was trying to do… to Orix. I doubt you'll approve."

"I can't," Noni said, and she was shivering now.

"Why's that?"

Eadgith moved far more quickly than should have been possible for an old woman. She set her bowl down, stood, and reached into the pocket of her skirt.

"He's too angry!" Noni said. "He spits hatred and roars!"

"Because of his shame!" Anskar retorted.

Eadgith flung a pinch of white powder at Noni, who jerked upright, sighed, and slumped forward. She took three labored breaths, then appeared utterly relaxed, as if nothing out of the ordinary had just happened.

Noni popped a green leaf into her mouth and chewed slowly. "He's gone," she said with a shrug.

As Anskar picked at his food, he caught Jaeloi watching him. She quickly dipped her eyes, then turned her head to whisper to Kentha.

"None of that, you two," Eadgith said. "You have something to say, say it so we can all hear. And that means loudly, lest either one of you wants to scrape out the wax from my ears."

"Forgive me," Jaeloi said. "I was wondering…"

Kentha put a hand on her shoulder. "We were wondering about you, Anskar DeVantte. Is it true? Are you really the *Melesh-Eloni*?"

"Carred thinks so," Eadgith said. "And that should be enough for you."

"But you're different to what we were told to expect," Jaeloi said. "Everyone in the camp says as much."

"You mean I was supposed to be a girl?" Anskar said. "Believe me, I was just as surprised as everyone else when I found out who I was. I thought my parents were knights killed in the war. I was supposed to be a knight of the Order of Eternal Vigilance. I even believed I'd be honoring my parents' memory once I was fully consecrated."

"And you know it's true?" Kentha asked. "How can any of us be sure you really are the Queen's son and heir?"

"Oh, it's true," Noni said. "That doesn't mean we have to like it. But you have to work with what you're given, however meager."

The next day it was raining again, intermittent icy sheets driven by a harsh wind, and the mood in the rebel camp appreciably soured. Most people remained in their tents, only emerging to go into the trees to relieve their bladders. A few sat in the entrances, glowering at the gray skies and periodic downpours, as if they could dissolve the cloud cover with a strong enough intention.

As he left his tent, Anskar noticed a man, hooded and cloaked against the rain, shadowing him from within the treeline. So, he was still being watched. The rebels didn't trust him yet, and that was understandable.

Anskar paused in the lee of a tent, waiting until the man walked past his position, then doubled back and entered the forest behind him. The man drew up sharp and glared in the direction of the tent Anskar had been hiding behind, then found a tree to lean against, muttering something as he glanced at the skies and the rain spattering the leaves above his head. When he cursed and pushed away from the tree to approach the tent, Anskar followed.

"Anything?" Anskar asked.

The man spun round. "Shit on you!" he growled. "You nearly gave me a heart attack."

He wasn't as tall as Anskar, though he was broad-shouldered; not exactly fat, but not exactly lean and muscular either. Beneath the hood, he was wide-eyed and clean-shaven, his red-skinned face turning plump. He had more the look of a shopkeeper than a warrior, and maybe he was. Whereas many of the women and men in the camp looked like seasoned veterans who had probably fought at Naphor, there were others who looked as though they had never hefted a sword until circumstances, or a sense of duty, had forced them to.

"Have you seen anything out there?" Anskar asked.

The man frowned in confusion, then seemed to understand. "On patrol, you mean? No, nothing. But that don't mean there's nothing there."

Anskar smiled and held out his hand. "Anskar DeVantte."

"Baylon," the man said, taking it. "You'd be better off staying in your tent. Don't seem no end to this blasted rain."

"I was looking for someone," Anskar said.

"Let me guess: the pig-boy?" Baylon said.

"Pig-boy?"

"Sorry. I meant the Traguh-raj lad, Orix. Pig-boy's what Carred used to call him."

Baylon seemed to be the type to talk too much and overshare. Anskar decided to push his luck. "Is that before she started sleeping with him?"

Baylon gave a disapproving snort. "Seems Orix has fallen out of favor. We all do, sooner or later, Vilintia says, and I'm inclined to believe her, considering what happened to her man, Taloc. Didn't know him too well myself, but our Vilintia was sweet on him, and Carred left him behind."

"Maybe Carred has an explanation. It can't have been easy, leading a rebellion all these years."

"Maybe," Baylon said. "And maybe we'll get to hear it if ever she comes back."

"So have you seen Orix? Is he in his tent?"

"Left camp first thing this morning. He's gone with others to the town down in the lowlands. Vilintia sent them for arrows, bread, jerked meat, and a few of the horses have thrown shoes, so…”

“Where are the horses?” Anskar asked. He’d not seen any since he’d emerged from his tent the day before.

Baylon jerked his head to the south. “There’s good pasture a half mile that way. We got two dozen folk there, keeping watch over the horses.”

“Vilintia told me she didn’t want people going to the town unless they had to,” Anskar said.

“She’s decided we should move out—find a new camp in the next week or so.”

“Because of me?”

“I doubt that,” Baylon said. “Dargul’s too good to have been followed, and the way he tells it, there’s a false trail from Dorinah that’ll have the Order’s knights scratching their heads for days, if not weeks. No, we never stay long in one place. We’d run out of grazing, for one thing, and the locals get nervous once they know we’re around. There’s always the chance of one of them ratting on us, too.”

“That happens? Niyandrians betray you?”

“You’d better believe it. Maybe not so much out here. This place is pretty much untouched by the invaders. Folks here are loyal to the old ways. I reckon they know what we’re about, and they approve.”

“Have you…” Anskar started, not sure where he was going with this. He sighed and continued, “Have you spoken with Orix?”

“When I have to. You speak pretty decent Niyandrian, but he doesn’t even make a bloody effort.”

“You don’t seem to like him.”

Baylon looked as though he were chewing gristle for a while, and then he spat. "I don't have an opinion on him."

"Orix and I were friends once," Anskar said. "Only…"

"You don't need to tell me," Baylon said. "Happy as a pig in shit, he was, rutting with Carred, till she wouldn't stop talking about you."

"Because of who I am?"

"I don't know nothing about this *Melesh-Eloni* business. I was talking about jealousy, plain and simple. New meat, Anskar. Carred's always on the lookout for new meat. Piggy was flavor of the day for a while, but even his dull little mind worked out you were next in line."

"That's ridiculous," Anskar said. "She doesn't want me in that way."

"Course, I could have gone there myself," Baylon said. "I've seen the way she looks at me—and not just me, I tell you. But I ain't interested in leftovers, if you know what I mean."

"Where I come from," Anskar said, "we show our leaders more respect."

"Respect gets old," Baylon said, "when you don't get results."

"Anskar!" a woman called above the sound of the rain.

"Hey ho," Baylon said, slapping Anskar on the back. "Looks like she's done mourning Taloc."

Waving from the entrance of her tent was Vilintia.

Vilintia had clearly been lying on a bed made from old blankets heaped atop a sheepskin. There was a streaming mug of tea on the ground beside the makeshift bed, and on top of the ratty blankets lay an open book with a cloth-and-board cover in gray and red and embossed with gold lettering. Anskar looked from the book to Vilintia. It must have cost a fortune. All the books he had ever seen were copied out by hand, the pages stitched together—all except a newish copy of the *Book of the Five Aspects* that Brother Tion had proudly shown him a few years ago. That had been cloth-and-board bound like this one, and the words within had been printed, not written.

"Where did you get that?" he asked.

"You mean, did I steal it?" Vilintia asked. "I haven't always been an outlaw, you know. I used to be a soldier in the army of Queen Talia. Used to command my own division back in the day. There was a time, though it's hard to believe, when Niyas was for Niyandrians. We are not the barbarians you mainlanders make us out to be."

"I never said you were."

"I wouldn't blame you if you did," Vilintia said. "Your mind has been shaped since you were able to walk. You think like a mainlander, act like one, and, save for your eyes and the slightest tinge of red to your skin, you even look like one."

"None of which is my fault," Anskar said.

"Isn't that what I just said? I said I wouldn't blame you… for making assumptions about a people you scarcely know anything about."

"My mother's people," Anskar said.

He started at the feel of Vilintia's hand on his shoulder. "*Your* people, if only you'll give us the time to prove it to you."

"We have time," Anskar said, meeting her eyes. "I'm not going anywhere, so you can call Baylon and the others off."

"Are you giving me your word? The word of a knight of the Order of Eternal Vigilance?"

"Former knight. But yes, my word." For what it was worth.

He'd broken his word and vows to himself so many times he didn't know who he truly was anymore.

Vilintia's hand moved from his shoulder to his face.

"You wanted to see me?" he prompted.

"Not for anything special. I just popped my head out for some air and saw you were up and about. Starting to settle in?"

He sighed and rubbed the stubble that had grown on his cheek. "It's not easy. Orix has changed—and I don't just mean his face. And the feeling around the camp…"

"What of it?"

"People seem… I don't know… Like they don't particularly want Carred to come back."

"Are you surprised? We love Carred, Anskar. We all know how much she tried. But this has gone on too long. I used to support Carred against the naysayers, those who want to take the fight straight to the Order, but now…" She shook her head.

"This is about Taloc, isn't it?"

"It's about failure. It's about years of running and hiding. It's about…"

"Vilintia, it's all right to grieve. I've lost people, too… my father, whom I didn't even know was—"

"Don't," Vilintia said. "Don't presume to know what's going through my mind. Yes, I blame Carred for Taloc—for taking him on her madcap quest, but mostly for not even bothering to tell me in person what happened. And for leaving him. Leaving him! But that's not what this is about."

"Baylon said—"

"Baylon! Baylon's nothing but a gossip. He used to be a merchant, so it comes as no surprise. Always running his mouth off. You think I'm unfair to Carred? He's worse, and all because she wouldn't sleep with him, while he denigrates her for sleeping with everyone else."

"And does she?"

"Sleep with everyone?" Vilintia shook her head and smiled. "Not everyone. And no, before you ask, not me. Some of us made sacrifices for this rebellion. My focus has always been on the cause. *Was* always on the cause."

"Until Taloc…"

"Until I let my guard down. And look where that got me. I'm sorry, Anskar, I shouldn't have called you over. The book I was reading is a very good book, and it's the only thing right now between me and a day of dismal boredom in this insufferable rain." The way she looked at him caused Anskar to swallow.

"What's it about?" Anskar asked.

"You don't take a hint, do you?"

Vilintia stooped to retrieve the book from the top of the blankets and handed it to him. The pages smelled damp, and the cloth of the cover was dog-eared. He glanced at the open pages she had been reading. The words were Niyandrian, the print tiny yet perfectly clear. He had to sound out the words one by one. "'The leash of the living is the vision of the dead'?"

"The vision of the dead risen," Vilintia corrected, taking the book from his hands. "Carred was reading this before she left. It's a copy of an ancient folio from before the time of the Necromancer Tain, a work that's supposed to have inspired him." She closed the book and ran her thumb over the embossed title on the cover. "It's called *The Governance of a People of Bone*. It was a popular read during your mother's reign."

"Popular?"

"Naphor possessed Wiraya's first printing press, or didn't your Order tutors tell you that? The means of reproducing texts efficiently, an alternative to the weeks and months, if not years, it takes to copy a book by hand. They have one in Sansor, I hear. Just one stolen idea among many. Soon they'll have printing presses all over the mainland, and some rich Kailean noble will no doubt take the credit for their invention."

"I expect you're right," Anskar said. He'd seen enough of Sansor to know that she was. "*The Governance of a People of Bone?*" he asked. "It's an odd title."

"It's a speculative work based on some of our most ancient beliefs."

"About the dead rising?"

"It's about more than that. Raising the dead is but a baby step on the road to the fulfillment of our destiny. Your mother knew that, and she was the most accomplished of all our necromancers. Ever. The oracles in our distant past foresaw a time when our dead would not only rise from their graves but would have newly constituted bodies that would never decay, age, or die again: bodies of bone. Not bone like ours, but diamond hard, impervious to all the ravages of time and trauma. The book explores what such a new life of bone might be like, whether we would still need to eat and drink, whether we would tire, whether there would be any more need for… procreation."

Vilintia slung the book back down on the blankets. "Much of it's nonsense, as far as I can make out, but it's good to know what our ancestors believed."

Vilintia feigned a yawn and seated herself cross-legged on her makeshift bed. Her eyes tracked his every movement as he leafed through the pages, making him feel uncomfortable. He handed her back the book.

"Baylon said you sent Orix and some others to the town for supplies."

"As I said, Baylon has a big mouth. Not as big as his stomach, but big nonetheless."

Anskar smiled, and some of the tension lifted.

"But Baylon is correct. It's time we were moving on. Carred never likes to linger too long in any one place, and we've been here a good few weeks now."

Vilintia picked up her book and resumed reading.

Anskar waited, in case she chose to speak again, but when she didn't, he understood that he had been dismissed, and he went back out into the rain.

TWENTY-THREE

WATER!

At least it looked like water.

Whatever it was, Carred dropped to her belly at the side of the running stream and cupped it in her hands, drinking greedily. It tasted sweet, with an aftertaste of chalk.

She drank and she drank, then splashed her face and hair. The dust and dirt on her face turned to a sheen of mud, which she washed off with handfuls from the stream. She rubbed water on the back of her neck, over her ears, and even used a finger to wash inside her nostrils.

Carred was tempted to throw herself into the stream to get relief from the relentless sun, but then she saw something moving beneath the surface: wriggling purple worms the size of her pinky finger. Lots of them.

She pushed herself back from the water's edge. Too tired, too utterly drained to resume standing, she rolled onto her side and let the sun dry her hair.

She must have dozed off, and while she dozed, she dreamed of Nally and of Queen Talia's frigid bed, and of Marith's warm one—when it wasn't blisteringly hot. The thought made her smile, still half-asleep. Truth be told, it made her horny too. Theltek, she missed Marith. When would she ever stop missing her?

It was a good question. She wasn't usually one to get hung up on lovers. Oh, she loved them all, and at times she would miss them, but Marith had always been… more than the others. In a different life, without Talia's demands from beyond the grave, without the constant threat of agents from the Order of Eternal Vigilance, Marith would have been family, she had no doubt about it, and the farmhouse in the woods would have been their shared home.

A shadow fell over her. She rolled to her back and opened her eyes.

Staring down at her from where it hovered ten feet above the ground was a ball of what she first took to be rock, but then saw was some kind of flesh covered with armor-like brown scabs. It peered down at her with a plate-sized eye, all white save for a pinprick pupil of black. It had been watching her earlier. It had been following.

A horizontal slit opened beneath the great eye: a mouth with spines instead of teeth. Words came out, guttural and malformed. A request? She couldn't tell. She couldn't speak the demon language of Nazgrese.

The lipless mouth moved again, this time the tone of its utterance sounding more like a command.

Without thinking, Carred put a hand on the hilt of her sword.

The creature's great eye tracked her movements. It blinked, and when it opened fully again, the sclera had turned green.

A warning?

Deciding to err on the side of caution, Carred released her sword hilt and raised her hands.

Another blink, and this time the great eye turned violet. The creature's mouth opened again, and strings of saliva shot over her, sticky, like the strands of a web. The saliva hardened as Carred tried to wipe it off, and as it hardened, it branched and grew, smothering her from head to foot, covering even her mouth and nose. She panicked then. She couldn't breathe. Nor could she raise her hand to her face to clear her airways.

Through the rock-hard webbing that cocooned her, Carred could clearly see the creature hovering directly in front of her.

"No," she tried to say, but her mouth wouldn't move. "Theltek, Talia, Marith, no!"

But the creature just hung there, suspended in midair. As if it were waiting. But waiting for…?

A shape appeared behind the floating ball-creature: two arms, two legs. Pale skin, platinum hair, golden eyes. Naked. All ribs and bones, yet somehow strikingly beautiful. A woman.

Before the great eye could turn to face her, the newcomer raised a hand. Shards of ice burst from the palm, and the ball-creature dropped to the ground with a thump.

"Oh, you poor dear," the woman said in perfect Niyandrian. Her golden eyes seemed to caress Carred wherever they looked. She felt a tickling touch inside her skull, and a pleasant warmth suffused her skin. "You are so lucky I came along when I did."

With slender, long-nailed fingers, the woman picked away at the fossilized webbing holding Carred. Her progress quickened as the strands started to come away in clumps. Once her arms were free, Carred managed to break off the rest of the cocoon herself.

"Thank you," she said. "What was that thing?"

"Is," the woman corrected, glancing toward the ball-creature, which was motionless on the ground, frozen in ice. "It's still alive. Come on, before the ice melts."

"Can't you kill it?"

"That would not be wise." She held out a hand, which Carred tentatively took. "Let's go."

"Where?" Carred asked.

"Where would you like to go?"

She let go of the woman's hand, brushing hair out of her face as she tried to think. How much should she say? She decided she didn't have much choice.

"I'm looking for the lord of this realm."

Just saying it aloud brought the niggling concerns at the back of her mind to the forefront.

"You're a friend of Lord Domatai?"

Talia's father. The lord here—in some gods-forsaken part of the abyssal realms. A demon lord? Why had she agreed to come? Then again, why would Talia have sent her if there were no chance of succeeding? Trade. That was the key. She had something this Domatai presumably wanted. It was a simple exchange: Wirayan star-metal for demonic void-steel, and then he'd send her on her way, this oh-so-reasonable demon lord, whom Talia had hidden from all her life. What could possibly go wrong?

"Not a friend exactly," Carred said. "I've come here to trade."

The woman's golden eyes widened, and at the same time the warmth flooding Carred's skin seeped into her veins, her muscles, her bones. She closed her eyes and let out a sigh, part relief, part pleasure.

"If you like," the woman said, "I can take you to Lord Domatai."

"You'd do that?" Carred couldn't keep the smile from her

face. She almost wept with joy.

"He will thank me for bringing you safely to him." Again, she held out her hand, and again, Carred took it.

The standing stones seemed to part for them as they approached, and the pale-skinned woman stepped lithely between the concentric rings, taking Carred with her.

The sun no longer felt hot and oppressive to Carred. She was both warm and cool, and she bristled with newfound energy.

Within moments that could have been hours, they emerged from the last ring of standing stones. Ahead, a salt-and-pepper desert rolled away into the distance, where the horizon was dominated by an immense, perfectly symmetrical mountain that shimmered every imaginable color.

"Is that it?" Carred asked. She felt so happy; a little girl once more.

"Oh, you poor innocent thing," the woman said. "You don't want to go to that nasty place. It's a good job I found you. Just you follow me, now. I'll take you where you need to go. You'll see."

TWENTY-FOUR

ANSKAR WATCHED FROM THE ENTRANCE of his tent as the party Vilintia had sent to the town returned. Seven Niyandrians and Orix were toting bulging sacks, and bags stuffed with produce hung over their shoulders. Orix was wearing his hood again, and he stumbled as he walked, either from fatigue or from poor coordination due to his misplaced eyes.

Movement drew Anskar's gaze, and he saw Vilintia emerge from her tent. She barked out commands, and a score of men and women went to take charge of the new supplies.

As Orix made his way to the tent he shared with Noni, Anskar waved, but Orix dipped his head as if he'd not seen.

Anskar had just opened his mouth to call out a greeting when a voice from behind startled him.

"He doesn't see well, with his eyes the way they are, but don't worry, I'll soon have him right again."

Noni.

Had she been waiting for him, watching his tent from the forest?

"I intend to rewrite his face," Noni said. "But I'm not sure whether to restore it to what it was before or to improve it."

"Does it matter?" Anskar said. His heart was racing after she'd made him jump, and the words came out harsher than he intended. "I thought you loved him despite his face."

"He asked me to help him. Begged me. But if he should change his mind and want to stay as Tain made him, I'll still be here for him. How about you? Will you stand by him? I know Carred won't."

"I doubt it was Orix's face Carred was interested in," Anskar said. "But you'd know more about that than me."

Noni flinched at his words, and for a moment she became faltering and uncertain. "Carred hurt him. I won't do that to him, and I won't let you hurt him either."

"Me? Why would I hurt Orix? We're friends, Noni."

"I don't think he believes that anymore."

"Because of something you told him?"

"Because of what your mother did to me."

Anskar grimaced as he nodded. "And I'm sorry about that. Truly I am. But I'm not responsible for what Queen Talia does. I'm as much her victim as you were."

"I am no one's victim, *Melesh-Eloni*. You will see."

"What does that mean?" It sounded like a threat.

But Noni brushed past him and skipped toward her tent like an overexcited child. Orix turned in the entrance, and the two embraced before going inside. Anskar couldn't tell if his friend had seen him, but if he had, he gave no indication.

His hands tightened into fists at his sides, and acid burned in his veins. The strength of his reaction shocked him, and he uttered a prayer to Menselas to calm him; but it was a hurried prayer, almost disdainful.

And he resolved that he would be the one to fix Orix's face, rather than Noni.

"Come," Vilintia said, striding toward him, bow in hand, another strung over her shoulder. "You look like a man who needs to learn a thing or two about hunting. It's about time you started to contribute. Assuming, of course, you're going to stay with us a little longer."

Baylon glanced their way as he supervised the unpacking of the supplies.

"I'm still not sure I have a choice."

Vilintia smiled—it made her look younger. "Come on now, Anskar, do you really think we could stop the *Melesh-Eloni* from leaving, even if we wanted to?"

"I have no catalyst…"

"Neither did your mother, and look what she achieved."

Over the next few days, Vilintia taught him how to hunt with a bow, and they talked about the way things used to be on Niyas before the coming of the mainlanders. But whenever the subject of Carred Selenas came up, Vilintia grew sullen.

"You liked her a lot, didn't you?" Anskar said. "Before… Taloc."

"She should have told me," Vilintia said. "She should have come back here and told me about Taloc. I'd still have been angry. Likely I'd have punched her. But I would have respected her. Instead, what did she do? She went on with her mission, doing your mother's bidding, as if Taloc were just some henchman to be discarded like trash."

"I'm sure that wasn't the case," Anskar said.

"Oh, then how do you explain it, wise one? Were you there?"

During the times Anskar was alone, Baylon was an ever-present shadow except when he was relieved of his duties by an old warrior named Finati, a gray-haired woman who was always immaculately dressed in mail and a patched but well-cared-for blue cloak, which she claimed she had worn at Naphor. The pretense that they were not following Anskar and ensuring he didn't leave the camp had been dropped, but neither Baylon nor Finati was good company. Baylon did little but complain—about the mainland scum, as he called them, and the practice of slavery (although Finati told Anskar that Baylon had once collaborated with the slavers back when he'd been a merchant. Made a tidy profit off the trade, too). Most of all, Baylon complained about Carred Selenas, saying how, if he'd been in charge, he would have done this and not that. He described Carred as an indecisive leader, and he disparaged her as "a field frequently furrowed." For some reason, that made Anskar angry, and after that he resolved to speak as little as possible with the man.

Finati, on the other hand, was all seriousness and tradition, and though Anskar might have learned a good deal about the Niyandrian culture he'd been deprived of, Finati looked down on him as if he were tainted by his mixed blood, and her condescension started to grate.

The rest of the Niyandrians were constantly busy, it seemed, taking their clothes and bedrolls down to the brook to wash them, then drying them on the low branches of trees; sharpening weapons with whetstones; setting fires upon which to cook the increasingly scant fare brought back by the hunters. And when they weren't working, they were lounging in the entrances of their tents, scowling at the ever-gathering clouds threatening yet more rain. Either that or they were arguing. Fights began to break out among them, and one woman, when she wouldn't stop beating her former lover bloody with her fists, was publicly flogged.

"It's the only way some of them learn," Vilintia told Anskar as they walked the perimeter together, but he saw no evidence of the discipline working: the rebels remained as volatile as ever.

To his mind, they were bored and restless and in need of something to do. Vilintia saw that too, and she admitted it was part of the reason she wanted to move out as soon as they had word back from the scouts she had sent out looking for a new hideout.

"There are other, smaller bands of rebels throughout Niyas," she said. "Maybe we'll join up with one of them. Carred established a network of riders for communication. We used to use trained birds too, but their keeper, Maggow, is no longer with us. Carred told me you had something to do with that."

"I did? I don't know who Maggow is."

"Maggow was a sorcerer, killed at sea not far from Atya."

"Oh…" Anskar said. "I remember."

He went quiet as he recollected decks flooded with gore, the clash of steel amid the crash of waves, and how he had infiltrated the old Niyandrian's sorcerous defenses on the strength of an intuition. It was an effort forcing himself back to the present, but when he did, he asked, "Would it not be better to gather all the rebels together in one place? Strike an occupied town hard, win a decisive victory?"

"That's what I wanted to do, along with several others, but Carred's instructions were clear: harry the enemy, but don't fully engage." Her tone took on a mocking edge: "Not till the time is upon us."

"But those instructions… Carred was doing as she'd been told by my mother?"

"She never said, though she did nothing to disabuse us of the notion. Carred used to put it like this whenever the dissenting voices grew too loud: We lost the war, even with Queen Talia at our head. What chance do you think we would have now, a ragtag band of defeated Niyandrians?"

"But if you all came together… There must be thousands of you scattered about the island. Out of the mainland allies who fought at Naphor, only the Order of Eternal Vigilance remains. The rest of the mainland population is settlers and merchants."

"And priests," Vilintia pointed out.

"You fear their sorcery? Trust me, I wouldn't."

She shook her head. "I fear their lies and their intention to eradicate the ways of our people. They undermine our efforts to unite. They sow seeds of doubt, divide us from our gods, and ultimately from each other. But as to a major attack, a pitched battle: if we were to lose, it would spell the end for Niyas."

"So, you agree with Carred?"

"She has an impossible task," Vilintia conceded. "All we ever do is wait. But wait for what?"

"For the *Melesh-Eloni*, I assume," Anskar said. "For me."

"And then?"

"I have no idea. You must be disappointed."

It made no sense, though. Even with his discarded dawn- and dusk-tide abilities, he would have been no substitute for his mother, and Queen Talia had failed despite having the full might of the Niyandrian army at her command. Yes, against the Order of Eternal Vigilance, the rebels might enjoy some initial successes, but then what? What would happen once news of the uprising reached the mainland? Would the allies reassemble? Probably, he thought; but then again, with what he'd seen of the tensions mounting between the City States and Kaile, not to mention the resentment and ambitions of the Kingdom of the Thousand Lakes, maybe there would be a different result this time.

"Carred always thought that when we found Queen Talia's child and heir, her work would be done," Vilintia said. "I think all she wanted to do was retire and go live with Marith."

"Who is Marith?"

Vilintia's eyes were moist, as if she too wanted it all to end so that she could make a quiet life for herself. She was probably wishing it could have been with Taloc.

"Carred has lovers all over the place. It's a running joke among us. But the one she really wants to be with is Marith."

"A woman."

"As was your mother, another of Carred's lovers. Actually, she might have been the first."

Anskar swallowed and tried not to think about that. "What I don't understand," he said, "is what we're supposed to do now. I'm here. You have me. What did Carred think would happen next? That the earth would open and disgorge an army of the dead? That the veil between worlds would be torn apart, and my mother would drift down on a cloud? What am I supposed to do? What are any of us supposed to do?" He knew he was being disingenuous. He knew the answer to his question involved the Armor of Divinity in some way, but he wasn't sure how much Vilintia knew, nor how much she was supposed to know.

Vilintia studied him for a long while, but he could read nothing from her expression. "You notice you said 'we.'"

"Your point?"

"'What I don't understand,' you said, 'is what we're supposed to do now.' Does that mean you're done with the

Order? Really done."

Anskar shook his head as he tried to make sense of his feelings.

"Don't answer that," Vilintia said. "You're still so conflicted, an outsider among us. And you've not yet started your lessons with Eadgith. So we have to wait a little longer for you to grow into yourself. Your true self, that is, not the lackey indoctrinated by the knights."

"And if I don't? What if this is my true self?"

Vilintia shrugged. "Carred will know what to do. And if she doesn't return… Well, maybe then we'll call it a day and all go home."

"I don't think that's very likely," Anskar said. "Queen Talia would never permit it."

Vilintia looked round at the sound of leaves scrunched underfoot.

"Baylon," she said, "I told you I'd be with Anskar this morning. I thought you'd appreciate the time off."

"It's you I came to see," Baylon said. "Someone's arrived."

"Someone?"

As Baylon looked behind, a ferret-faced man in an ostentatious cloak of blue velvet trimmed with ermine stepped from the trees with four armed and armored Niyandrians in tow.

"Fult Wreave," Vilintia said with a weary sigh. "And there was me hoping you'd gone for good."

"A little more respect, Commander Yoenth," Fult Wreave said. He ended with a sniff and a wipe of his massive nose.

"Respect for my betters?" Vilintia said. Then to Baylon, "It's all right, you can go now. Get some rest. His Majesty won't be any bother. Will you, sire?"

"You may mock," Fult Wreave said, "but the day is coming— perhaps it is already here—when the—"

"Blah, blah," Vilintia said. "When the last miserable toe-rag of the tragically deposed Ickthal Dynasty resumes the throne of Niyas."

"Illegally deposed, not just tragically!" Fult Wreave said, looking round at his men for support. None of them reacted in the slightest. "That demonic hag you fanatics still serve slaughtered my uncle the king, then hunted down every last one of my relatives. And there will be a reckoning!"

"So you keep telling us. I still don't understand how Queen Talia rooted out your entire clan, yet you somehow managed to elude her. Of course, you've yet to provide proof that you are indeed the last remaining Ickthal, and even if you are, who's going to follow you? The last thing Niyas needs is a return to your family's politics of appeasement. The mainlanders despise us and all we stand for, and that didn't change when we gave them our territories overseas."

"Niyas has land oversea?" Anskar asked.

"Not anymore," Vilintia said. "Fult's uncle made sure of that, enriching himself at our loss and the mainland's gain."

"Propaganda," Wreave said. "More of the Necromancer Queen's lies!"

"You hear that, Anskar, the way he speaks about your mother?"

Wreave's mouth dropped open, and he wiped his perpetually dripping nose with the back of his hand. "This is…?"

"The *Melesh-Eloni*," Vilintia said. "Queen Talia's son."

"But I thought…"

"So did we all, but I have it on good authority that Anskar is a boy, not a girl. Perhaps you'd like to see for yourself."

"Don't be so impudent!"

"Unintentional," Vilintia said. "I assumed the rumors were true."

"What rumors?"

One of the armored men with Wreave covered his mouth with his hand, stifling a laugh. His comrade nudged him to be quiet.

"Let's get down to business, Fult," Vilintia said. "Why are you here? I thought we'd seen the last of you before Carred left."

"As did I," he said. "Then I heard a rumor of my own: that our beloved leader had failed to come back."

"As of yet," Vilintia said. "But she'll be back, you can be sure of it."

Anskar looked at her askew. He thought she might have winked.

"So, where is she?" Wreave said. "Cementing her hold over the resistance now she has her precious heir? Assuming, of course, this—what is he, a half-breed?—Anskar really is the bitch-queen's son."

"I don't like your tone," Anskar said, taking a step toward him.

Wreave stumbled back a pace, and all four of his armed men move forward, hands on the hilts of their swords.

Darkness seethed through Anskar's veins and formed in tongues of shadows at the tips of his fingers. Interesting. But still no conscious control.

"You don't get to decide if this young man is the heir, and neither does Carred Selenas," Wreave said. "That requires the discernment of a full council, and you don't have the authority to call one. Who's going to respond to *you*, Vilintia, a mere soldier?"

"Carred—"

"Yes, yes, she has the Queen's authority, though why anyone believes that when there's no official record of the delegation, I'll never know. Face it, Vilintia: Carred's control of the rebellion was already tenuous, to put it mildly. Daily, people come over to my side. And now, with her gone, what do you think will happen? You seriously think the displaced nobility of Niyas is going to turn to you for leadership?"

"Well, when given the choice of me over you…" Vilintia said. "But it's not my intention to lead. Unlike you, Fult, I know what I am and what my limitations are."

"Unlike me! I know what I am."

"A chinless cretin with a bad cold?" Anskar said. "And repositories as tiny and as flaccid as your prick no doubt is."

"Anskar!" Vilintia said with feigned shock.

And now the armed men with Wreave laughed openly.

Wreave turned and slapped one round the face. The laughter stopped, but Anskar didn't miss the look of anger in the man's eyes.

"There must be a council," Wreave said. "A half-blood, the heir to the throne of Niyas! We'll see about that!"

Then, with a final sniff, he turned and strode away.

"Staying?" Vilintia asked the armored men.

They exchanged looks, and Anskar felt certain they were tempted.

"Sorry," one of them said as they made to follow Wreave. "You know how it is."

TWENTY-FIVE

"A POX UPON THE DAWN and the dusk," Eadgith spat. "And the dark is no more than a stinking slurry from the Urygion's warted anus. You'll get by without a catalyst, mark my words."

It was twilight, and they had come a short distance from the camp so that they wouldn't be disturbed. Baylon had tried to follow, but Eadgith drove him off with a threat to putrefy his manhood.

The dusk-tide whispered all around Anskar, rather than gusting through him. It felt faint, weaker than before, as if he had grown insensitive to it. He wondered how long it would be before he didn't feel it at all.

"Urygion?" Anskar asked. "Don't tell me: another Niyandrian god?"

"The father of all demons."

"The demons have a father?"

"Everything that exists must have a creator. The demons are

the living turds of Urygion, so our old ones say."

"Which old ones?"

Eadgith sighed and rolled her eyes. "Them that wrote our lore books. The first necromancers, of course."

"And they knew this father of the demons?"

"How should I bloody know? All they do is name him, and if it ain't written down in their lore books, there's no way of knowing, is there?"

"But you trust what is written?"

Eadgith slapped him around the head for that.

"I was thinking about the scriptures of Menselas," Anskar protested, "and whether I still accept them as a reliable guide."

Eadgith frowned. "You mean you once did?"

Anskar felt foolish admitting it. "It's how I was raised: to believe without question."

"And now you have questions?"

"And some answers too. But faith… I think my faith may have shifted course…"

"But it's not quite dead?" Eadgith said. "Then let's hope it soon will be. Now, enough with the questions. It's time for you to learn—real knowledge, not fancy words and formulas that make you guilty for touching yourself. You've felt the earth-tide before, you say. You've experienced its power over the dead."

"But that was my mother working through me."

Eadgith slapped him again. "Don't interrupt my train of thought. Shut up and just listen. You say you sometimes hear the dead, that you've even spoken with them?"

Anskar nodded, not daring to speak.

"Noni is the same; only her talents are too raw, her mind too scrambled to train adequately. Truth be told, I'd refuse to teach her at all, if she weren't so darned insistent."

"She wants to…" Anskar stopped himself before she hit him again.

"Go on," Eadgith said.

"She wants to fix Orix's face."

"Don't you think I don't know that? The girl's lovestruck—though Theltek knows why. And that kind of love's another type of madness, if you want my opinion."

"But you'll help her anyway?"

"Aye, daft cow that I am. I'll help her."

Eadgith crouched down and placed her hand on the ground, shut her eyes, and tilted her head as if listening. She sniffed and opened her eyes, then stood and led Anskar deeper into the woods and farther from the camp. She repeated the action beneath the branches of a sycamore, and this time when she stood, she grunted with approval.

"Right," Eadgith said, "now you try it."

"Try what?"

"Don't be an idiot. Like I said, you've felt the earth-tide before—so feel it again. Direct all your senses into the ground and follow them down. Then, when you reach the source of the flow, see where it draws you."

"Where it draws me?"

Eadgith just glowered at him, so Anskar did as she had done and crouched down, touching the ground. He shut his eyes and strained to listen, to smell, to taste and feel.

It came far easier than he had expected: that same putrid essence that bubbled up towards the surface. He felt it as a tingling sensation in his fingertips, then an itch in his veins. He became aware of its steady prickling beneath his booted feet. He tasted it on his tongue—like slimy spinach that had been left too long—and its scent was of rotting meat. And there were sounds too, echoing whispers that came from afar, and deep below the ground he thought he could hear mournful, groaning cries.

"Good," Eadgith rasped in his ear. "So you're not completely useless. Now, see where it wants to go."

Anskar tried to marshal his thoughts, bind them together into one, a simple directive of his will. He frowned in concentration, and his head began to throb with the effort.

"Relax," Eadgith chided. "Let the earth-tide go where it's naturally drawn. The trick is to get out of its way."

Anskar drew in a deep breath and let it out slowly. His knees ached from where he was still crouching.

"Stop thinking about yourself," Eadgith said. "You are nothing. You exist only as a channel through which the flow must pass."

Anskar could feel the polluted rush in his veins, rising from his guts and turning to bile. But it seeped from his pores too, escaping into the forest around him. So he breathed deeply again and gave himself over to the noxious flow flooding through him. He found himself caught up in its current, drawn violently along the leaf-covered floor, then felt it stop abruptly, as if it had hit a wall.

He opened his eyes and stared at a spot amid the gnarled roots of a large oak. He glanced at Eadgith, who scowled in return.

"Don't look at me," she snarled. "Go there. Bring me what you find."

As Anskar approached the tree's roots, he felt the putrid crawl of the earth-tide in his veins, itching, burning, oozing. He stooped beneath the branches, then dropped to one knee as he saw what it was he had sensed and been drawn to: the tiny skeleton of a bird, half buried beneath brown and yellow leaves. Gently, he picked it up. It tingled to the touch. The bird, he reasoned, must have fallen from its nest. Either that or it had been ousted.

As he stood, Eadgith peered over his shoulder, causing him to jump.

"You feel the earth-tide within the bones?" she asked, holding out her hand.

Anskar passed the dead bird to her. "I think so."

He found himself wondering if the creature had been reduced to a skeleton through the slow process of rot and decay, or whether it had been picked clean by scavengers.

"The earth-tide leaves a residue in bone. It solidifies there. Calcifies, you might say. That's what drew your senses. Bone and flesh and blood are insulated from the earth-tide in life—except in those who deliberately seek it out—but in death they're like lodestones that absorb the transformed essence rising from the world's core. Blood congeals, then dries and slowly disintegrates. Flesh putrefies until it is no more. But bone endures. This is what makes bone so useful in the art of necromancy."

"And blood isn't useful? Nor flesh?"

Eadgith chuckled. "Oh, they're useful, right enough, but they have a different application. There's an order to these things, a hierarchy, if you like." Eadgith pocketed the bird's skeleton. "Later I'll show you how to powder the bones, and you'll learn how bone's density makes it the perfect agent for slowing the release of the earth-tide contained in blood, which is the most potent and explosive agent of all."

"Blood is better than bone for necromancy?"

"Not necessarily. Bone holds the earth-tide and, when used, only releases it slowly. That makes it ideal for the crafting of simple items of power, or even weapons."

"My mother—working through me—used shards of bone as weapons. I flung them, and they ripped a woman apart. She was a Tainted Cabalist," he added, as if that made it somehow more acceptable.

Eadgith's eyes widened, and then she scrunched her face up. "That would require a massive infusion of earth-tide, far beyond anything I've ever managed. I've tried a similar sorcery myself, but each time the bones have crumbled to dust. Queen Talia was a far greater necromancer than I could ever hope to be."

"And blood?" Anskar asked. "You said blood can also be used."

"The fresher the better. The blood of one still warm is the most potent, but its effects are almost impossible to contain. The earth-tide that resides in blood is greater than that in bone, but it's all used up in one massive burst of sorcery."

"And without bone, blood, or flesh, there can be no necromancy? But how was I able to hear the dead and speak with them?"

"You don't need to be a necromancer to see and hear the dead. Noni has an uncanny ability, yet she hadn't even started her training with me when it began to manifest. Her parents were simple folk, neither of them necromancers."

"Perhaps further back in her ancestry?" Anskar suggested.

Eadgith wrinkled her nose at the idea, and Anskar thought of Braga, who had also seen spirits, and to whom Queen Talia's shade had come, demanding that she follow Anskar to Wintotashum.

"But that doesn't account for the time my mother wielded earth-tide sorcery without any of the three: flesh, blood, or bone."

"You have blood, don't you? Flesh and bone?"

"But I thought you said they had to be dead in order to attract the flow. Life, you said, insulates us from the earth-tide."

"You're the get of a necromancer, Anskar. Perhaps the greatest to have ever lived. Queen Talia had one foot in the realm of the dead long before her death at Naphor. The atmosphere of the grave polluted her entire being, so it seems reasonable to assume some of it passed from her to you. You felt weak after? Sick?"

"Yes, terribly," Anskar said.

"It may be that she made use of your substance without you even knowing."

"You mean she used up my flesh and blood and bone?"

"Just blood, most likely. It would've burned off without you realizing, save through weakness. See, you can't work the earth-tide without an exchange of essence. Death resides within you, Anskar, though it's swamped by the currents of life. With your mother, it was the other way around. According to the old ones' lore books, the more you draw upon your own substance to fuel necromancy, the more death will be pulled into you from the earth's core."

"Until I die?"

She shook her head. "Until you change. Until you're both present in the world and not."

"Like the wraithes?"

"They weren't always the way they are now," Eadgith said. "Your mother drew closer to them, so close she might one day have become as them. She grew frail, emaciated, and was wasting away. It was long thought that she had the rot and would soon die, but then one day her decline stopped, and she grew once more wholesome."

"What happened?"

"No one knew it at the time, but I'd have to say her condition improved when she got herself pregnant."

"But how would that have helped?" A baby drew nourishment from its mother while in the womb, so if anything, Talia's condition should have worsened.

"Keep on asking yourself that."

Unless… "She was siphoning off my substance even while I was in the womb?"

"I don't know enough about it. All we can do is speculate. But yes, she could have drawn the earth-tide from your blood and bone and flesh and used it to reshape a tumor, for instance, until it no longer drained her. And I expect it was a two-way street. The more she took from you, the more she probably gave you in return. That, though, was likely her intention all along: to imbue you with as much of herself as she could—knowledge, power, aptitude. You were to be her heir, after all, and the one to bring her back."

And what would I be if she returned, once the task she'd birthed me for was done? "But where is this knowledge? I mean, I've felt the power at times, but seldom under my conscious control. I have intuitions, but there's no more than that."

Eadgith shrugged. "How should I know? Your mother was an exceptional sorcerer, but she didn't reveal her secrets lightly, and even if she had done, there are few who would have understood them. The more you learn, the more you're put in touch with who and what you are, the more likely it is that you'll reject your mother's enemies."

"The Order of Eternal Vigilance?"

Eadgith spat. "Them and the five-faced god they worship. Not to mention the real power beneath it all on the mainland. No one talks about that."

"The wealthy nobles? The Church of Menselas?"

"Beneath even that. Layers upon layers of deception and control. Your mother taught me that, and even she couldn't fathom the full extent of the corruption. You should ask her about it sometime."

"It's too late for that," Anskar said. "The healers drove her out of me, remember?"

"For now."

"I still don't understand what you expect from me," Anskar said. "What you want."

"What I want," Eadgith said, "what we all want, is our land back. Our culture. Our pride."

"Not Queen Talia?"

"Oh, we want Queen Talia," Eadgith said. "Because without her, there's no way to win. The mainlanders are too many, too rich, and too strong."

"But she failed before," Anskar said.

"Did she? What if death was always part of her plan? And what if you were, too? Never assume you know all there is to know, Anskar."

Before he could ask any more questions, Eadgith held up a hand. "Now, tell me what you think you know about the earth-tide."

"You said it comes from the core of Wiraya," Anskar said.

"I didn't ask you to tell me what I said. What do *you* think you know?"

"Unless I've misunderstood," Anskar said, "the earth-tide has its origins in the other tides—the dawn and the dusk, at any rate." He'd gathered as much from a dream in which he had seen the tides of dusk and dawn seeping into the ground, filtered through the bedrock, but not cleansed by it; polluted in some way. He told Eadgith of his idea and added to it Zek's speculation that all the tides might come from the same source. "Why not the earth-flow as well?" he concluded.

Eadgith scoffed. "That's your theory? Theltek's teeth, you really do sound like a priest of the Elder!"

"Do you have a better one?"

She didn't answer, and instead started off through the trees, back toward the camp.

After a moment's hesitation, Anskar followed.

TWENTY-SIX

AS EADGITH BUSTLED OFF AHEAD of him through the forest, Anskar felt he had angered her, though he was hard-pressed to understand how. By the time he reached the fringes of the rebel camp, he had lost sight of the old woman and decided at last to jog to catch up with her.

"He's waiting for you," a mocking voice cried out.

Anskar stopped in his tracks and spun around.

"Colvin's waiting," Noni said, gliding out from behind a tree. She was shivering, but even so, she wore a fierce grin, and her eyes sparkled with mischief. "His father's agents will find and kill you, and when your soul arrives in the realm of the dead, Colvin will be there to greet you."

A fist of ice enclosed Anskar's heart, and rage grew inside him, threatening to overwhelm his senses. Before he knew what he was doing, he raced at Noni and grabbed her by the front of her tatty dress.

"Shut up!" he warned, spittle flying from his mouth. "Shut your stupid mouth!"

Noni giggled then, and Anskar let go of her dress and staggered back a pace. He'd come this close to hitting her. It was the fear, he told himself, but even so…

Noni stopped her giggling and just stared at him, her eyes no longer sparkling, but dark and empty. "You leave my Orix alone, you hear me? If you come for him, I'll… I'll…" She seemed to refocus her eyes, then frowned at Anskar. "I'm sorry," she said in a little girl's voice. "What happened? What did I say?" Her mouth dropped open in shock—the feigned shock of a bad actor, to Anskar's mind. "I didn't want to scare you. It was Colvin. He made me do it."

Anskar narrowed his eyes. "Let me guess: he controls you, like my mother did, from the realm of the dead? Are you really so weak?"

Noni's eyes widened. She'd not expected that—and to be honest, neither had Anskar. He knew he was being unreasonable—cruel, even—but he couldn't stop himself. What if he was wrong? What if she wasn't acting?

"He made me," she repeated, and then began to sob.

Anskar rubbed the back of his neck, and that seemed to release some of the tension. Violence ebbed away from him, and he struggled for the right thing to say—the sort of consolations a devotee of Menselas was supposed to utter. "It's all right," he said lamely, taking a step towards her, but she flinched, so he stayed still. "I won't let Colvin's spirit harm you, I promise. This is between me and him." And Orix. "Tell him if he uses you like this again, I'll summon him from the realm of the dead and—"

"He doesn't want to harm me," Noni said, her sobbing stopping abruptly. "He promises he'll leave me be once he has his revenge. But don't let him harm Orix, please. I know what you are. You have the power to stop him."

"His father's agents, you said. Archduke Peleus has sent someone from the mainland? Do they know where I am?"

Noni just stared at him blankly.

"Ask him," Anskar said. "Ask Colvin. Possession is a two-way street. You've had my mother's spirit inside you. Did you learn nothing from her? *Make* him tell you."

"I can't," Noni said. "Not yet. Eadgith says I have the touch but not the strength. But she's teaching me, and I will learn. Maybe even faster than you."

"You still think you can fix Orix's face? Eadgith has no knowledge of shaping matter with the earth-tide, so how will you learn that?"

"How will you?" she countered.

"I have the aptitude," he said, "to work things out for myself."

"Do you? Or is it simply the gift your mother left you?"

"She told you that… when she possessed you?"

Noni shook her head. "But as you guessed, her presence within me left impressions. I, too, can intuit how to use the earth-tide, but first…"

"But first you need to learn how to access it." So in that, they were at the same stage and both dependent upon Eadgith to teach them.

"We don't have to be rivals in this," Anskar said. "Orix is my friend too. We could help him together."

She averted her eyes, hands gripping her tatty dress.

"Is it only voices you hear," Anskar asked, "or can you see into the realm of the dead?"

She nodded and swallowed a lump in her throat.

"Who can you see right now? Anyone I'd recognize?"

"Right now, no one. I have to choose to look where the shades abide, and I choose not to."

"Choose now," Anskar said.

"And lose more of myself? There's so little left."

"There was a boy I used to know," Anskar said. "Naul was his name." Naul who had died when the Niyandrian kidnappers came for Sareya.

Noni gave a little shudder and closed her eyes. Within moments, she nodded. "I see him."

"Who else?" Anskar asked.

"A big man. Curly beard. Black-singed eyebrows. Ginger hair—not on top, but just at the back of his head, where it hangs in ringlets. He's squinting at me. Now he's smiling. He only has two teeth. Both yellow."

"Hrothyr," Anskar said. "The blacksmith from King Aelfyr's forges in Wintotashum." His heart began to race with hope then. "And his wife? Is she there? Ask him about his wife, Braga."

"Nothing," Noni said bleakly, and Anskar's hope evaporated. Braga had been ripped from the shadow-step as he'd tried to save her from the demon that had entered the forge, her essence scattered and lost. "There's no Braga here. A tall man, though. A giant." Suddenly Noni's voice changed, growing deeper than should have been possible. "Make not an enemy of Rindon or Nul," she said. "Consider what you are about, Anskar DeVantte."

"Borik?" Anskar said, but before Noni could reply, he heard the crack of twigs underfoot and the rustle of leaves.

"Are you coming?" Eadgith snapped as she approached. "You too, girl. Might as well kill two birds with one stone." Then she chuckled at what she must have thought was a good joke and took the skeletal bird from her pocket, holding it up. "Two birds!" She sighed and shook her head. "Well, I thought it was funny. Does everyone have to be so bloody serious these days?"

Eadgith turned and headed towards the camp.

Anskar hesitated, watching Noni, expecting to hear more from Borik, but she shook her head as if to clear it and said, "Come on."

And together they followed Eadgith.

"It ain't just about talking with the dead or raising them," Eadgith said. "Nor is it just about shaping matter—something I know bugger-all about. The earth-tide has other applications. For example, you'll learn soon enough that there's no need for your god's power for healing, not if you learn the ways of blood and bone."

They had returned to the tent Eadgith had moved to. The other two women seemed to have moved out, or more likely had been told by Eadgith to leave. In place of their bedrolls were a dead badger, the skin flensed from its face, which was nothing more than bleached bone now, two freshly killed squirrels, and a small wooden chest.

Anskar was instructed to watch as the old woman hammered the bird skeleton into pieces then ground them into a fine powder using a mortar and pestle.

Noni was even now placing a pinch of the bone powder into the half dozen glass vials Eadgith had removed from the chest, sealing each afterward with wax from a candle as thick as Anskar's forearm and almost as long.

Eadgith nodded approvingly as Noni sealed the last of the vials and then carefully placed them all back in the chest. "Well done, girl. See? You are good for something after all."

Noni managed a feeble smile.

"There's not much you can't achieve with the bones of animals, though those of people make for stronger sorcery, and dead necromancers the strongest of all. I don't know why, but your mother had a theory it was because we necromancers invite the earth-tide so much, it makes a home in us. And we already know how the tide calcifies in bone, so it makes a certain kind of sense."

"But there's still a need for the other tides, isn't there?" Anskar asked. When Eadgith sneered, he pressed on. "Our healers—the priests of the Healer aspect of Menselas—have the ability to knit bone, close wounds, or transfer disease from the victim to themselves. I've seen this. I've done it myself."

"Through the god's mark that afflicts you," Eadgith said. "Not through the tides."

"God's mark? But isn't that just another name for the mark of sorcery some of us are born with?"

"Who told you that? I thought the priests of Menselas made the distinction between the two kinds of marks, or have I heard wrong?"

It was Zek who had speculated about the god's mark being the mark of sorcery seen from a different perspective, and Luzius Landav, the sorcerer who had fitted Anskar's catalyst, had said something similar. But what if they had been wrong, or trying to deceive him for some reason?

All his life, the priests who had taught him, Tion among them, had insisted there were two kinds of marks, and that some—and only a very few in comparison with the general population—bore one or the other of them. In extremely rare cases, individuals had both, along with the capacity—or the calling—to be sorcerers and priests, though the former was always frowned upon, officially, at least. He had assumed that was the truth of things until Landav had planted that first seed of doubt.

He looked at Eadgith. "I have a god's mark that is distinct from my sorcerous one? You can see it?"

"Like someone shat on your soul."

"That doesn't sound good."

"It's a hook the Five has in you. It's Menselas's way of making his puppets dance."

"So, you believe in Menselas?" Anskar glanced from Eadgith to Noni, who was watching him with wide, empty eyes.

"No use denying what's real," Eadgith said. "I believe in all the gods, old and new."

"And which is Menselas?"

"A bit of both. They say he didn't always have five aspects, you know. He started out as one, then gathered others to him."

"How? Why?"

Eadgith shrugged. "How does anyone become a god? You might want to start with that question."

"You're saying Menselas wasn't always a god?"

"Course he wasn't. None of them were, save maybe one, and no one remembers who that was, or is, or will be. But those we worship the length and breadth of Wiraya were people once, no different to you and me, save for ambition. They're the ones who clawed their way to the top of the hill, more often than not climbing on the still-twitching bodies of their rivals."

Anskar frowned in confusion. He looked again at Noni, expecting her to share his bewilderment, but her eyelids had drooped shut, and she was mouthing silent words to herself.

"But I don't even feel my god's mark. I have no way of knowing it's there."

"Yet you must have used it for healing," Eadgith pointed out.

"It felt like the tides. I was convinced it was the tides." Maybe it was, he told himself. Why should he trust anything Eadgith told him, any more than he trusted Landav or even Zek?

"Then the power will have been stripped from you when the catalyst was removed. And, to my mind, the god's mark is not unrelated to the tides. These mortals who became divine did so on the strength of the tides and the sorcery flowing through them. Any mark they give to others must itself be manufactured from the sorcery of the tides. But as to your power to heal, your repositories"—she half spat the word—"are but empty skins now. So heal this."

Eadgith lashed out and grabbed Noni by the wrist. The girl's eyes snapped open and she whimpered, and then she yelped as Eadgith raked the skin of her arm with curled and filthy fingernails, drawing blood.

"Go on," Eadgith challenged Anskar. "Heal it, if you're so clever."

Anskar flinched at first, but then steeled himself to try. Instinctively, he reached for his dawn-tide repository despite knowing that it had withered away to almost nothing. He reached out and clamped his hand over Noni's wound, then tried to retrace the steps of the vicarious healing Gisela of Gessa had shown him.

Warmth flared within his veins, and almost at once he felt the stinging pain of scratches on his arm. Noni gasped, and Eadgith smacked her lips in satisfaction.

There was no longer any blood on Noni's arm, no trace of scratches. It was now Anskar who bled.

He laughed aloud in astonishment. "I never expected…" he started, but then Noni gasped again and cried out.

The bleeding scratches had vanished from Anskar's arm, his skin unscathed; but Noni was now staring at her own arm, which was not only scratched and bleeding but rank with infection, and an angry redness was visibly spreading beneath her skin.

"So much for your useless bastard gods!" Eadgith cursed as she bustled to the side of the tent and grabbed the badger with the flensed skull. With the badger grasped in one hand, she covered Noni's spreading wound with the other. There was a sudden stench of rot. Eadgith shuddered, Noni's skin writhed, and when the old woman released her, the festering wound had gone.

But so had the remnants of the badger's hair, skin, and flesh. All Eadgith grasped now was a skeleton, and then even the ligaments disintegrated, and bones clattered to the ground until she was holding nothing but the skull.

"I was saving that for something special," Eadgith grumbled. "Now it's wasted."

"What…?" Anskar started, intending to ask how Eadgith had effected the cure. Clearly something had passed from the dead badger into Noni… some kind of transfer of substance, but…

Eadgith must have misunderstood where he was going with his question. "What happened? The whim of a capricious god is what happened. Menselas toyed with you, then withdrew his favor." She leaned in close and smirked. "My, what have you done?"

A lot of things, Anskar thought, a knot of dread tightening in his guts. Too many things. He had even begun to wonder if Menselas really existed, but this… There was a sort of proof even in his failure to effect a permanent cure of Noni.

Had he really fallen so far?

And whose side was he now on?

The anger rising atop his shock and disappointment almost answered the question for him.

"I don't understand," Anskar said. "If the healing came through the god's mark, and if Menselas has abandoned me, then why did it work at all?"

Eadgith studied the badger's skull in her hands. "Maybe Menselas was trying to lure you back, but then changed his mind. More likely, he wanted you to know that he is real, a power to be reckoned with, a power that you have run athwart of."

"Menselas is merciful," Anskar said, repeating the very words Brother Tion used to repeat day in, day out.

"Then tell him you're sorry," Eadgith said. "Collect your things and leave us. I'm sure he'll give you the power back if you do."

Anskar stared at her blankly, then shook his head. "But what if you're wrong? What if I'm cast out forever for being Queen Talia's son?"

"You were always that," Eadgith said. "Or did you think Menselas didn't know? He's a god, isn't he? Gods know everything. Or at least they like you to think they do. No, Menselas marked you, same as you were marked for sorcery. He wanted you, Anskar; that much is clear to me. Wanted you badly. But why? Have you ever asked yourself that? Why does a god need people like you? What did he have planned for the heir of the Necromancer Queen?"

"You accuse him of scheming, of using the innocent? It's hardly my fault. I didn't choose to be who I am. You're wrong about this. Menselas is a god of five aspects in balance. He is just, not evil. He would not condemn me for the sins of my mother."

Noni sniffed. Anskar had all but forgotten she was still there. There was a new light in her eyes, as if Eadgith's macabre healing had given her more than she'd had before; as if it had revitalized her, as well as removed the taint of infection.

"I've bought goods from the market that were weighed in a balance," Eadgith said, "and I was short-changed. See, I used to have my own scales, and they always said something different. It's all very well being a god of balance, but that don't mean to say the balance is true."

All Anskar had to go on were the teachings he had received from Brother Tion and the other priests and knight-tutors at Branil's Burg. But how could any of them really know the mind and will of a god? What if they were making things up? Or what if they had been deceived by a being far greater than anything they had ever imagined in their pious books and liturgies? What if they had written and taught about a god they wanted to believe in while deafening themselves to the reality of the being they professed to serve?

But how could he know? How could he know anything? And there was always the possibility that Eadgith was trying to mislead him as much as she claimed the Order had done.

Either Menselas was what the priests said he was, or he was something altogether different. Capricious, like Eadgith said. Malevolent.

Eadgith was watching him intently, a thin smile curling her lips. "Think on it no more. You'll find your roots first, then you'll find your way."

"My Niyandrian roots?" Anskar almost snarled.

"You are, whatever else you are, Queen Talia's son and heir, and Vilintia Yoenth, acting in the place of Carred Selenas, who has been revealed as the *Melesh-Eloni*'s guardian"—Eadgith sneered at that—"has asked me to help you find yourself."

"With bones and blood?" Anskar asked, eyeing the badger's skull and the squirrel corpses lying on the tent floor.

A hungry look came into Noni's eyes, and she smirked at Anskar.

"With bones and blood," Eadgith confirmed.

TWENTY-SEVEN

NAKED AND PALE-SKINNED, THE PLATINUM-HAIRED woman led Carred across plains of black-and-white sand. Things scuttled out of their way—things with chitinous bodies and dozens of glass-like legs. A two-headed snake undulated through the sand, always some way ahead of them. The sun blazed down, causing the woman's golden eyes to blaze, but Carred felt only a refreshing breeze. And they skipped and they talked—happy talk, funny talk. Only Carred could grasp none of it, nor why she was constantly laughing.

"When will we be there?" she asked.

"Are you excited?"

She certainly felt excited, but a scratching sensation at the edge of her awareness said she should be scared, or at least a little worried.

"What's he like, this Lord Domatai?" she asked.

"Very wise," the woman answered. "Very mighty. Everyone

loves him."

"Everyone?" Pity it wasn't that way back home, with her and the rebellion.

"Oh, yes, everyone."

"You think he'll like me?" Carred asked. She clutched her hands to her chest, as if she were holding Nally.

"I know he will. Hush now, we're almost there."

The desert dropped away into a gulley with walls of pockmarked stone. She could smell cooked chicken. At least she thought it was chicken. As the gulley widened into a natural amphitheater, she could see two men crouched beside a firepit, above which half a dozen of the two-headed snakes were roasting on a spit.

The men looked up as the woman and Carred approached. They too were naked, and Carred couldn't stop herself from bursting out laughing. Not that it seemed to bother them any. They both just stared at her with the same golden eyes as the woman. One of them was grotesquely fat, with a distended belly and breasts bigger than hers. The other was tall and seemed much older, his pallid skin cracked and wrinkled.

"What you got for us, Jacari?" the fat man said, slobber dripping from is jaws. "Looks a pretty little thing."

Carred could understand him, as if he spoke in Niyandrian, yet the sounds that reached her ears were alien to her—probably Nazgrese.

"Older than I'd have liked," the woman—Jacari—said. "But there's fire in her."

"Enough for all three of us?" the older man asked. He ran his golden eyes over Carred, provoking another fit of giggling. He curled his lip, as if the laughter annoyed him.

"More than enough. And after we've partaken of the fire, we get to eat."

"I don't know," the fat man said. "Mature meat is so stringy." He glanced at the older man. "No offense, Clax."

"None taken, Rogo."

"Such lovely names!" Carred clapped her hands. "Oops, I dropped Nally," she said, but when she looked at her feet, the ragdoll wasn't there.

"Shame for you, they're not our real names," the fat man— Rogo—said.

"Else I'd have power over you?" Carred asked in a quavering voice, as the mist shrouding her mind dissipated and she came back to her senses. "What did you do to me? Some kind of glamor?"

"I prefer 'natural magnetism,'" Jacari said. "Something I have in abundance. Which is why I'm the one to go out hunting while these two sit on their backsides all day."

"We cook," Rogo said.

"I cook," Clax corrected. "You just eat."

"And you want to eat me?" Carred asked, no longer laughing.

"After we drain you of all your fire," Rogo said. "And absorb everything you are: memories, places, names… feelings. Oooh, I just love the succulent ones! Makes up for the stringy meat on old bones."

Carred's hand went to her sword but found only air.

"Looking for this?" Jacari asked, producing the sword from behind her back.

"That's some strong glamor," Carred said. Akin to the glamor that had led her to Talia's bed that first time.

The two men stepped away from the fire. As Carred backed away, Jacari moved to intercept her. Red light effused from between Jacari's breasts and then from the chests of the two men. Clax was erect, whereas moments before there had been nothing between his legs to speak of. If Rogo was aroused too, it was hidden beneath an apron of flab.

The three formed a loose circle around Carred. She thought about running, but her fatigue had returned, along with her thirst and her sweat from the blistering sun.

"Good girl," Jacari said. "There's no use fighting."

Red light bathed Carred's skin now from the fire on their chests. It didn't burn, but she felt… something: a stirring of buried memories, a swell of emotions—fear, abandonment, lust, anger, frustration.

Clax threw his head back and sighed, one hand grasping his swollen cock. Rogo jiggled his belly and made sharp, sucking noises, as if he were slurping soup.

Carred spun round to see Jacari caressing herself and moaning, as the fire in her chest flared and flickered.

She tried to run then, gave it all she had, but her knees buckled and she pitched to the sandy ground. Heartache tore through her chest, causing her to sob. Then joy, ecstasy, the slump after a battle. She saw places in her mind's eye—the woods from her childhood; Marith's farm; Atya, Niyas… And there were names, ripped from her memories and siphoned off: Kovin, Jada, Noni, Orix, Taloc, Tain, Mother, Father… Talia. Theltek. *Melesh-Eloni.* Anskar.

Convulsions wracked her frame. Her guts flipped inside out. Drool leaked from her mouth. She was empty. Scraped clean. Nothing left inside…

Jacari's scream brought it all to an abrupt end.

Carred lifted her head to see a smoldering spear tip sticking out between Jacari's breasts, purple blood blooming over her chest. Behind her: a winged demon, armored in shadow.

Someone grunted, followed by a heavy thud, then a lighter one. Carred was too weak to turn, too weak even to crane her neck. She was saved the trouble, though, when a severed head rolled across the ground and came to rest in front of her, golden eyes staring. Clax.

She heard Rogo gibber and shriek, begging for mercy—cut off by a pulpy splat.

Something passed between Carred and the sun, a moment of blessed shade. She blinked until she could see the silhouette of a large ball floating before her. Blinked again and found herself staring at a huge, lidless eye, white save for the pupil.

"The ice thawed?" Carred said, voice reedy and thin.

The ball-creature said something, but the words made no sense. The armored demon who'd impaled Jacari yanked his spear free of her body, letting her crumple to the ground. Two more demons came into view, stepping out from behind Carred. Both wore armor of shadow. One held a cleaver, the other a poleaxe.

The demon with the cleaver spoke in clumsy Niyandrian: "Anything caught in the stone web belongs to the lord of the mountain."

"Stone web? You mean the standing stones?"

"Only the Lord of Vulthanor may use the portal."

"Then tell him I apologize," Carred said. "I didn't know."

"You will tell him yourself."

"Fine, I will." She bit down on her lip and willed herself to stand. Wavering on her feet, she glanced at the naked dead bleeding out on the ground. They had wanted to drain and eat her!

"Poachers," the demon with the cleaver said. "They knew the rules."

"They spoke in Nazgrese," Carred said, "yet I understood every word."

"They are parasites with power over the minds of their victims."

"I suppose you're going to tell me I was duped," Carred said, "and that this Lord Domatai lives at the multicolored mountain?"

At a gesture from the demon with the cleaver, the ball-creature floated closer to Carred, its white eye turning blue, then green, then red in swift succession. Blue, green, red. Blue, green…

And Carred drifted down into a dark and bottomless pit.

TWENTY-EIGHT

"HUH?" ANSKAR GRUNTED AS HE rolled over, clutching his blanket tight for warmth. "What is it?"

He grew suddenly alert. Someone was in the tent with him. He threw off his blanket and leaped to his feet, and there she was.

Noni was standing in the entrance, holding the flap open with one hand. Dawn's golden light shone through the opening.

"There's something I have to show you," she said. "I've been working all night."

Anskar frowned. He'd not felt the dawn-tide. Sometimes he didn't, when indoors or if he slept too deeply. But out here, in the forest, with only a tent between him and the tide… He should never have had his catalyst removed. The absence of the dawn-tide rushing through him felt like a bereavement. *Well, what's done is done and there's no use crying over it.*

At Noni's gesture, he put on his boots, strapped on *Amalantril,* and followed her outside.

"Where's Orix?"

"Still sleeping. Come on, it's all right."

The camp was still, save for the scattered guards on watch. Noni waved at one of them, and the woman waved back.

Anskar followed her into the woods.

They walked for perhaps half a mile, till Noni brought him to a clearing. Anskar stopped at the edge, initially too shocked to go in. There were bones scattered around the perimeter… the tiny bones of birds and rodents. There were half-rotted squirrel carcasses too, a badger rigid in death, and half a dozen live mice in a rusted iron cage.

"You've been experimenting?" Anskar asked.

"Eadgith gave me the start I needed." Noni squatted down in front of the cage. She opened it and snatched a mouse before shutting the cage door once more. There was a flurry of movement within the cage, which stopped abruptly when the mouse clutched in Noni's fist emitted a squeak.

"You crushed it?" Anskar asked as she stood.

"No." She took hold of the mouse by its tail and watched it squirm as it dangled. "They're more potent alive. Didn't Eadgith teach you that?"

Anskar nodded. "She said something about it." *The blood of one still warm is the most potent…* "She also said that blood— warm blood—is the most volatile conduit for the earth-tide. She made it sound wasteful. Explosive."

Noni frowned down at the skeletal birds and rodents that littered the clearing. "Oh…"

"You've been siphoning off their essence, haven't you?" Anskar asked. "I assume this is all for Orix?"

A smile cracked Noni's face, and her eyes glittered. "I've had some success," she said, producing a vivid green blade of grass from inside her dress.

Anskar took it from her and studied it. "I don't understand. It's just grass."

Noni capered in a circle, cackling like a witch. "Look around you! All the grass is brown."

"It always is at this time of... You turned a brown blade of grass green?"

She nodded excitedly.

"Just the one?"

"I changed it, Anskar. Altered the grass with the earth-tide."

"And a lot of dead animals," Anskar observed. What a waste of life. Whatever breakthrough Noni thought she'd made, the cost was far too high.

Noni held the mouse by its tail in front of her eyes. "You must be right... about the blood burning up too quickly. These birds, these mice... they were living, moving creatures one instant, then husks or skeletons the next."

"You need to mitigate the flow," Anskar said. "Didn't Eadgith teach you that?"

"She said I wanted to run when I could barely walk."

She was right. And all the dead animals were the cost. Anskar nodded. "I know what that's like. You're getting ahead of yourself. You must... you must really care for Orix."

"We're in love."

"Does he know that?"

"We are betrothed."

"So soon?"

Noni twirled as she danced around the clearing. "My spirit recognized him the first time we met," she said. "And once he was free, he recognized me."

"Free from what? From Carred?"

"She possessed him, just as your mother possessed me. And then she sought to drain him with her lust. To Carred, he was no better than these birds and mice."

"Carred's no sorcerer. I saw that much for myself."

"Sorcery isn't just confined to the tides. You know that. There are some who prey on our feelings and needs. Some who arouse in us passions that enslave. You know this. Your mother's spirit within me witnessed the things you did."

Anskar felt heat flood his face. "She saw?"

"All I have are the impressions she left behind. I carry her imprint, Anskar. Does that connect us? I think it does." She came to a stop in front of him, the hand that held the mouse behind her back as she leaned in till he could smell her breath—sickly sweet and metallic, as if she had bleeding gums… or had been drinking blood.

Anskar handed her back the green blade of grass.

She took it with a grin and thrust it into her dress pocket.

"Your mother loves you, Anskar," she said, taking a step toward him for each step he took back. "I feel her love for you. In some ways, I feel you."

"Noni…" Anskar cautioned, circling away from her, back into the center of the clearing.

"Orix won't mind," she said, her head dipped to one side as she appraised him with mad eyes. She brought the mouse to her lips and kissed it.

"Orix already hates me," Anskar said.

"Silly man. Hate is just one extreme of love. Now that, your mother said to me when she was inside. Words like that, you don't forget."

"You wanted to show me what you've been up to," Anskar said coldly. "Well, you've shown me. I'm heading back now."

"Wait. There's more. Look."

She bent down, still holding the mouse, and extended her free hand over a fallen pinecone. Anskar's stomach rebelled as he felt Noni plunge down deep below ground in her spirit. He gagged at the stench of the earth-tide that bubbled up through her, then surged into the mouse. The creature squealed and thrashed for an instant, then its fur melted away before his eyes, followed by skin and muscle. Noni opened her fingers, and tiny bones dropped to the earth. The pinecone was nothing more than a pile of dust.

"That's it?" Anskar said. "How is that going to help Orix? It's no different to the decay involved in necromancy."

"Hand me another mouse," Noni said.

"This is so wasteful. Unnecessarily so," Anskar said, yet he felt compelled to see what she would do next. He grabbed a mouse from the cage and passed it to her.

"Next time," Noni said, "I'll come prepared with powdered bone. I'll slaughter the animals and mix their still-warm blood with the bone. That's what Eadgith meant, isn't it?"

"You should wait; learn more from her. Far better to take your time and—"

"And what? Eadgith knows nothing of the shaping power of the earth-tide. All she knows is how to access the tide and use it for simple necromantic tricks. But with the intuitions I receive from your mother's lingering footprint within me, and with—"

"Me?" Anskar said. "You expect me to help you?"

"I expect you to help Orix. You said you were his friend. Alone, I might learn how to heal his face eventually, but together... we can do it. I know it to be true."

She took the mouse from him and again plunged her spirit below ground. This time, as the mouse withered and turned to bone, the pile of dust shivered as its particles clumped together. Noni moaned and swayed back on her haunches, sweat streaming from her brow. Anskar steadied her with his hands as she completed the sorcery. And then she slumped into his arms, pointing proudly at the fully formed pinecone, looking as though it had just fallen from a branch.

"You used the earth-tide to…" Anskar couldn't find the right word. "The earth-tide breaks down, causes things to decay…"

"And it shapes…" Noni said, sounding close to sleep. "I don't know how, but I changed something within the pinecone. I reversed the decay by shaping… its essence? What is a pinecone made up of, anyway?"

"The priests of the Elder say all matter is made up of ever smaller parts. But I don't understand… You re-ordered the parts? You somehow shaped them to re-form life?"

"Isn't that the basis of necromancy?" Noni said sleepily. "It's the first step in Orix's cure, I'm sure of it."

Was the rotting stench he usually smelled really the earth-tide, or some kind of discharge, a waste product? "Wait," Anskar said, releasing her and clutching the pinecone in his hand. "I have an idea."

Without thinking, he did as she had done and plunged his awareness down through the ground. It came much easier than he'd expected: not an actual journey to the core of Wiraya—there was nothing to see, just queasiness, a sense of dislocation, a pervasive stench, and then a sensation of stagnant water surging through his veins.

The pinecone throbbed in his hand, started to grow, then change. *Fool!* he told himself. He'd not decided on what change he wanted to affect; had merely intuited how to direct the tidal power sluicing through him. The first thing that came to mind was an apple, then he worried that might be too large and require more matter than the cone contained, so he pictured instead an acorn.

It was easy! he thought as the cone grew smoother and firmer. He felt it first, then saw it morphing in the palm of his hand. How had Eadgith not thought of this, not mastered so simple a use of the tide? But then again, was it simple? His intuition had led him here, but he was no nearer to knowing what it had discerned, or why.

Suddenly, he doubled over as his stomach clenched. Acid burned beneath his scalp. His skin prickled and then pulled taut. With a gasp, he felt his cheeks suck in and his muscles contract.

Pain erupted from his cheek and he stumbled back, ears ringing. At the same instant, the earth-tide drained away back into the ground, and in his hand he once again held a pinecone.

Noni, he realized, had slapped him round the face.

"Silly!" she said, handing him a mouse. "Use this."

More than a fool! Anskar chastised himself. *I'm such an idiot.* It could have proven a costly mistake. "Of course," he said. "A conduit for the earth-tide, and matter to provide the energy for the transaction."

"Otherwise the earth-tide uses up your own," Noni said. She nodded enthusiastically, and her eyes were feverous when they met his.

"Energy," Anskar said, another intuition he didn't fully understand. "There's a transfer of energy between the sorcerer and the object he wishes to change. The mouse is a surrogate, a sacrificial victim."

"Imagine something bigger than a mouse," Noni said, the inkling of an idea bright in her eyes. "A badger, perhaps. A person…"

"No," Anskar said. "I'd never do that. This is to help Orix, but I'll not harm another person to achieve that."

"I would," Noni said. "A lot of mice, then? Or several badgers?"

Or perhaps there was a way to store the energy of living creatures? To take a small portion from many, so none needed to be killed. "First things first," Anskar said. "Let's see what this little fellow can do for us."

He squeezed the mouse tight and again plunged his consciousness through the earth. The stench came even faster this time, as if it knew him now and knew where he wanted it to flow before he willed it. Rank effluence sluiced through his veins. The mouse squealed and started to twitch. Its fur grew warm, then melted away. Skin sloughed through his fingers. The mouse grew hard and leathery, then contracted as it atrophied. Now it was a desiccated husk. Now just bones. Bones so hot they scalded, and Anskar dropped them on the ground.

In his other hand, an acorn now sat in place of the pinecone.

Noni hopped from foot to foot, clapping. "Better than I did!" she said. "Already we have both outstripped Eadgith. She's nothing but a dull old witch!"

"Without her, you'd never have accessed the tide," Anskar said. "And neither would I, now my mother's spirit has gone."

Noni looked at him askew. She curled her lip, baring yellow teeth. "Your mother... what she did to me..."

"Was unconscionable," Anskar said. "Yet you seem to blame me for it."

"It was in your name," Noni said. "Everything she did to me was in your name. She used me to speak with Carred. All she wanted was for Carred to find you and prepare the way for her return, and for the rebirth of Niyas. She cared not at all for me, for what she did to me. Niyas is bigger than one stupid girl, she used to say, and she might be right. But it still hurts. It was still a violation."

"And in her absence, you need someone else to blame?"

"Maybe," Noni said. She took the acorn from his hand, bit into it, then spat out what she'd tasted. "It's a real acorn. Much better than my green blade of grass. Orix will be pleased."

"I thought you wanted to be the one to heal him," Anskar said.

"And now, with what I learned from watching you, I'm one step closer! Promise you won't heal him if you gain the power before me."

She stepped in close—too close—and rubbed her body against him. She pressed her face up close to his, tangling her fingers in his hair.

Anskar turned his face aside and held her at arm's length. "I promise."

"Noni!" a voice called from the direction of the camp.

"Orix!" she said, throwing herself into Anskar's arms and straining to kiss him. He shoved her off, but too late.

Orix had seen.

He stood glaring from the edge of the clearing, in one hand a garland of brightly colored flowers.

"My love," Noni said, running towards him. "Did you weave that for me?"

"Orix!" exclaimed Anskar. "This isn't—"

Orix let go of the garland and it fell to the ground, then he turned and ran back through the trees.

TWENTY-NINE

ANSKAR STORMED THROUGH THE TREES, Noni scurrying behind, clutching the garland Orix had made.

"You did that deliberately," he said over his shoulder. "Why would you do that? Not just to me, to Orix!"

"What did I do?" she pleaded. "I don't understand."

"You know. You knew perfectly well what you were up to. What were you thinking? Were you trying to make Orix jealous? Do you want him and me to be enemies?"

"Why would I want that?"

"I've no idea. You tell me. So you can have Orix to yourself?"

"By upsetting him? No, that's not what I want."

Anskar stopped and spun round to face her. "Then what? Why did you do it? You pressed yourself against me. You tried to kiss me!"

"No!" Noni swooned. She looked as though she were going to collapse, but Anskar wasn't falling for it.

"A fine performance," he said. "You should be an actress. You'd get all the good parts."

She bent double, panting, hair falling over her face. Not panting, he realized: she was sobbing.

"That won't work on me," Anskar said.

"Please," she said through sniffles. "I didn't mean to… Forgive me, please."

"Why? So you can do it again?"

"I'm sorry. It's all I know… It's how I… Growing up… Affection…"

"What are you talking about?" Anskar asked.

"I was happy. Don't you understand?" Her hair fell away from her face as she straightened up, her eyes perfectly dry. "Your success with the earth-tide… added to my own. I… I didn't know how to celebrate. I was happy for Orix."

"I bet you were," Anskar said. "Is that what you're going to tell him by way of an excuse?"

Noni's eyes flashed with anger. "How can you be so callous?"

"I thought you'd have worked that out by now," he replied. "I'm the son of the Necromancer Queen. Now, get out of my way."

He left her standing there, a look half shock, half rage on her face, then ran the rest of the way back to camp.

He smelled the early morning cookfires first: the bread baking and the meat roasting for breakfast. It smelled like pork but was probably squirrel. As the first of the tents came into sight, he could hear raised voices—some sort of commotion.

He spotted Vilintia and several warriors confronting a Niyandrian man wearing a bulging backpack. Behind him were six more Niyandrians, most of them youths, all carrying sacks and bags, and leading a train of four ponies, who were even more heavily laden.

"We asked for no such supplies from your town," Vilintia said.

"I know that," the man said. He was mostly bald, but the little hair he had was the color of iron. "But some of us was talking, see, after your folk came for horseshoes and the like. We worked out who you was."

"You mean, who you think we are," Vilintia said.

"You're Captain Carred Selenas, survivor of Naphor. It's you that's been keeping the spirit of the old days alive all this time."

Vilintia raised her hands. "Sorry to disappoint: ten fingers, see. Carred has the tips of two of hers missing."

"I didn't know that," the man said. "I just assumed… Is she here? Carred Selenas is a legend to my people."

"And these gifts you bring are for her?"

"For all of you," the man said.

"Carred's not here. She has business elsewhere. She left me in command. My name is Vilintia Yoenth. Now turn around and go back to your town. You shouldn't have come here."

"But why?" the man retorted. "You've nothing to fear from us. We're all Niyandrians in Joltham, untouched by the mainlanders."

"And I had hoped to keep it that way," Vilintia said. "Why do you think I kept most of my people away from your town? Tongues wag; gossip spreads. The less we know of you, the better; and if you don't have any contact with us, better still. Because if the Order of Eternal Vigilance come here one day and start asking questions, they'll know if you're lying to them. And then what do you think will happen?"

The man turned to the youngsters behind him. "Me and the other elders discussed that, and we all agreed the risk was worth it. There's more to life than hiding away. Niyas has so few defenders left, and though we can't do much, we'd like to do what we can to help."

Vilintia glanced at Anskar, a look of frustration etched into her face. "What I would like…" she said to the man. "No, first tell me your name, seeing as I gave you mine."

"My name? Forgive me, I didn't mean to be rude. I just never thought… I mean, I'm just a carpenter from a long line of carpenters."

"I'm waiting…" Vilintia said.

"Believe me," one of the youngsters said with a grin, "we know the feeling. Sul's never been one to get to the point. He's not a man of few words by any stretch."

"Sowath's my name," the older man said. "Sul Sowath. A carpenter, as I say, and an elder of Joltham. Speaker of the Elders, in point of fact, which is why it was me that came and not—"

"I wish you hadn't, Sul Sowath," Vilintia said. "We're leaving soon. We never stay long in one place, because we are constantly hunted. If those hunters track us here, they'll come to you expecting answers."

"Look about you," Sul said. He gestured to the rebels coming from their tents and standing around in a broad semicircle. "These people of yours, these heroes of Niyas, they look tired to me. Run-down. Disheartened. No doubt all that running from one place to the next, fighting the odd skirmish, then running again. Not that I'm saying you shouldn't do that. It's brave, is what it is. Valiant. But when did any of you last go home to visit family and friends? Not for a very long time, I'm guessing, by the looks of them."

Some of the rebels grumbled their agreement, and Vilintia rolled her eyes.

"All I'm saying is," Sul said, "that folk need a rest. They need to know they're appreciated. They need things to celebrate. And they need to remember."

"Remember what?" Vilintia asked.

"Don't you know what day it is?"

Vilintia frowned. "Of course I do. It's…" She looked at the rebels nearest her for support. Baylon shrugged, but a woman began to answer when Sul interrupted.

"I don't mean what day of the week. I mean the date."

Anskar frowned his incomprehension. Truth be told, he had no idea of the day, never mind the date.

"Enlighten me," Vilintia said.

"Today's the anniversary of the fall of Naphor," Sul said.

Vilintia's mouth hung open, and she blinked several times. "I was there," she said. "How could I not know it was the anniversary today?"

"But *we* know," Sul said. "You can't be expected to keep track of dates, the way you live, but we remember for you. And not just us, I'll wager. All Niyandrians who managed to keep out of the way of them mainland bastards. We remember the way things was before they came here. We make sure to preserve them ways. We remember our Queen Talia, may she be ever adored. And we remember when the great city fell. That's why we brought these supplies, see. So you can honor the fallen and raise a glass to the future of our land."

"Celebrations are for the victors in war," Vilintia said cynically.

"What does it matter whether the victory is in the past or in the future? Remember Naphor, and let the bitterness of your recollections drive you on to a glorious triumph one day. And most importantly, let us not forget what was done to us, nor that we remain Niyandrians, and that we are not without hope. It's my belief, and it's the belief of the good people of Joltham, that these fighters of yours deserve a feast."

A cheer went up from the rebels, and Vilintia looked helplessly at Anskar, who just smiled. Until he noticed Orix toward the back of the rebels, his face obscured by a hood once more. Even so, Anskar had the distinct impression his old friend was scowling—whatever that would have looked like.

"Come, what say you to a feast to remember Naphor?" Sul said. "And to celebrate the victory to come when the *Melesh-Eloni* walks among us and Queen Talia returns."

Vilintia raised an eyebrow at Anskar.

"Then you have our thanks, Sul Sowath, and we shall have our feast."

Later, when the feast started, Vilintia insisted that Anskar sit with her on a blanket beside one of the fires. Orix was seated at another fire, next to Noni, who seemed to have been forgiven, judging by the way she nestled into him. When Anskar caught her eye, she glared and mouthed what looked like a curse.

Vilintia seemed awkward in his presence, despite having been the one to suggest they sit together. He assumed she wanted to speak about Carred, about his mother, about his role and responsibilities as the *Melesh-Eloni*, but she said nothing, just glanced around at the others seated at fires dotted about the camp, occasionally casting looks up at the darkening skies.

Jagonath was a crimson crescent monitoring the proceedings. Chandra had not yet risen. She was late making her appearance in the sky at times, though no one had ever convincingly explained why. The priests of the Elder had their theories, but whenever Anskar had been forced to listen to one of them, his eyes had glazed over. Whatever else he was—knight or sorcerer, or the great hope of Niyas—he knew one thing for certain: he was no tedious, long-winded, pontificating priest of the Elder. But just thinking about the Elder's priests added another level to his moroseness. It made him think of Brother Bonavir, whose insistence that they make use of the Necromancer Tain's notes to construct their own Armor of Divinity had led to the priest's horrible death.

Anskar puffed out his cheeks and sighed. Vilintia offered him a wry smile, then turned back to troubles of her own. Some celebration this was turning out to be.

It had taken all day to prepare for the feast. More supplies arrived on the backs of packhorses. Trestle tables were erected for all the food and drink, and blankets were laid upon the ground. Musicians made their way up the escarpment, carrying silver pipes and curling horns, lutes and hand drums. Finally, just before dusk, the townsfolk had come in droves. They mingled with the rebels, sharing tales, drinking beer and mead, and one or two couples crept off into the trees as the musicians played their reels and jigs. Yet all Anskar and Vilintia had done was just sit there and watch. Finally, he could stand it no longer.

"What was it like?" he asked. "Naphor, I mean."

Vilintia stared at him for a long while, chewing on a bite of one of the savory pastries the townsfolk had brought for the feast. She swallowed and then took a sip from her earthenware mug of mead. Anskar thought she wasn't going to answer, but eventually she said, "It was hopeless. So many deaths. So much suffering." She seemed to withdraw into herself, remembering, reliving the last day of the New Niyandrian Empire.

Anskar looked over at Orix and Noni. He had the feeling they were listening in, plotting against him, but Orix had turned his back on them and was watching the group settled about a neighboring fire. He seemed particularly interested in a lithe young woman who had come up from the town.

Noni looked as if she had fallen asleep where she was sitting, the only evidence she hadn't being the barest movement of her lips as she muttered under her breath.

Eadgith, Anskar saw, was lurking beneath a tree at the fringe of the gathering. Some sort of animal stood beside her, the size of a large dog. It was hard to see what it was in the gloom. Only its eyes stood out, yellow and gleaming. Eadgith held the end of a leash fastened around its shaggy neck.

"Carred and I often speak about that day," Vilintia said. She gave a little laugh. "It's funny, because I resented her so much at the time. I was older by several years—not that you'd believe it these days," she said, running a hand through her hair, and glancing at Anskar in case he didn't agree. "After the Last Cohort's Captain was killed outside Dorinah in the early days of the war, everyone assumed I would replace him. When Carred was chosen—with half my experience and less than half my kills in battle—we all knew why. Do you know what we used to call her in those days? The Queen's bed warmer."

Anskar gritted his teeth and looked away.

"Sorry," Vilintia said. "That was insensitive."

Anskar shook his head. "No, it wasn't. And I already knew. Whatever happened between Carred and my mother, I don't pretend to understand. Nor do I care. Please, carry on. Spare me nothing. I just want to hear the truth."

"So you can decide where your allegiances lie?"

"It will certainly help if I know the Niyandrian perspective."

Vilintia met his gaze and held it. "You suspect the Order's knights have lied to you?"

"Not just me. Isn't that always what happens in war? Each side paints the enemy as demons?"

"In war, yes. It's what's called propaganda, though I've heard generals call it morale building. But I didn't mean just during the war. From what I hear and observe, the Order of Eternal Vigilance projects an image of sanctity and high-sounding morals, yet…"

Anskar nodded. "I know. It sells slaves in Atya. Its knights only observe the rules when they're in public. The Grand Master…"

"Yes?"

"It's best you don't get me started on him."

"Is it true he likes young boys?"

"Let's change the subject," Anskar said. "Please."

"What would you like to talk about?"

"My mother. If she was as powerful as everyone says, why did Naphor fall?"

"There is much that can be achieved with sorcery and much that can't," Eadgith said, causing Anskar to jump and Vilintia to reach for her sword. They'd neither heard nor seen the old woman approach. "Sometimes it's a case of powerful sorceries canceling each other out."

Eadgith looked into Anskar's eyes, as if he of all people should understand what she was saying. At her side, held on a short leash, stood a creature with the body of a wolf, the head of a gigantic black cat, and six scaled legs with knees that bent backwards, ending in talons like a bird's.

"I thought I told you not to parade that thing about in public," Vilintia said. "And didn't Carred tell you to put it down?"

The cat's head hissed. A tail of nothing but bone whipped and snapped through the air.

"I wanted the *Melesh-Eloni* to see, and to know that I ain't been entirely truthful with him."

"You lied about your abilities?" Anskar said. "You knew all along how to shape using the earth-tide?"

"I wanted you to work out how to shape things by yourself. Sorcery must be earned, not handed to you on a platter."

"Does Noni know?"

"Course she knows. How do you think she succeeded in turning brown grass green? The problem with Noni is a matter of aptitude and power. You, on the other hand, have all the advantages."

"But she has my mother's imprint, she claims…"

"What good is that without brains or a repository that's up to the task? The girl's good for hearing the realm of the dead, but not much more than that. Any skills she acquires is through mimicry, and that will only get you so far. Dead, most likely, with her unrealistic ambitions."

Anskar could see why Noni had called him into the woods now, to see what she had achieved. She had hoped competitiveness would force him to respond; to build upon her scant accomplishments. So she'd observed everything he did with the intention of imitating the improvements he made on her initial successes.

"She wants to be the one to restore Orix's face," Anskar said.

"I was planning on letting her do just that," Eadgith said, "or at least, letting her think she was the one to do it. But now I'm not so sure. Maybe you should be the one to do it. Gestures like that can reconcile friends who ain't friends no more."

The hybrid creature strained at its leash. Around the camp, people were casting nervous looks at the beast.

"Take that thing away," Vilintia said. "I don't want to see it out of its cage again. When Carred comes back—if she comes back—she can decide what to do with it. Bala was her dog, after all." To Anskar's enquiring gaze, she said, "Carred fed a stray that wandered into camp, then couldn't get rid of it. Then Eadgith took it upon herself to alter poor old Bala with sorcery."

"You'll be glad I did one day," the old woman said. "Come on, Bala, back to your cage, lovey."

"Wait," Anskar said. "What were you saying about sorceries canceling each other out? Are you saying the allies had powerful sorcerers at Naphor who could thwart my mother?"

"Powerful's a matter of perspective," Eadgith said. "There are degrees to these things."

"Then why…?"

"There are limits, *Melesh-Eloni*. Even your mother's sorcery had limits. But where sorcery fails, iron and steel often prevail, and the engines of war that wealth makes possible. On the mainland, there are rumors of a powerful consortium—merchants, nobles, the Church of Menselas, and others. It's them that pulls the strings of government. Their tentacles are everywhere. Together, they can move mountains or overthrow Empires. The allies never lacked for resources. They bombarded our walls, they matched our sorcerers—"

"Even my mother?"

"She was so thin, Anskar. A delicate twig of a woman. I sometimes used to think if someone squeezed her too hard…" She broke off and looked away, absentmindedly petting her hybrid beast. "Queen Talia was by far the most gifted sorcerer I've ever known. She could do things other sorcerers had attempted to do and failed at for centuries. Even her own people feared her, at least as much as they loved her. But she was so frail; not the goddess she aspired to be. You must've felt it yourself, the draining effects of the tidal forces sluicing through you."

"I have," Anskar said.

Eadgith studied him for a moment, then gave a curt nod. "I've a notion you need no further instruction from me, but in case you do, you know where to find me."

"Thank you," Anskar said as the old woman walked away through the trees with Bala at her side.

"The cage is a fair way from camp," Vilintia said. "The people were getting frightened. Eadgith walks out to it every morning and evening. Theltek alone knows what she feeds the beast."

They were both distracted as Baylon pushed himself to his feet. The young woman from the town had seen him watching her, and to Anskar's surprise, she smiled and held out her hand. Baylon glanced at Anskar and winked, then went to her. Orix, who had also been watching, looked sharply away, only to find Noni glaring.

"I do so love a good feast," Vilintia said, finally starting to relax now that Eadgith and Bala had gone, and all talk of Naphor had abated. "People are so much more at ease with life, don't you think?"

"This is my first feast," Anskar said, then corrected himself. "My first Niyandrian feast. At Branil's Burg, before the first of the trials we have to undertake for knighthood, we had a banquet. The knights all had sumptuous meals and fine wine, but we postulants… they gave us stale bread and water."

"And that surprises you? Isn't that just like everything else with the Order of Eternal Vigilance?"

"I think it was a test… of discipline, I suppose. Of patience."

"Course it was," Vilintia said. "But tell me this: I've heard that love isn't allowed in the Order. Romantic love, I mean."

"Not between comrades, and not outside of wedlock."

"Mainlanders are so stuffy. Their weird religions make them act out of step with their nature. We Niyandrians couple as the urge takes us, and never more so than at feasts. It's how the ancient gods made us."

Anskar felt heat rise to his cheeks, and he looked down at the food heaped on plates set around their blanket.

"Not me," Vilintia said. "Not because there's anything wrong with it—your priests are insane to think that there is. But because of our cause. When Naphor fell, it was just we of the Last Cohort that remained of Niyandrian dignity and pride. Everyone else just gave up or hid away, unnoticed by the conquerors, like these good people of Joltham. I vowed never to love again, till Niyas was once more ruled by Niyandrians. Till the return of the Queen. Carred took the same vow, but in her case it lasted about a month. Still, that was better than many of us expected."

"And did it help?" Anskar asked.

"Not having sex? I don't think so. It made me irritable and self-righteous—I'm sure as a devotee of Menselas you know all about that!"

"Maybe once," Anskar said. "But I've not always lived up to the teachings of the Church."

"No," Vilintia said, appraising him with her eyes. "No, I don't suppose you have."

"So what happened?" Anskar asked. "What made you abandon your vow?"

"Besides years of frustration, and all for nothing? I mean, it's not as though we achieved any noteworthy results. You have no idea how many people left our resistance, claiming Carred was cursed, a failure. But what changed me? Not a conscious decision. I neither needed nor wanted anyone to share my bed at night; but then, what did I know? Carred freed some slaves before they could be shipped to Atya and sold by your holy Order. Noni was among the slaves she brought into our rebellion. And then there was Taloc."

She went quiet for the longest time, staring up at the sky, where hundreds of stars were now showing.

"Nothing last forever." She sighed. "We must be thankful for the brief moments of happiness we have." She looked searchingly into Anskar's eyes. "Don't you agree?"

When he hesitated in responding, Vilintia said, "I'm sure you must have had lovers, despite the regulations."

Anskar shut his eyes and sighed. "More than I would have liked."

Vilintia laughed. "You would sooner have remained a virgin, like those prudish priests of the Healer?"

Anskar chuckled. "They're not as prudish as you might think. Not all of them."

"Oh?"

He was remembering Tion, and he was sure Tion wasn't the only one who had violated his vows. As for the knights' injunction not to form romantic attachments with their colleagues, he'd seen enough to tell him not everyone abided by the rules. Least of all the Grand Master.

"No," he decided at last. "I don't regret what I've done. I did, but now… I don't know what I feel."

Vilintia watched him, her expression inscrutable. "That makes two of us."

Anskar began to feel awkward with the direction the conversation was taking, so he reverted to what they had been discussing before.

"So, my mother could have raised the dead to fight against the enemy at Naphor?"

Vilintia gave him a delicate smile. "Eadgith was one of the court sorcerers who assisted Queen Talia. She says your mother did raise our fallen soldiers at first and return them to the ranks, but the mental strain was too much to continue. She pushed herself to the limit, Anskar, and beyond. And when she saw, as we all did, that our defense was futile, she saved her energy for one last act of defiance."

"She destroyed the city," Anskar said. He'd heard the tale often enough: how Queen Talia had risen on a crest of sorcery and swelled with unimaginable power until it exploded, destroying the city of Naphor, the inhabitants who hadn't evacuated, the invaders within the walls, and Queen Talia herself. The supreme sacrifice, as far as Niyandrians were concerned, and also the seed from which the new Niyas would grow.

He noticed that Vilintia was trembling.

"I'm sorry," she said. "I know you want to talk about your mother and Naphor and all that's happened since her death, but I can't stop thinking about Taloc. This is so stupid. I should be stronger than this."

He reached out and tentatively touched her shoulder, causing her to face him and give a fragile smile. Tears glistened in her eyes, and almost in a daze, Anskar wiped them away.

The enchantment was broken as the musicians struck up a wild and jaunty jig. People—townsfolk and rebels—drew together in pairs, stomping, whirling, joining hands and matching each other step for step.

Vilintia's smile widened. "I don't suppose you want to—?"

"You're not dancing?"

It was a town girl who had spoken, her red skin glistening with sweat. She was scantily clad, leaving her arms and legs and way too much of her ample breasts exposed. Anskar had tried not to notice her making the rounds of the campfires.

"I'm not," he said.

"Then come dance with me."

"I'm sorry, but I'm talking," Anskar said, tearing his eyes away from her.

"Half-blood!" she said as she spun away. "Half-*man*!"

"Then why did you want to dance with him?" Vilintia called after her. "Still, you surprise me, Anskar. She is pretty."

The young woman made her way over to Orix's fire, but when Noni spat at her, she flounced away toward the dancers, where at last a thick-set rebel pulled her into an embrace.

"What were you about to ask me?" Anskar asked.

"Ask? I can't remember," Vilintia said. "Probably nothing."

He felt certain she'd been about to ask him to dance, and his mind was awash with excuses not to. Not for any reason other than he had no idea how to dance, especially in the way the Niyandrians were dancing.

"Look at Eadgith!" Vilintia said.

The old woman had returned without her beast, and was in amongst the revelers, dancing a wild caper that belied her age. An old man from the town joined her, took her hand, and spun her around.

Vilintia stood. "I'm going back to my tent."

"Are you tired?" He wanted to ask her to stay, or if he could accompany her, but Anskar held his tongue.

"There are things I need to think about. Several of our scouts returned during the afternoon. They spotted a good deal more Order activity than usual, all of it far from here. They seemed to be searching for something."

"Seneschal Monash," Anskar said. "She's a different sort of governor to Vihtor, my... my old Seneschal."

"It makes no difference. We won't be here much longer, and we know how to cover our trail. We've still to decide upon a new campsite, one remote enough and large enough for as many of our splinter groups to come together as possible. Our scouts have already informed the closest groups that we've found the *Melesh-Eloni*, and they're keen to see you for themselves."

"You told them about me?" Anskar said. "Why? Won't that increase the risk of the Order finding out? And what if I want to leave?"

Vilintia stooped and touched his cheek. He thought for a moment she was going to kiss him.

"Eadgith says you're a quick learner, Anskar. Stay a little longer. Learn more."

"About who I am?"

"About who you may yet become. At least wait until Carred returns. *If* she returns. Give us a little more time, please."

Vilintia turned and walked away, and Anskar was shocked to realize he badly wanted to follow.

"You fool," he told himself, and shook his head to clear it of the lustful thoughts starting to rise to the surface. She was old enough to be his mother, for the Five's sake. And she was still in the depths of grief. Whatever she might have felt right now was likely a phantom, a way to hide from the pain. And besides, he had probably misinterpreted things. Maybe she was just trying to be friendly, to put him at his ease.

He glanced over to Orix's fire and had the impression his old friend had just quickly looked away.

"Enough of this nonsense," Anskar muttered to himself. He wasn't going to let this situation go on for one moment longer.

But before he could stand, Orix got up and strode away toward the tents, and Noni went running after him.

THIRTY

ANSKAR MADE HIS WAY THROUGH the village of tents
with the pounding of drums, the din of lutes and pipes and
laughter trailing him. The revelry sounded mocking. His skin
prickled with heat, and his heartbeat thudded in his ears. The
dark-tide in his veins burned. It made him want to crush, to
throttle, to kill.

And that shocked him.

He slowed his pace and came to a stop amid a cluster of tents.
What was he doing? What was he going to do? He'd intended
to confront Orix about Noni—reveal her for the liar she was.
He was going to make the case for their friendship, over and
above any idiotic relationship Orix might have with her. He
was going to remind him of… what? That they were brother
knights of the Order of Eternal Vigilance? Hardly. Brothers in
infidelity to the vows they had both taken, perhaps, but it went
no deeper than that.

Slow down, he told himself, breathing deeply and letting the air trickle out through his lips. He wasn't himself. Something had possessed him every bit as much as Queen Talia had possessed Noni. A knight—even a lapsed one—must not be the slave of his emotions, Vihtor had once said, at a memorial for the dead of Branil's Burg. Words that had stayed with Anskar, albeit buried most of the time. But was it mere emotion that was driving him, making him impetuous and enraged? Or was it in the blood? His veins seemed to fizz and pop and bubble with the darkness that had taken up residence within them.

"Menselas, please," he breathed. "Come to my aid."

A weak petition to a phony god, an errant thought retorted.

Images flashed across his inner vision: Gann coming at him, possessed by the Warrior's Fire. Borik's shattered sword. The Abbess grinding away above him. Vihtor, Sareya, Seneschal Monash... And in the background, like the coming of the tides and the whistle of the wind, he could hear his mother's laughter.

With a gasp, he jolted himself out of his vision, only to find himself staring at the tree line on the edge of camp, straight at two figures—a man and a woman—gesticulating violently at each other. Orix and Noni, cursing one another, imploring understanding, pleading, weeping. *All emotion,* Anskar thought. They were enslaved by it. *Weak. Pathetic.* Let them think what they liked about him. Let them say whatever they wanted—*do* whatever they planned. He was better than that. So much better. And it occurred to him that he need not ever be the slave of passion again. Emotion itself could be enslaved. And not just his, the dark-tide within him seemed to say: the emotions of others.

He suppressed the urge to laugh out loud. He knew it would have sounded crazy, even to him. But the intuition stayed with him, a temptation as irresistible as Sareya on that first night in the smithing hall. As Carred Selenas had been for him when the Abbess had worn her guise. *They* had done it to him. They had beguiled him with feelings, aroused the passions that had ensnared and controlled him. Why shouldn't he do the same?

Tion's face rose like a ghost behind his eyes. The healer shook his head in warning, but Anskar dismissed Tion as the hypocrite he was. Vihtor came next. *Did you do it?* Anskar challenged. *Did you rape my mother?* The image fled.

Suddenly overwhelmed with guilt, Anskar buried his head in his hands and shuddered as he wept.

What was happening to him? He was buffeted this way and that by every changing feeling. He was like a ship at sea with no anchor, no harbor. He turned a slow circle, not knowing which way to go.

His eyes came to rest on the wavering light of a lamp coming through the canvas of a tent, and the slender shadow it cast. He moved toward the tent as if there were no other option. Not possession, he realized. Not lust out of control. But nevertheless, he acknowledged it as a need.

Steeling himself at the entrance, he gritted his teeth, then pulled back the tent flap and held it open.

"Anskar?" Vilintia said.

He had startled her; that was plain by the tightness of her voice. She was seated atop her bedroll in the middle of pouring herself a mug of wine from a bottle.

Anskar swallowed, and whatever resolve he'd mustered evaporated like morning mist. He struggled for something to say, at the same time scanning the interior as if he were interested in the contents: several changes of clothing, neatly folded; a mail hauberk laid out on a blanket, gleaming from a recent oiling; a scabbarded longsword; polished boots. The only thing that seemed out of keeping with the image he had formed of Vilintia—the long-suffering soldier and loyalist of the rebellion—was the open book on her bedroll.

Vilintia frowned as she followed his gaze, then took a sip of wine. "Why are you here?"

"Orix stormed away from the feast," Anskar said. Quickly, breathlessly, he told her about Noni leading him into the woods and almost kissing him.

"And Orix saw?" Vilintia said when he finished.

"I think he was meant to see."

"Just goes to show," Vilintia said. "You shouldn't be too quick to judge with the eyes alone." She knocked back the wine in her mug and poured another. "Anyone in their right mind can see you two are friends."

"Well, Orix isn't in his right mind," Anskar said. "He hasn't been since…"

"Since Carred?" Vilintia said. "Well, no surprise there. She knows how to hook them, and there's no easier prey than a young man just out of boyhood." She measured him with her eyes, and though he expected to find it, Anskar saw no hint of mockery there, merely a probing sort of interest, and was that concern?

"I have another mug somewhere," Vilintia said. "Or should we just share?" Her cat's eyes widened, and it was a few second before Anskar got her meaning.

He stepped inside the tent and let the flap fall closed behind him.

"Should I hood the lantern?" Vilintia said, already doing it and plunging the interior into semidarkness. She laughed. "Otherwise someone might see two silhouettes on the canvas outside. We don't want to give the wrong impression. You know how people misinterpret what they see, and you still have a reputation to keep, knight of Menselas."

Anskar took a couple of wary steps through the dark, then lowered himself to sit on the floor opposite her.

"The bedroll's more comfortable," she said with a slight slur.

"Are you drunk?" Anskar asked.

"Does that bother you?"

"It hit you hard, didn't it?" he said. "After so long alone, then finding someone, only to lose…"

"Shush," Vilintia said. He heard the plop and glug of her pouring more wine into her mug.

"How are you going to find that second mug now?" he asked, straining to see in the semi-darkness.

He heard her shift on the bedroll; then she was leaning close to him, mead and wine on her breath. She fumbled about for the back of his head and drew him gently toward the mug she held.

Anskar sipped. The wine was sour, but that didn't stop him from taking a second sip before allowing Vilintia a turn.

He could see her a little more clearly now in the reddish moonlight filtering through the canvas. Her eyes, so close to his, glinted, and he caught the flash of her teeth.

"I'm surprised Baylon didn't follow you," Vilintia said.

"He was otherwise occupied."

Vilintia took another drink. "More?" She offered the mug to Anskar.

"I probably shouldn't." He started to rise, but Vilintia's hand caught his arm. She was trembling.

"Don't go," she said.

"Vilintia… you're grieving."

"And you'd know all about grief, wouldn't you? You with so many years and so much experience behind you."

"That doesn't mean I haven't known grief," Anskar said. "My

father…"

"Huh!" Vilintia snorted.

"You didn't know him! Whatever you might have heard, whatever you think, it's not true."

"Try telling that to your mother, *Melesh-Eloni*. You think the Queen of Niyas would lie with a mainlander by choice?"

"Why wouldn't she? It's not like Carred's fussy about who she sleeps with—Orix, for Menselas's sake! Why would the Necromancer Queen be any different? She used Vihtor, I've no doubt in my mind. Beguiled him with sorcery and took from him what she wanted."

"And so what if she did?" Vilintia said. "If you truly believe that, would it be so bad? The mainlanders were the aggressors in the war. Why shouldn't our Queen do whatever it took to protect us?"

"But it didn't protect you, did it?" Anskar said.

"Maybe not. But it gave us a slender hope for the future. I just hadn't realized how slender!"

"I shouldn't have come," Anskar said, starting to stand.

"Forgive me. You're right. This is grief. It's why I left the feast when I did. Theltek's eyes, why should Taloc's death affect me like this? I barely even knew him."

"But you did know him," Anskar said, settling back down on the bedroll. He pulled Vilintia's head into his chest and ran his fingers through her hair. "And he knew you. That's how love happens, sudden, unexpected, beyond our control."

"And you know this how?" Vilintia asked as she nuzzled her face into him. "So wise, yet still so young. You'd make an excellent priest of the Elder."

"Now you're getting nasty," Anskar said.

"I can feel your smile." Vilintia's fingertips brushed his lips.

"You should do it more often."

As gently as he could, he pried her hand away from his face. "We don't have to do this," he said. "I'll stay and talk, but anything more... With you in this state, it doesn't feel right."

She shoved him back and held him at arm's length. "Don't tell me why I'm doing this! And who said I am doing anything? You assume much, *Melesh-Eloni*. I'm no Carred Selenas, flinging herself at your mother or anyone else who takes her fancy."

"Then what *is* going on?" Anskar asked.

"You tell me. You're the one who came here. It's not like I invited you."

"Fine. Then let me leave."

She leaned so close he could smell the wine on her breath. Her cat's eyes glistened through the dark.

"Are you crying?" he asked.

"No." She sniffed.

"Vilintia, please. Please listen. Just now, before I came to your tent, I was filled with such rage and—"

"Towards Orix?"

"Towards everyone, everything. It scared me. I wasn't myself. And I feel... I keep feeling such..." He shook his head and pulled away from her. "Such need."

"Need can be good," Vilintia said, inching closer.

"Not this kind! This is new. It started with... Never mind."

He was going to say it started at the Abbey of the Hooded One, but was that strictly true? Hadn't it started even before that, with Sareya?

"It started with the fitting of my catalyst," he said, rather than admit to the depravities he had suffered from the Abbess. "And when my catalyst was removed, it only grew worse. I don't know what's happening to me."

"What's happening? You are becoming yourself," Vilintia said. "That's what is happening. You're freeing yourself from the unnatural restraints of the Church of Menselas and the knights that raised you."

"No," Anskar said, "this is more than that. There's something inside me."

Vilintia grew very still. All he could hear was the sound of her shallow breaths. "Your mother? I thought…"

"Not her. Something different. Or at least I think it's different. I don't know. The priests of the Healer banished her from me. But this… It's like a dam has burst. I can no longer sense my dark-tide repository."

The atmosphere chilled between them. Nyandrians were accomplished sorcerers familiar with the dusk- and the dawn- and even the earth-tide. But the dark: save for Queen Talia, it seemed to play little to no part in their culture.

"It's gone, Vilintia, but the dark-tide flows through me, through every vein and pore. It feels… it feels as though I'm becoming the tide."

Vilintia hesitated before replying. "And this is where your rage comes from? Your… other feelings?"

"What am I, Vilintia? What am I becoming?"

She embraced him, and now it was she pulling his face into her chest. No floral scent, no musk to inflame him, only a faint odor of sweat.

"Oh, Anskar, what are we like, the pair of us? Perhaps it would have been easier if we'd just given in, done what we both wanted to do, and moved on." With a hint of playfulness in her voice, she said, "We still could if you like."

"Why do I think that would only encourage the dark to grow?"

"Maybe it's supposed to grow," Vilintia said. "Have you

considered that? You are the heir to Niyas, the son of the Necromancer Queen. No one knows the full extent of Talia's powers, not even Eadgith, not even Carred, who was closer to your mother than anyone alive."

"But what does that say about my mother—about me?" Anskar said. "This darkness within isn't natural—for mainlanders or Niyandrians. Besides my mother, I've only encountered it in my dealings with the Tainted Cabal. But I fear it is natural for me, a part of me."

"Perhaps Queen Talia was a demon?" Vilintia suggested.

"That's not funny."

"No," Vilintia said. "No, I don't suppose it is. Well, Eadgith says your mother was always studying, always researching the different tides of sorcery. Who knows what she uncovered?"

"And what she passed on to me?"

"But ask yourself this, Anskar: Where is all this worry, all this speculation getting you? Where is it getting either of us? I can reason that Taloc is the cause of my grief, of my vulnerability when it comes to… situations like this, but so what? All we are is the gods' playthings, and if I've gleaned anything about gods, it's that they're capricious."

"Even Theltek?"

"Shush," Vilintia said as her hand slipped behind to the small of Anskar's back. "He has a thousand ears. He might hear!"

Anskar savored the heat of her belly pressed against him.

"Don't tell me I'm controlled by my grief," Vilintia said. "I'm Niyandrian, remember, not some mainland prude bound by the rules of Menselas. It took Taloc to remind me of that, and rather than wallowing in sorrow, I should be grateful to him. But how about you, Anskar? Are you Niyandrian, or has your other half won out? Do you still wish to be a eunuch for the sake of the Five?"

She touched her lips to his. "Just don't tell me we have to marry after."

"Please," Anskar said, pulling away and wiping his lips. "I can't. Not now."

"But you would if it were Carred and not me?"

Yes. Maybe. "No. If it's not grief, Vilintia, it's the wine."

"We don't have to drink," she said, and she slung the mug across the tent. There was a dull thud as it hit the ground. "Nor do we have to do anything else. We can't go having anything remotely like fun now, can we? But if you just want to talk, then let's just talk."

"I…" Anskar couldn't think of anything to say. "What should we talk about?" he asked.

Vilintia lay her head in Anskar's lap, making a pillow of his hardness. "Well… how does it feel to be without your catalyst?" She quickly rethought her question. "What was it like in Thousand Lakes? Do you think the new Seneschal will really make it a priority to scour us from the isle?"

"I think she will," Anskar said. "She was some sort of troubleshooter before. A general."

"The mainland lords have grown tired of our presence?" Vilintia said. "Costing them too much business?"

"Maybe," Anskar said. "Though I used to think otherwise."

"You used to think theirs was a pious conquest? That they sought to bring the light of Menselas to us baby-eating heathens?"

"It's what I was taught, yes. But I saw a few things in Sansor and along the way. I didn't know about the slaves."

"You've gone soft," Vilintia said, nestling her head into his groin. "See, I told you we could just talk."

Anskar stroked her hair, caught up in his thoughts.

"So," Vilintia said, "you've seen behind the mask of the Order. What will you do now?"

"You make it sound as though I have a choice. My mother had all this mapped out for me. I'm just a tool for her to use."

"Yet you had her cast out of you," Vilintia said. "That hardly sounds like part of her plan. Give us a little time, Anskar. Stay with us a while longer, get to know the others. You could learn from Eadgith…"

"Learn what? How to change dogs into part cat, part reptile?"

"Maybe she could help you understand this darkness within."

"I doubt that," Anskar said. "It frightens me. There are layers within me I know nothing about. Latencies buried since my birth. I don't know whether they're natural to me or planted."

Anskar sighed, and now he was the one trembling.

Vilintia raised herself level with his face. "So, you had your catalyst removed…"

"I thought…" Anskar said, "I thought that all my troubles had begun when it was fitted, and that if I had it taken out…"

"You could go back to being a good little knight?"

Anskar pulled away from her.

"I'm sorry," Vilintia said. "It's the wine talking—and to think, I don't normally drink."

"It was a childish dream," he said. "I know now there can be no going back."

"Only forward?" Vilintia said. "Does that involve acceptance of your Niyandrian nature?"

She darted her head forward and pressed her lips to his. Anskar gasped as her fingers made their way inside his shirt to trace the ridge of his catalyst scar.

And then he was kissing her greedily, and nothing else mattered.

THIRTY-ONE

ANSKAR AWOKE TO FIND VILINTIA lying naked beside him. The scent of their lovemaking clung to his nostrils. It seemed a remedy; a ward against the stench of the earth-tide.

"Were you watching me while I slept?" he asked as he rubbed the sleep from his eyes.

She smiled and traced patterns on his face with her fingertips. He pulled them to his lips and kissed them.

It was still dark outside, but there was no more sound of music, just the occasional muted moan or distant laugh from deeper in the forest.

"It'll soon be dawn," Vilintia said.

Once, Anskar would have felt the thrill of anticipation as he rose and waited for the dawn-tide, but not any longer. He was surprised to find he no longer viewed it as a loss—more as a liberation.

He had never felt the tides before the implantation of his catalyst, and that alone made him question just how natural his dawn- and dusk-tide ability had been. What was it about mainlanders— about their culture—that severed the link with the tides, or at least caused their repositories to atrophy to the point they needed the help of a crystal? Zek had told him the Soreshi made no use of catalysts, and neither did the Niyandrians. Although Vilintia's repositories were underdeveloped, as were Carred's. He smiled to himself. She compensated in other ways, though.

"What's the matter?" Vilintia said. "Why so pensive?"

There was concern in her eyes, as if she thought he were dissatisfied with her.

"Last night…" he said. "Were you making up for lost time?"

She frowned, then seemed to get it. "All those years of celibacy, you mean? Theltek, I was a dozy cow."

When she kissed him, he responded fiercely, aware all the time that this was not love. It wasn't even a need for closeness. It felt more primal. Akin to hunger.

When they had finished and lay in each other's arms, the east side of the tent was bathed in red as the sun finally rose.

"So, you like how we celebrate our feast days?" Vilintia asked.

"Drinking, dancing, and feasting, you mean?"

"And making love," Vilintia added. "We weren't the only ones, you can be sure of that."

Anskar smiled, and though she smiled too, a new sadness entered Vilintia's eyes.

She encircled his wrist with her fingers, feeling the vambrace that invisibly adorned his forearm. "It glowed a little during the night," she said.

"Jagonath was bright. The vambrace is visible under moonlight. I thought my mother wanted me to learn from it, so I could make a full suit of Armor of Divinity. In Wintotashum,

I started to try. We procured the necessary components, had access to a forge hot enough to work divine alloy… I even stole the necromancer Tain's notes from the Scriptorium."

"But you made no progress?"

"A little, but it soon came to a stop."

"What happened?"

"People died." Hrothyr, Bonavir, Braga. "I suppose that's why my mother sent Carred to find a suit of armor from the past: I'm taking too long."

Vilintia dabbed at her eye with a finger.

"I'm sorry," Anskar said. "I've set you off thinking about Taloc, haven't I?"

"Taloc? Don't know what you're talking about," she said.

"You're a terrible liar."

"An attribute I'm proud of," Vilintia said, "because the world already has too many good ones."

"What made you become a soldier?" Anskar asked. "Like this—the time we've spent alone—you're so…"

"Nice? Normal?"

"Both. When I first met you, you seemed so hard."

"Maybe I need to be. That's what the war did to people like me. But I'm not the only one."

Vilintia rolled on top of him and bent her head to kiss him on the lips, but she looked around as the tent flap parted and Baylon poked his head inside.

"Sorry to interrupt," Baylon said. He coughed, as if he were embarrassed, but made no attempt to look away. "Pig-boy's gone, and he's taken the loony with him."

"Orix?" Vilintia said. "Noni?" She rolled off Anskar and stood, oblivious of her nakedness.

Baylon averted his eyes. "He was seen leaving during the feast."

"And no one stopped him?"

Baylon met her gaze then, and there was a hint of belligerence in his tone. "Was he being watched? I don't remember you giving that order."

Anskar was already pulling on his pants. "I went to speak with him, but he stormed off with Noni. When I saw them arguing beneath a tree, I came..." He glanced at Vilintia. Whether it was Baylon's intrusion or the dawn light coming through the opening, she looked so different now: colder, harder. "I had no idea they would leave the camp. I'll go after him."

"Why bother?" Vilintia said. "You're better off without him. As for Noni, I can't be expected to mother her forever."

"I have to find Orix," Anskar said, "because of Archduke Peleus. I tried telling him about the blood feud, but I don't know how seriously he took it."

"He's his own person, Anskar. He can look after himself."

"You don't know that. And besides, there's his face. Noni will never be able to fix it, whatever she says. I must go. Please don't try to stop me."

He saw Baylon exchange a look with Vilintia, his hand resting on his sword pommel. For a second, the darkness seethed in Anskar's veins. And then Vilintia let out a sigh.

"You're the *Melesh-Eloni*. You're aware of that now, and aware of your responsibilities to the people of Niyas. You will fulfill them, or you won't. I've no authority over you." No claim on you, either, she might have added.

"Thank you," Anskar said. "I'll come back. I promise you that."

The slight wrinkling of her nose was a reminder that she hadn't asked anything of him save a night of festive lovemaking. He got the impression she couldn't care less if he came back or not. Or was she just acting indifferent? Anskar gritted his teeth. He'd never understand women.

Baylon stepped aside as Anskar moved to the entrance.

"You think Orix will go back to Branil's Burg?" Vilintia asked.

"I don't know where else he'd go."

"Want me to ready a horse for you?" Baylon asked.

"Yes, please."

Baylon disappeared outside, and Anskar finished dressing.

Vilintia stood there naked, thinking. Hard-bodied and lean, with none of the softness Sareya possessed. And then he took it one step further—or rather, his intrusive thoughts did. Vilintia was mutton to Sareya's lamb, just one small step away from the Abbess.

The comparison was unfair, he realized, unjustified. Vilintia was still an attractive woman, but the damage was done. All he felt—all he would ever feel—in the face of her nudity was an icy clumping in his guts.

"I don't like this," Vilintia said. "If this Archduke Peleus should find Orix... if he should find you... We move camp today."

It threw Anskar that she hadn't reacted with bitterness to his thoughts, but then, why would she? It wasn't as though she could read his mind.

But that was how it felt: that the criticisms, the derogatory things he had been thinking, even those moments he was almost overcome with lust, were accessible to others. He had the growing suspicion that everyone he met knew exactly what he was thinking and judged him by it.

"The others won't like it," Anskar said. "Most of them are hung-over from the feast."

"We'll head north into the hill country," she said, at last grabbing her clothes.

Anskar had the impression she was lying to him, deceiving him about where she was really planning to go, in case he was captured. Did she trust him so little? Perhaps he couldn't blame her, even after what they'd shared last night.

"I'll send scouts ahead of us," Vilintia said. "Be swift. I'll give you until noon, and then we have to go."

He pulled her to him and kissed her, and she shivered from where he brushed the small of her back.

Maybe he wasn't the only one whose perspective had changed with the coming of day.

Anskar rode east. The horse Baylon had readied for him was dapple gray, light and very fast. He cantered through woodland until he reached the road, which was little more than a track scored through the grass, and then heeled the horse to a canter.

A mile or so along the road, he passed recent horse dung, and that seemed to him a good sign. He was no tracker, but it seemed obvious this was the spoor of but one horse, and at no point did he see any indications of another.

The question remained, though: if Orix had come this way, if he was indeed heading to Branil's Burg, how far could he have come, especially if he and Noni were sharing the one horse? Would he have ridden through the night? How much would the dark have slowed his pace? There seemed nothing for it but to press on, but already Anskar's horse was lathered in sweat, so he slowed to a trot and then to a walk.

He rode on for another couple of miles. Either side of the road the forest grew denser, pine trees shadowing the way ahead. He stopped at a plank bridge spanning a stream that split the road and allowed his horse to drink.

When he got underway again, he picked up speed. After a while, the track became more distinct, and there was evidence of stone poking through the dried mud, where in ages past there had been a paved road.

The horse's hooves clipped loudly here, and the forest to the left side thinned out, revealing that the road ran along an elevation. He could see down into a valley and across the hazy distance to where a scatter of smallholdings stood out from crop fields of yellow and green. Smoke plumed from one or two chimneys, and there were sheep and goats out to pasture.

The road rounded a bend, and Anskar pulled on the reins, then brought the horse to a stop.

There was a lacquered black carriage blocking the road, its back toward Anskar, the team of horses harnessed to it facing away from him.

And there was a figure in the road, seemingly waiting: a man in a dark gray coat. A varnished mask of blackwood covered his face. There were no long ropes of braided hair, just mussed-up locks the color of flax. No sign of the twisted leg, either, but there was no doubt that this was one of the Ethereal Sorceress's functionaries.

Anskar dismounted and approached, leading the horse by the reins. There was something familiar about the functionary, and it wasn't just the attire. He drew up a few feet in front of the man. There was nothing but darkness through the eye slits of the mask.

"Your debt is due," the functionary said, and although he spoke with a flat monotone, Anskar recognized some quality of the voice.

"Blosius?"

"Leave the horse. Perhaps it will find its way back, perhaps it won't."

"This needs to wait," Anskar said. "I'm following someone. It's urgent. Orix? You remember him?"

"Your debt is due," Blosius said again. He touched the fingertips of one gloved hand to the palm of the other and made a deft circle. Immediately, Anskar released the horse's reins.

The door on the left of the carriage opened, seemingly of its own accord.

"You will step inside," Blosius said.

"Blosius," Anskar said, "we don't have time for this. Tell Sheelahn I'll come to her depot as soon as I'm done."

Again Blosius traced a circle on his palm. Anskar swore and then obeyed, walking to the carriage and climbing inside.

Another functionary was seated on the bench that faced the rear. He too wore a gray coat and a blackwood mask, but this one had the long braided hair, and Anskar saw that his leg was twisted.

"Sit," the man said, gesturing to the forward-facing bench opposite.

Anskar sat, and Blosius climbed into the carriage, shutting the door behind him. He seated himself next to the other functionary, and both of them stared blankly at Anskar. Was Blosius just deeply involved in his new role? Or had the Ethereal Sorceress done something to his mind?

Though Anskar had seen no driver, the carriage pulled away, and he could do nothing save sit and wait and be taken where he didn't want to go.

It reminded him of the time a golden-eyed crow had visited him in his room at Branil's Burg and led him in the daze of sleep across the wilds to the top of Hallow Hill.

THIRTY-TWO

"YOU KNOW BLAICE RANCEY," THE Ethereal Sorceress said without looking up as Anskar entered.

The masked functionary—Anskar was more convinced than ever that it was Blosius—shut the door behind him.

Sheelahn was sitting at a polished blackwood desk carved with miniature monkeys scrambling over fruit-bearing vines. Anskar saw one was picking its nose. Sheelahn was scratching at a ledger with a slender gold pen, and he took the opportunity to look around.

It was a small chamber, the walls overcrowded with ornately framed oil paintings, all of them portraits, all of cruel-faced men and women Anskar would not have liked to meet. He noted briefly their strange attire—frills and ruffs, a preponderance of gold—but he hadn't been brought here to admire artwork. He'd not wished to be brought here at all.

He acknowledged Blaice Rancey with a glare, and instead of

the mocking roll of the eyes he had expected—or a lascivious pout—she looked down at the floor, as if she had seen something crawl across the green carpet.

Blaice was dressed in thick-weave pants, knee-length boots, and a brown leather jacket with too many pockets, all of them bulging. Her dark hair was braided close to her skull, and there were silver studs piercing her nose and top lip. She had a new tattoo as well, Anskar noted: a seven-pointed star on the side of her neck. It struck him as an odd vanity, and one her former lover, Niklaus du Plessis, would not have approved of, for it would have lessened Blaice's resemblance to his goddess.

Anskar glanced furtively toward her chest, where previously she had worn an open-necked shirt that revealed the serpent tattoo weaving its way between her breasts. There was no sign of the tattoo now, save for the serpent's head on her throat. Beneath her leather jacket, she wore a plain black shirt buttoned to the top. She looked all business, ready for some long and arduous journey, but there was something sullen about her too. She looked as resentful as he presumably did.

Anskar dragged his gaze back to the Ethereal Sorceress, who was once more wearing her usual stiff robes and orichalcum mask, which covered her entire head. And he wondered if this was the same woman who had greeted him so differently last time: the woman with the empty eye sockets, Haeth Ho'akopeth. He waited until she had finished writing and set down her pen.

When the Ethereal Sorceress turned on her chair to face him, he simply said, "I assume my stock has gone back up."

"I made some inquiries," she said. "Your usefulness is reaffirmed, and our bargain has resumed."

"Not now," Anskar said. He was aware that he was grinding his teeth. "I have to find someone."

"A trivial matter," Sheelahn said.

"What do you know of it?"

"No action of yours can avert what must come."

Anskar frowned at her, shot a last look at Blaice, who had lifted her eyes to study him, and then he turned and pulled open the door.

The masked functionary blocked the entrance, arms folded across his chest.

"Blosius, if that's you," Anskar said, "get out of my way, or do I need to remind you what happened when we fought in the trials?"

The Blosius he had known at Branil's Burg would have obeyed in an instant. He wouldn't have wanted to get hurt. But the functionary stood his ground. He didn't even flinch.

"Last warning," Anskar said, reaching for his sword. His fingers encircled the hilt, but try as he might, he couldn't pull the blade from the scabbard.

He narrowed his eyes at the functionary and tried again; then giving up, he surged forward, intending to shoulder the man aside. It was like running into a wall.

Anskar turned back to the Ethereal Sorceress, who watched him impassively through the empty eye-holes in her mask. Blaice shook her head, a wry grin curling her lips.

"You may shut the door," the Ethereal Sorceress said, and the functionary obeyed. "Debts must be honored, Anskar DeVantte. Is that not so, Blaice?"

"With interest," Blaice said bitterly.

"That remains to be seen. Blaice, as you well know," the Ethereal Sorceress said, "has a reputation for procuring rare merchandise."

"She has a reputation for leaving her companions behind," Anskar said. "Dead."

Blaice snorted a half-laugh at that.

"This time she will not," the Ethereal Sorceress said. "Not without leaving herself behind. And my contacts assure me there is none so suited as you for this task, *Melesh-Eloni*." The weight she gave to the title made it seem ridiculous, a joke. And perhaps that was what it was in her eyes. "Fortuitous, was it not, that our paths had already crossed?"

Anskar doubted fortune had anything to do with it. "Sheelahn... Are you Sheelahn, or must I call you Haeth Ho'akopeth now?"

"Circumstances decree that I am Sheelahn at this juncture."

Anskar was about to ask what that meant, but what would have been the point? "Why can't this wait until I find Orix?" he asked.

"Because the stakes are too high."

"What she means," Blaice said, "is that someone else will run off with all the plunder."

"I think that most unlikely," Sheelahn said. "But in any case, there are other factors in play besides profit."

"If you mean power," Blaice said. "I doubt you know much of anything else, you and your friends in the Consortium."

Sheelahn waved her hand, and Blaice clutched her throat, gasping for breath. Her eyes bulged from their sockets, and she stumbled.

"Stop!" Anskar said. "Whatever you're doing to her—"

"Has already ended," Sheelahn said, dropping her hand.

Blaice rubbed her throat and coughed to clear it. She glanced at Anskar, her face red. "I didn't know you cared."

Anskar drew in a long breath, held it for a second, then slowly released it through his nostrils. It didn't work. He was still angry. "Whose side are you on?" he asked Sheelahn.

"The one with all the cards," Blaice said.

Sheelahn's hand twitched, and that was enough warning to silence Blaice. "This is not about the Order of Eternal Vigilance," she said, "or the Last Cohort and Carred Selenas. It is not a matter of sides, but of preserving and shaping. I am not alone in this."

"This Consortium..." Anskar started, but Sheelahn cut him off.

"Has no existence outside the heads of those who see conspiracy everywhere," Sheelahn said. "Do not mention it again."

"But by your actions, you've imperiled the Niyandrian rebels," Anskar said.

Even if Vilintia moved to a new camp, the Order would learn the location of the old one from Orix should they capture him. They could use it as a starting point. A large group like the rebels... there would be tracks. And the village at the foot of the escarpment... Questions would be asked. There would be consequences if answers weren't supplied.

"I am innocent of interference," Sheelahn said.

"How can you be innocent?" Anskar asked. "It was your functionaries—Blosius and the other one—who got in my way. Blosius did something to me, some kind of sorcery. He compelled me to come."

"Do you deny that you owe me two debts?" the Ethereal Sorceress asked.

"No, but—"

"Debts enslave," the Ethereal Sorceress said, "until they are paid."

"Unless you die beforehand," Blaice observed caustically.

"Why do you think I brought Anskar in on this," the Ethereal Sorceress said, and for the first time Anskar heard a note of irritability in her usually mellifluous voice, "if not to preserve your life?"

"Then you have more confidence in him than I do," Blaice said. "Frankly, I wasn't impressed by his earlier performance." She turned a sly look on Anskar, and as heat prickled his cheeks, she smirked. "Maybe you've matured since we last met. Gained more experience." She raised an eyebrow. "We'll have to put it to the test."

And there it was again: the feeling that someone—Blaice—was reading his mind. Was she referring to what he'd just done with Vilintia? But how would she know?

"We will not be putting anything to the test," Anskar said. And he meant it. He had found Blaice's tastes somewhat depraved. Not anything as bad as the Abbess of the Hooded One, but still depraved. His only regret was that he had succumbed the one time. He would not do so again.

"I'm hurt," Blaice said with feigned sincerity. "Another woman? She must be good in bed."

"Anskar will preserve you," the Ethereal Sorceress said, and now there was no music in her voice, only ire. "His blood will preserve you."

"My blood?"

"Where the dark now resides. Or rather, has revealed itself."

Had she seen? Had she seen what he had only felt: the dissolution of the great pit of dark-tide essence that had squatted at his core? Its shift into his veins—a move that felt more like a return?

Anskar felt the appraisal of Sheelahn's empty eyes keenly then. He was utterly exposed to them, and the realization served to increase his paranoia and his mounting sense of impotence. After finally shutting his mother out and thwarting her plans, here he was embroiled in someone else's. Was that to be his lot in life? If it was, he refused to accept it without a fight. If anything, it told him his mother's ambitions hadn't been entirely wrong. How could you oppose the tyranny of the powerful without rising to power yourself?

He tried to outstare the Ethereal Sorceress, but he grew lost in her vacant gaze and looked away.

"What do you know about me?" he asked. "What do you *think* you know?"

"That you are fitted to this task."

"And I can't refuse to go?"

"How else will you repay your debt?"

The implication was that there might be another way, but what would it entail? He thought about Blosius and what he had become. Or was there some worse form of servitude that the Ethereal Sorceress reserved for those who refused to settle their debts?

Anskar shook his head. "How many of my debts will be paid if we succeed in this task?"

"You wish to be absolved?"

Blaice scoffed, as if the idea were ludicrous.

"I do," Anskar said. "Entirely. I should never have come to you for aid."

"Yet you did," Sheelahn said. "And incurred a debt."

She stood, and her robes straightened themselves into stark lines and folds that hung too perfectly all the way to the floor.

"Return with that which I seek, and I will consider all your debts repaid."

"And with me alive," Blaice put in.

There was a slight pause before Sheelahn responded. "That would be preferable."

"I assume this is no easy task," Anskar said.

"No tasks I set are easy. But this is not impossible."

"Tell me this, first," Anskar said. "Why is Blaice so important to you?"

The Ethereal Sorceress didn't answer, merely looked at him with her empty eyes. After an uncomfortable silence, it was Blaice who spoke.

"Because I'm an asset. I owe her too many debts, and she wants to make good on her investment. This mission will make a dent, but not much more."

"How many debts do you owe her?" Anskar asked.

Blaice glanced at the Ethereal Sorceress and shrugged. "I don't think either of us can remember."

"There is a ledger," the Ethereal Sorceress said. "There is always a ledger."

"Ah, but who keeps the tally?" Blaice said. "And how can we trust them?"

"This is business," the Ethereal Sorceress said. "Business cannot long survive without trust."

"Oh, I don't know," Blaice said. "In my experience, the reverse tends to be true."

"Can you both just stop?" Anskar said. "Whatever this is about, there are more important things I have to attend to. So let's just get this over with. What is it you want us to do?"

And so Sheelahn told him.

THIRTY-THREE

SOMETHING STANK.

It couldn't be her. Last Carred checked, she didn't smell of pepper and mold and rotten fish. And if she ever had, no one had ever mentioned it. Marith would have said something, for sure.

She yawned and stretched. The bed beneath her was hard as rock, and she was stiff all over from it. Perhaps because it wasn't a bed?

She opened her eyes onto a dismal cell. Murky green light came from the walls—from some kind of slimy ochre growth that clung to them. The ceiling sagged in the middle and was both cracked and riddled with mildew.

She was lying on a stone bench. When she sat up, a chain rattled; it was attached to her ankle by a dark metal manacle. It could have been void-steel, the very substance that had gotten her into this mess. That made her check for the star-metal she'd brought to trade. Gone. Her pouch had been removed.

A squat figure sat on a stool by the opposite wall, watching her. Legs like a frog's, big bloated belly, and a man's face, pockmarked and scabbed. His hooked nose almost touched his chin, and his ears resembled trumpets.

He grunted something, stood, and walked into the wall—and right through it.

That was when Carred realized there was no door.

Standing, she approached the same wall and gingerly touched it. Solid. And slimy. She wiped her hand on her shirt, picked up the stool the squat man had been sitting on, and used it to prod the walls all around the cell. At length, she gave up. No way in or out. At least, no way for her.

She returned to her bench and sat.

So, what did she know? That she'd trespassed in something known as the "stone web." She'd been captured, first by poachers, then by three demons and a flying ball of scabby flesh. Before the ball-thing had rendered her unconscious, one of the demons had mentioned Lord Domatai, to whom she could apologize for her trespass herself. *Anything caught in the stone web belongs to the lord of the mountain.* Is that where she was now? Somewhere inside or beneath the multicolored mountain?

Not very promising if she was, though. Not if they'd stuck her in a cell and taken the one thing she might be able to bargain with: her pouch of star-metal shavings.

And what of this Lord Domatai? Was he Talia's father, the man she was meant to trade with? It would have been helpful if Talia had given her a letter of introduction, if he was. Although the way Talia spoke of her father, it was unlikely he'd read it. Talia had taken great pains to hide from him, and had used her considerable sorcerous ability to set up protective wards all around her palace in Naphor. Sometimes, Carred wondered if that was why the Queen had ordered her to share her bed: so that Carred could protect her if her father ever found her.

Nice of Talia, then, to send Carred all the way to the abyssal realms to see him. Nice to know how much she cared. The reality was, all Talia cared about was her precious son, and then only because she needed him to bring her back from the realm of the dead.

So, why go along with her schemes? Carred thought, not for the first time. All these years of service, all the while suspecting she was being used. More than suspecting: it had been obvious from the first. It showed how well Talia knew her. Knew how much Carred hoped for a free Niyas. Hoped for the greatness of her homeland to be restored. Hoped that she was needed, respected, wanted, loved—and not just an abandoned child in the woods, crying for her ragdoll.

She started at a shift in the light. The wall opposite bulged, and someone stepped through. Someone so large, he had to stoop so that his head didn't brush the ceiling.

And it was a big head: four times, at least, the size of her own, pinched and long, and impossibly old. The skin had a granular quality, like porous stone. It was a sad face, the mouth drooping, a fang-like tooth protruding on one side. But there was nothing either sad or old about the eyes: they were like crescent moons blazing violet.

His body—she couldn't tell if he was naked, because he was wearing what looked like his skeleton on the outside. It might have been an effect of his great height, but he looked emaciated, withered, and yet, at the same time, she could feel the weight of his presence, as if he were the most solid thing in the cell, or even all the worlds.

Tucked under one arm was a helm of sorts, made of bone,

with crescent eye slits and an opening for the mouth rimmed with jagged fangs and flanked by curved tusks as long as her arm. Just looking at the helm set her teeth chattering, and she looked away at the ground.

She heard the creak of ancient joints, followed by the relieved sigh of the giant seating himself on the stool opposite her bench. She risked a look. His massive head pivoted left and right as he sniffed the air, then he brought his violet eyes to bear on her. Instinctively, Carred sniffed at her armpit. Maybe it was her after all.

"You bear my daughter's taint."

Carred just stared blankly at him.

"Queen Talia of Niyas?"

"Is dead," Carred finished for him. "I saw her die."

"Indeed. I was reliably informed of the events at Naphor. But she's not quite gone, is she? She still reaches into Wiraya from the realm of the dead. Hmm? Am I right?"

Carred wracked her brains. Tell him the truth or be evasive? Or stall until she could decide?

"I assume you are Lord Domatai?"

No answer. He just held her gaze, the merest of smiles tugging at his lips.

"I didn't know I was trespassing," Carred said. "I want to apologize."

"Really, there's no need. I assume my dear, sweet Talia told you about the portal on the grounds of my mansion. I rarely use the place. Haven't done, in fact, since Talia was born. Do you know, with your luscious red skin and your black hair, you remind me of Talia's mother."

"Talia never mentioned her mother," Carred said. Admittedly, Carred rarely mentioned hers, and with good reason. "What happened to her?"

"Why, she spawned us a child, that's what. After that, I ate her. It's something of a tradition in certain dynasties. I still remember the taste: quite succulent she was, though stringy from fright. Far better to strike when the prey isn't looking, don't you think? We live and learn."

His face tightened into a grimace. "Regrettably, I also recall her bitter aftertaste. I suspect she cursed me. She was, after all, what you Niyandrians call 'moontouched.' As you can see from my infirmity, I still suffer the effects of her sorcery. So you needn't worry. Niyandrian is not a meal I intend to savor again.

"As to your apology: did Talia not mention the stones?"

"They must have slipped her mind."

"It's easily done. She was so young when she left home. The stone circles comprise a system of wards to alert against intruders coming through the portal. And of course, there are others who roam the circles looking for easy prey. We refer to them as poachers. I'm so sorry you ran into some.

"So, tell me, why are you here? And what possessed you to bring this?"

He opened a shovel-sized hand to reveal Carred's pouch of star-metal.

"I know what it contains. The star-metal burns a little, even through the pouch. So, I ask again: why did you bring it here? You've not the look of an assassin about you."

"You're right," Carred said, "about Queen Talia's taint."

"I know I am."

"I don't understand what that taint is exactly. I can't smell it or feel it, but you clearly can."

Domatai dipped his huge head modestly.

"She spoke to me through a young woman who might be

moontouched, might just be crazy."

"Perhaps a bit of both, if she can channel voices all the way from the realm of the dead," Domatai said.

"Talia told me to come here, find her father—"

"She really told you to find me? I'm touched. You're going to tell me, of course, that she was desperate. That she needed something only I could provide."

"Void-steel," Carred said.

"Well, that certainly makes sense," Domatai said. "Star-metal for void-steel. Ordinarily, it would be a good trade, but you've brought so little."

"I used some on the way here."

He studied her face with those probing violet eyes. He seemed to see everything, deep below the surface. "Yes, I'm sure you did. Well, I'll take what little you have left."

"And you'll give me void-steel?"

"What does Queen Talia of Niyas want with void-steel? It'll play havoc with her sorcery."

When Carred didn't answer at once, Domatai stood and turned to face the wall he entered through.

"Wait!" she said.

"I think not." He looked back at her, over his shoulder. "Stalling is the wrong tactic to use with me…"

"Carred. Carred Selenas."

"Oh, a gift of your name. How generous of you. But really, you ought to be more careful. It's not just demon names that grant others power over them. But don't fret, Carred, my dear, I'll not divulge your secret to anyone else here."

"It doesn't bother you that I know yours?"

"Pish," Domatai said. "The first few syllables won't give you power over me. Didn't Talia tell you what kind of lord I am?"

"I worked that out for myself."

"Besides Samal and Nysrog, there are none to rival me. A demon lord cannot be controlled using a mere fraction of his name. For that, you would require all twenty-seven syllables, and even if you possessed them, one error in pronunciation… Well, I'm sure you can appreciate the risk you would be taking."

"Please," Carred said, "let me tell you why Talia needs void-steel." She didn't want to be left alone in the cell. What if Domatai forgot about her and never returned?

He smiled, as if he felt her fear.

"We will talk about it later."

And with that, he walked through the wall.

THIRTY-FOUR

IT WAS TO THE VERY foundations of her strange building that the Ethereal Sorceress brought Anskar and Blaice, a dank chamber with a low, vaulted ceiling with struts like gray ribs. Three alchemical globes were suspended from silver chains, providing a dim but steady illumination. The chamber was defined by four arches that bore the weight of the structure above. There was no green carpet here, just a floor of gleaming obsidian. A large circle of silver-blue metal had been riveted to the center of the floor, and around its circumference were painted words in Skanuric and another language, one Anskar had hoped not to see again: Nazgrese. He understood little of Skanuric and even less of the language of demons.

But he shouldn't have been surprised to find such an inscription here, not after Sheelahn had told him and Blaice what she wanted them to do.

"And I thought you hated demons," Blaice had said.

"Your thoughts have not led you astray," the Ethereal Sorceress replied.

"But you love profit more?"

"You mean coin? There are many things more valuable, many of them not physical. Business cannot be swayed by likes and dislikes, Blaice Rancey. You of all people should know that."

The functionary with the injured leg limped from beneath one of the arches. He was carrying a small chest, which he set down on the floor outside the circle and opened. From within he removed a disk of crystal, which began to glow red as he set it upon the circle's edge. He took more disks from the chest and set them farther around the circumference, returning to the chest for more, until two dozen red disks added their glare to the light of the hanging alchemical globes.

The Ethereal Sorceress waited, silent and still, until the functionary closed the lid of his chest and took it back out through the archway.

"What now?" Blaice asked. She spoke around the fingernail she was gnawing on, but the Ethereal Sorceress ignored her, turning instead to the archway through which they had entered.

The other functionary—Blosius—approached along the corridor beyond, and he was carrying a blackwood box that reminded Anskar of the box his catalyst had been in before Luzius Landav, the sorcerer, had embedded it beneath his skin.

The Ethereal Sorceress held out her gloved hands to accept the box from Blosius.

"You will need this." Sheelahn removed a circular contraption of brass from the box and passed it to Blaice. Anskar stepped closer for a better look. "It will guide you to the star-metal. The problem I have is that a demon lord, or his minions, have infiltrated one of my depots on the mainland, and they have stolen weapons made from star-metal, which is inimical to demon-kind."

Blaice seemed familiar with the device, and flicked open its lid to reveal a face of crystal inside the brass shell. A filament of silver, like a miniature bolt of lightning, arced between the center of the crystal face and a point along its circumference. It sparked and shivered, then started to spin.

"The lodestone will stabilize once you are in the abyssal realms." Sheelahn returned the box to Blosius and walked with him back to the archway, where they conferred in murmurs.

Anskar sidled up to Blaice. Whether Sheelahn's concern was for what the demons might do with such a stockpile, or whether this was a matter of punishing them for the audacity of raiding her premises, she hadn't said.

"What's really going on here?" he whispered.

Blaice glanced at Sheelahn, then back to the lodestone. "Star-metal weapons were forged centuries ago for use in the war against the demon lord Nysrog. Without them, the people of Wiraya would have been without hope."

"Has this demon lord Sheelahn mentioned taken away the means of the world's defense in the event of another demon war? Is an invasion imminent?"

Blaice's attention was still on the lodestone. She tapped the crystal face and gave the device a gentle shake.

"Demons work on a much longer timescale to us," she said. "So if that is their plan, it doesn't mean there's an immediate threat. It could be a problem a hundred or more years from now, though. No, this is about reputation and control of the goods, as far as Sheelahn is concerned. I bet the bloody Consortium are mad about it and have pressured her into taking action."

"The Consortium again…" Anskar said.

"Best not to ask. And even if you got answers, no one of any import would admit the truth of who our rulers really are behind the scenes, nor even that the Consortium exists. You'd be labeled a madman or a fool. And if you persuaded them otherwise, you'll wind up dead or disappeared."

"How do you know this?" Anskar asked.

"I sleep with all the right people. Or the wrong ones, depending on how you want to look at it. Shush now," she warned as Sheelahn glided over to them.

"You are also going to need this," the Ethereal Sorceress said, producing another object, this time from beneath her layered robes.

It was a tiny model of the depot, exact in every detail, seemingly made from the same stone. She gave it to Anskar, and it fit snugly into the palm of his hand.

"What's it for?" he asked.

"Blaice will show you when the time is right."

"Why not just give it to me to look after?" Blaice said.

"Because you must have need of each other," the Ethereal Sorceress said. "Without the miniature depot, neither of you will return, yet if you have the depot, Blaice, along with the knowledge of how to use it…"

"I might leave poor Anskar behind? I'm hurt that you think so little of me," Blaice said.

"Anskar is necessary. Until the end of your mission, he is necessary."

"So don't get me killed," Anskar said. "Like you do everyone else."

Sheelahn turned her orichalcum mask on him. "Keep the depot safe, Anskar. Do not lose it. I am seldom given over to anger, but in such an instance…"

"Her fury would know no bounds," Blaice quipped, though she looked far from mocking. "And you had better believe it. Too many didn't in the past."

"What happened to them?" Anskar asked.

Blaice deferred to Sheelahn with a look, but the Ethereal Sorceress didn't deign to answer.

Instead, she gestured toward the center of the circle, and Blaice and Anskar took up their places.

Anskar rubbed his thumb over the tiny model of the depot. In some way he couldn't fathom, it felt a ponderous weight—not a physical weight; it was more akin to the weight of guilt, though subtly different. He turned the model over, inspecting it for any clue as to its true nature, its purpose. But then, beneath her mask, the Ethereal Sorceress began a monotonous incantation, and he pushed the model deep into his pocket.

Though Anskar couldn't understand the words Sheelahn intoned, he was reminded of the ritual he had experienced at the Abbey of the Hooded One. For someone who despised demons, Sheelahn sure had a good grasp of their language.

"Wait," he said. It wasn't just the chanting that reminded him of the Abbess's summoning of Nysrog: even the circle was similar.

Sheelahn studied him with her empty eyes. Her chanting stopped. "You are committed, Anskar DeVantte. There is no turning back now."

"But this is a circle of summoning," Anskar said.

"It is not. If you understood anything of Nazgrese," Sheelahn said, "and if you were more proficient with Skanuric, you would perceive that this circle is the reverse of a summoning circle. Its purpose is to send, not receive."

"But why not use the *izindel*?" Anskar asked—the mode of

transportation she had previously used to send him across vast distances in next to no time.

"Because there are no depots where you are going," Sheelahn said, as if it were a foolish question. "Which means no terminus. Your journey would be without end. I doubt you would like that."

The Ethereal Sorceress resumed her incantation, her voice at once sonorous and melodic, and then like light striking a prism, it seemed to fragment. One voice became two, and two became three, until the incantation became a symphony, a chorus of a hundred voices. This wasn't the barbarous chant Anskar had heard at the Abbey of the Hooded One, but a complex melody, dark and mournful, a threnody of words he almost recognized but did not. A poem beyond speech—at least any speech he had heard.

The atmosphere in the chamber grew charged and heavy. Anskar felt it as a pressure in his head, and he had to check his nose repeatedly to see if it was bleeding. He glanced at Blaice, who was grimacing, one hand clenching and unclenching, the other clutching the circular lodestone.

Menselas, why did I agree to this?

Because he'd been given no choice, that was why.

Anskar's throat tightened to the point he found it hard to swallow. White-hot needles of pain lanced his scalp, and he jerked, then started to shudder. They pierced the skin of his face, his arms, his chest, back, and legs. As invisible spears perforated his flesh, Anskar tried to scream. *I won't go! This is madness. I won't go!*

Beside him, Blaice seemed to thrash, though she was standing perfectly still. Her face stretched and distorted. Her limbs grew impossibly long, then undulated as they began to fade along with the rest of her.

This was sorcery beyond any Anskar had experienced. Was

Sheelahn a sorcerer become almost a goddess, like Queen Talia? Or something altogether different?

He flung out his senses on instinct, and at first they failed him. He winced at a twist of pain from the flaccid remnants of his braided repository. But then a different sense responded, at once old and new. Not from any repository this time; it was as though a dark and inky vein peeled away from beneath his skin and lashed toward the Ethereal Sorceress. He caught a brief snatch of the complex mesh of forces—dusk and dawn and dark and something else—something that permeated all three, or encompassed them and bound them all together... But then a wall snapped down inside the Ethereal Sorceress, and his thread of awareness whiplashed back into him.

He saw then that Blaice was gone, vanished into the air.

Anskar glanced at his hands—ghost-like. He could see the bones. He forced open his mouth to scream, and his jaw fell all the way to the floor. He disgorged the words of his protest, as if birthing boulders from his mouth. "I won't go!" he said again. "I. Won't. Go..."

His voice was an echo from another room, another place.

Another world.

Crushing force pressed in on him from every side, shrinking him, squeezing him, compacting him.

He became aware of a pinprick of darkness where his feet should have been. It hungered for him, sucked at him. He tried to pull back, but there was nothing left of him to resist with. The pressure was relentless, and it was still mounting. The pinprick of darkness was an infinitesimal point drawing him in; but it was also a yawning void—he had no sense of proportion.

All he had was agony and panic and horror.

And then, with a crunch, the void consumed him.

THIRTY-FIVE

ANSKAR COULD SMELL FEAR, CONFUSION, resentment. It wasn't his own. Odd he should scent emotion, but it didn't feel entirely unnatural. And he could smell something else, too, though at the same time, as with emotion, it didn't have an odor in the ordinary sense of the word. He could smell darkness.

A darkness that churned and seethed and bubbled. A darkness that defined him.

A darkness that swelled and popped.

Anskar slopped to his knees upon unforgiving ground.

The model of the depot in his pocket felt heavy beyond belief, and it was burning hot.

He shielded his eyes from the glare—red turning into bronze, then back again. He risked opening his eyes to slits.

Blaice was a silhouette looming over him, backlit by a crimson sky across which clouds of many colors scudded.

Anskar knelt upon porous, jagged rock glittering with crystals that reflected all the burning colors of the clouds. Shimmering plains extended for miles in every direction, broken only by outcroppings of rock and long, low mesas of the same perforated limestone. Pillars touched the sky, as if they were the only thing stopping it from falling. Ripples of light ran across the sparkling ground, giving the impression of water.

A vast alien sun throbbed with bronze light. Wind gusted, hot and scorching, reminding him of the tides he no longer greeted.

He tried to stand, but the weight of the mini depot kept him pinned. He tugged with all his strength, but his hand was stuck, as if the depot weighed as much as a mountain.

Blaice chuckled as she stooped down, and her fingers touched parts of the model in sequence. It whirred and clicked, and its heat turned to cold.

"Here you go," she said, lifting the model as if it weighed no more than a feather. She inspected it for a moment, then tossed it back to him. Anskar caught it and stood, turning the model over and over in his hands.

"Make sure you don't lose it," Blaice said. "That's our only way back."

"What did you just do to it?"

She touched a finger to the side of her nose. "Knowledge is a privilege."

He thrust the mini depot into a pocket. "If we're to work together…" he began.

"All I'm prepared to say for now is that this is how it always begins—how the Ethereal Sorceress and her friends in shadowy places expand into new markets. Though I'm less and less certain that profit is her motive."

"She plans to trade with the abyssal realms?"

Blaice smiled, then gazed off into the far distance, drinking in the view.

"It looks different from the last time I was here," Anskar said, still shielding his eyes from the strange light. He had passed through the abyssal realms briefly once before, an experience he had not planned to repeat.

"This is Vulthanor," Blaice said. "There are many abyssal realms; hence the plural."

Anskar blinked against the glare of the bronze sun, then found himself staring at the seven-pointed star tattooed on Blaice's neck.

"Insurance," she said, touching her fingertips to the star. "Sheelahn might have every confidence in your ability to keep me alive, but I do not."

"Thanks," Anskar said.

"You're welcome."

Blaice opened her palm to reveal the circular lodestone the Ethereal Sorceress had given her. The lid sprang open, and Blaice turned a slow circle as she studied the crystal face.

"So what is it—a ward?" Anskar said, meaning the star tattoo.

"Can't you work it out for yourself?" Blaice said, still turning, still studying the lodestone. "You're the sorcerer."

Anskar reached out with a gossamer thread of dark-tide that peeled away from beneath his skin and darted at Blaice's star. And whiplashed back into him.

"Well, that's encouraging," Blaice said. "I was starting to think the Orgols had ripped me off."

"Orgols?"

"Half Orgols, actually. Associates of mine from back in Atya."

"Those two women? I remember."

"Orgols are unsurpassed at sorcery," Blaice said. "And this pair, half-bloods though they may be, claimed to have firsthand experience of demons—and not just the brute guardian demons you encounter in ruins, either: higher-order demons with a good grasp of the dark-tide and an ability to scent fear from a mile away, like a sharp-tooth scents blood in the water."

"And this tattoo prevents them doing that?"

"For me it does. You'll have to rely on your own means. Just don't use the dusk- and the dawn-tides, though. Not here. Those tides are inimical to demons and will make even the dumbest lesser demon aware of your presence."

"Not much chance of that," Anskar said. "My catalyst was removed. I have no dawn- or dusk-tide ability now."

"Voluntarily?"

He nodded.

"Interesting," Blaice said. "Yet you still probed my ward with something, and I can imagine what. Sheelahn said you were suited to this task, and I'm starting to see what she meant."

Blaice pocketed the lodestone and started walking.

She was a lot sharper than she looked. Anskar licked his lips, cast a look around, and then hurried after her, feeling like a sheep being led to the slaughter. "You called this place Vulthanor," he said. "Have you been here before?"

"This is my first time," Blaice said. "Do you recall your first time? Judging by your fumbling, I'd hazard a guess it was me."

Heat prickled Anskar's cheeks, and it wasn't from the wind. "You were not," he said.

"Then I pity the poor woman who was."

"She had no complaints." At least he didn't think she did.

Sareya had been hungry for him, insatiable. Until they had stopped seeing one another in that fashion. But then, Sareya had changed so much since Anskar had been away in Thousand Lakes. She showed no signs of hunger for him now. Quite the opposite. He started to wonder if Blaice were right, if Sareya had been disappointed in him, but then he saw Blaice watching him with an amused glint in her eye. She knew she'd touched a nerve. She'd won their little joust.

"But back to Vulthanor," Blaice said. "Sheelahn may have spared you some of the details of our quest, on account of you playing the role of a grunt, but Vulthanor is apparently on the cusp of the realm of Shimrax, where demons are exiled, though what they do to deserve such a fate, I have no idea. Shimrax is about as low as you can go in terms of the demonic hierarchy."

"So this is a lowly realm?" Anskar asked. He assumed the higher-order demons inhabited the higher realms, which implied that the threats they would face in Vulthanor would be somewhat diminished.

"Vulthanor means 'dung heap' in Nazgrese," Blaice said. "But even dung heaps in the abyssal realms are presided over by a demon lord."

"A lesser lord?" Anskar asked.

"Is there such a thing? You seem quite the expert on demons, Anskar. Why is that?"

"I..." He clamped his mouth shut. He wasn't falling for her bait again. The less she knew about his time at the Abbey of the Hooded One—the less anyone knew—the better.

As they walked, Blaice sporadically checked the lodestone, and each time Anskar glanced over her shoulder at the crystal face. The silver filament no longer shivered erratically; it was a solid line now, always pointing the way directly ahead.

Hour after hour they went on, the ground beneath their boots hard and ungiving. Anskar felt heavier somehow, as if the red sky were a weight pressing down on him, and his hair grew hot under the sun.

Mineral deposits in the rocks all around them glittered with every conceivable color. The few plants they saw were as tall as trees, with long, drooping petals bristling with thorns. Crab-like creatures the size of a hand clustered together beneath the umbrella formed by the petals, and their shells had a metallic tint, sometimes bronze, sometimes brass, sometimes silver. They had sinuous tails, segmented and ending in a bony hook.

"We should have brought water," Anskar said. His mouth was dry and his lips cracked and sore.

"There'll be water soon enough," Blaice said. She had removed her leather jacket and now carried it slung over her shoulder. Her black shirt clung to her body, heavy with sweat, and her pace had slowed appreciably.

"Did Sheelahn tell you that?"

"Allegedly, the city stands at the hub of eight canals."

Canals. Again he was reminded of his void-steel ingots and *nietan* horn, probably resting somewhere in the muck at the bottom of a canal. He hoped that was where his sack was, at any rate, and safe. "So a city is our destination," Anskar said.

"Artuum-Nak'Urdim. The Mountain of Plenty. Where did you think we were going? Did you expect the stockpile of star-metal to be buried in the middle of nowhere?"

"I don't know what I expected. I hadn't really thought about it."

Blaice gave a weary sigh and patted him on the head. "Then it's a good job you've got me, isn't it?"

"I still don't understand why demons want star-metal if it's so harmful to them."

"Don't our healers always strive to understand diseases and poisons and all the things that do us harm? The principle's the same."

"The priests of the Elder say star-metal fell from the sky over many thousands, if not millions, of years," Anskar said.

Blaice rolled her eyes. "Hence the name. How's that model depot? Still in your pocket?"

"Of course."

For the past hour they had been drawing nearer to one of the tabletop mountains that blistered the plains. This one was much broader than most they had seen, though it only rose to a height of maybe a hundred feet. Checking the lodestone once more, Blaice led them through a narrow, winding pass, where there was blessed shelter from the burning winds and the glare of the bronze sun.

On the far side, the ground dipped into a vast basin that filled the space between the mesa they had just passed beyond and a sweeping escarpment opposite, which was shaped like a horseshoe. Within the basin, water glimmered, changing color as it reflected the racing clouds. Already, Blaice was hurrying toward the water.

"Is it safe to drink?" Anskar asked, jogging to keep up with her. An odor like rotting eggs came from the water.

"We'll find out soon enough," Blaice said. She flung down her jacket at the lake's edge, dropped to her knees, and scooped water into her mouth with cupped hands.

Unable to endure his thirst a moment longer, Anskar abandoned his concerns about the quality of the water and started to drink. The water had been kept cool by the shade of the surrounding mesas, and he sighed as he gulped it down despite the metallic taste.

Blaice took off her boots and dangled her feet in the lake. "See there," she said, pointing across the lake to the far side, where the water flowed in a broad channel through the rock face. "Must be one of the canals."

"It leads to the city?"

Blaice shrugged. "I guess. This must be some kind of reservoir."

Anskar's stomach rumbled. Now that they had stopped, he realized just how hungry he was.

Blaice gave him a mischievous look. "I've got something you could eat."

"You have?"

She rolled her eyes, and heat rushed to Anskar's face.

"You didn't complain before," she said.

"Yes, well, that was before," Anskar said.

He wished he was back at the rebel camp right now. If only he'd caught up with Orix and persuaded him to return…

"I was joking, stupid man," Blaice said, slapping him on the arm. "If you think I want to be getting up to funny business out here, you're dumber than you look. Did you see those crab things earlier? Makes you wonder what other nasties are creeping around, just waiting to take a nip at our sweating, naked flesh."

Anskar looked around and saw nothing save for a rippling of the water and tiny bubbles a mere few yards from where they were sitting. Blaice saw too and quickly removed her feet from the water.

"Come on," she said, pulling on her boots. "We should get going. Maybe they'll have a restaurant at Artuum-Nak'Urdim. It is, after all, the Mountain of Plenty."

"Yes," Anskar said. "But plenty of what?"

"You've a filthy mind!" Blaice said.

"That's not what I… Oh, forget it!"

Blaice took them on a course around the lake, skirting the water, which continued to ripple from time to time. Once, Anskar saw something sinuous break the surface, though it was too far out to see what, and it quickly ducked back under.

Even though they kept to the shade of the mesa walls, sweat poured from Anskar's forehead and stung his eyes; and though they were sheltered from the wind, still there was an abrasive quality to the hot air, which had grown stultifying within the basin's ambit.

It took them the best part of an hour—at least Anskar estimated it to be about an hour, though time seemed to move at a different rate here, judging by the position of the sun, which had remained stationary ever since they had arrived. It was a surprise, then, as they approached the channel through the opposing mesa to the one they had entered from when darkness fell with the swiftness of an axe blade. Not an absolute darkness. It wasn't even black, but more of a deep jade, heavy and oppressive. It felt almost solid.

Something screeched overhead, and Blaice swore. "I thought we had longer till nightfall. We should find cover."

Moving slowly now, owing to the poor light, they entered the rift between the mesa walls and followed the course of the canal. Overhead, a pallid disk now stood in place of the sun—in the exact same place, as if nightfall had somehow transformed the sun into a moon.

Again a screech sounded from overhead, and this time it was followed by a cry that sounded almost human. Something huge and winged passed across the face of the moon, and in its talons a smaller creature thrashed and struggled. All Anskar could see was its silhouette: two arms and two legs. A person? He recalled something Malady the demon had told him: *If you were to linger too long in the abyssal realms, every demon within a hundred miles would pick up your stench.*

So why hadn't they? Blaice had her star tattoo, but what

about him?

"In here," Blaice said.

She had spotted the dark mouth of a cave in the mesa wall. Then Anskar noticed: there were hundreds of openings in the wall ahead of them on the left-hand side, but whether they were natural vents for lava or water, he couldn't say. They seemed too uniform for either.

He followed Blaice inside, then bumped into her because she had stopped.

"What is it?" he asked.

"Can you summon light?"

He almost reached for his braided repository. "Not anymore. But I can see well enough to guide us."

His ability to see in the dark had improved with the change that had come over his eyes since his Niyandrian captors had altered them—or revealed them for what they really were.

"After you, then," Blaice said, and Anskar took the lead.

The interior of the cave appeared in varying shades of gray to his altered sight. The walls, floor, and ceiling had the consistency of a desiccated sponge; and it was more of a passageway through the body of the mesa than a cave.

The beat of leathery wings caused Anskar to turn back towards the entrance. A shadow swooped across the opening, and a shrill screech followed in its wake.

"What can you see?" Blaice asked. She fumbled for Anskar's hand and, when she found it, gripped it tightly. She was trembling.

"Just a passageway," Anskar said. "It turns a corner a few dozen yards ahead of us."

"Let's go, then," she said. "Before one of those things from outside gets daring."

"It's not like you to be scared," Anskar said.

"How would you feel if you couldn't see? I like seeing. It's others who are usually left in the dark."

Anskar led her to the bend in the tunnel, then cursed as he trod in something soft. Phosphorescent lime-colored spores puffed into the air, and he covered his mouth and nose as he took a step back.

"Some kind of fungus," Blaice said, releasing his hand and covering her own mouth and nose as she watched the shimmering spores float gently down to the ground, where their light instantly went out.

"Are they poisonous?" Anskar asked.

"In my experience, it's always best to assume so."

She took hold of his hand once more once the passage through the rock had returned to gray for Anskar, and for Blaice, he assumed, pitch black.

Together they rounded the corner and the tunnel widened, eventually opening into a cavern, the walls of which Anskar couldn't see, it was so vast.

"What is it?" Blaice asked.

"A cathedral cavern, I think. Should we stop here and rest?"

"I don't want to go any deeper," Blaice said. "Not without light."

"Then why don't you try to get some sleep?" Anskar said. "I'll keep watch."

What he really wanted was some time in which to explore the dark-tide that had shifted within him, becoming part of his blood. Perhaps some intuition would strike him, some means of brightening the darkness around them. It seemed unlikely, though. Light, he had to assume, was antithetical to the dark-tide. Or was it, if Zek had been right about all the tides originating from the same source?

He regretted the removal of his catalyst. In fact, the gloom and the screeching of winged creatures outside was making him wish he hadn't had his mother exorcized either. If anyone could have guided him in such a place, he felt certain it was Queen Talia.

"It's too dark to sleep," Blaice said.

"You need to see in your sleep?"

"You know what I mean. I don't want to wake up and find you've left me alone in here. I might never find my way out."

"I'm not like you," Anskar said. "I would never do that."

"Even so, we sit and we wait, and you bloody well make sure I can feel where you are. Actually, I've an idea about that." She fumbled for his chest and Anskar slapped her hand away.

And then a thought struck Anskar.

"What about the lodestone?" He didn't need to say anything else for Blaice to grasp his meaning.

"Idiot!" she said. "Me, not you. Well, both of us, maybe."

Taking the metal casing from her pocket, she flipped open the lid and was immediately rewarded with the silvery glow of the filament that pointed the way. It wasn't much—a candle's glow against a sea of darkness—but in its scant illumination, Anskar saw the smile of relief it brought to Blaice's face.

"Maybe I'll take that sleep after all," she said, settling down on the hard floor and folding her jacket to use as a pillow. "Wake me as soon as it's light outside. Shouldn't be more than an hour or two."

Anskar lowered himself beside her, orienting himself so that he sat facing the passage they had entered by. Blaice fidgeted and shifted in search of a comfortable position, and when at last she found one, she sighed. Soon after, her breathing settled into a gentle rhythm.

And so Anskar turned his focus inwards, towards the dark-tide flowing through his veins. At first he had thought that it had mingled with his blood, but now he perceived it differently: it *was* his blood, or at least a constituent of his blood.

And it felt quite natural, as if this was its true state rather than being corralled within a fathomless reservoir beneath his dawn- and dusk-tide repositories. If anything, *that* had felt contrived, unnatural, the work of someone else. But he'd not known that at the time. He'd just assumed that was the way it was meant to be: three repositories of different—yet related?—powers lying within, waiting to be recognized and tamed. Although the dark had never seemed amenable to taming. It had shown an inclination to do as it wished, to dominate rather than be bridled.

So the dark-tide was in his blood—*was* in some way his blood. *His blood will preserve you,* the Ethereal Sorceress had said. How many layers of concealment had his mother wrapped him in? How deep did this go? He'd always assumed he'd inherited his dark-tide ability from Queen Talia, but the dark-tide wasn't common among Niyandrians. Save for Sareya, he had sensed none within anyone else. Yet Sareya's dark-tide potential was minuscule compared to his, a mere fissure within her, for the most part untapped. It seemed, if anything, an opening onto something else. Or perhaps it was a flaw, some kind of inner scar that had allowed something alien to enter her? Sareya had experienced great trauma as a child, and it couldn't have been easy at Branil's Burg, with people like Tion taking advantage of her. So was that how dark-tide ability started: with suffering?

That answer didn't satisfy him. It might explain Sareya, but it didn't account for his blood. He clenched up with what felt like anger, then realized it was fear.

A door slammed on his speculation. What did it matter

where his dark-tide ability came from? All he needed was to master its use.

He tried once more to lay hold of the dark-tide and shape it as he had been able to before, but still it eluded him. Perhaps if he pricked his finger... made use of his blood, accessed the darkness directly? He had half a mind to draw his sword and break the skin of his finger along *Amalantril's* ever-keen edge, but that seemed sick somehow. Depraved. It was bad enough what Eadgith had taught him about the use of life to pay the cost of earth-tide sorcery; what Noni had shown him with her mice. But this was worse. It was a slippery slope when a sorcerer started to use his own blood.

And then he noticed an absence. At first he couldn't say what it was, but as he let his senses roam free within him, he realized his guts were free of corruption. He panicked then. First the dark-tide out of reach, and now this: the absence of the earth-tide. It had been a tangible force within him before they had left Wiraya. Perhaps there was no earth-tide in the abyssal realms?

How quickly he had gone from having control of four sorcerous currents to having control of none. And to realize his absolute impotence here of all places, surrounded by the dark, with winged predators patrolling the skies outside! All he had left now were the skills of a knight, skills honed by an Order he no longer believed in.

A sharp exhalation from somewhere in front made him grasp *Amalantril's* hilt.

Blaice sat bolt upright. "What was that?" she whispered.

Anskar glared at the passageway, straining to see.

At first there was nothing but layers of gray, but then, out of the gloom loped a figure, mannish yet with yellow eyes that gleamed in the darkness and skin a darker gray than its surroundings, bristling with thorny spines. Its jaws opened as it exhaled again, revealing jagged teeth and a flicking, sinuous tongue.

A lesser demon—like the ones Braga had saved him from when he fled the Abbey of the Hooded One. Poor Braga.

Slowly Anskar stood so he could draw his sword. Blaice rose beside him, shrugging into her coat. The silver glow of the lodestone in her hand cast her face in shadow and glinted from her nose piercings. With her free hand, she took a pouch from one of her jacket's many pockets.

A scuff from behind made Anskar turn.

Another of the spine-covered creatures was creeping up from behind.

"Demons," Blaice said, using her teeth to loosen the pouch's drawstring.

"You don't say." Anskar did his best to keep both creatures in sight. They faltered as Blaice got her pouch fully open.

"Lesser demons," she said dismissively. "Bottom of the pecking order. The last demon I faced was much more impressive, but even he was burned and blinded by star-metal." She shook the pouch. "I've enough shavings left for both of them."

A third demon emerged from the darkness.

"Shit," Blaice said.

Then a fourth, a fifth, a sixth… They kept on coming out of the shadows, dozens upon dozens of hissing, snarling forms.

Blaice tucked her pouch back away inside her jacket. "No point wasting the shavings. There's too many of them."

"What do we do?" Anskar asked as the demons encircled them. They stank of rotting meat, and their yellow eyes burned with hatred and something else…

Lust, he realized to his horror; for now they were nearer, he saw that each of the demons was shamelessly, all too visibly, aroused. What the demons would do to them once they were overrun, he didn't want to think about.

"Do something!" Blaice hissed at him. "You're supposed to be the sorcerer."

"I trained as a knight," Anskar said. "Not a sorcerer. And I no longer have a catalyst."

"Bet you regret that now. Do something else, then. Sheelahn sent you along to keep me alive, remember. So keep me alive."

Anskar feinted with his sword towards one of the demons. It hissed and took a step back. He reached inside with his senses, tried once more to gain control over the dark-tide flowing through him, and again he failed.

The demon he had driven back advanced once more. Anskar lunged for its chest, but it was fast—far quicker than he could have imagined—and it slid around his blade and leapt at him.

Anskar pivoted, and Blaice stabbed the demon in the face with a dagger he'd not seen her draw. Purplish blood gushed. The demon dropped into a crouch. It lifted a taloned hand to its face, tasted its own blood, and grinned.

The other demons surrounding them took that as a signal. Abandoning their caution, they shrieked as they swarmed over Blaice and Anskar.

THIRTY-SIX

ANSKAR CAUGHT ONE OF THE demons coming in and raked his blade across its chest, but then it was on him. Hands wrapped around his throat, throttling him. He struck two more demons, drawing purple blood, and then went down as more demons piled on top. He heard Blaice scream. Heard the lustful hoots and growls of the demons, felt their urgency.

"Menselas!" Anskar cried. "Menselas!"

The pressure suddenly relented, and the demons fell away from him, leaving him gasping and panting beside Blaice on the rocky floor.

Surely not! Menselas had heard his prayer? And responded?

There had been a voice, he was certain of it. Amid the cacophony of howls and roars, his own and Blaice's screaming, he had heard a man's voice, deep and rumbling and stern.

Blaice rolled to her knees and stood. Her hair had been pulled from its braids and stood out in a frizzy halo. Her jacket had been ripped in several places, and she was white-faced and breathing hard, but otherwise unscathed.

Anskar pushed himself to a sitting position, reclaimed his sword, and stood. He looked for the owner of the voice.

At first he could see nothing but the ravenous demons surrounding them, straining towards him and Blaice, apparently restrained by some invisible force. But then the demons on one side parted, and a tall man came through.

At least Anskar thought it was a man. But it was taller than any man he had seen—at least two feet taller than he was, and he was by no means short. In the scant light from Blaice's lodestone, the man-thing's skin appeared gray and abrasively grainy. He had long, oily hair, intricately braided with silver ribbons, and unlike the spine-covered lesser demons, he was clothed: coarse-woven and much-patched pants, buttoned up at the sides; a frayed woolen jerkin; the tattered remnants of a high-collared cape; and turn-down boots that came up to its knees, scuffed and riddled with holes. But it was the eyes that gave it away: the same searing yellow as the lesser demons, though these eyes were not bestial; they conveyed a fierce intelligence and a slyness that went way beyond brute cunning.

His thin-lipped mouth parted and a slew of words tumbled out—the rumbling bass Anskar had heard amid the commotion, the words gargled and barbarous. He should have known! Menselas wouldn't answer his prayer—not after the things he'd done. Not after he had reneged on the simple vows he'd made to the Order.

"A higher demon," Blaice whispered. "That's all we need. At least those other demons aren't defiling us."

The lesser demons snarled and growled, but the newcomer clapped his hands and they prostrated themselves on the floor and started to gibber.

The higher demon's gaze fell upon Blaice briefly, and his face twisted into the semblance of a smile. He looked her up and down, shaking as he chuckled—a gurgling, throaty sound.

And then he focused on Anskar, nostrils flaring, and he took an eager step toward him.

"What here have we?" the demon said in broken Nan-Rhouric, pausing to widen his eyes at Anskar to see if he was impressed with his language skills. His tongue darted rapidly and repeatedly between his lips, his gurgling laughter interspersed with slurping, sucking noises that recalled the sound of a draining ditch. "What bring me my hunters?"

The demon stepped even closer, then sniffed at Anskar's chest, his throat, his mouth.

"That smell know I. Fear, yes, it fears, but more just than fear. Something else I know."

Anskar stepped back, but he could go no further without treading on one of the prostrate lesser demons. He brought *Amalantril* up between him and the higher-order demon.

The demon extended a taloned finger, touched it to the keen edge of the blade, then snatched the finger away and sucked at it, purplish blood staining his lips. "Star-metal?" He took a wary step back.

Anskar felt the seethe of dark-tide within the demon—not a repository, for he could sense none; as with himself, the demon's dark-tide essence originated in its blood.

But star-metal? Of course! Star-metal was one of the elements of the astrumium shavings Luzius Landav had brought to Branil's Burg, and Anskar had melted it into the steel of his sword.

But before he could gain confidence, the dark-tide surged from within the demon and a blade of shadow appeared in his hand—a blade that continued to grow until it was almost twice the length of *Amalantril*. The demon extended his shadow blade so that its tip touched Anskar's throat.

Out of the corner of his eye, Anskar glimpsed Blaice reach inside her jacket. The demon noticed too and turned his yellow eyes on her.

"Show," he said. "Pocket what you have in."

Blaice frowned, pretending she didn't understand. Before the demon could press its demand, Anskar blurted, "What is it you think you smell on me?"

"Think?" the demon said. "Think I do not. Know I do."

"You said you could smell fear," Anskar said, "but you're wrong about that, just as you're wrong if you think you can speak Nan-Rhouric properly."

Not strictly true. Anskar was terrified, close to panic, but doing his best to disguise it with arrogance, with anger. The important thing was to distract the demon from whatever it was Blaice was trying to do.

"Half-blood you is," the demon said, then frowned. "Half-blood you are."

Anskar bit down his automatic response: that he was not Niyandrian—because he was. He had accepted that now. He drew his shoulders back and was about to say "So?" when the demon corrected itself.

"Not half… less than half. But you mixed, no? Yes, mixed you is—are."

"Oh, he's got Niyandrian blood all right," Blaice said. She had one hand behind her back, and Anskar did his best not to give it away. He kept his eyes fixed on the demon. "But you'll never guess which Niyandrian."

Anskar flashed her a glare. What game was Blaice playing?

Why reveal who he was to this demon?

"Niyandrian, Soreshi, Traguh-raj, Inkan-Andil… all matter not," the demon said. "All weak. All worthless. Demon blood… That what matter. And not low order. This high." The gurgling laugh took on a triumphant note.

"Demon?" Blaice frowned at Anskar.

"What are you talking about?" Anskar said. He clenched up inside. He already knew. The speculation he'd shut the door on—he'd seen where it led. The dark-tide in his veins shivered and seemed to pulse more strongly.

"But high how much?" the demon said. "A lord, think I. A lord! Which lord, though?"

He made a sharp swipe with his shadow sword, and Anskar yelped as the blade broke the skin of his neck. Faster than he should have been able to move, the demon lunged forward and grabbed a fistful of Anskar's hair, then sniffed at his jugular.

The demon stepped back, yellow eyes wide.

And Blaice cried out, "Hey!"

The demon spun toward her, and Blaice flung shavings of silver in its face—star-metal. There was a blinding flash, and the demon howled, and in the same instant, Anskar swung *Amalantril* with such force, he sheered straight through the demon's neck. Purple blood spurted into the air. The demon's head hit the ground first, then his body jerked and shuddered and collapsed. It twitched for a few moments, and then it was still.

There was a sudden commotion as the lesser demons who had lain prostrate around them screeched and howled. They leapt to their feet and fled.

"Well done," Anskar muttered, without looking at Blaice. He felt as though he had a mouthful of sand. A fist of ice gripped his heart first, then his lungs. What the demon had said… He still wanted to dismiss it as a lie, but his body—*his body!*—recognized the truth, and had done for some time. His eyes were fixed to the demon's severed head as whorls of dark vapor seeped from its mouth, nose and eyes.

"But now we're out of star-metal shavings," Blaice said. "I was saving them for…" She broke off. "Are you all right?"

Anskar didn't answer. He couldn't. Without knowing why, he ran his blade along his forearm, drawing blood, and then pressed his cut against the weeping, severed neck of the demon.

Blood against blood. Essence against essence.

Threads of dark-tide essence peeled away from his veins—dozens of them. They thrashed about his body, and he glanced at Blaice, as if she could help him; as if she could explain what was happening to him. But then he realized, by the way she frowned and then shrugged, that she couldn't see what he could see.

"Anskar? Hello? Is there anyone there?"

Anskar gasped as the dark-tide threads whiplashed toward the demon's head. Where they struck, the threads wormed their way into the demon's skull, then converged upon what seemed to Anskar's senses a pit of bubbling acid. The threads twisted together and plunged into the pit, and Anskar screamed. Lightning streaked through his veins. His back arched and he threw his arms out as he shook violently. And then dark-tide poured along his threads, flooding him. And not just the dark-tide: something else came with it—fear and rage, urges and lusts. Then came memories, fleeting and ephemeral. Then knowledge too fast to absorb.

The threads withdrew from the demon's skull and whipped back into Anskar. He lowered his arms and turned a blank gaze on Blaice.

"What just happened?" she asked.

Anskar shuddered. He opened his mouth to speak, but no words came. His tongue felt thick and awkward, as if it were no longer his. His body, too. He took a faltering step toward Blaice, and his knees buckled. He would have fallen had she not caught him.

But then he felt the rush of the blood in his veins. It scoured like fragments of glass, briefly it burned, and finally it settled until everything felt normal once more.

But he had changed. At first he didn't know how, but some instinct caused him to raise his hand. A dark flame sprang up on the palm.

Blaice gasped. She could see it this time.

With a thought, Anskar quelled the flame. Another thought, and it returned. Dark-tide sorcery.

"Did you just...?" Blaice started. She hesitated when Anskar met her gaze. "Did you absorb something from that demon?"

"No," Anskar said. And then he laughed with elation. "No, I did not. I absorbed everything—his essence, his memories. Who he was."

Blaice swallowed and took a tentative step towards him. "His power?"

Anskar couldn't answer that. It was too early to know. All the things he had taken from the demon were within him somewhere, but he couldn't locate them. He had glimpsed the demon's memories, but now they seemed lost. He had felt the warring emotions that smashed against the cage of reason the demon had built to contain them, but nothing of them remained. He felt only calm. Calmer than he had ever been.

There was something else different about him, too. He turned his senses inwards and perceived it at once. The dark-tide in his blood no longer slipped through his fingers. When he reached for it with his mind, he could grasp it, weave it into patterns, mold it. And he didn't need to figure calculations and speak cants to effect it, to shape the power. He just… willed it.

He raised his arm and wreathed it in shadow, and Blaice looked at him with fear in her eyes. Another thought, and the shadows seeped back beneath his skin.

Blaice's eyes widened. "Your throat," she said. "Where the demon's blade broke your skin…"

Anskar touched the spot with his fingers, expecting it to sting, expecting the feel of congealing blood. But there was nothing, not even a scratch.

"Has that happened before?" Blaice asked. "Have you healed like that?"

"Never." Anskar became aware that he was sweating. His hands were trembling. "Malady, the dwarf-demon who was with Carred Selenas…"

"After we escaped from Yustanwyrd," Blaice said. "I remember."

"She said that demons evolved by absorbing the essence of those above them." *There is always some lesser demon skulking in the shadows, stalking us and waiting for just the right opportunity.*

Blaice didn't say anything. She didn't need to. She'd heard what the demon had said about the blood flowing through his veins. She wasn't stupid.

"Your mother was the Necromancer Queen," Blaice said. "So, your father…"

"It wasn't him," Anskar said. "Vihtor Ulnar was no demon spawn."

"The Seneschal of Niyas was your…?" Blaice looked impressed. "Then it must have been her—Queen Talia. Well, that explains a lot: a necromancer and a demon."

"But how much of a demon?" Anskar wondered aloud. His mother had passed as a Niyandrian.

He became aware of the lesser demons creeping out of the gloom once more. Feral glances passed between them as they grew in confidence. They started to fan out, teeth bared, tongues flicking.

Without a thought, streams of shadow burst forth from Anskar's fingers, and he cracked them like a whip. The demons shrieked and howled and scattered back into the dark.

"I guess they know who's boss now," Blaice said. She put the lodestone back in her pocket.

"What do we do now?" Anskar asked. He needed time to experiment with his newfound dark-tide control, but out here with danger all around, it wasn't likely.

"We repay our debts—a task that might just have become that much easier. I assume this is what Sheelahn meant about your blood." She angled a look down the tunnel they had entered by. "It's growing light outside."

"You said it wouldn't be long."

"This isn't Wiraya, you know. Time works differently in the abyssal realms. If Sheelahn's to be believed, we could have been away for days already, if not weeks. Or maybe even a few minutes. Come on, let's get out of here."

Anskar followed Blaice down the gloomy length of the tunnel until they emerged in the valley between the mesas. He glanced back in case the lesser demons had once more found their courage, but there was no sign of them. No sign either of the winged creatures that had stalked the night sky. Instead he saw only the bronze sun, and clouds shifting in color from lavender to rose, shimmering with prismatic brilliance that was reflected by the crystal deposits that encrusted the rocky ground.

"This way," Blaice said, not using her lodestone this time. She headed towards what looked like steps hewn into the face of the mesa they had emerged from.

As they climbed, they spoke about the demon Anskar had slain and somehow absorbed. "It must have been a rogue, an outcast," Blaice said. "Higher-order demons like that are creatures of law and community. It must have fallen out of favor with the local demon lord or committed some crime. Lucky for him he wasn't exiled to Shimrax."

"Do demons have laws that can be broken?" Anskar asked.

"From what I've heard, there are more laws here in the abyssal realms than even in the statute books of the Order of Eternal Vigilance."

By the time they reached the mesa's summit, they were both breathing heavily and soaked with sweat. Together they stood at the edge, gazing out across the hazy distance. The valley they had been following led onto a vast, open plain, where in the far distance stood what appeared to be a lone mountain. Only it was a mountain bedizened with all the colors of a rainbow as, like the mineral deposits, it reflected the light of the clouds illuminated by the sun.

"What's that?" Anskar asked, pointing at the shimmering lines that radiated from the base of the mountain like the spokes of a wheel; they extended for miles in every direction, and one led into the valley between the mesas they had earlier been following.

"Canals," Blaice said, with a satisfied grunt. She seemed to know where she was now. "All eight of them, leading to and from Artuum-Nak'Urdim."

"That mountain's the city?"

"What did you expect, another Sansor? Or thatched roofs and wattle and daub? Didn't I say it was called the Mountain of Plenty?"

"And over there, to the—is that west?"

"It's hard to tell, with the sun not moving," Blaice said. She visored her eyes and peered into the far distance to their left. "Oh ho," she said. "Pity the poor fool who goes that way…" Then she frowned at Anskar. "Unless they're a demon, of course."

"Why?"

"Tell me what you see," she said.

"Circles. Are they stones?" All he could see was specks from this distance. "But they must be massive, and the circles within circles they form…"

"Like ripples after you throw a pebble in a lake," Blaice said. "Only in this case, they spread out from the locus of a transfer, if you'll excuse my Skanuric."

"A what?"

"I've seen something like this in one or two of the ancient ruins—the ones that date back to the demon wars. That is one of the two poles of a portal. The other, I assume, is somewhere on Wiraya. The stones are the first line of defense against invasion."

"Demons fear an invasion from Wiraya?"

"Fear might be putting it a bit strongly. Perhaps a better way to think about the stone circles is if you imagine them as a spider's web. Touch a single strand, and the spider senses its dinner has arrived."

"Then it's a good thing we didn't come that way," Anskar said.

THIRTY-SEVEN

IT WAS A DIFFERENT KIND of heat as they made the long trek along the banks of the canal and emerged from the shade of the valley between the mesas. Scorching. Blisteringly hot. Anskar sucked in deeper and deeper breaths, but still his lungs felt empty. The air was stultifying, and the wind that greeted them on the open plains was lacerating.

Despite the heat, Blaice put on her leather jacket and did it up as protection from the abrasive gusts. She grumbled repeatedly about not bringing the broad-brimmed hat she had worn when they first met in Atya. All she could do was cover her face with her hands and peer between her fingers.

Anskar had more protection from his cloak and mail, but still the breeze stung. And then an idea occurred to him. Reaching into the dark-tide that now seemed to define him, he separated out threads of essence from his veins, and with the merest of thoughts, wove them into a barrier against the wind, a sphere of mists and shadow that was not altogether unlike the sorcerous ward sphere he had once been able to cast using the dawn-tide.

He extended the barrier around Blaice, and she smiled her thanks. After that, Anskar increased his pace, and Blaice matched him. He could feel the steady trickle of dark-tide seeping through his pores. He guessed there was some way to go yet, but in time he would be depleted, and what that would mean for him, he had no way of telling.

Previously, too much use of the dark-tide had left him spent, utterly bereft; but now that it no longer resided within a repository, now that it was a part of his blood, what would happen if it ran out?

There was something else he felt within him too, something other than the slow bleed of the dark-tide. He sent his senses questing inside himself until he found it: a hardness within his mind. Not a physical hardness, but a sensation that had not previously been there. It felt dense, and to his inner sight it appeared vaguely egg-like. An egg of glistening blackness. And it had a pulse. He could feel it now, out of kilter with his own heartbeat. He sent a feeler of awareness into it, but the feeler recoiled. He tried again, more gingerly, felt around the surface of the dark egg, and he saw. Saw that the demon he had slain had not simply been absorbed and dispersed into the ether. It was here—all its experiences and memories, its ineffable powers, locked away within his mind behind the hard-yet-not-really-hard shell of the egg.

At once he was tempted to crack it open, if that were even possible, but a niggling voice warned him to tread carefully. Already what he had absorbed had changed him, or at least liberated powers that had lain dormant within him. What would happen were he to unleash the full force of the demon's life force, its experiences, its puissance? Malady had claimed that lower demons advanced by absorbing the essence of those above them, but was there a risk? What if the demon he had killed was still a power to be reckoned with? What if the cracking of the egg that contained its life force overwhelmed him in some way? What if he were the one to be absorbed?

So he withdrew his senses and decided to proceed—if at all— warily. Perhaps it would be better if he left the egg alone until he could find someone to guide him. And again he rued the decision that had led to the exorcism of his mother.

An hour's walk away from the shelter of the mesas, Anskar's keen eyes picked out the smudged form of some kind of settlement amid the heat haze. He pointed it out to Blaice, but it was still too far off for her to see.

"Should we avoid it?" Anskar asked.

"Why would we do that?" she replied. "It's our way in to Artuum-Nak'Urdim. Sheelahn's contacts told her about the barges that use the canals. If we can smuggle ourselves on board, we may avoid detection. There are no certainties in this game, after all."

"Sheelahn has contacts in the abyssal realms?" Anskar asked.

"Apparently."

"What I don't understand," Anskar said, "is why you're involved with her."

"Same reason as you. I was stupid enough to incur debts to her."

"But why are you indebted?" Anskar asked. "What did she do for you?"

"I could ask you the same thing," Blaice said, "though I'm not sure I want to hear the answer. We all need something—at least we think we do. And people like the Ethereal Sorceress have a knack for giving us just what we want—or think we want—at the moment we most need it. It's too easy to say yes to her terms. Too addictive to keep on saying yes. One debt leads to another, and before you know it…"

"Before you know it, you're in the abyssal realms," Anskar said. "It sounds like a morality tale from the *Book of the Five Aspects*."

"Now I regret not having read it when I was at the academy," Blaice said.

When Anskar glanced at her to gauge whether or not she was being serious, she smirked.

"Seriously, it sounds like a riveting read."

"I don't think the morals of Menselas would be to your liking."

"Nor yours, apparently." Blaice stopped walking for a moment and took hold of Anskar's hand. The dark-tide ward swirled around them, a sooty veil. "What I said earlier… about it being your first time… I was being a bitch. You did all right."

"No," Anskar said.

"I wasn't offering. Well, not right here, right now; but let's keep an open mind."

"All that is behind me."

"You've rediscovered piety? Oh no, wait; it was another woman, wasn't it? No! Not Carred Selenas? But she's almost old enough to be your mother!"

Anskar resumed walking, and Blaice came with him. "So are you," he said.

He glimpsed her frown, the doubt that entered her eyes, then she focused her gaze on the way head.

"But no, it's not another woman." Not Vilintia Yoenth and, he told himself, certainly not Carred Selenas.

Still lying to yourself, a niggling thought said. He throttled it at the source. He was done with being governed by feelings the

Abbess had aroused in him. That charm of beguilement was over. *Over!*

By the time they reached the outskirts of the settlement, Anskar was shivering despite the heat. Cold sweat beaded his skin, and a growing void had been steadily blossoming within him. Too much dark-tide, he told himself; or at least, too much too soon. When would it be night again—that brief interlude of darkness? Perhaps then he would be able to replenish himself.

Extending away from the shimmering waters of the canal, which reflected the multi-colored sky, was a sprawling conglomeration of structures that resembled blisters of the same porous rock the mesas were formed from.

The buildings—for they had oval windows and arched entrances—were dome-shaped, and they varied in size from barely large enough to accommodate one person to enormous hill-like growths—how else could they have come into existence?—as large as any basilica of the Five.

Narrow streets threaded between the buildings, paved with flags of coarse, grainy crystal that dazzled with reflected rainbow light. The odd thing was, the streets were immaculately clean: no dust, no footprints, no waste. It was as if they were as warded as Anskar and Blaice had been on the way there from the detritus thrown up by the wind.

"Try to look like you belong here," Blaice said, striding with purpose toward the settlement.

Anskar scurried after her. "But we look nothing like demons."

"They'll assume we're shifters," Blaice said. "Some demons can take on different appearances. You know that."

Malady, the dwarf-demon, had turned into a serpent.

"The important thing is that we smell like demons, and don't do anything a demon wouldn't do," Blaice said. "Lower-order demons are brutish in their intelligence, and the middle-order ones aren't exactly bright. It's only the higher-order demons who might suspect something."

"Smell?"

Blaice touched the star tattooed on her neck—the ward she had paid the Orgols for. He sniffed the air, but could smell nothing unusual save for the faintest tinge of fear exuding from Blaice's pores. He frowned, still not used to this new sense.

Once they came within the shelter of the strange buildings, Anskar dropped the dark-tide warding that had kept the wind off. It felt as though a huge weight had been lifted from him, but it left him weak and in need of food and drink.

There were demons everywhere, tall and gray-skinned—not at all like the spine-covered lesser demons they had encountered beneath the mesa. But neither were they like the demon Anskar had slain. They looked like gray-skinned humans. They wore boots and pants, and silken tunics of every conceivable color. Males and females all dressed the same, only distinguishable by the natural contours of their bodies and the disparity in musculature. The men were mostly huge, at least a head taller than Anskar, barrel-chested and thick of limb. The women were just as tall, yet they were stick-thin and gangly, and many had absurdly long fingernails curled into claws.

Demons turned to watch them as they passed, but they were curious looks, not threatening. Some muttered in Nazgrese—words neither Blaice nor Anskar understood, but he felt they were commenting on the color of their skin. Or rather, his. No one seemed to pay the slightest attention to Blaice, which struck him as odd. Another quality of her star tattoo?

Blaice led them along the fringes of the settlement, following the embankment flanking the canal. There were dozens of barges moored to the stone banks, some being loaded, others unloaded, several of them covered with oiled tarps and apparently going nowhere.

Most of the domes by the canal were large warehouses, their arched doorways revealing the stacked goods within: piles of quarried crystal, ingots of green-tinted metal, dark wooden crates—was it blackwood? There were sacks and barrels, rugs, crockery, long-poled tools. He saw warehouses stacked with armor and weapons and shields; some housed livestock: six-legged lizards the size of ponies, scaled goats, some kind of winged beasts, part bird, part horse.

Goods poured into and out of the warehouses in a near-continuous stream. Muscular demons working in teams labored to carry or drive or goad, and in among them Anskar glimpsed demons of a different kind, men and women, closer to human-sized, their skin a lighter gray, sharp-eyed, their hair intricately bound with ribbons in all manner of elaborate styles. And they were dressed differently, too: knee-length coats of brocaded dark cotton embroidered with swirling patterns in gold, silver, or crimson.

It wasn't just their appearance that made these demons stand out, it was their *smell*: brash, disdainful, superior. These were the demons in charge, and by their bearing and scent, Anskar knew they thought of the majority of taller demons as no better than chattel. And the dark-tide emanating from them... it almost choked him, it was so strong. But was it really? he asked himself.

He sent out threads of awareness as they passed one such demon supervising the loading of a barge, and as he had intuited, he perceived a moderate flow of the dark-tide within the demon's blood, but nothing to rival that within his own. And he wondered then at the intuition. Where had it come from? He withdrew his senses from the demon and turned them instead inwards, onto the hardness of the black egg within his mind—the essence of the demon he'd subsumed.

A hairline fissure was perceptible to his inner sight. It was seeping a sooty sort of essence. Anskar threw threads of dark-tide at the crack, weaving them around it, binding and sealing. And he was successful, but not before he caught the stench of the burning malice within. An entity. And it had exuded scorn and disdain for the coated demon overseeing the loading of the barge. Worse, it had seethed in rage at Anskar. Rage and insatiable hunger.

The coated demon by the barge turned its dark eyes on Anskar, head cocked to one side. The demon's sorcerous senses tickled at Anskar's scalp, seeking entrance, and he denied it with such firmness that the demon visibly flinched. Its eyes widened as Anskar glared at it, and after a moment, the demon dipped its head in a slight bow.

"What was that about?" Blaice asked as they move away.

"It tried to read me. I forbade it."

"And it bowed to your superiority? Your first victory at a pissing contest, then."

"Must you be so crude?"

"And there was me thinking you liked it. I'll never understand you pious types. I assumed all that holiness was a smokescreen for something else. It just goes to show!"

They stopped a little way along the wharf to watch a massive barge being loaded with sleek black crates of some substance that had the appearance of rock. What the crates contained was a mystery, but whatever it was—even the substance that comprised the crate itself—was extremely light, so easily did the demons toss the crates about.

One of the higher-order demons, a woman with grainy gray skin, her black hair braided into three tails with scarlet ribbons, and wearing a long coat the color of fresh grass, barked something at the demons doing the loading. It sounded to Anskar as though the loaders grumbled, but then they set about organizing the tossed crates into neat stacks with gangways between them.

Still more of the dark crates were being brought from the domed warehouse the barge was moored outside of.

"This might suit our purposes," Blaice said.

"We stow aboard?"

"Well, I assume it's heading to Artuum-Nak'Urdim. There's nothing much back the way we came."

"And if it doesn't?" Anskar asked. "If it stops at another settlement along the way?"

"Then either it will take on more supplies, and we'd better not get ourselves seen. Or if it stops there, we get off and find another ride—which is the story of my life."

"And how to you propose we board without being seen?"

"I'm sure you'll find a way," Blaice said. "My pious little sorcerer."

Anskar's hands clenched at his sides, but already he was thinking about what he could do. "How long do you think it will take them to finish loading?"

Blaice shrugged. "A couple of hours?"

"And how long till sundown?"

"Your guess is as good as mine. Could be any minute. Could be hours, maybe even days. All I know is that night, when it comes, never lasts long."

"But long enough for us to stow away on board." And hopefully long enough to refill him with dark-tide essence.

"Demons can see in the dark," Blaice said.

"But not in shadow." At least not the kind he planned to wrap around them in an obscuring cloak.

"I'll have to take your word for that," Blaice said. "But we can't stand here all day watching the barge, and I for one am starving."

"You're going for something to eat? Here?"

"Demons eat, same as we do. Well, not exactly the same. It may take a little getting used to."

"They eat brains, I heard," Anskar said. Tion's stories had been quite specific about that. "Hearts and livers."

"They do like their meat," Blaice conceded. "But then," she said with a wink, "so do I."

Anskar rolled his eyes. "But neither of us speaks Nazgrese, so how will we order?"

"*Sul luk ka na vilix ka'ath,*" Blaice said.

"What did you say?"

"You'll find out soon enough."

"You speak Nazgrese? But I thought—?"

"Just a few words and phrases," Blaice said. "It's not chance that's kept me alive all these years, and it's certainly not divine intervention. It's study and preparedness."

He narrowed his eyes at her. "How long have you known about this mission?"

"Longer than you. I knew it was coming. Sooner or later, I knew it would come."

"So Sheelahn had this planned for you all along, as repayment of your debts?"

"Some of my debts; not all of them. And I suspect this was

planned long before I approached her and got myself into debt. In fact, I'm certain she offered her services to make sure, when the time came for this mission, that I owed her."

"And then she threw me in as fodder?"

"Don't be so hard on yourself," Blaice said. "I suspect she had good reasons for sending you along—not least of all your blood. Who knows what connivances she works on the world stage? But think upon who you are and what you represent. There are no coincidences in the dealings of the Ethereal Sorceress, of that you can rest assured. And besides, I think Sheelahn likes you. Come on, I really am starving."

"But how will we pay?"

"With these."

Blaice opened one of the many pockets of her leather jacket and produced a coin purse. She opened it and withdrew a thin square of what looked like quartz, though there were filaments of crimson within. They could have been capillaries.

"Demon coins," she said brightly.

THIRTY-EIGHT

THE HEADS ON THE EATERY walls glared at Anskar. Some of them were skulls; some of them were fresh. They were mostly the heads of beasts: gigantic lizards, a tusked cat, goat skulls and sheep, familiar yet different. Trophies, Anskar assumed, but Blaice corrected him: they were samples of the kind of fare the eatery had to offer—a menu of sorts. Those with skin had still been bleeding when placed upon the hooks set into the walls, leaving now-dried trails of purplish blood streaking the walls. Save for the lizards, whose blood was green. The cats' heads were spiny, like porcupines, rather than furred. The boar's head wasn't hairy but was covered with bony protrusions. The sheep's skulls had elongated snouts and jaws bristling with needle-sharp teeth. And all the skulls were black, but whether that was from charring in the cooking process or their natural state, Anskar couldn't tell. Natural, he assumed, when the food Blaice ordered arrived at their low stone table, for the meat—all of it—was uncooked.

The few other patrons glanced with unabashed hunger at the immense dish set on the table before Anskar and Blaice. There was pink flesh and white, brown, yellow, and black, all of it seeping blood, some of it purplish, some of it green. Strips of roughly equal length and thickness had been intricately layered in a complex pattern that must have taken both skill and time to arrange. Whatever they were, and despite their appetite for raw meat, these demons were certainly no base animals. They took as much care over the presentation of their meals as they did in the binding of their hair with ribbons.

The server, a long-limbed demon woman with unbound hair and insolent eyes, set down a second dish, this one of sausages, each the size of Anskar's forearm, glistening with oil and marbled black and purple.

"Congealed lizard blood, if I'm not very much mistaken," Blaice said in a low voice, already reaching for one. She had warned Anskar about being overheard speaking Nan-Rhouric, as that would give them away, even if their appearance and scent had not.

"Blood?" Anskar wrinkled his nose. "But how do they get it into that form?"

"Sausage shape? I'll leave that to your imagination." Blaice bit into one and sighed. Purple blood smeared her lips as she chewed.

The drinks came next: a bottle of some astringent-smelling spirit, with a couple of stone bowls to drink it from. Anskar decided to try the drink before the meat, in the hope it would dampen his disgust at the meal. He poured one for Blaice, another for himself, and Blaice watched him take his first sip, an amused glint in her eye.

Anskar spat it out. "Goat's piss!" he exclaimed.

Blaice pressed a finger to her lips. "Shush."

"Sorry," Anskar muttered.

"You know what goat's piss tastes like?" Blaice said as she lifted her bowl and took a long drink. "And I was starting to think the rumors about you worshipers of Menselas were false."

"Of course I don't," Anskar said. But how else could he describe it? Acidic, burning, and vaguely tasting of cabbage.

"Well, now you do."

Anskar glanced from his drinking bowl to a goat's head adorning the wall. Its dark eyes seemed to mock him, and he pushed the bowl across the table. "You're joking, aren't you?"

"Not if it means I get to drink yours too." Blaice downed her bowl, then started on his. "Of course, much of the alcohol in the demon realms is smuggled here from Wiraya. Demons have created many wonders, but distilleries are not one of them. And as with everything else—as with their passions, their hungers— demons are unbridled in their desire for strong drink. At least, the lower-order ones are. The fact that you're not drinking will lead these poor bastards here to assume you're some refined upper-order demon, one step shy of a lord. See how they're trying not to look at you?"

Anskar glanced round, and true enough, several demons were glancing his way. He felt a tickle of senses around the egg of darkness that contained the demon's essence he had absorbed. Eyes widened and murmurs passed between the demons. They didn't sound disapproving, though; they sounded awed, as if he had accomplished something they could only dream of. As if they both envied and feared him.

But had he in truth absorbed the demon's essence? It felt more like an intrusion. He checked with his newfound senses. The egg was still intact, its fracture sealed. But its weight, if it could be said to have weight, had increased somehow, as if it were growing denser, ready to explode. As if the trapped essence within were gaining confidence. Anskar shook himself and turned his senses outward.

Blaice devoured strip after bloody strip. He had never seen anyone eat so ravenously. She must have detected his disgust, as she paused in her chewing long enough to say, "I'm insatiable… but you already knew that, didn't you? Go on, try some. It's not nearly as bad as it looks. They do eat raw meat in some places on Wiraya too, you know. Well, you would if you traveled a bit."

The room behind Blaice was a blur of severed heads and blackened skulls, but he anchored himself on her violet eyes— eyes that had obsessed Niklaus du Plessis, a man cursed to forever pursue his goddess.

"You're going to starve," Blaice said, a sliver of meat dripping green blood in her fingers.

Something shifted inside Anskar, and he was suddenly ravenous. As if he had always eaten his food uncooked, as if he relished blood and cold flesh, he snatched up a strip of raw meat and crammed it into his mouth.

The proprietor—an enormously fat demon—smiled benignly as she wandered over and asked something in Nazgrese. Anskar had the excuse that his mouth was full not to answer. Blaice replied in Nazgrese, and the proprietor frowned.

Above the stench of the meat there was a different kind of scent, not remotely olfactory: Anskar smelled suspicion, wariness, indecision in the proprietor. The smell was smothered by gratitude, though, when Blaice slipped her one of the red-veined crystal squares that passed for currency here.

As the proprietor moved away to the meat hooks, where demons with cleavers were preparing the food, Anskar swallowed what he was eating and took a slurp of goat's piss or whatever it was.

Blaice popped more meat into her mouth and reached for another strip, then withdrew her hand. "Too much of a good thing," she said, clutching her stomach and wincing. "So, what do you want to talk about while we wait for nightfall?"

"I don't care."

"Then let me start. I was wondering about your time in the company of Carred Selenas."

"There's nothing to tell. I wasn't with her for long."

"But before you were brought to the Ethereal Sorceress's depot, I thought that you came from the rebel camp."

"Carred wasn't there."

"How disappointing for you. Where was she, then?"

Anskar shrugged. "How should I know?"

But he did know. Vilintia had told him what Orix had told her, about some kind of portal near to Naphor. Carred had come here, to the abyssal realms, at the bidding of his mother. But which of the realms? And what did it mean that they had both traveled to the demon lands at the same time? Coincidence? Not likely, given the way Queen Talia worked. Although… did his mother even know about the mission the Ethereal Sorceress had sent him on? The healers had exorcized her beforehand, so maybe Queen Talia assumed he was still on Wiraya, maybe even still at Branil's Burg. He had to suppress a smile. If that was the case, this was the first time he had kept her in the dark, and it felt good.

"Tell me about the Order of Eternal Vigilance," Blaice said, changing tack. "What was it like growing up with enforced celibacy? Did it drive you to touch yourself?"

"I've a better idea," Anskar said. "Why don't we just leave and get this over and done with?"

"Because the barge doesn't get underway until right after the next dark."

"How do you know that?"

Blaice shot a look at the proprietor, who was sampling the meat of a freshly killed tusked cat, blood gushing from its opened throat to pool on the floor.

"When I ordered our food, she told me so. No one wants to get caught in the blackness, she said, when the hunters fly."

"That thing we saw last dark," Anskar said. "The creature with wings... So, how long do we have to wait?"

"I didn't ask. She was already suspicious of my questions about the barges. But when night falls, we'll only have an hour or two in which to stow on board. Hopefully the wharfs will be deserted then."

"Save for the hunters," Anskar said.

"You'll just have to ward us. So, if Carred Selenas is off-limits, and you won't divulge any juicy details about the Order of Eternal Vigilance, what should we do to pass the time? They have rooms out back..."

"We talk," Anskar said, "about you."

"My favorite subject. What do you want to know?" Blaice eyed the meat plate again, then chose to pour another measure of spirits into her bowl instead.

"It's not really goat's piss, is it?" Anskar asked.

Blaice chuckled and poured one for him.

"What do I want to know?" Anskar said. "Who you are. Where you're from."

"How I ended up the best in the game?" She said that wryly, as if the idea were wearing thin, even for her. "How I ended up in debt to the Ethereal Sorceress?"

Anskar nodded as he sipped his drink.

"What's there to tell?" Blaice glanced around the room, eyes alighting on the grisly animal heads that glowered from the walls. "My father was a rich noble from the Pristart Combine. My mother was not. And no, before you go thinking it, she wasn't a whore."

"I wasn't about to suggest that she was," Anskar said.

"Of course you weren't. She was a scholar and the curator of the Museum of Kaile in Sansor."

"Sansor? But how—?"

"People travel, Anskar, or hadn't you noticed? And Kaile is just to the north of the Pristart Combine. My father traveled. A lot. Business associates in Sansor. You know the sort."

"The Consortium?"

"He was connected," Blaice said, "but not *that* connected."

"So, your mother relocated to the Pristart Combine when they married? It must have been hard, giving up her position."

"Must it?" Blaice said. "I never said my parents were married. And my mother never gave up her position. She was removed from it. Suddenly. Brutally."

"What happened?"

"She was murdered."

"By your father?"

"Don't be ridiculous. That fat bastard lacks the energy for violence, and his interest in my mother was, shall we say, conditional. No, lore hunters killed her. Broke into her house— because she was the only one with access to the parts of the museum they were interested in."

"And she refused them?"

Blaice shook her head, then turned to meet Anskar's gaze. Her eyes were moist. "They did things to her... in order to persuade…"

Anskar looked away, wanting so much for her to stop. He wished he hadn't pried.

Blaice seemed to sense the change that came over him, and immediately her tone lightened. She sniffed and then said, "They got what they wanted. Next morning, the museum had a new exhibit: my mother's mutilated corpse."

"And you went after the killers?"

"I was thirteen years old."

"Then what? They didn't get away with it, did they?"

Blaice smiled and looked at her hands, fingers interlaced on the tabletop. "They did not. My mother had contacts, so I looked one of them up. A contact who knew a good deal about the movement of precious artifacts. I told her what had happened. She had the artifacts retrieved, even had them returned to the museum. The thieves? I didn't ask, but I think their fate was unpleasant. That was my very first debt to the Ethereal Sorceress."

Anskar frowned. He felt far too angry, as if this tale were much closer to home. What was wrong with him? He didn't usually get so bound up in another's grief. When had he become so… sensitive? "So Sheelahn has enslaved you since the age of thirteen?"

"Oh, I repaid that debt quite handily, but the idea had been sown. If things got difficult in the future, if I needed information, or an advance, or help with a rival… Because the one good thing that came out of all of that was that it got me interested in the kinds of things you sometimes find in museums, the things that people—some good, some bad—will pay a fortune for."

"You weren't interested while your mother was alive?"

"No child ever is."

Anskar didn't know about that. He had no experience of parents and children. Was that why he was so attracted by the powers that his deceased mother had wielded, the dark-tide and, more recently, the earth-tide that could rouse the dead and shape matter?

"But now…" Blaice said, sounding pensive. "Now my debts to Sheelahn seem just a little insurmountable." She reached for her bowl and took a long drink. "Maybe one day I'll pluck up the courage to kill her. Please don't tell her I said that."

"Is that even possible?" Anskar whispered the question. Irrational as it seemed, he couldn't quite suppress the idea that the Ethereal Sorceress might hear.

"Probably not. Besides which, I'm not one for murder. Now listen," she said, again changing her tone and apparently her mood. "I wasn't joking about finding a room. All this meat's made me horny."

Anskar started to stammer a reply, but night chose that moment to fall, suddenly, shockingly, plunging the eatery into blackness. What sounded like a grumble went up from the demon patrons, and within moments the walls and ceiling started to effuse a soft, reddish glow. It was enough to see by inside, but outside, beyond the arched doorway, it was black as pitch.

"I suppose it's just as well," Blaice said. "We can't have you getting too attached to me now, can we? I know what you men are like."

Anskar scowled.

Blaice palmed the lodestone and called out something in Nazgrese to the proprietor as they left. Outside, she flipped open the lid so that the silver filament could light her way.

Anskar's senses strained, in case anything came flying in from overhead, in case there were demons still on the wharves—those who might take more risks in the dark. But there was nothing. No activity. The canal banks were dead save for the gentle lapping of the water.

Nevertheless, as they drew near the barge Blaice had earmarked, Anskar separated out veins of dark-tide and once more wove a shroud of shadows around them.

"You can never be too careful, eh?" Blaice said, snapping shut the lid of the lodestone and gripping Anskar's hand.

He led her to the gunwale and parted the heavy tarp that covered the stacked crates they had earlier seen being loaded. The only part of the barge that wasn't uncovered was the aft, where a stool sat next to the steering oar. On the way to the settlement, he had seen one demon piloting the barges while another, armed and armored, stood guard over the merchandise. Hopefully, this would be the same, and no one would inspect the crates until they arrived at their destination. And that, he hoped, would be Artuum-Nak'Urdim, the Mountain of Plenty.

He stepped on board and guided Blaice after him. Then they hunkered down in one of the narrow channels between the crates and waited for the brief dark to lift.

THIRTY-NINE

CARRED SAT; THEN SHE DOZED. Sat and dozed. There was nothing else to do.

Well, she'd added her own stench to the cell; she'd done that. There had been no food, no water, no one even to check on her in… she didn't know how long. Hours? Days? She had no way of gauging the passage of time. But she'd still had to go, and so she had gone, in a specially dedicated corner. And with that, her exhaustion had returned as a crushing depression. She was worse than an animal to these demons, and she was starting to feel that way about herself.

She'd always considered herself a failure. How could she not, after all those defeats? And, truth be told, she'd always needed others to make her feel worth something. Sex helped with that, more than it ought to. But so did the camaraderie of the rebel camp. So did Talia and her unreasonable demands—it was better to be needed than not. But her whole life, she'd carried around the wound of abandonment, of being left alone to scream in the woods. There was never a day when she wasn't aware of that, but what good was self-knowledge when it didn't change anything?

She stared at the wall. Always, she stared at the wall. Stared so much, the wall sometimes writhed and shifted—though of course that was probably her eyes growing tired. Sometimes as she drifted off, a figure stepped through the wall. Usually it was someone she knew. One or two she begged to stay, but people never seemed to do what she wanted in her dreams. Kovin stayed awhile. Marith too. But other than them, phantoms could be so bloody uncooperative.

When the surface of the wall blistered, she pinched herself to make sure she was awake. Pain was the great dispeller of illusions. This time, there was a slurp and a pop as a demon came through.

He was an ugly toe-rag: blue-gray skin, hairy neck, hairy arms, hairy face—hairy everywhere save his bloated belly, which was veined and translucent and reminded her of a jellyfish. He glared at her through slitted eyes of puce and growled something incomprehensible. He was carrying a pole with a metal loop at one end.

The demon's nostrils flared. He turned to face Carred's corner of shame and made a gurgling, rasping sound that might have been a laugh.

"Glad it amuses you," Carred said. "I assume you mean to take me somewhere? That"—she indicated his pole—"won't be necessary."

As she stood, the demon backhanded her across the face and knocked her back down to the bench. If she'd had the strength, she'd have gouged his slitty little eyes out for that, but instead she remained still while he clicked the metal loop shut around her neck. Controlling her from behind with the pole, he shoved her toward the wall. She threw her arms up, but it was like hitting treacle. There was a brief sucking sound, the momentary buildup of pressure, and then she was on the other side, standing in a dank, dripping corridor.

The demon emerged behind her, forcing her ahead with the pole. Her neck chafed from the metal collar—it wasn't exactly smooth. Even when she complied, the demon alternately shoved and pulled on the pole, gurgling away in amusement at her lurching discomfort.

The corridor branched at the end, and the demon goaded her left, up a ramp that rose at a steep incline. At the top, they came to another corridor, this one with a mosaic floor of what looked like marble and jade, arranged into patterns of straight lines—triangles, pentagons, octagons. Looking at it made her head hurt. Brass panels covered the walls, engraved with images of winged and horned demons in all manner of poses she could only think of as heroic.

At the far end, they came to louvered swing doors made from bone. Steam curled beneath the doors, sweet-smelling and mildly arousing.

The demon roughly released her metal collar then shoved her in the back, sending her flying through the doors to land sprawling on her face. He didn't enter behind her.

Soft hands helped her to her feet.

"I do apologize," a female demon on Carred's right said. She was gray-skinned and naked, and undeniably beautiful. Save for her color, and her yellow eyes and the slight scaly texture of her skin, she could have passed for a human.

"The lesser demons can be so uncouth," a second naked woman, on Carred's left, said. Her scales were more pronounced, her skin tinged with blue, and one eye was pink, the other orange. Her tongue flitted between her lips as she spoke, long and moist and sinuous. "Tolak especially so. I apologize for any mistreatment, on behalf of Lord Domatai."

"You speak Niyandrian?" Carred asked.

"We speak many tongues," the first demon said. "Lord Domatai regrets that he has had no opportunity to speak with you further."

"He's so busy all the time," the second demon said.

"Undeniably busy," the first concurred. "He has asked us to assure you that you have not been forgotten. Between you and me, I think he likes you."

"He's always been partial to Niyandrians," the second demon said.

"Well, they taste so good," the first said. "My little joke. Come, Carred—I may call you Carred, mayn't I? You may call me Scaal, and this is Varda. We serve Lord Domatai."

"In many and varied ways," said Varda.

"Not your real names, I assume?"

"Of course not!" exclaimed Scaal. "Names are filled with power."

"You speak Niyandrian well," Carred said, although it was a somewhat archaic form, the preserve of the old nobility.

"Why, thank you," Varda said. "Though languages come easily to demon-kind."

Arms looped in Carred's, they led her deeper into the room—a huge, steamy interior with soft, reddish lighting. The floor, hidden beneath a carpet of curling steam, was spongy underfoot. She couldn't see the walls for the steam. Couldn't see much of anything at all, until the women brought her to a carved stone bathtub filled with water.

Without asking her permission, they began to peel off her

soiled, stinking clothing.

"We'll have it washed and dried," Scaal said. "Don't you worry."

Shadowy, crab-like creatures scuttled across the floor and dragged Carred's clothes away.

"Let me help you," Varda said, guiding Carred up the single step to the tub and supporting her arm as she settled into the warm, scented water—cloves and musk and maybe honeysuckle.

Scaal came behind Carred, cradled her head, and massaged her scalp. Varda leaned over the side of the tub and began scrubbing Carred's arms with a rough cloth.

Carred sighed and closed her eyes, letting Scaal take the weight of her head. She smiled as Scaal poured warm water over her hair, then rubbed in some kind of sweet-smelling oil. Marith used to do the same for her on the rare occasions they could be together for more than a snatched hour or two.

Varda next went to work on her legs, scraping away dried skin and grime. Then she set down the washcloth and began to rub Carred's feet, knowing just where to press to elicit moans of… pleasure?

Scaal placed a rolled towel under Carred's head on the edge of the tub, her hands gliding to Carred's breasts.

"Are you feeling more relaxed?" Varda asked, placing Carred's foot back in the water.

The only response Carred could muster was a sleepy moan.

"You like this?" Scaal asked, as her thumbs brushed Carred's nipples. "Because we wouldn't do anything you didn't want us to."

Carred had to think about that. Not for long. She was too tired to object and way past caring. This was the first time anyone had been gentle and kind and sensual with her since that last night at

Marith's, when the assassins came.

She opened an eye at the plop of something entering the water. Varda was leaning over the end of the tub, her tongue trailing as long as a snake, its tip underwater, running along the inside of Carred's thigh.

"Oh…" Carred said. Should she be repulsed? Would she be, if she weren't so tired?

Maybe not, she decided, as the tip climbed higher and made her gasp.

Scaal silenced her with a kiss—hot and wet and sugary. Carred writhed and groaned. Her hips bucked, splashing water out of the tub. She could feel nothing save for Scaal's lips and Varda's tongue. Hear nothing save the splash of water and her rapid breaths. See nothing behind her closed eyes, save for Marith's head bobbing between her legs.

"Marith," she cried. "Ah, Marith!"

And then she was gasping and weeping and shaking all at the same time, and after, she sank back in the water as the two demons stroked her skin.

"We wish you could stay longer," Varda said.

"Memories are made here," Scaal added.

Carred wished so too, but the lesser demon Tolak was waiting with his pole when the demon women ushered her outside to the corridor.

His nostrils flared, and he gave a contemptuous sniff at her freshly cleaned clothes.

"So unrefined," Scaal said. "Such a base creature. But then, weren't we all, once?"

Tolak fitted the metal collar round her neck and pushed her ahead of him. Carred cast a longing look behind, where Scaal and Varda were waving. And then there was nothing to look forward to but her cold, damp, stinking cell.

FORTY

A CIRCLE OF CANDLES SURROUNDED Marith where she sat in meditation on the tree-stump stool she'd lacquered and painted with flowers and clouds—the full extent of her artistic talent. She was proud of the stool, just as she was proud of the sturdy wooden shelf she'd erected for her grandmother's statue of Theltek. The statue had become enormously important in her life after the assassins came for Carred. She'd cut the wood for the shelf a few summers ago, seasoned it in the woodstore, planed it, sanded it, and stained it all by herself. And she had to say, Theltek seemed much happier now that he stood looking out over the workshop as if he owned the place.

She liked to think the god of a thousand eyes guided her in her meditation, and she'd come to accept that her intuitions were gifts from Theltek. She hoped that if she concentrated hard enough, she might even hear his voice—or voices, given that he had so many mouths. But the only voices she heard were those that came at night, the machinations of "the bankers," as she'd come to think of them. Whatever they were, they sounded arrogant, condescending, too assured of their combined power.

An intuition struck her as she sat making a futile attempt to quiet her ever-chattering mind: sorcery wasn't the divided discipline she'd been led to believe. Yes, the tides each had their own characteristics, their own applications, but what if they all came from the same unified source? The dawn had no meaning save in relation to the sun. Same with the dusk. Same with the dark, she had to think, albeit in a negative sense, though the dark-tide wasn't something she gave much thought to. And the earth-tide, about which she knew even less, being that it was the province of necromancers... wasn't that supposed to be a reservoir more than an actual tide? The pooling of the three known tides beneath the ground, filtered through rock and rot and carcasses until it became polluted and unnatural.

"Don't go messing with the dark- or the earth-tide," her grandmother used to say. "One's for demons, the other's for the dead."

"But the dead are our friends," little Marith once replied.

"Not all of them," Nan said. "And till you know which ones are which, stay away from the earth-tide, I tell you. Otherwise I'll stop teaching you."

And so Marith had stopped. Not entirely: she'd still read what little there was on the subject. Necromancers like Tain were revered for their earth-tide abilities, but there was always something dubious about them in the stories. They seemed cursed.

As to the dark-tide, she had no capacity for it. So few did, outside of the abyssal realms, and those few had sold their souls for the ability—at least if the poets were to be believed.

But Queen Talia had wielded the dark-tide...

Marith glanced up at Theltek on his shelf, his six eyes glinting in the candlelight, goading her on. Was that for real? The hairs on the back of her neck prickled, and there was a chill in her veins, some kind of connection with something not of this world. A spirit? A demon? A god?

"Is it you?" she asked Theltek.

The statue's six eyes stared back blankly.

"What are you trying to tell me? You want me to experiment with the tides?" She was already a master of the dawn and the dusk. "How about I try the earth-tide? Is that what you want?"

Theltek said nothing, which wasn't exactly a denial.

She rose from her stump and went to one of the huge cobwebs that hung down from the corners of the workshop. She selected a desiccated wasp that had been trapped there for Theltek only knew how long and placed it on her open palm.

She smiled at her own foolishness. At least, it felt foolish, and not a little disrespectful to her grandmother. But, hey, Theltek was Theltek, and she wasn't about to argue with a god. Even the statue of a god, which hadn't said a word to her.

"Crazy," Marith said to herself. "If only Carred could see you now."

She returned to her stump, sat down, and removed her shoes.

She started with her feet—both set firmly on the packed dirt ground. She tried to feel the earth-tide seeping up from the core of the world, but all she could feel was cold earth and the tickle of an ant crawling over her foot.

So what was she supposed to do? Imagine the earth-tide? But as what? A stinking mist? A putrid flow? Brackish water? Whatever she tried, it didn't work. Maybe she was the problem. After all, she had the imagination of a brick.

She switched her attention to the dead wasp in her hand,

bringing it close so she could see the fine details of its wings, sniff it, and when that didn't work, taste it with just the tip of her tongue.

Instantly, she was surrounded by the stench of rot. Her stomach clenched and she leaned forward to vomit. When she'd emptied her guts, she wiped her mouth with her sleeve and flicked the dead wasp to the ground.

"Sorry, Nan," she said. "You were right."

That left her with just the dark-tide. Only demons—and those foolish enough to bargain with them—had access to the dark-tide. But was that strictly true? Though it was said to be strongest there, the tide wasn't exclusive to the abyssal realms. She'd felt the pitter-patter of its touch during the full-dark when the dead-eyes were on the prowl. Felt it, but had no repository in which to store it. If she did, she might be able to contact Carred.

And you still might, a chorus of voices whispered in her mind.

She glared at the statue of Theltek. "Was that you?"

The reflected candlelight in the statue's eyes gave them an eerie sort of animation, the glint of amusement.

"How?" she asked, glancing behind to make sure no one was there, watching her make a fool of herself. "How do I contact Carred?"

You've seen where she is, came the harmonized reply. *Images are the gateway of the spirit.*

Then it was a pity she was so bad at holding images in her head. Nevertheless, it was worth a try.

She began by closing her eyes and trying to picture again the red sky and the bronze sun. The sun was easier than the sky, as if it had literally burned itself into her memory. She tried to recall the ragged breathing she'd heard, but all she achieved was to make her own breaths labored.

"Idiot!" she chastised herself. She didn't lack imagination for this; she had too much imagination. It was all in her mind: Theltek, the voices of the bankers, the vision of red sky and a bronze...

That smell.

Sweet Theltek!

Carred...

Her musk and her sweat.

She turned at the sound of Carred moaning, but there was nothing there. Odd: it had sounded as though Carred were in the workshop with her.

But she could still smell her, hear her panting, the way she did when they made love.

Then, clear as a bell, though impossibly far away, she heard Carred in ecstasy, calling her name.

"Marith. Ah, Marith!"

And she could feel her now. No longer in the throes of passion. Alone in the dark. Afraid. Devoid of hope.

The little girl lost in the woods Carred had told her about.

"Oh no, my love," Marith said, useless, unable to help. "Please don't despair."

Then she stood and went face-to-face with Theltek.

"Whatever it takes, whatever it costs, give me a way to help her. You hear, Theltek of the thousand ears? Even if it kills me."

FORTY-ONE

LIGHT CAME AS SUDDENLY AS it had vanished. It fell like an axe—or the great sword the Grand Master's executioner had used on the Niyandrians at Branil's Burg.

Almost at once, footsteps approached the barge, as if whoever it was had anticipated the return of the sun. To Anskar, the alternation of night and day seemed chaotic and unpredictable, but maybe it wasn't so to the denizens of Vulthanor.

"They're coming," Blaice said needlessly. She had done nothing but fidget since they came aboard. "And about bloody time, too. I'm stiff all over."

"That'll be your age," Anskar said wryly. "But did you notice? The dark lasted only an hour or so this time."

"It felt like a bloody millennium."

She was nervous, that much was clear. But a woman of her experience—all the ruins she had raided—perhaps she felt less confident with only Anskar beside her; just one companion to use up as fodder this time.

The barge rocked as someone came aboard and moved toward the stern. Anskar heard the grate and clunk of the steering oar being released, and then the barge rocked again as a second demon boarded. Two, then, as he had observed before: one to steer, the other to guard.

Anskar was tempted to reach out with his senses to see if he could gauge their strength, but thought better of it, on the off chance that one or both of them might detect his intrusion. The last thing they needed was a fight in the midst of the settlement.

His dark-tide reserves had barely diminished since he had shrouded them in shadow. The brief snatch of night had partially replenished him, till his veins seethed with virulence. What would happen if he had an opportunity to fully welcome the dark-tide? The thought both frightened and intrigued him.

A flash of light out of the corner of his eye made him turn. Blaice had opened her lodestone so that she could check the alignment of the silver filament. Anskar placed his hand over the top of it.

"When we get underway," he mouthed.

Blaice rolled her eyes, and he could understand why. Beneath his shrouding darkness and the heavy tarp, there was little to no chance that the demons at the stern would spot the light. But still, you could never be too careful.

It seemed an age before they got moving. A demon barked something unintelligible from the wharf, and one of the demons at the stern shouted back. There were a few brief minutes of the two demons on board muttering to each other, then a yelled signal from the wharf, and the hull began to thrum.

Anskar glanced at Blaice, who shrugged.

Slowly at first, but gaining speed, the barge began to move

through the water. Only Anskar had no idea how the demons were doing it. All he had seen was a steering oar, but nothing that would assist with propulsion.

After a while, he grew accustomed to the hum and vibration coming through the hull, and then he realized that Blaice had fallen asleep. Of course she had. She had not really settled in the cave beneath the mesa, and since that time it had been all go: miles and miles of hiking, then feasting on raw flesh and strong spirits. She must have been exhausted. So should he have been, yet he remained alert. He was too anxious to sleep. Anxious about being found, but more anxious about where they were going. No, he wouldn't risk sleeping, so he decided to spend the time examining the kernel of demon essence that seemed to reside somewhere within his skull.

When he probed it this time, it seemed to harden against him. The thing was sentient, he was sure of it. Sentient and scheming against him. Part of him wanted to oust it at once, but he didn't know how. Another part rose to the challenge, though, wanting to break its way inside and do combat with the demon—sorcerous, spiritual combat, wherein one would absorb the other. For that was what he was certain must happen.

He fashioned the tip of a ribbon of dark-tide into a sharp point before he realized he was doing it. It felt natural, almost familiar. Then, with that sharp point, he scraped away at the casing of the egg within his mind. When that achieved nothing, he refashioned the ribbon so that its end resembled a tiny axe. And now he chipped away at the kernel, his excitement growing as fragments of darkness broke away. He kept striking the shell, slowly excavating what lay beneath. It was both intangible and impossibly dense; it felt as solid as a mountain yet as ephemeral as smoke.

At last, though, a hairline fissure split the shell, and something escaped in whorls of mist. In a sudden panic, fearing he had gone too far, too soon, Anskar sealed the fissure with a surge of dark-tide, but not before a contact had been established.

He had a name now: Sicth-Na'Jagalot.

He had an order: Thirty-Seventh.

And more than that, he felt a hunger, an insatiable desire to break free of the kernel that contained it and smother him, consume Anskar's own essence, his soul.

For Sicth-Na'Jagalot, demon of the Thirty-Seventh Order, Anskar perceived, as if they spoke the same language, recognized him as one who was steeped in the dark-tide. And that meant only one thing to such a demon: opportunity. Lust for power.

It wanted nothing more than to rise to the challenge and consume him.

Anskar and Blaice remained hidden from the oarsman and his guard, but when the barge came to a stop, crashing against the stone of the wharf, Anskar decided it was time to take a look outside the tarp. He left Blaice sleeping and waited till the demons had clambered onto the wharf and moored the barge. They exchanged words he could not understand, then moved off—he assumed to relieve themselves or do whatever it was that demons did.

Anskar hesitated a while longer, then decided to risk his senses. He sent out threads of awareness to scour the wharf, but the demons had passed beyond his range. Taking that as a good sign, he found an opening in the tarp and pushed his head out.

They had stopped in the middle of nowhere, but he guessed the demons needed a break, for they had been traveling a good few hours. He saw them now, a few hundred yards from the canal. The armed guard had his spear leveled at something on the ground, while the pilot stood by, drinking from a canteen.

Anskar glimpsed a small settlement back the way they had come. Mercifully, they had not stopped there. Farther from the canal, in the midst of sparse, sprawling plains dotted with the same tree-like plants they had seen earlier, Anskar spotted several more clusters of blister-like huts, and when he looked ahead in the direction they had been traveling, he saw more and more such buildings bunched together in what he took to be villages and towns.

And directly ahead, still miles in the distance, loomed the mountain that was in reality the city of Artuum-Nak'Urdim, their journey's end. The canal, it seemed to him, ran straight toward the center of the city, and he could just about make out the haze coming off several more canals intersecting with Artuum-Nak'Urdim, which sat at the center of eight such channels, and by extension, the center of this region of Vulthanor.

He squinted, the better to see, and realized the mountain was different to any he had seen before: it was too perfect, too symmetrical. At intervals it shimmered and glinted with the reflected colors of the clouds. Thready veins of blackness formed a halo about the summit that shivered, twitching in response to some unseen touch; or perhaps they were attuned to sounds or the shift of sorcerous tides? Maybe they could feel him watching?

He looked away, exposed and discomfited, then ducked down out of sight as the demons headed back towards the barge, one of them dragging the carcass of a man-sized lizard behind him, which he must have just killed. So they had stopped for breakfast—or was it lunch?

He sat clenched up, gripping his knees beneath the tarp,

listening to Blaice's fitful snores and the sounds of the demons ripping and chewing as they devoured their catch on the bank of the canal.

At length, when they had finished and clambered back aboard, Anskar closed his eyes as they got underway. He wanted so much to pray; but pray to whom or what? Menselas would never again listen to him—if he had at all in the past—and who else was there? Theltek of the Thousand Eyes? He knew nothing of the Niyandrian gods, save that everyone cursed by their names. Again he yearned for his mother's spirit within him, but could even the Necromancer Queen aid him here?

Maybe, the dark-tide sluicing through his veins seemed to say. *Probably.*

The lapping of the canal water against the prow and the gentle rocking of the barge must have lulled Anskar to sleep. He woke to voices—some guttural, almost growling, others high-pitched and musical. None of them were speaking words he could understand. He recognized the voices of the two demons from the barge, one of them grumbling and the other making a rumbling sound that could have been laughter.

He turned his senses inwards, to make sure his dark-tide cloaking was still in place, and then he poked his head out from beneath the tarp.

It was cool outside. They were in shadow. At first he thought it was a cave, but then he saw light streaming in from every side, and there was water all around. He crawled to the gunwale, and what he saw made him want to slink back beneath the tarp and hide.

The barge was moored at a jetty on the edge of what Anskar at first took to be an inland sea, it was so vast. But as his eyes adjusted to the gloom, he could see they had come to rest within a circular lake hundreds of yards across. This body of water—clearly artificial—was fed by eight canals that entered it in perfect symmetry. Even now barges were coming and going, and others were moored at the hundreds of jetties that jutted into the water from the retaining wall that ran around the entire circumference.

But it was above that held the greatest shock. A ceiling of shimmering blue rock, veined with glittering seams of purple, shaded the entire lake. Rope ladders hung down from openings in the ceiling, and armies of gray-skinned demons ascended and descended. Robed demons stood on the wharves, conducting business with the barge crews, smaller, pale-skinned demons standing by with ledgers, upon which they checked off quotas using silvery styluses.

Several of the barges were stacked high with massive crates, one of which even now was being hoisted toward a trapdoor in the ceiling by a block and tackle.

But a ceiling without walls? Anskar turned his head to take in more of the surroundings, and he saw pilings driven into the bed of the lake, massive pilings—or should he call them pillars?—of some glistening black metal that extended to the ceiling some fifty feet above. There were dozens of them, he now saw, all around the perimeter of the lake, all as thick as ancient trees and supporting the immense weight above. For he realized then that this was no mere ceiling, no platform raised on black metal pillars. The barge had come to a stop beneath a mountain. They had arrived at Artuum-Nak'Urdim.

Anskar ducked back under cover as traps opened directly above and rope ladders dropped down to the deck of the barge. He peeked above the tarp to see that demons were already swarming down the ladders, and the two demons who had crewed the barge were striding along the jetty to greet a robed demon and his ledger man.

Covering Blaice's mouth with one hand, Anskar shook her awake. Playfully, she bit him. Her eyes snapped open, and she frowned a question.

"Demons," he whispered. "Everywhere." He removed his hand.

"We've arrived, I assume. And they're everywhere, you say? Can you still cloak us?"

"The cloak obscures, but it doesn't blind them. We're not invisible. But I think I know what to do."

The dark-tide within his veins no longer ran through his fingers like water. He could grasp it now, and he could direct it.

The barge rocked under the weight of demons dropping from the ends of their ropes. They tramped across the deck, inspecting the cargo and calling out to one another. He had to make his move and make it quickly.

"Hold my hand," Anskar said.

"I thought you'd never ask."

"This is going to feel very strange. Have you ever shadow-stepped before?"

"Of course I have," Blaice said. "Depends on what you mean by shadow-step."

"I'll take that as a no. Just hold onto my hand, and hold your breath. It might stop you from being sick all over me."

Before Blaice could say another word, Anskar made a conscious connection with the dark-tide in his veins, feeling it shiver in response. Then he stared at the shadows pooling at the base of one of the black metal pilings and poured his awareness into the darkness. His mind melted and drained away. When he and Blaice re-formed beside the massive pillar, Blaice retched, but Anskar dragged her by the hand to the far side, away from the activity on the lake. At the same time, he refashioned cloaking shadows around them.

"Hah!" Blaice whispered. "I didn't throw up." She promptly did. "Oh…" she groaned. "Oh!"

"Quiet," Anskar said. "This cloak of darkness does nothing to dampen sound."

"All right, all right," Blaice said. She spat bile from her mouth and grimaced. "So, what do we do now? Camp out here till it's dark again?"

"No," Anskar said, tracing his hand over the outline of a circular hatch set into the wall of the piling. At his touch, the panel shuddered and popped open, and Anskar jumped back, alarmed.

"How did you do that?" Blaice asked.

"I don't know. It's as if… it knew me."

"You felt that, just from touching it? That's… disturbing."

She wasn't wrong there. His blood was still bubbling and seething from the contact. Yet the panel was open. But what had drawn him to it in the first place?

"Wait," Blaice hissed. "Before we go in there, and perhaps never come out again, let me check this."

She drew out the lodestone from her pocket and frowned down at it. Anskar looked too. The silver indicator was whirling erratically back and forth.

"It won't settle on a direction," Blaice said. "Some help this piece of junk turned out to be."

"But it only works on one plane," Anskar said. "North, south, east, and west. What if we're right below the target—this stash of star-metal?"

Blaice glanced up at the bluestone ceiling, where the stream of demons going up and down the rope ladders showed no signs of slowing.

"Or what if it's below us?"

"How can you tell which?" Anskar said.

"I can't." She moved to the open hatch and peered inside. "But unless you can climb like a spider…"

"I think I can," Anskar said, feeling the thrill of dark-tide effusing from his fingers and toes. "I did it before."

"Yes, well, I can't, so our choice is made for us."

She stood back from the opening so he could see. There was a ladder of the same dark metal as the pilings leading down into the dark. Above, there were only the bare walls of the inside of the piling, perfectly smooth, as if they had been molded in one piece.

"After you," Blaice said.

Anskar shook his head. What would be the point in arguing?

"Is this why you always survive?" he asked.

"It's one of several reasons."

The instant his hands gripped the ladder, Anskar's blood turned cold—literally. The cloak of shadows that had covered them vanished, and he could no longer feel the dark-tide coursing through his veins.

"Quickly," Blaice said, "before one of them sees us."

Anskar started to descend, glancing up as Blaice entered through the hatch and closed it behind her.

Then, with the sound of their boots on the metal rungs, their ragged breaths in their ears, and the feel of the ladder the only thing to guide them, they descended into the stygian darkness.

FORTY-TWO

THE LADDER DESCENDED PERHAPS TWO hundred yards before they reached solid ground. No sooner had Anskar released his grip on the ladder than the dark-tide in his blood began to seethe and bubble once more.

"How're those cat's eyes of yours holding up?" Blaice asked, fumbling for his hand in the dark. "Because I can't see a bloody thing."

Neither could Anskar: the darkness was a little too absolute, even for his Niyandrian eyes. But he could feel the dark-tide goading him, willing him to—what?—to embrace an intuition that had not even fully formed?

"You think your Theltek would have this problem?" he asked. "Out of those thousand eyes, surely at least one must be able to see in the dark."

As he spoke those last four words, he felt the dark-tide stir in his blood, and a mauve glow started up on his palm. He held his hand in front of his eyes and felt both satisfaction and dread. What else could he do that he didn't yet know about? And without the usual calculations and Skanuric cants he'd thought all sorcery needed… Perhaps most, if not all, demon sorcery was instinctive; ingrained rather than extrinsic.

The radiant sphere of mauve swirled in his open hand. Its glow didn't extend beyond itself: it shed no light like a candle or a lamp. Yet, as soon as the sphere had appeared, everything else—Blaice, Anskar, the walls of the massive tunnel they now stood in—was limned in the same mauve glow.

"How did you do that?" Blaice asked.

Anskar chuckled. "Maybe Theltek sent us one of his eyes."

"Don't be absurd. That's an effect of the dark-tide, isn't it?"

"I'd like to hear the priests of the Elder explain this," Anskar said. "Darkness that produces light."

They stood at a crossroads, with no way of differentiating among the four passageways that moved away from them. Each was a vast tube of dark metal, half again as tall as Anskar and wide enough for three people to stand abreast.

"Is this…?" Blaice started, brushing the surface of the wall nearest her with her fingertips. She turned wide eyes on Anskar. "If this is void-steel… do you have any idea how much this stuff is worth?"

"Always thinking about profits," Anskar said. "We're here to pay off debts to Sheelahn, remember? Nothing else."

"But—"

"Stay if you like, but once we've found what Sheelahn sent us here for, I'm leaving." The abyssal realms had introduced a level of discomfort he wasn't used to, not to mention revelations about himself he wasn't willing or ready to accept.

"Which way?" he asked.

Blaice studied the face of the lodestone, then swung toward the right-hand passage.

A terrific cry went up from somewhere above, followed by an enormous splash. A voice like thunder blared out, causing the tunnel they were in to shake. Anskar threw his arms out to keep his balance.

"What was that?" he asked, heart racing.

Blaice held up a hand for silence. Up top, it had gone quiet. "I don't think it has anything to do with us, otherwise there would be sounds of pursuit. It sounded to me as though they dropped something—something really heavy. You saw those massive crates they were unloading. Maybe a pulley snapped."

"Maybe," Anskar said. He hoped she was right. "Come on. This place gives me the creeps."

"Welcome to my world," Blaice said, gesturing for him to take the lead once more. "Most of the places I explore give me the creeps. It's why I need to drink and do other things to relax as soon as my missions are over. I'm sure you're going to feel the same way when we get back."

He couldn't see her expression in the dull mauve light, but he could imagine it.

"Do you ever stop?" he asked. She was far worse than Sareya had been when they were postulants together.

The tunnel ended abruptly at a ramp of black metal limned with Anskar's mauve light that descended at a steep gradient.

"It's wide enough for a horse and cart," Blaice observed as they went down, boots clanging no matter how softly they tried to tread.

The ramp continued for about twenty yards then came to an L-shaped landing that switched back and led to another ramp down. Each ramp they came to led deeper and deeper below the lake, forming a zigzagging descent that seemed to go on forever. At every landing, Blaice would check the lodestone and find its indicator spinning wildly. But once they started to descend again, the indicator would settle.

"I think we're going the right way," she said. "And I think we might be getting close."

"To the star-metal? How can you tell?"

"The indicator hardly moves except when we come to a new level, and then it goes crazy, like it did before we entered the piling. We could be directly above the stash."

"Or below it," Anskar said, "and getting farther away."

"No, it's below, I'm sure of it," Blaice said. "I have a special sense for these things."

"I'm beginning to think neither of us has any sense at all, to have accepted such a mission from the Ethereal Sorceress," Anskar said.

"You act like we had a choice."

"We did… before we asked Sheelahn for favors."

"Mainland bankers are the same," Blaice said. "Only they call it credit."

Finally, they came to a landing longer than the others, and it was straight, not doubling back on itself. At the far end was a door of the same dark metal—void-steel?—as the corridor. Set in the center of the door were two gemstones, one of sparkling quartz that chased away some of the gloom, the other of gleaming amethyst. To the right of the door, some kind of green phosphorescence had formed into the likeness of a mouth with fangs and thin lips. On the left, another mouth. Beneath each was a series of letters that Anskar recognized but didn't understand.

"Nazgrese," he said.

"The left-hand one says, 'One of us always deceives,'" Blaice said. "The right, 'One of us always speaks the truth.'"

The lips of the left-hand mouth moved, and a tinkling voice spoke.

"What did it say?" Anskar asked.

"It said I was wrong… I think," Blaice said.

And now the other mouth spoke, its voice resembling the growl of a wild animal.

"Then again…" Blaice said.

"The right-hand mouth said you were correct?"

Blaice let out a world-weary sigh. "It must have been a mid-order demon who came up with this! Not exactly the original thinking you'd expect from a higher-order demon or a demon lord."

"You've seen something like this before?"

"Several times, in some of the older ruins. You're supposed to ask the mouths how to open the door—in this case, which crystal to press, I assume." When nothing happened, Blaice said, "Let me rephrase that," then proceeded to speak in guttural words that must have been Nazgrese.

Both mouths spoke at the same time.

"Let me guess," Anskar said. "No and yes?"

"Ignore them," Blaice said. "There's a method to this. A companion of mine—a priest of the Elder, if you'd believe it, called it logic."

"I suppose he didn't survive."

Blaice puffed out her cheeks. "Afraid not. It was a trap like this that killed him. He worked it all out and pronounced the solution with all the pompous hyperbole of his kind, and then pressed the wrong crystal. He realized at once, of course, but by then it was too late."

"What happened to him?"

"He dissolved into a pile of goo. I couldn't get it off my boots. Had to throw them away."

Anskar eyed the mouths warily, then tried to connect with the amethyst using his dark-tide feelers.

"Whatever you're doing," Blaice said, "stop."

Anskar swallowed, then drew the feeler back into himself, where it dispersed into his veins. "I thought I might—"

"These mechanisms, if that's what you call them, are obstinate things. You have only one way of opening the doors, and any attempt to do so by other means—especially sorcery—will trigger either an alarm or a trap. What we do is pray to your god of five aspects that I have remembered the priest of the Elder's reasoning aright. I would ask Theltek, only a thousand minds is a lot of minds for him to make up, and I'm likely to end up more confused than when I started."

Anskar shook his head. "You're not taking this very seriously, are you? Is it really so easy?"

"Of course it's easy; otherwise how do you think the demons come and go? Now, be quiet while I try to remember." She began to muse aloud: "One mouth always lies, the other always tells the truth. I assume," she said, "that I am only permitted one question as regards how to open the door." She translated her question into Nazgrese.

Both mouths replied. Anskar could guess what they said this time.

"Well, that was helpful," Blaice said. "Best to assume one question, then. All right, here we go. If you are the liar," she said, jabbing a finger at the left-hand mouth, "you would tell me to press the wrong crystal. And if you always tell the truth, you would tell me to press the correct one. The problem is, how do I know which of you tells the truth and which lies? And for the record, I'm being rhetorical."

Neither mouth responded, presumably because they only spoke and understood Nazgrese.

Anskar tried to work it out. "If you ask the left-hand mouth how to open the... No, wait, it might be lying."

"I just said that," Blaice said. "Now, do be quiet while I... Aha! I think I recall."

"You'd better be sure you do," Anskar said.

"The priest of the Elder worked it out," Blaice said. "You have to ask one mouth what the other mouth would say and then do... do what? The opposite? Or do what it says? This is where the priest made a mistake. He was so bloody cocky, it served him right. The rest of us got through after that, and the loss of one life was actually a remarkably small price to pay."

"Don't let me stop you from being the one to press the crystal," Anskar said.

"Have you always been such a coward, Anskar DeVantte?"

"Only when on a mission with you."

"Fine, I'll take the risk," she said, then made a show of deliberating, going over her logic.

"All right, I'm ready," she said, squaring up to the door, hand hovering over the crystals. To the left-hand mouth she asked, "If I were to ask the right-hand mouth which of these crystals I should press to safely open the door, what would its reply be?"

Nothing happened.

Blaice slapped her forehead. "You could have told me to speak in Nazgrese this time!" She tried again, and the left-hand mouth gave a one-word reply.

Blaice's hand moved to cover the quartz crystal, wavered there for a moment, then moved to the amethyst. Anskar could almost hear her mind grinding out the calculations. "No, that's what

Brother Diwalf did, the arrogant fool. He was so concerned about his reputation and his beckoning fame should we return from the mission intact, I fear it blinded him to what must, to him, have been patently obvious."

Her hand darted back to the quartz crystal, and Anskar winced as she pressed it.

"Ta-da!" Blaice said as the door slid open with a rushing sound. A wave of hot air hit Anskar in the face.

"You were just trying to scare me," Anskar said. "You knew all along which one to press, else you wouldn't have taken the risk yourself. You'd have made me choose."

"Do you think so little of me?" Blaice said, peering through the open doorway to the passageway beyond.

No more black metal here: the walls, ceiling, and floor looked to have been bored out of the same porous rock as the mesas they had passed on their way to Artuum-Nak'Urdim. Every surface glistened with water and was scabbed with black, furry growths.

"I think you have a knack of surviving at the expense of your comrades. Are you going to explain the riddle?"

"I'd have thought you would have worked it out by now," Blaice said, "a clever sorcerer like you. Whichever mouth you ask, always do the opposite. The truthful mouth will tell you the lie its counterpart would give, and the lying mouth will lie about the answer the truthful mouth would give. Easy, see?"

"It's easy now you've explained it," Anskar said as he followed Blaice across the threshold.

The air in the passageway was humid and smelled of mold. It was difficult to breathe, and when he tried to fill his lungs, the stench of the mold grew overpowering and made him sneeze.

"Shush," Blaice said. "Unless you want to announce our presence to any demons who happen to be down here."

Anskar couldn't help himself: he sneezed again, trying to muffle the sound with his sleeve.

Blaice consulted the lodestone, then led them to an intersection, where she took the right-hand path. Here, the passageway had been smoothed over and finished with some kind of plaster, and there were circular doors of frosted crystal all the way along the walls on either side. When Anskar pressed his face up against one of the doors and tried to peer inside, Blaice grabbed him by the earlobe and tugged him away.

"We're here for one reason, and one reason alone," she said, eyes on the lodestone's indicator as she strode ahead.

Anskar followed her through a labyrinth of passageways, past hundreds of crystal doors, some of which were open onto storerooms heaped with sacks and crates, and one in which the carcasses of dozens of large lizards were hanging from meat hooks above trays of glowing red stones. The entire room smelled of chicken and spice and caused Anskar's stomach to rumble.

"Keep going," Blaice said over her shoulder. "Unless you want to be numbered among those I've left behind."

As he ran to keep up with her, she said, "See, this is why I lose so many companions. The idiots lose sight of the very specific reasons we enter the ruins. Get what it is you're looking for and get out is my motto. But by all means, if you want to stuff your face on spiced lizard, go ahead. Just don't blame me if you don't make it back to Dorinah alive."

She rounded a corner and stopped outside a crystal door so abruptly, Anskar bumped into her.

"Really, Anskar, now is not the... Aha! I think we've arrived."

Anskar peered over her shoulder at the lodestone. The silver filament was spinning so fast, it was no more than a blur.

"Don't you think it's odd," he said, "that we've seen no demons down here? I mean, if this star-metal is so important to them—"

"Dangerous to them is what it is," Blaice said. "Perhaps they have good reason to keep away."

"So, how do we open the door?"

Blaice ran her hand over the crystalline surface. "I don't know. I've seen similar doors in the ruins that open to the touch, only it depends on who does the touching." She looked askance at him. "Perhaps you should try?"

"Oh, no," he said. "I'm not falling for that. You're the expert. You get it open."

"If you insist. I'll try, but as you can see"—she pressed her palm to the crystal surface—"it doesn't appreciate my touch half as much as you seemed to."

Anskar almost snarled as he pushed past her to look for himself. "No sorcerous mouths," he noted. "No riddles."

Blaice widened her eyes mockingly and nodded as if she hadn't already noticed.

"Try pushing it," he said. "Put your shoulder into it."

"Why don't you?"

Anskar gritted his teeth. "Blaice, if you know something, please tell me."

"I know as little as you, save for what I told you. I've seen doors in the past that open to touch, but…"

"Not everyone's touch, I know. Is this why Sheelahn sent me along? Because she knew I could open this door?"

"How would she know that?" Blaice said.

"I imagine you both knew, and that you discussed it at length before I was brought to the depot. Sheelahn is no fool. She knew about my blood. I assume that's what you're implying… That the door will open to the touch of a demon."

"Of that I have no doubt," Blaice said. "But will it work for a part-demon? Sheelahn was quite clear the better part of you was anything but. What confused her was where the demon part came from."

She stood back from the door and gestured for Anskar to approach it.

"Why would such a valuable stash of star-metal be accessible to just any old demon?" he asked.

Blaice held his gaze. "I, too, have wondered about that. Perhaps Sheelahn was wrong, or perhaps she knows something we do not." She nodded toward the door.

With a sigh, and with his heart thumping in his chest, Anskar raised his hand and pressed his palm to the door. The crystal was initially cold, then suddenly grew hot and caused his skin to tingle. A thrill ran along his nerves, and something like a bubble of air popped within his skull, leaving him with the sense that he was known, that he was... permitted.

The crystal door slid open.

"Did I mention that I'm the best in the business?" Blaice said. With an expansive gesture, she invited Anskar to look inside.

It was a large storeroom that, unlike the others they had glanced into, was neatly organized. There were crates stacked to the ceiling in each of the four corners, and around the walls, animal skins, many of them reptilian, hung from hooks. But it was to the center of the room Anskar's eyes were pulled. There, a cylinder of swirling shadows rose from the floor to the ceiling, and within it he could just about make out the shapes of more crates, of weapons, and of a huge chunk of smooth, shiny rock.

"Have you got any idea what that shadowy cylinder is?" Blaice asked. "Because I haven't. But according to the lodestone, we're in the right spot. That's one big heap of star-metal inside."

"We'll never be able to carry it all," Anskar said.

"We won't have to... unless... please don't tell me you've managed to lose the miniature depot?"

"Of course I haven't." But just to be sure, Anskar reached into his pocket and felt the contours of the model. "But how does that help?"

"Oh, you'll be surprised, and not a little impressed. When I give the go-ahead, all you need do is twist the base and make sure you continue to hold it. I, naturally, will be holding your hand."

"It's a teleport?"

"It is not. It's far more interesting than that."

"So what are we waiting for?" Anskar asked.

"We are waiting for you, the sorcerer, to come up with a way to remove the ward, or whatever you call that cylinder of blackness around the star-metal."

Anskar ran his eyes over the gaseous barrier until it made him nauseous and he had to look away.

"It appears similar to the cloak of shadows I wove with the dark-tide," he said.

"But is that all it is?"

Anskar sighed. Was this the trap that would see him slain and Blaice the sole survivor of another expedition? "I don't know." But she clearly expected him to find out.

Already the darkness in his veins was shivering with anticipation. It was as though it wanted him to draw upon it. It also seemed to prompt him this time, for it felt more like a suggestion than an intuition. Instead of his usual feeler of awareness, filaments of dark-tide spurted from his pores, hundreds upon hundreds, thrashing and swaying, straining to be unleashed.

He glanced at Blaice, but she had a look of strained patience on her face. She raised an eyebrow, as if to tell him to get on with it, but clearly she couldn't see what Anskar could with his senses.

With the merest thought, he gave his consent, and the filaments lashed towards the dark cylinder. Again, he had the sensation of being known, of his authority being recognized.

What now? he wondered.

He could feel some kind of warning conveyed through his dark-tide filaments, but whatever threat there was, it seemed, was not aimed at him.

He decided to try something, and, while holding onto his rudimentary communion with the filaments, he willed the cylinder to vanish in the same manner he could dispel his cloak of shadows. And, to his complete and utter amazement, the cylinder did just that, evaporating into the air and leaving only swords and spears, axes, glaives, ingots, and tiny balls that might have been sling bullets, all of them glittering with unnatural intensity, and at the center of the hoard, a boulder of dark brown rock with seams of silvery ore running like veins across its surface.

"Well, that was worryingly easy," Blaice said. "I suppose Sheelahn knew what she was doing after all. Just look at that," she said, indicating the rock. "Those are veins of virgin star-metal. The rock must have fallen from the sky, according to your beloved priests of the Elder."

"What if someone's been alerted?" Anskar said. "Usually, with sorcery, there's someone maintaining it, or at the very least monitoring."

"Then we'd better get a move on," Blaice said, stepping into the room. "We need to stand at the center of the stash for this to work. On the rock is as good a place as any."

Anskar followed her into the room, but before they had crossed half the floor space, there was a shift in the shadows and movement from above.

"Shit—!" Blaice cried, covering her head with her arms.

Anskar looked up in time to see the ceiling, like some massive cloak, drop down on top of them.

FORTY-THREE

SOMETHING WAS DRIPPING. IT WAS more of an irritation than a concern. Anskar cursed under his breath and tried to go back to sleep. Or was it sleep? he wondered as he drowsed. The thought occurred to him that he could be in a grave, one of the restless dead, and that the dripping sound was water seeping into his coffin. To his surprise, the thought comforted him. Restless he might be, but at least it was still existence, of a kind.

He rolled over but couldn't get comfortable, and at the same time he knew he wasn't dead: his lungs were burning from lack of air—unless that was just a memory? Even so, he gasped and then began to suck in great gulps of damp air that smelled faintly of hot metal or the aftermath of a lightning strike.

He remembered a little more then: the ceiling coming down on top of him and Blaice, but not in any way he would have expected. It had rippled as it fell, like the unfurling of a sail from its mast. It did not crush; it smothered the two of them.

There had been a brief struggle, his limbs growing ever weaker. He couldn't breathe… Menselas, he couldn't… After that, he remembered no more.

Again he heard water drip, and he opened his eyes. A peculiar glow effused from the walls of the cell he found himself in—as if the bronze walls were on fire. The ceiling was comprised of some other material, clearly not up to the task. It sagged in the middle and was riddled with hairline cracks. Its original color might once have been gray, but the entire ceiling was coated with furry black mold. In several places, water was dripping from the mold, running out of the cracks webbing the ceiling. Did that mean he was still somewhere beneath the lake? Where was Blaice?

Anskar pushed himself up on one elbow. He was lying upon a wooden bench, and the thought struck him that he hadn't considered that there might be carpenters among the demons. Most of those he had previously encountered were brutish, no better than wild animals or the dead-eyes who haunted the wastes of Wiraya. But craftsmanship—or at least the ability to trade for it—should have come as no surprise. He had learned from the Abbess and from Malady that there was a hierarchy to demon society, and that the higher a demon rose through the orders, the more refined its intellect became, the more civilized its behavior. Allegedly. The most powerful demon he had thus far seen was Nysrog, during the Abbess's summoning, and he'd seen nothing civilized in that monster. Still, Nysrog had supposedly lost his mind after the priest Morudjin had summoned him. Nevertheless, there was obviously culture of an advanced kind here in Vulthanor: the immense structure of Artuum-Nak'Urdim was testament to that.

He sat up and promptly began a coughing fit. It felt as though his lungs were filled with tar, and as he coughed, he caught the stench of rotting fish that clung to his nostrils. He remembered the smell, then, from when the ceiling had engulfed him and Blaice: the rotting stench, the oily air within the confines of the cloak-like ceiling as it tightened around them, diminishing the available air until they must have both passed out.

His coughs turned to retching, and then the relief of vomiting—a long stream of acrid muck that burned his throat as it came up. After he had finished, Anskar spat, then wiped his mouth with his sleeve, only then realizing he was still wearing his mail.

Did that mean…? He checked his pockets. The miniature depot was still there. So he still might escape. But would the depot work here, or only where it was meant to be used? He wasn't sure. All he knew was that the depot was to be activated, Blaice had said, from the center of the stash of star-metal. Use it now and he would presumably fail the mission—especially if he returned without Blaice, a valuable asset to Sheelahn.

The only thing that was missing—other than Blaice—was his sword. He stood and gave a cursory scan of the cell, but not surprisingly, there was no sign of *Amalantril*, just piles of what looked like chicken bones but on closer inspection turned out to be the skeletons of lizards.

It was then that he noticed the cell had no door. It was essentially a tube of gently glowing bronze with a stone floor and mold-covered ceiling. The realization sent him into a panic, and he circled the cell, running his hands over the concave walls, seeking the outline of a door. In his frantic mind, he was back in his cell at the Abbey of the Hooded One, sullied by the things he had been forced to do there. He turned back to the center of the cell in disgust, kicking through the detritus on the floor in case there should be a hatch or a trapdoor. Nothing, not even amid the mold on the ceiling.

Anskar's heart raced. He spun frantically, in case there was something he had missed. Again the sensation that he'd been buried alive took his mind captive, only this time there was no peculiar comfort from it, only panic. He struggled to breathe, and as he snatched in air with shallow gasps, he again began to cough.

Why had he come here? He should never have asked favors of the Ethereal Sorceress. He should never have put himself in her debt. Then, with a sudden suspicion rising to the surface of his mind, he ceased coughing and instead grew angry.

Blaice.

What were the odds she had somehow evaded capture? More likely, she'd been in collusion with the demons all along. What if she was with them now, laughing at how she'd led him into a trap? She might even have found her way back to Niyas without him. He could almost hear her boasting about being the best in the business. And he could feel his knuckles splitting against her teeth as he knocked the smirk off her face.

"You fool!" he said, slapping himself on the forehead. "There must be something you can do. Think!"

He plunged his senses within and clutched dozens of dark-tide threads, peeling them from his veins. He would do the same as he'd done when he'd caused a sphere of dark light to burn upon his palm, only much larger, much fiercer, and he'd use it to blast his way out of the cell. More than a fool, he'd been an idiot to have his catalyst removed. How much more powerful an explosion could he have made with the added virulence of the dusk-tide?

Setting aside past mistakes, past regrets, he focused all his attention on the space between his raised hands, willing the dark-tide to coalesce there, but nothing happened. The instant the dark-tide escaped through the pores in his skin, it dissipated like whorls of mist.

"No!" he muttered, then he shouted, "No!"

It was something about the cell, about this doorless cylinder of—was it really bronze?—interfering with his sorcery. But of course it was. This was a city and a land of demons. The cell was designed to thwart the attempts of demon captives to escape using the dark-tide that was innate to them.

He hammered the walls with his fists, cursing at the top of his voice. Where was Menselas? Where had Menselas ever been? Nowhere, that's where. The god of five aspects didn't exist! Or if he did, he was impotent, utterly useless. When had he ever come to anyone's aid, let alone Anskar's?

Before he could retract his blasphemy, or before he could add to it, water sluiced down from above in a tight stream, and then a pair of boots plopped through the ceiling as if it were made of fluid. Tattered pants followed, a hunched and twisted torso riddled with spines, then a skullish head with a thin layer of gray skin scraped across it like butter. Last of all came two gangly arms.

Anskar took a step back as the demon dropped to the floor and turned slitted eyes of maroon on him, its tongue flicking between black lips as it gargled and hissed. Water briefly cascaded over and around the demon until the black mold that coated the ceiling shifted—it actually moved, as if somebody had adjusted a tablecloth—to stem the leak, and the water returned to a steady drip, drip, drip.

The demon's tongue continued to dart in and out of its mouth as it made loathsome, ululating sounds, gargling and slurping as it formed words at the back of its throat—Nazgrese words that Anskar couldn't understand, but from the way the demon's eyes narrowed and the aggressive posture it took, Anskar had the impression it was cursing him. The stream of what felt like abuse petered out, replaced by a hideous gurgling laugh; and then, taking a step towards him, the demon opened its mouth wide and ran its tongue around its palate. At first Anskar thought it was planning to attack, to bite him, even to eat him. But then the demon's tongue glided over sharp teeth and made little darting movements, like the death throes of a blind snake.

"Here doing, what are its, hurgh?" It was Nan-Rhouric of a kind.

Anskar backed away to the wall, which thrummed when he touched it and sent a thrill—almost painful—through his nerves. The demon slobbered as it laughed.

"Where is Blaice?" Anskar demanded.

"Blaice? Blaice? What Blaice is?"

"My companion," Anskar said. "The woman who was captured with me."

The demon's yellow eyes widened till they resembled not so much slits as glowing coins. "Argh, Blaice. Yes, Blaice. She no demons, no. Nurgh. Eats her, we does."

"You've eaten her?"

"Maybes both yous we eats, and the other creeping one."

Anskar's hands balled into fists at his sides. If the thing took another step closer, he'd…

"Other one? What other one? Someone else, like me, like Blaice?"

"Shuts its gob! Talks no more. Eat we may, yes, urgh, but not yets, though, nurgh. Firsts, things we must do. The bosses will expect it."

A snaggletoothed grin split the demon's skull-like face as it raised a hand, fingers splayed. The nails were long and curled, and they gleamed with the same light and color as the bronze walls of the cell. Their tips looked painfully sharp.

"Firsts," the demon said as it pressed up close to Anskar and touched its bronze claws to his throat, "speaks we musts."

Anskar tensed, but with those talons so close, he dared not lash out at the creature. Instead, he swallowed thickly and held himself back.

The demon ran its abrasive tongue up the side of his neck, then, with a sharp sniff at his skin, pulled away.

"In you, it is! Or it, you is. Nurgh, no, gurgh. In your bloods it is… and something…"

The demon backed away, eyes wider than ever, mouth hanging open in shock. "Higher, gargh! Highs enough to raise us! Nurgh, no, too high for us, it is. We'd never wins it. Too strong, it is, gargh. Too strong. And that not fairs, it isn't. Nurgh. And we's was so hungries, yargh. But now it's not for us, nurgh. Splits our skulls, it woulds, if we tries to absorbs it. No, to the bosses you must go. The bosses knows what with you to do, they wills. Maybes the bosses absorbs it. Gurgh."

And with that, the demon leaped into the air. Its hands stuck momentarily to the ceiling, which then parted like oil. The demon shot upwards, as if someone had pulled him from above, and the ceiling closed up once more.

Leaving Anskar alone again.

Alone with questions he had no way of answering.

Alone with his fears.

Who, or what, were the bosses?

He started at the sound of a muffled scream from somewhere beyond the walls of his cell. Was that a woman? Was it Blaice? Would he care if it was? The callousness of that thought stunned him. Of course he cared! All life was valuable in the eyes of… *No, it's not*, some other part of him said. *For Menselas's sake, does the Warrior value all life? Of course he doesn't!* The Warrior was always depicted slaying the enemies of the Five with hammer, axe, or sword, and his priests were some of the most violent men Anskar had ever known—especially under the influence of the Warrior's Fire.

Nor did the Hooded One value life. How could she, when she was also known as Death? Brother Tion had taught him a one-sided version of a five-faced god! Tion had taught piety and love, and then done whatever it was he wanted to do, and with whomever he wished. *And no, I'm not being unfair,* Anskar thought before he could mount a defense of his old mentor. *Tion's a hypocrite. They're all hypocrites!*

He paced the cell, careful not to come into contact with the bronze walls. What if the tingling sensation was a warning shot? What if a second touch would result in something much worse?

His head buzzed with thoughts both alien and familiar. And as he struggled to work out what he believed and what he did not, he became aware of the seething of his blood, the seepage of dark-tide essence through his pores.

He glanced up at the ceiling. Did the coating of mold just move again? He watched it intently till his neck hurt. He couldn't be sure, but he thought the fine hairs on the mold rippled from time to time. If the demon had exited the cell that way, perhaps he could as well? It seemed a long shot, but all the same, it was better than no shot at all.

Dipping his knees, Anskar jumped into the air with his hands overhead. His fingers struck the ceiling and found it solid. At the same time, the mold shivered, and a stinging sensation ripped through his fingers and along his arms, ending with an excruciating pain beneath his scalp. He cursed and doubled over in agony, clutching his head, scratching and pulling at his hair, until the pain abated.

He had barely had time to catch his breath when a droning hum started up. It seemed to be coming from the bronze walls.

Coldness seeped into Anskar's bones. He wasn't sure if it was from fear or some effect of the walls, for now they started to move. A single revolution at first, only discernible because of the shifting of the dim light in the cell. Then the cylinder that was the cell turned again, a complete turn, which caused Anskar to feel giddy and lose his balance.

He stumbled and threw out his hands to steady himself, only for the walls to revolve again, and again, building speed, until the cell dissolved into the shimmering and flashing of bronze light, flickering faster, faster, faster...

Anskar could smell hot metal and sulfur. His lungs burned when he inhaled. He shut his eyes against the flash coming off the walls as they spun and spun, but the light was somehow inside his head. He stumbled and swayed. His guts clenched, and then, with an audible suck and a pop, he was gone.

FORTY-FOUR

A SANDSTORM BLASTED THE INSIDE of Anskar's skull. The cascade of rubble deafened him. Lightning coursed through his veins and exploded from his eyes, and he flopped, invertebrate, to a hard floor. He tried to move, but none of his muscles would respond. His head rested on his arm, which was flaccid, amid an agony of pins and needles. He groaned and tried to twitch his fingers, and when nothing happened, his heart thudded as he started to panic.

When he opened his eyes, they were met with a gleam coming off the metallic floor, which, as he blinked, he could see was engraved with hundreds, thousands, millions of minute symbols, some of them Nazgrese letters, others geometric shapes, and still others in the form of simplistic pictures denoting waves, lightning, fire, and all manner of birds, reptiles, fish, and beasts.

There was a sudden pressure on the back of his neck, a clenching of the collar of his mail, and then he was hoisted into the air, suspended a foot above the floor, utterly limp and unable to feel anything below the neck. He knew only that it was a hand that had grabbed him—a hand belonging to someone or something massive, and with monstrous strength.

He couldn't turn his head to see, but he felt the weight of the presence holding him aloft, perceived it as dark and impossibly dense. The sensation was of the mass of a mountain packed into a gigantic humanoid form—perhaps eight or nine feet tall.

Anskar could only see directly ahead, where he was confronted by a semicircular dais of some dark stone that might have been onyx, upon which were seven thrones that looked as though they had been molded out of bronze. Seated upon each of the thrones was a figure swathed in shadows. Anskar had the sense of a solid form beneath the shadow-woven robes and hoods. One of the figures, even seated, was far taller than Anskar. Another, if standing, would scarcely have come up to his waist. One was broad, with the impression of huge muscles beneath the obscuring cloak of shadows. One was painfully thin, with long, slender fingers like the tines on a rake. All seven radiated colossal amounts of dark-tide essence.

His eyes were drawn to a silver crest on the concave wall behind where they were sitting, an engraved oval depicting some kind of coat of arms or symbol of office in the shape of a clenched fist beneath a floating eye. He caught sight of his reflection in the silver, dangling like a hooked fish, limp and lifeless. And he glimpsed the reflection of the one holding him: a massive, muscular demon wearing scaled armor of obsidian and a black hangman's hood with only narrow slits for its eyes. The exposed skin—shoulders and arms—was coarse and gray, and the little of the eyes he could see through the slits was violet.

Anskar tried to speak, but the only sound that came out was

a gurgling moan. Frantic, he reached inside for his dark-tide power, but all he felt was absence. Instead, he turned to the earth-tide, but the result was the same as before. Nothing.

One of the seated demons said something—it sounded like a command, but it was in Nazgrese. The demon holding him pulled up Anskar's sleeve to reveal his vambrace shining with scintillant colors, utterly visible. That should have been impossible. The vambrace only revealed itself in moonlight, although it had once become visible in the lost city of Yustanwyrd when the wraithes had confronted him. Anskar could see no source for the blue-tinted light that illuminated the chamber.

In perfect Nan-Rhouric, the demon holding him asked, "What is this for?" When Anskar didn't answer, for he still couldn't form words—not due to the effects of the transportation here, or from any sorcery the demons were using on him; he was literally shaking with fear. Without control over the dawn- and dusk-tide he was defenseless, a babe in the woods. What a fool he'd been to remove his catalyst!

The tallest of the seated demons said, also in perfect Nan-Rhouric, "There is void-steel in this vambrace you wear. Where did you come by void-steel?"

"He must have stolen it," the short demon said.

"Indeed," the tall one concurred. "Is that why you have come here to Vulthanor now—to steal more?"

Still Anskar could not speak. He whimpered and moaned, and tears stung his eyes. He hated himself for his weakness. He wasn't a child. It was shameful to feel like this. But what else could he do? Save for his mouth and his eyes, he was unable to move. Yet that wasn't the source of his terror. Neither was being confronted by this court of demons, he realized. His fear was something else altogether... something sorcerous.

His suspicions were immediately confirmed when the tall demon made a clutching motion with his hand and calm descended over Anskar. He could breathe properly now, fully and deeply. Then, at a nod from the tall demon, the demon holding him lowered him to the ground, where he crumpled into a heap, unable to move a muscle. The demon produced a black rod from a sheath at its side and touched the tip of the rod to Anskar's head. He gasped and then cried out as his skin prickled from head to toes, pins and needles scouring his veins as blood resumed its flow.

The seven demons opposite sat patiently, waiting until he had recovered, then the demon in the hangman's hood gestured for Anskar to stand. At first, he was unsteady on his feet and stumbled, but after wiggling his toes and stomping his feet, sensation returned, along with his balance.

"I didn't come here to steal," Anskar said.

The tall demon held up a hand for silence. "That I doubt very much. One of your companions admitted she had come for void-steel."

"Blaice wanted void-steel? That's news to me. Wait... What do you mean 'one of my companions'?"

"You deny there are three of you?"

"Yes, I deny it. Of course I deny it. It's just me and Blaice. Blaice Rancey. She was captured at the same time as I was."

"In the storerooms, yes. Void-steel I can understand. Your puny sorcerers are always trying to acquire it for their trinkets, but star-metal..."

"Your people stole it," Anskar said.

"Why would we not, when your kind would use it against us? Is that why you came here—to profit from void-steel and to take back weapons intended to harm demons? What is it you plan, the three of you? An attack on Vulthanor? An invasion of the abyssal realms?"

"You know that's not true," Anskar said. "With so few weapons, what could any invasion force hope to achieve?"

"You are assassins, then?"

"No!"

"Then why are you here?"

Anskar didn't know if he should answer that. He knew so little of the relations between the abyssal realms and the Ethereal Sorceress, but his impression was that they were not good. If he admitted that Sheelahn had sent him, would he be executed as a spy, as a thief? But what should he tell them, and would they know if he lied?

"I would advise you to answer," one of the seven said, the obscuring cloak of shadows lifting momentarily to reveal a lean, muscular woman with slate-gray hide and violet eyes as big as plates. As if she realized he had seen through the veil, she blinked rapidly and the shadows re-formed around her.

"You will tell us, at least, what you are," the smallest of the shadow wreathed demons said. "The jailer was correct: you are no mere human."

"And something is within him," the tall demon said. "You feel it? A coalescence, a knot of the dark-tide. One of our kind. It should not be there. Would not be if he were a mere human. So, what are you, a half-blood?"

"I've been called that before," Anskar said. "My mother was Niyandrian. My father was a knight of the Order of Eternal Vigilance."

The tall demon waved its hand, as if this were of no importance. "What are you... really?"

Again the veil of shadows dissipated, but only around the

tall demon. He could have passed for a slender man save for his yellowish skin, mottled all over with clusters of black marks that resembled bruises or perhaps mildew. The demon wore a long scarlet robe that left both his arms exposed—arms knotted with sinewy muscle and ending in tiny hands with glistening, manicured nails. His face looked as though it had been pinched in the middle: a broad, high forehead, sunken cheeks, and a curved chin. It had a piggish snout with flaring nostrils, and tiny eyes set in deep calderas of shadow—silver eyes that glinted like stars.

"You will answer," the demon said. At the same time, the demon with the hangman's hood slammed his fist into his palm. There was a resounding clang, which was when Anskar realized both the demon's hands were sheathed in black-metal gauntlets.

"Answer!" the tall demon demanded, standing and extending his hands toward Anskar. "Answer!"

The silver eyes flared. Pain ripped through Anskar's skull, spreading to his arms and legs. He jerked violently and collapsed to his knees, screaming as lightning seared every nerve in his body.

"Stop!" he tried to yell, but his lips were jelly. "Please stop!"—no more than a scream that would not leave his head.

He fell back, bucking his hips and arching his back as spasms wracked his body. Something cracked within Anskar's head… something not quite solid, not quite there. Through the agony, he felt the seep of dark vitriol beneath his scalp, and the furious pounding of… it had the sound of a heartbeat.

The agony stopped abruptly, leaving Anskar gasping on the floor. He felt warm dampness on the front of his pants, and his cheeks burned with shame. A dreadful stench reached his nostrils, and he squeezed shut his eyes. "Oh, Menselas," he groaned. "Menselas."

Chuckles passed among the seven watching demons. The

demon in the hangman's hood remained silent, but he stood directly above Anskar now, a threat waiting to be unleashed.

"Found your tongue yet?" the tall demon said.

Anskar tried to answer that he had, that he was willing to tell them anything they wanted to know, but the truth was, his tongue was limp, beyond his control. When he started to speak, drool trickled from his lips.

"So weak," another demon said—Anskar couldn't raise his head to see which.

"Pathetic," a female voice concurred.

"Is that what you think?" a tinkling voice asked.

This time Anskar craned his neck so he could see the speaker: no longer obscured by shadow, it was an unimposing form, perhaps a man, no taller than he was, no broader. A man robed in scarlet who sat with great poise and barely moved as he spoke, as if he were supremely confident in his power to command attention. And that would have been the truth. Despite the little he could see through the veil of shadows, Anskar couldn't take his eyes off the demon.

"While you have been employing your crude torture," the tinkling voice went on, "I have been discerning. You might want to do the same, Adjudicators," it told the other six. "Tell me what you find."

The air thrummed, and shadows dispersed, revealing all seven demons, each of different stature and with different hues to their skin. Some had slitted eyes, others oval or round. Some had scales, others porous hides like pliant sandstone. All wore uniform robes of scarlet.

Barbs snagged Anskar's nerves, but not to torment him this time: to infiltrate. He felt the crawl of multiple threads of awareness questing through his body, probing his blood, scouring his mind.

He didn't even bother trying to ward against the intrusions. What would be the point? His sorcerous powers had been taken from him, or at the very least, blocked. And even if they had not been, he knew he would have seemed an ant in sorcery compared with the dark-tide essence emanating from these demons. They were nothing like the creatures that had attacked him when he fled the Abbey of the Hooded One; nothing like those he'd seen above, loading and unloading the barges. Even the demon jailer had been nothing compared with these seven, little more than a beast with the ability to speak and perform one or two functions. But here, under the inspection of these seven red-robed demons, Anskar knew that he was the primitive beast in their eyes, his sorcery no better than a child's plaything.

And there are others still who far surpass even them, a grating voice said within him—it seemed to vibrate through his marrow and find its echo in his mind. The echoed words gave way to a heartbeat, faint at first, but growing stronger, growing faster as if it were racing toward some goal.

"Hah!" one of the seven cried. "Diluted but plain to see!"

"Once you muster the intelligence to look," the demon with the tinkling voice said. "It astounds me how you six ever rose so high. Who could have been foolish enough to allow you to absorb them?"

"I don't know what you are talking about," another said. "What do you mean diluted? Oh… Oh, now I have it! That's disgusting."

"Who would demean themselves so?" the tall demon said. "A higher-order demon, rutting with… with what?"

"There is mixed human blood, but the strongest strain is Niyandrian," the tall demon said. "I think we all know which Niyandrian!"

"Oh," said the woman. "*That* Niyandrian!"

Mocking laughter followed, then sneering remarks:

"The Necromancer Queen of Niyas!"

"Should have been put down when she slid from her mother's womb like the snake she was."

"I liked the look of her mother. So red, so succulent. Never did get a taste of her meat."

"His Lordship refused to share her," the demon with the tinkling voice said. "After she had served his sublime purposes. I have to say, I'm glad he didn't, considering the side effects of such a venomous meal."

"Unnatural is what it is," the tall demon said. "Rutting with a witch. Nothing sublime about sating appetites that should have long since been mastered."

"Ah," the tinkling voice said, "but the rules of self-mastery no longer apply to those who have ascended so high, or had you not noticed?"

"Oh, we've noticed," someone muttered, and the others grumbled in agreement.

"But are you saying…?" a demon asked. "Are you saying this is the son of Queen Talia of Niyas? But that would mean…"

"I wonder if His Supremacy is even aware," the tinkling voice said, then gave a gloating laugh.

Listen to them! the voice in Anskar's marrow said. It resounded louder in his head now, as if it had stepped through a wall into the same space where he was. The heartbeat quickened, pounding ever louder. Anskar heard the sound of something tearing, a succession of cracks.

Lust for the power we all do, of those above us, the voice said. *These fools no different are, and am I neither. Strong only survive. Absorbed the weak are. And weak you are, grandchild of a demon lord!*

The heartbeat raced to a gallop. Crack after crack after crack rent Anskar's skull. Heat bloomed between his eyes and bubbled like lava to fill his head. He swayed on his feet, clutching his ears against the pound, pound, pound of the heart. Dimly he heard the gasps and anxious cries of the seven demons: "What is happening?"; "What is he doing?"; "Stop that! Stop it at once—I command you!"

Command! the voice inside Anskar said. Only it came from his lips now. "Command of yours refuse I!"

"Is that—?" a demon asked in a shrill voice.

"Sicth-Na'Jagalot," Tinkling Voice said, "of the Thirty-Seventh Order." Then with a tinge of panic, it added, "A powerful higher-order demon, one who could one day become as we are!"

"Out of it stay, Adjudicators!" the voice speaking through Anskar said—Sicth-Na'Jagalot, the demon he had absorbed back in the cave he and Blaice had rested within. "Not permitted it is for you to interfere!"

Anskar flinched as the demon in the hangman's hood raised a metallic fist.

"No!" Tinkling Voice said. "Sicth-Na'Jagalot is correct. We cannot stand in the way of a fight for absorption."

"What does that even mean?" Anskar protested. "I already absorbed him!"

A couple of Adjudicators laughed at that.

"Apparently, you did not fully assimilate the essence of Sicth-Na'Jagalot," Tinkling Voice said. "Even the most lowly and bestial demon understands the need to do so. In the abyssal realms, we grant no second chances."

"I am no demon," Anskar said.

Again he clutched his head at the pressure mounting inside

his skull.

"No, you are not, despite the bloodline you belong to, albeit in a form so diluted you are tainted beyond redemption. The essence of Sicth-Na'Jagalot coalesced inside you. It sequestered itself in the shadow parts of your mind… gestating… ready to hatch like a serpent's egg. Ready to resume battle for dominion."

The heartbeat was now the hammering of rain on a window, the fierce patter of a deluge, the cascading downpour of a storm at sea. Anskar swayed, screaming against the pressure in his head. Crack after crack seemed to split his skull. The egg of hardness at the center of his mind started to split.

And then, with a fizzing pop that was surprisingly gentle, the hardness ruptured, and its contents swilled out into Anskar's mind. Not just his mind: every vein, every nerve, every pore and every marrow-filled channel in every single bone.

The seven demons in front of Anskar grew blurry to his sight, and what he saw of them no was longer moving. Any sound they made was just a muffled, long drawn-out echo that howled at the periphery of his awareness. It felt as if he were in another place entirely, alone, just he and the growing weight of a presence.

Darkness smothered the remnants of his blurred vision, obliterating the chamber in which he stood. And in the absolute black, he became aware of a silvery glow emanating from his body. He raised his hand to see the fingers mere outlines of argent; looked down to find his legs the same, defined by nothing more than starlight.

He looked up at a flash, also of silver. A single tongue of silver flame flickered in the air before him. It shuddered—seemed to breathe—and expanded. Shuddered again and grew till it stood in front of him, the same height, the same width, the exact same stature. Crudely etched as outlines of silver, even the eyes were the same, the mouth, the nose: all his, a mirror image of the sketched form of himself Anskar had become.

"It's not real," Anskar breathed. "This is not real."

"Oh, but it is," came the grating response from his silver-lined double.

And then it leaped at him.

FORTY-FIVE

SICTH-NA'JAGALOT'S LEAP TURNED INTO A drift as he slowly fell towards Anskar, his silver-lined form leaving a blurry trail in the air. As if he were moving through molasses, Anskar shifted to his right, out of the path of the demon, yet still a fist connected, glancing from his temple. There was pain—real pain—but it was the agony of the wracking nerves at the precise point Anskar had been struck.

As if in response to the contact, Sicth-Na'Jagalot's silver outline grew solid, filled out with flesh and tone and color, until he perfectly resembled Anskar. A glance at his hand showed Anskar that he, too, had transformed from an outline to his real form.

All around Anskar—even beneath his feet—as he circled away from his double was blackness, absolute and disorienting. In the background, spectral as ghosts, he could see the dim outlines of the seven demon Adjudicators, motionless yet apparently watching, and to the other side, the demon in the hangman's hood.

398

Sicth-Na'Jagalot lunged, his attack wafting and slow, yet Anskar's defense was equally torpid. The demon overextended when he threw his jab, and timing it better than he had the initial attack, Anskar slipped it and came over the top with a right hook. He knew he was going to miss, so slowly did his fist travel towards the target, but as with his own defense, Sicth-Na'Jagalot was late to evade. Anskar's knuckles impacted the demon's jaw, turning his head. Sicth-Na'Jagalot spun to his knees, then shuddered as a jolt of the wracking nerves ripped through him.

"Quick learn, you do," Sicth-Na'Jagalot said. It was jarring, the sound of the demon's gurgling voice coming from the lips of Anskar's mirror image. "But not enough fast, think I. Who would believe the blood of a lord so washed-out would be? Weak, you are. No match for—"

Anskar wasn't about to give Sicth-Na'Jagalot time to recover. He spun a heel kick into the demon's face, his heart thumping wildly in his chest as he waited for the lagging impact. Equally as slowly, Sicth-Na'Jagalot's head snapped back, and droplets of silver that might have been blood, might have been the essence that defined him and kept him in existence, sprayed from his mouth.

The demon wiped mercury from his lips—Anskar's lips! Sicth-Na'Jagalot's tongue darted out repeatedly as he emitted a slurping laugh. He circled Anskar warily now, still playing for time, seeking any advantage. "Want you to know why you alike I look?"

"No," Anskar said, gliding forward with what should have been a quick two-step. He stretched out a languid jab, but Sicth-Na'Jagalot shuffled back out of range.

"Tell you, I will," the demon said. "Not a body of my own anymore have I. Defeated Sicth-Na'Jagalot you did, only, stupid you are. Waited, I did, in here." He tapped his own temple, then frowned and pointed at Anskar's head. "Waited, and stewed, and waited more. Should have absorbed me, you should. Should have assimilated Sicth-Na'Jagalot. Ignorant fool. Ignorance get you dead, it will. Take your body, I will. Take *your* essence. Absorb! Assimilate!"

Anskar glanced at the seven Adjudicators, but they remained motionless. He wasn't even sure if they were still watching his fight with Sicth-Na'Jagalot. Though he could see them, they might as well have belonged to another place, another time. But they had permitted this contest. There were apparently laws that bound demons every bit as much as those reputedly binding sorcerers. They had been obliged to let Sicth-Na'Jagalot make his challenge.

The demon leaped at Anskar—far faster than before. Anskar's reaction, though, was still slow, as though he were moving in a nightmare. A fist identical to his own crashed into his jaw, and he wafted away from its impact like a leaf in the breeze. But the pain was far from gentle. He shrieked as white-hot barbs ripped through his mind and flayed his nerves.

"Hah!" Sicth-Na'Jagalot said, coming towards him with a speed that—while normal—felt preternaturally fast. "A trick I use! Could have been your trick, but take it you did not when chance you had. Assimilate you should have, foolish human."

Whatever this unnatural slowness was that had overcome them both, the demon had found some way to overcome it. If it were some kind of glamor, the sorcery had been dispelled—for the demon. And with that realization, lore that had just now been buried within him—snippets of the demon's memories and powers—burst like a sudden dawn into Anskar's mind. He ducked beneath a hook and slammed an uppercut into

Sicth-Na'Jagalot's chin. The demon grunted, and he spun as he scrambled away.

Anskar followed, keeping the advantage. He kicked the demon in the chest; then, as Sicth-Na'Jagalot tried to counter, clinched him and pounded him with knees to the ribs. He could feel Sicth-Na'Jagalot's entire frame shuddering under the assault of the wracking nerves. Froth spilled from the demon's mouth, but then, with a triumphant howl, Sicth-Na'Jagalot wrapped his arms and legs around Anskar and dragged him down.

Together they fell, tumbling yet still intertwined. They hit the ground hard, the demon on top now, hands switching to Anskar's throat as he tried to throttle him. Sand spewed into the air from their impact. Above, clouds of many colors scudded across the face of the bronze sun. The hazy peaks of mountains loomed on the horizon.

For an instant, the new terrain confused Anskar. One moment he had been inside the demon city, the next…

His lungs were starting to burn. Sicth-Na'Jagalot was still throttling him. He drove his arms in between the demon's and thrust upwards, at the same time forcing his body weight back. Sicth-Na'Jagalot cursed as he lost position, Anskar shifting onto his side then kicking off against the demon's hip. He rolled to one knee, poised to spring, but the landscape shifted again.

They were beneath charcoal skies now, yet it was the same bronze sun. Buildings of brass sprang up from the ground in every direction, stretching into the distance. Anskar expected to see movement—demons walking the streets of iron, winged shapes filling the skies, but there was nothing, no movement. It was as if…

Sicth-Na'Jagalot reached for him, one fist raised, and Anskar knew exactly what the demon had done—knew with some unknown sense he'd not been aware of before, a sense he must have unknowingly acquired when he'd first absorbed the demon's essence.

As he ducked inside Sicth-Na'Jagalot's reach and slammed an uppercut into his ribs, he formed a picture in his mind, making manifest a memory of his own.

They were atop the parapet at Branil's Burg now. Not really there; there was no breeze and no movement in the streets of Dorinah below. It was an image thrown up by Anskar's mind, no more, a rendering in three dimensions that encompassed them both. This power he had stolen from the demon was nothing short of an ability to work illusions—but illusions where? Inside his own mind, or outside in the world he shared with others? That wasn't yet clear, and when he looked for them, the Adjudicators and the demon in the hangman's hood were nowhere to be seen. For all he knew—and it did seem most likely—while they were fighting in different locations, he and Sicth-Na'Jagalot were still in the chamber before the Adjudicators. Perhaps only Anskar was present to the observers—physically present, that is. Perhaps his demon double had no existence outside his mind. But if Sicth-Na'Jagalot won… What would happen then?

The demon snarled, but at the same time he retreated a step, casting a nervous glance down at the ground so very far below. He knew that Anskar had worked out his game—his only advantage—and he looked terrified.

The demon frowned, and then they were deep within a forest of writhing, shifting trees. Anskar countered with a memory of his own, and they were in the tomb at Hallow Hill. He took satisfaction from the demon's fearful look at the statue he had taken the vambrace from: the statue of his mother.

Another shift—the demon's move—and they were on the

shore of a violet sea—one more location Sicth-Na'Jagalot had sought out from among his memories. The sparkling surf coming off the waves startled Anskar at first, then he had the growing sense that he had been here before. Or had he? Was the distinction between his memories and Sicth-Na'Jagalot's getting harder to discern?

The demon pounced, knocking him to his back. Anskar rolled as soon as Sicth-Na'Jagalot leaped atop him, hammering a fist repeatedly into his face. Pain ripped through Anskar's nerves, yet he gritted his teeth and refused to scream. Then, hands on the demon's hips, he pushed, at the same time thrusting with his legs and twisting. The demon cried, and as he fell off to one side, Anskar shifted their location again—back to Branil's Burg.

Back to the parapet.

Sicth-Na'Jagalot screamed as he rolled from the edge.

The demon reacted quickly. Shadow wings burst from his back, and he soared skywards, reversing his course to sweep down at Anskar.

As Anskar braced for impact, the scene shifted to the cave within the mesa where he had first encountered Sicth-Na'Jagalot. Anskar dived and rolled, and when he came up, they were in the lost city of Yustanwyrd, and this time the demon froze in shock and fear.

For Anskar had gone one better. No simple place memory this time. This time he had wrought creatures to populate his memory, and birds woven from shadows swooped down at the demon. Before they struck, Sicth-Na'Jagalot shifted the fight to an atoll in the midst of a raging sea, where sharp-toothed leviathans broke the surface of the waves both within and without the ring of coral they stood upon.

So the demon could learn from him as well.

Sicth-Na'Jagalot grabbed Anskar and spun him toward the sea within the atoll's ambit, but Anskar threw up a new image, and they were in the crystal caves where he had found the *nietan*.

The creature stood there waiting; not a child made of crystal, but the beast Anskar had seen it become, gigantic and taloned, and with a scorpion's tail made of the same crystalline substance as their surroundings. The barbed tail stabbed down at Sicth-Na'Jagalot, who screamed as the tip pierced his chest. But then he realized this was just an illusion, and he wagged a finger at Anskar as he smiled.

Anskar smiled back, and with an effort of will, he plunged them both deeper into the illusion, made everything more substantial, more... real, till he could hear the crystals crunching underfoot and the thud of the *nietan*'s paws as it stamped toward the demon. Sicth-Na'Jagalot tried to back away, but the *nietan* smothered him and then disappeared, leaving the demon encased in crystal.

Anskar sensed Sicth-Na'Jagalot's panic, but then the crystal casing started to crack. As the demon burst forth, he wailed, raising his hands to his eyes. His body—the very double of Anskar's body!—was now formed of crystal.

Another layer deeper into the illusion, Anskar thought. As the demon shrieked, trying to work out what to do, how to match Anskar's mastery, Anskar willed another illusion: a sword in his grasp.

Amalantril.

Sicth-Na'Jagalot's crystalline eyes widened as he saw the flash of silver coming towards him. He threw up hands of crystal, but *Amalantril* smashed right through them both and slammed into the demon's neck, and the crystalized body shattered into a million pieces.

Anskar collapsed on the floor of the Adjudicators' chamber, panting and ragged. Lightning struck his veins and boiled his blood. Tremendous forces raged through his limbs, causing him to moan, to cry out, then to scream. His scream became a triumphant roar, and as it died down, he was left with a pleasant fizzing sensation beneath his scalp, and then even that was gone.

But he knew things—things he had not known before. Sicth-Na'Jagalot's home. The demon's family, his followers. The horror of the other demons Sicth-Na'Jagalot had absorbed. All were flowing through him, settling in his mind: so many demons, each higher than the last. And now he had assimilated the demon who had assimilated them all! Oh... the elation. He rolled to his knees. The power!

"Now!" a tinkling voice commanded—the Adjudicator who had spoken before.

Anskar tried to stand, but hands of metal restrained him, and all his new power bled rapidly away.

He put up a token struggle, but he was too weak to fight, exhausted from the mental battle he had fought. Something about the demon in the hangman's hood—about its hands that held him—had nullified the dark-tide that had reawoken within him once he absorbed Sicth-Na'Jagalot. Metal hands. Dark metal.

Anskar tried to will them both away to some other place—tried to imagine *Amalantril* embedded in the hangman demon's heart—but nothing happened. More than that, he was no longer holding *Amalantril*. The sword he had shattered Sicth-Na'Jagalot's crystal form with had been a product of his own illusion.

The Adjudicator with the tinkling voice laughed. "The mind games only work during the contest for dominance. You must absorb a demon first, then assimilate it. But you will be absorbing no one here. Not without the use of the dark-tide.

As our prisoner, you have been deprived of that which runs in your veins."

"Let me go!" Anskar snarled. Then, weaker: "Let me go."

"I don't think so," the tallest of the Adjudicators said. "I think we are going to enjoy…"

Its gloating words trailed away as a sudden pressure built in the chamber. There was a smell like molten metal, a crack and a pop, and a shadow fell over the room.

Anskar's innards turned to ice and his limbs trembled. His teeth chattered so hard he feared they would break. All he could think of was fleeing, but the metal hands still held him, and his legs felt as though their bones had been removed. Terror such as he'd never known consumed him. His vision blurred, then contracted to a sliver, then to a point.

He felt himself crumple as the metal hands released him. Blackness pressed in on every side.

And then the chamber shook, though the voice that had spoken was measured, almost whispered.

"You seek to deprive me of what is rightfully mine, Adjudicators? Surely not! Surely even you wouldn't be this foolish!"

"No," several of them replied in frantic tones. "No, no, no."

"I assure you, Magnificence…" the tinkling voice said, but it never finished its sentence.

One after another, seven thuds sounded, echoing in the newly descended silence. Then, with an eighth thud, something hit the ground next to where Anskar lay.

He cracked open an eye, and the effort almost killed him, he was so weak, so helpless, so petrified.

It was the demon in the hangman's hood that had fallen beside him, rigid and smoldering, its flesh the texture of coal.

And then Anskar felt cold eyes rake across him—felt but did not see, because he had squeezed his eyes shut once more as he curled into a ball and shivered.

"Look at me," the whispering voice said, its echoes rumbling around the chamber.

Anskar tried, but he was too afraid to raise his head. He glimpsed a massive fist of bone, clutching the hilt of a sword.

His sword.

Amalantril.

"It is my will that you should look!" the voice said. This time it tore through Anskar's mind, scouring his every nerve.

And so he looked.

Gibbering with fright, stuporous, he looked but did not see.

All he perceived was dread; overwhelming dread. Infinite power. A presence too great for all the worlds to contain.

And he was nothing before it, less even than an ant. He was nothing. Worse than nothing. He lacked the right to exist.

And so, he ceased to be.

FORTY-SIX

LIGHT FLICKERED. OR WAS IT the darkness that moved?

A guttering candle cast its dying glow on…

On what?

No, not dying: the candle had already been snuffed out. If it was a candle at all.

There was nothing now. There *should* have been nothing! He was supposed to be dead.

He could smell meat; cold meat that had been left out too long.

He…

Anskar.

Behind his eyelids, there was gray light now, glowing between black slats. Anskar's jaw felt numb, and his teeth ached from so much chattering. His eyes were still squeezed closed, not out of necessity: out of fear. Yet the fear had passed. He was no longer trembling.

And he was no longer where he had been—in the courtroom, facing the Adjudicators.

He opened his eyes.

Everything was blurry and indistinct. He blinked his eyes into focus, till he saw that what he had taken for slats were in fact bones—monstrously large bones, black and glistening. The bones formed the framework of a hall: joists, girders, pillars, lintels, and arches. Between the gigantic bones that held up the ceiling was some kind of coarse canvas. It might have been skin. But this was no tent. The ceiling was of gleaming brass, and he had the impression of rocky solidity behind the canvas walls, which now struck him as some sort of stretched-out tapestry. There were marks upon the canvas—sigils and wards of bewildering complexity, combinations of symbols he thought he might have seen on his adventures, but intertwined with others into forms that hurt his mind when he looked at them too long.

He became aware of a background susurrus, a rhythmic rush like the wind, and behind it a low, steady thrum. The hall's dim light, ruddy and warm, alternately faded and intensified in time with the breathy sound: the source of the flickering he had perceived upon waking.

He was on his back, staring up at the brass ceiling from a hard, cold, ungiving floor. A floor also made of brass—not the entire floor, just the circle of brass he was lying within. Staked out. His wrists and ankles were chained to metal cleats on the edge of the circle. Dark metal. The air was charged like it was before a thunderstorm, carrying with it the iron smell of a forge. His skin prickled, and he felt every particle that constituted his body settling back into equilibrium after the separation and agitation that followed a teleport.

A presence tugged at his attention, and he craned his neck

to see the shadow-wreathed form of a massive figure reclining in a comfortable chair festooned with cushions. Beside it on a round table of bronze sat a helm the color and texture of bone. It resembled the skull of some exotic giant: crescent-shaped eyeholes, an opening for the mouth lined with jagged fangs, and twin tusks the size of scimitars. Just looking at the helm made the hairs on the nape of Anskar's neck stand up, until he switched his attention from the helm to the creature in the chair.

But there had been something else on the table with the helm: a scabbarded sword. He was sure it was *Amalantril*. Shadows expanded and contracted around the scabbard with the rhythm of breathing.

"No longer trembling?" the giant on the chair said. The voice was the same one he had heard in the Adjudicators' chamber, yet it no longer resonated with the force of thunder. It was frail, grated, slightly lisping: the voice of an old man. "Perhaps you are not afraid now because I have exposed myself to you as I truly am."

Shadows flitted away from the figure, and Anskar gasped at what he saw. The giant's flesh—if that was what it could be called—was withered and gray, but it was encased in bones, as if it wore its skeleton on the outside. Standing, the man would have been at least twice Anskar's height. He was slender, but there was about him a solidity, a density that seemed to tug Anskar toward him. If not for the metal restraints pinning him to the floor, he felt certain he would have been pulled into a collision with the man, and that he would not have survived it. Indeed, the entire room seemed to strain against being sucked into this gigantic figure on the chair, who commanded attention and seemed the focal point, wherever Anskar might have looked.

It was an odd face that watched Anskar. Odd, but not exactly terrifying. It was large—the size of four normal men's heads, and it was impossibly wizened, creased with a million wrinkles, scarred either by disease or the cuts of many weapons. The mouth turned down at the edges. It looked a sad mouth, though the one snaggletooth visible hinted at danger underlying the sadness. The crescent-shaped eyes were violet, and there was nothing dim about their glow. They were eyes of fierce intelligence, brilliant, god-like.

"What do you think?" the giant man said—the demon. "Old, infirm, so terribly, terribly weak?" He smiled, and it was a smile that belied the former impression of frailty. It was a smile full of hunger, not necessarily for flesh or indeed for food of any kind. But there was malice in that smile. Cruelty. And there was condescension—Anskar was all too familiar with that from his tutors at Branil's Burg. "Would you rather cower, stinking of your own excrement, your thighs chafing from the incontinence caused by fright? Have you even asked yourself why you were a gibbering wreck only moments ago, but now you are quite— well, not quite, perhaps—calm?"

The demon reached a lazy hand toward the bone helm and drummed long fingers knotted with arthritis on its crown.

"Without it, I am as you see me, and I have quite a convivial visage, don't you think? But once I put the helm on…" He narrowed his eyes and stuck out his tongue—forked and yellow, veined with purple. "Roar," he said in a voice laced with mockery. "Roar, roar, roar!" That last word shook the chamber, and the demon chuckled as if amused by his own antics.

"But why is the helm necessary? I hear you ask. Why would one so mighty make use of an artificial aid? My answer: age. Great age. Eons take their toll, you know. You can see just how much in the lines on my face." He chuckled—it sounded good-natured to Anskar.

The remnants of Anskar's terror dissolved in the sound of the demon's mirth, and he was filled with a rush of euphoria, coupled with warmth, belonging, and trust. Yet a fragment of his awareness still registered the bonds that held his ankles and wrists; asked why there was a need for him to be tied spread-eagled within the brass disk on the floor.

"Go on," the demon said, "ask away. Ask me anything you like. I am in a good humor and feel inclined to grant you answers. It is so rare that I have visitors not from this realm."

Anskar responded to the invitation like a child enraptured by a story and dying to know how it would end.

"Demons grow old, just like us?" he asked. Even his voice sounded childlike, filled with awe and wonder. And, despite the disjunction between how he felt and the peril he knew he must be in, he couldn't wait to hear the answer.

"We age, it is true," the demon said. "But not like you. Although there is something different about you, as I'm sure you have noticed. The only question is, how different? Are we more similar than appearances would have us believe?"

Anskar said nothing. Now he felt like a naughty child on the verge of being found out and then chastised.

The demon's crescent eyes rested upon Anskar for a long moment, studying, contemplating, considering. With one hand, the demon stroked the top of the bone helm, absently—he might not have been aware he was doing it.

"I take pride in the fact that I not only noticed my declining powers, but that I acknowledged the decline to myself. It is not every demon who can admit that; but then, there are so very few of us who have lived so long—perhaps I should say 'survived.'

"I might not have survived, had I not 'fessed up to my waning abilities. Not mental, I might add."

He removed the hand from the helm and tapped his head.

"Mentally, I continue to thrive, even to excel. But it is the flesh that grows weak, even flesh that has for thousands of years possessed the quality of regeneration. If I had not disguised my growing infirmity, others would have noticed and profited from it, you can be certain of that.

"Have you any idea how demon society functions? How we rise through the hierarchy or, failing to do so, fall victim to those on the way up and die? Yes, I think you do; for you have experienced what it is like to assimilate one who is above you, have you not? Poor old Sicth-Na'Jagalot. First exiled, then absorbed. It has not been a good century for him. And he showed such promise. Another couple of thousand years and I would have to have kept an eye on him. But now he is yours, all that he was, all that he possessed, mingling with the sea of your being. How was it for you? First time? That's so sweet."

Anskar closed his eyes, trying to remember exactly what had happened, what he had done during the contest with Sicth-Na'Jagalot. More than that, he sought out any trace of the demon's lingering essence within him, but he found none. Anything that might have remained of Sicth-Na'Jagalot was his now, part of everything that defined him. Somewhere within, he possessed the power and the memories of a demon, but had the absorption changed him in any other way?

"This is all new to me," he said, and he loathed the sound of his voice, so innocent, so naive, so gushing with love and respect for this demon he didn't even know. What was it, some kind of glamor? If it was, he had no defense against it, nor did he desire one, save for that tiny part of his mind that observed. "I know what happened… with Sicth-Na'Jagalot… but I feel the same as before."

"And that is quite normal for a beginner. But what a beginner! It is usual for a lesser demon to absorb a demon of the next higher order, and on rare occasions a demon of two or even three orders above themselves, but this... what you have achieved... is quite unprecedented. Why do you think that is? What makes you so unique?"

Before Anskar could muster a reply, the demon stalled him with a raised finger. "The question was rhetorical. I shall arrive at the answers in my own good time. But first, let us continue our feeling-out process. We were talking about my infirmity, about my great age, and about my need for the bone helm to assert my dominance." A mocking edge had crept into his tone, and it was hard for Anskar to determine if anything this demon said was sincere. But even if the demon were speaking falsehoods, Anskar felt certain he would nod and agree like an obedient puppy.

"You are perhaps thinking that I do not need the bone helm in order to dominate you, or anyone else, for that matter," the demon said. "But I sense you do not know demons well. You have been insulated from that which mingles with your Wirayan blood. And what blood is that, we may ask? The reddish tinge to your skin..."

"Niyandrian," Anskar said without hesitation. "I'm half Niyandrian."

The demon's crescent eyes widened momentarily and then narrowed. It was hard to see if he was frowning, there were so many wrinkles creasing his ancient face.

"And the other half?"

"My father was from Sansor in Kaile."

"Was he now? So which one of your parents was the demon?"

"Neither!" Anskar said.

"Then perhaps I should rephrase my question: Which was

414

part demon? It's all right, don't answer. Permit me the fun of working it out. Let us continue."

Anskar clenched and unclenched his fists in an attempt to restore circulation. His hands were numb, tingling with pins and needles. He wiggled his toes and winced at the discomfort as blood returned to his veins. The demon cocked his massive head and smiled at him, then resumed his cordial speech as if Anskar were not a prisoner bound to the floor—to a circle of brass that served… what purpose?

"One does not like to admit one's age," the demon said, and now it seemed to mock the nobles of Kaile with the accent it adopted, an affectation. "But there comes a time when a crisis occurs and one is not as up to the task as one had believed. Forgive me, am I boring you? I do so like to ensure my visitors know with whom it is they are visiting."

"Why are you doing this?" Anskar asked in a quavering voice. He felt the sting of tears in his eyes, felt himself winding up to snivel and complain that it wasn't fair. "What have you done to me?"

"Done? Why, nothing, save to reveal to you what all men in essence are. Humans are such babies: one step shy of the brute beasts, two steps away from the swamp your ancestors crawled from."

"I can't feel my hands," Anskar said. "Please release me."

"I might," the demon said with a thoughtful rub of his chin. "Yes, I think I might. But we digress. My tale… you wanted to know about how I managed the decline that comes with thousands of years of life."

"I did not," Anskar said.

"Yes, you did. Of course you want to know. And I shall indulge you."

"Please let me go."

"Quiet, please." The demon touched a finger to his lips. "I beg you not to interrupt, it does so irk me. Now, where was I? Oh, yes: the crisis that revealed to me my growing infirmity. Nothing out of the ordinary for a high-order demon—would it be boastful to say 'demon lord'? A challenge from a demon beneath me. Actually, it was an ambush, and she didn't come alone. Three want-to-be demon lords there were, all above the Thirty-Seventh Order."

He gave a mock sigh and a roll of his violet eyes.

"Of course, I only saw two of them. The third was a shapeshifter. I toyed with them, as one is wont to do at my age. Instant victories, like instant gratification, can feel so hollow.

"And while I played, the shapeshifter—who had been disguised as a pillar behind me—took her true form and stabbed me in the back. Her blade didn't penetrate, of course: despite my overconfidence, I didn't forget to manifest my shadow armor and to render it invisible. But the shock of her attack was enough of a distraction to give the two demons in front an advantage.

"To cut a long story short, I won, but it was not an easy victory, and it took me several weeks to recover. Others noticed. Oh, they expressed concern and a willingness to offer their support should any future challenges occur, but concern expressed by demons of a lower order is never sincere. It is, rather, a statement of intent. I might just as well have painted a target on my back, or rather a sign that stated my powers were waning and my legendary fortitude was as atrophied as my once-impressive muscles.

"I weathered two more challenges before I realized that time was running out for me, and I had to do something if I wanted to stay at the top of the heap. Well, aren't you going to ask me what I did?"

Anskar found that he did want to know, that he had an overwhelming desire to know. Excitement bubbled up within him, then blurted from his mouth. "What did you do?"

"Something no other demon had thought of doing before: I paid a visit to your world—to the Jargalan Desert, where I took the Orgol god captive and forced him to work his peculiar sorcery. With a power so raw, so pure that it surpassed any I knew—any I still know—he shaped and welded bone together into the helm you see here on my table. And this power he drew from some tide unknown to me—perhaps all the tides in one? I still don't know. This power he did not think to turn on me, though I'm sure if he had, the result for me would not have been to my liking. He infused it into the helm, giving it a glamor, a quality of terror that radiates from it, but only when I wear it. I suspect it amplifies those qualities in my nature that tend towards dominance and control."

"This power," Anskar asked, "was it the earth-tide?"

"The earth-tide!" the demon said. "Certainly not. I have only encountered this earth-tide twice, in each instance from people you might describe as close to me. The earth-tide has little traction here in the abyssal realms, save in the blood of those who are born to it. It is a cursed tide, vile and polluted. No, I would never place a helm infused with that muck on my head! The act would addle my brains, if it didn't kill me and reduce my carcass to pus. No, whatever power the Orgol god used to make my bone helm, it was not the earth-tide. Nor was it the dark-, the dawn-, or the dusk-tide."

"And you can't identify it? Even one as mighty as you?"

"With my vast intellect? You would think I could identify such a power, wouldn't you? And I did try."

"What happened?"

"Come here and I'll show you. Oh, you can't. I'll come to you."

With a creak of ancient joints, the demon pushed himself out of his chair and straightened up as far as he was able. Even stooped as he was, he must have been over eight feet tall. With ponderous steps, his feet dragging on the floor, he approached until he stood looking down at Anskar. The demon splayed his arms wide as a series of cracks came from the external skeleton he wore like armor, and the entire rib cage opened up to reveal the gray hide of his chest, which had the texture of coral. Over the sternum there was a patch of white discoloration, where the skin was puckered and pocked with long-ago healed blisters.

"The power contained in the helm burned when I tried to isolate and identify it. And not just here, either." The ribs closed like the doors of a cage and the demon tapped his head. "My mind too. I can't tell you how many memories were scorched away, how many thoughts excised. My one attempt at identifying the power diminished me. I will not try again."

"What happened to the Orgol god?" Anskar asked.

"What did I do to him, you mean? Nothing very much. I released him after he had completed the helm, but I suspect he would sooner have stayed. His people were not kind to him in the long run. Why am I telling you all this? I hear you ask. Why give up my secrets to a stranger, an infiltrator, a potential enemy? One: because I discern in you nothing to fear. Two: because I don't think we are fully strangers, do you?"

"I don't know you," Anskar said.

"I believe you. I am not easy to forget. But I am starting to think I know you; or at least, where you have come from. Your name, if you please."

"Anskar." Still he spoke with the voice of a child, and not only could he not keep secrets from this demon, he did not want to. "Anskar DeVantte."

"Odd. Not a Niyandrian name, and certainly not the name I was expecting. Rather, I assumed you would give me your title first."

Melesh-Eloni? Had the demon worked that out for himself? The demon asked for no elaboration of his name, though, and Anskar felt no compulsion to reveal what had not been asked of him.

"And what is your name?" Anskar asked instead.

"Oh ho!" The demon laughed. "A good question, but do you really expect a full and truthful answer? Any name I might choose to give you will not be my real name. Do you think I would be a demon lord if my name were known?"

"Because others could control you if they knew your real name?"

"That might apply to the lower-order demons, but when you reach this level, it's a bit more complicated than that. Nevertheless, knowledge of a higher demon's name—even a lord—does give you certain advantages. But who, pray tell, knows the real name of a demon lord?"

"Nysrog," Anskar said.

"No, sorry," the demon lord said. 'There you are wrong."

"But…" Anskar was going to say he'd experienced the memories of Morudjin in the memory crystal the Abbess of the Hooded One had acquired from the Scriptorium in Wintotashum. The name had worked—at least in part—when the Abbess and her acolytes, and Anskar, had summoned the demon lord Nysrog.

"Nysrog is at best a fraction of a name. The full name would have syllables beyond counting."

"But Morudjin summoned Nysrog," Anskar protested. "Which led to the first demon war." And the first apocalypse to afflict Wiraya.

"Morudjin botched the summoning because he did not possess the full name. Nysrog, as he is known to you, was able to resist his summons, but in the ensuing struggle, his mind was damaged. He regressed, mentally, to the level of a lesser demon, little more than an enraged beast. If this fool of a priest had possessed Nysrog's full name, who is to say what would have happened? Nysrog might not have resisted the summons, but I can assure you, with the intellect he once possessed, he would have overwhelmed Morudjin, or outwitted or tempted him beyond his ability to resist. Imagine that! Nysrog, in possession of his full faculties as a demon lord, free to expand his sphere of influence to the whole of Wiraya. That would not have gone well for your kind, nor ours. We would have been forced to act to counter the imbalance in power. So, we other lords have the ignorance of Morudjin to thank for that situation not arising."

"But you don't care about the millions slaughtered in the demon wars?"

"Millions of humans?"

The demon lord returned to his chair and sat down with a sigh. Whatever it was he thought about the humans who had been massacred during the rampage of Nysrog, he chose not to say.

"Well, Anskar DeVantte, you have given me a name, though I am far from certain it is the name you were bequeathed at birth, so I shall make you the gift of one of mine. You may refer to me as Domatai, which is Nazgrese simply for lord."

"Domatai," Anskar said. "And you are a demon lord... the lord of this realm?"

"Vulthanor," Domatai said. "Yes, I rule here, though I'm told that dominion over one of the abyssal realms is very different to how your lands are governed. For us, the pursuit of dominance is our way of life—the only way of life. Life for a demon is a competition, a race to the top; a game, if you like, with consequences. And so, yes, I rule here, but that only means I am the one everyone else seeks to depose."

Anskar winced as he struggled in vain against his bonds. He gave up once more and did his best to relax.

"It must be difficult for you," he said. "Lonely."

Domatai laughed. "How can you know so little of demons when you possess demon blood? Did your life among humans blind you to what you are, to what you still might become? No, I am not lonely. I enjoy being alone. It is somewhat of an ideal to strive for: being forever without others. It is what every demon craves, ultimately: to be the last one standing, the only creature left in existence, no one to challenge you, no one to deprive you of food, no one to get in your way. Oh, what bliss, to be a demon alone!"

Anskar frowned. He'd been without friends for much of his life at Branil's Burg. Loneliness had been a daily burden, and he'd been desperate to make friends. Perhaps that was why he had been an easy target for bullying and vindictiveness. He shook his head as he remembered how Sareya used to mock him, only later on to become his lover.

"Our holy scriptures…" he started.

Domatai spluttered out a laugh, then waved for him to go on.

"The teachings of the Five," Anskar said, "tell us that to be alone is the worst of all afflictions, especially if our loneliness extends to the afterlife, and we are isolated for all eternity."

"No doubt the writers of your scriptures intended that as a slur on the abyssal realms. Your beliefs, it would seem, are diametrically opposed to our own. What you see as eternal damnation, we would describe as bliss. Other demons—other people—are for us the very definition of suffering. Not for all demons, I might add. The lower in the pecking order, the more a demon craves company, the pleasures of the flesh, alliances, friendships, loving partners. There is an abyss—spiritually—that must be crossed before our true nature is revealed, even to ourselves. It requires a leap in the dark, and the accumulation and absorption of many, many souls. Once that leap is made, there is no going back. When one becomes a demon lord, one severs all ties with the animal self that came before. One has ascended."

"You are a god?" Anskar asked.

Rather than answer, Domatai picked up *Amalantril* from the table beside his chair, gingerly holding the sword by its scabbard.

"You seem rather partial to star-metal, young Anskar. Is that why you were after my hoard?"

"Star-metal?"

"Blended into this sword."

Astrumium! Of course.

"Not nice if one is a demon. Not nice at all. But tell me this: how is it that one of demon blood wields a sword that contains star-metal? Your hands should be blistered. They are not: I inspected them while you were unconscious. Hold a sword like this too long, and you should be dead. But then, you are not a full-blood demon. Is that what protects you?"

"I..." Anskar said. "I made the sword myself, as part of the trials of knighthood. I was a postulant at the time, in the Order of Eternal Vigilance."

"Is that the secret to your Order's unsurpassable weapons and armor—star-metal? That still doesn't account, though, for how you can wield it when you have the blood of demons running in your veins. And how is it a star-metal sword shows the signs of nascent... life?"

"Life? I don't know what you mean." And he didn't, although he had sensed something about *Amalantril* since the removal of his catalyst: the presence of the dark-tide. But life? Dark-tide life, unharmed by the star-metal the blade contained?

Domatai leaned forward in his chair, all good humor gone. He no longer sounded amiable: he sounded cold and emotionless.

"What exactly are you, human? What are you comprised of? *Who* are you? Something beyond the ordinary, even for a demon. I sensed your presence when you were fighting with Sicth-Na'Jagalot just now in the Adjudicators' chamber. By the way, it was no small feat to assimilate him!"

"Is that why you came when you did," Anskar asked, "because you sensed me?"

"The lesser demon who was your jailer had the good sense to send me your sword, else he would not make it to the Fifth Order. The Adjudicators, though, failed to report what they had uncovered during their interrogation of you. Rather, they were seeking to use you in some way against me."

"Are they dead?" Anskar asked.

"Already replaced. That's the beauty of our society, if such it can be called. There's always someone coming up from behind, looking for an opportunity at your expense. But this grows tiresome. Already I desire to be alone once more, with my thoughts, with my glory. You are a mystery to me, young Anskar, and mysteries are an irritation I could well do without."

An itch started in Anskar's ankle—an itch he could not scratch because of his restraints. He tried to ignore it, tried to focus on something else, but the only thing he could see was once more right in front of him, looming over him: the demon lord's violet eyes, his condescending gaze.

The itch spread up Anskar's calf, then to his thigh. A second itch began in his other ankle, working its way up his leg. Both itches converged at his groin and then, like the march of a thousand insects, progressed up his stomach, his chest, down both arms, and up his neck into his head. He bucked and twisted, straining against his bonds, his jaw clenched in agony, as whatever the demon lord was doing to him infested his entire body. He felt its prickle within his blood, scratching across his bones. There was no sudden excruciating pain, as with the wracking nerves, but this was deeper, more invasive.

He could not look away from Domatai's eyes now. They held him rapt, and they expanded to fill his vision till he was drowning in a sea of violet, lost in its swirling eddies, plunging deeper and deeper into their depths. Heat rose to meet him, scorching heat. And then he was burning up in the fury of a violet sun. He screamed, but there was no sound, no body left to do the screaming. No one. Nothing.

"Ah, a third person with the sludge of the earth-tide in their blood," the demon lord said, his voice disembodied and distant as Anskar felt himself melting away—his skin, his muscle, his blood, his bone. "The first was a Niyandrian mate I took. The second was our daughter. And now the third appears in my very domain! The third who shares not only the earth-tide but my own demon blood."

Anskar slammed back to reality like a meteor rich with star-metal crashing to the ground. He grunted at the impact, though in truth he had not moved. He still lay there, spread-eagled, his ankles and wrists bound. His skin was slick with sweat, which ran into his eyes and stung.

"So it would appear," Domatai said, backing away and slumping into his chair, "I have a grandson."

FORTY-SEVEN

"WHAT LED YOU HERE, ANSKAR, descendant of mine, grandson?" Domatai said. The demon lord was slumped in his chair, shadows swimming in the deep grooves of his scarred face. Beside him on the table lay the bone helm that projected such terror. And *Amalantril*. "Not chance, surely. I have no belief in chance. Were we destined to come together, or is there scheming here? A plot?"

Without warning, the bonds holding Anskar's wrists and ankles released—simply vanished into the air as if they had never been real.

Anskar's veins ignited as power flooded them. It felt as though his blood had turned to tar and been set on fire. As it oozed, the tar grew diluted, till it flowed like oil, then water, but black water that might have been acid, so much did it burn.

Anskar thrilled in the burning sensation. It did him no harm, yet he felt it swelling within him, saturating every organ and bone and pore. He had never before felt the dark-tide so strong within him, never before felt so part of the tide itself. He could do anything! Anything at all!

With a surge of tidal power that came easier even than a thought, he raised his body to a sitting position. Another gush of dark-tide power and he was standing, then floating, an inch above the floor, suspended in midair by nothing other than his own power.

Shadows filled his mind, forming an opacity behind his eyes, but when he blinked, everything came sharply into focus: Domatai before him, rendered in shades of black and gray. This new vision made the demon lord seem frail, vulnerable, a thin figure cut out of paper.

Anskar grinned, then started to chuckle.

"Oh, you are no threat to me," Domatai said. "You see what I intend you to see. You have power enough, yes, but only because I permit it."

"No, you're wrong!" Anskar said, rising a full foot from the ground, shadows effusing from his skin and growing in solidity. In euphoria, he laughed as he ordered the shadows to smother the demon lord, but before they could move an inch, the shadows dispersed, the power gushing through his veins went cold, and Anskar hit the ground hard and crumpled into a ball.

"Everything you have is from me, one way or another," Domatai said. As if to demonstrate, he waved his fingers, and dark-tide roared through Anskar's body once more. A wink from the demon lord, and the power died. "Consider it an unwarranted gift."

"My powers came from my mother!" Anskar cried. "Not you!"

Feelings he was not used to flooded him now, and he shuddered as he sobbed, curled up on the floor.

"In a sense, true," Domatai said, "but where did she come by her own power—her real power, not the tinkering sorceries of Wiraya?"

Frustration turned to anger and Anskar rolled to his knees. "You gave her the earth-tide, then?" he asked. "Is that what you claim?"

"No," the demon lord said—his grandfather! "That foul power she earned for herself. But what would drive a person to that—a person possessed of demon blood? What would possess her to plumb the cesspit of Wiraya, where the stinking effluence of corrupted tides collects?"

"Like all Niyandrians," Anskar said as he made it back to his feet, "she wanted to live forever, to be a god."

"I could have made her a god!" Domatai said, and his voice cracked like thunder, causing Anskar to flinch and take a step back. "A god in my own image."

"But she didn't accept?"

Domatai returned to his chair and slumped into it. "Because she hated me. Feared me. Fled from me." The demon lord sat in silence for a long moment. "What about you, grandchild? Will you reject me too? Will you eschew my gifts?"

Darkness once more surged through Anskar's veins, swelling him with its power. His skin grew taut, his muscles full and ready to burst.

Domatai turned his huge head aside, as if he were bored. With a lazy wave of his hand, he said, "Go on—try out your abilities. See if I care."

Anskar hesitated to do so. Was this some kind of test? If he grasped at the forces surging within him, would the demon lord merely shut them down again? Would Domatai kill him this time?

"Come on," Domatai said, facing Anskar once more, a new glint in his violet eyes—it might have been capricious, might have been condescending. Anskar was certain it was nothing positive, certainly no indication that he was accepted now, that he was family in any but the basest of ways.

"Let me start you off," Domatai said. The demon lord's expression did not change, but Anskar felt Domatai's presence in his mind, then sluicing through his veins. "The power to protect oneself is always good when starting out. An additional layer of armor, perhaps."

The dark tide shifted within Anskar. He felt it effusing from his pores and weaving shadows around him. To his eyes, the demon lord was partially obscured by a swirling mist, but it was not Domatai who was sheathed with shadows: it was Anskar, and he was looking through the dark smog that had formed around him, and seeing only dimly.

"How do I achieve this on my own?" he asked.

"My intention is merely to show you what you can do, what you might one day become, not to spoon-feed you powers we demons must learn over centuries. Here, try this."

An itch started around one of Anskar's shoulder blades, then the other. The muscles beneath rippled, then spasmed. Dark tide essence flooded the region and coalesced there. He grunted as dark streamers burst from the skin that covered his shoulder blades, thrashing, weaving together, until by craning his neck, Anskar could see that he had grown wings of shadow.

Domatai gave a smile that was almost benevolent. "Go on—try them."

As if they needed no input from Anskar, the wings unfurled, and with a single, graceful flap, Anskar rose into the air. Effortlessly he began to glide, making a drifting circuit of the chamber before setting his feet back on the floor. Another mental connection from Domatai, and the wings retracted, then vanished.

"How are you enabling me do this?" Anskar asked. "Must I use my imagination? My will?"

"A little of both and more," Domatai said. "For manifestations such as wings, you must learn to isolate the muscles in that region, contract them, relax them, then channel the dark flow through them. It is the same with your hands."

Anskar gasped and clutched his wrist as a blade of shadow extended from his palm. It resembled nothing so much as a dark form of *Amalantril*. He closed his fingers around the shadowy hilt, only for the shadow blade to dissolve into the air.

"And your fingers," Domatai said.

This time, Anskar's right hand came up of its own accord, and shards of shadow shot from the tips of his fingers, impacting the wall opposite with a succession of black sparks. In their wake, there were now four smoking holes in the wall, a matter that seemed to cause Domatai some amusement.

"With the dark-tide, you can climb like a spider," the demon lord said.

"I know," Anskar said. "I've done it."

"Ah, but have you made a web of shadows to ensnare your foes? No? Have you used the dark tide to summon and bind lesser demons? Really? You should try it; just watch your back— lesser demons are bestial things, quite unintelligent, but they are cunning and always on the lookout for ways to break their servitude to you. And if you are really, really adept at using the dark tide, you can learn how to engender objects with a sentience differentiated from your own. Of course, you may have a leg up in that department, given the life blooming within your sword."

Amalantril.

"But I didn't will that. Whatever is happening to my sword, it has nothing to do with me."

"It has everything to do with you. Somehow—and this is new even to me—you infected the sword unconsciously."

"Infected?"

"Is there a better word? I'll have to think about it."

Anskar hung his head and wanted nothing more than for the dark-tide to drain away, but it didn't: it wasn't his to command. At least not yet.

"My mother..." he started, and Domatai leaned forward out of his chair. He held up his forearm, the vambrace clear as day despite the lack of moonlight. The way it had killed Hrothyr the blacksmith, the way it had fastened itself to Anskar's forearm against his will... Was that evidence of sentience?

"My Talia made that delightful vambrace? Splendid. I must admit to being a little surprised. I had no idea Talia had embraced her demon blood to such an extent."

"I'm not sure if she wanted to," Anskar said. He'd gathered the impression that his mother feared and hated demons, and loathed the fact that she was born of the union between a demon and a Niyandrian. "But I think she needed every advantage she could get."

"In her war against the mainland allies?" Domatai said. "Yes, I imagine she would. Then I wonder why she lost. The power of the dusk- and the dawn , the dark- and the earth-tide, yet Naphor still fell, and the Queen with it. Why do you think that was, Anskar?"

"You know, don't you?"

Domatai chuckled. "There are powers in your world far more dangerous than sorcery, and far more subtle. And there are alliances that take place under the table, so to speak, not always with the connivance of governments."

"How do you know this?" Anskar asked.

"Let's just say I have connections, not to mention a small role in the governance of your world—the real governance, not that exercised by kings and patriarchs and procurators. But let's not get ahead of ourselves. I was showing you your potential. The abilities you have inherited from your mother—ultimately from me—are still for the most part latent. Those that you subsumed from Sicth-Na'Jagalot are largely unconscious—to such an untrained and unglorified mind. But they will come, with experimentation and a helpful shove in the right direction."

"Why are you showing me all this?"

Anskar had the impression all these powers were nothing to the demon lord, that he had nothing to fear from them. Already he had demonstrated how he could turn off Anskar's abilities with the mere wave of his fingers. What did that say about the magnitude of Domatai's own power?

"It's exciting, don't you think," Domatai said, "discovering what you can do? I know it was for me all those millennia ago. You will be frustrated at first. The powers reside within you, but they will not easily come, not without my guidance and permission."

"Then they are not really my powers," Anskar said.

"Oh, but they are. Latencies, perhaps, but they are *your* latencies. The insights I have bestowed upon you are a catalyst that will speed your aptitude. Most of us take centuries to discover our full potential. But, a word of advice: do not be deceived by such semblances of power. The real accomplishment for demons is in the realm of the mind. These abilities you have glimpsed are no more than noise and dazzling displays compared with the fully developed intellect, the will, and the glamor that comes with each ascension. But now that I have given to you, what will you give me in return?"

"Given?" Anskar said. "These are abilities I was born with. Latent abilities, I grant, but they started to awaken before I even came here to Vulthanor. The rest, the new powers, I took from Sicth-Na'Jagalot when I absorbed him. I won those powers!"

"Spoken like a true demon. Only you are not a true demon, are you? Merely a quarter demon at best. But doesn't that beg the question? Which is dominant, demon or human? Can a half or a quarter breed become as powerful as a full-blood demon? I have a feeling that demon-ness wins out."

Domatai clicked his fingers, and all Anskar's dark-tide essence drained away. Clicked again, and the power came rushing back.

"I decide if you can access the dark-tide within you and if you cannot. How is that any different from the bestowal of a gift? You don't get to choose; I do."

Anskar had no answer for that.

"So let us start again. What will you gift me in return?"

"I have nothing you could possibly need," Anskar said.

"Oh, but you do. You can handle star-metal without harm. I cannot. Please—" there was no disguising the sardonic tone, the intimation of threat "—give this power to me."

"I don't know how."

"Then let me help you. You were not created in a vacuum. You, like all your pathetic race, do not exist independently. Everything you are, everything you have, comes by way of someone else. Me, for example. Your dark-tide ability comes from me. It is contingent upon my blood in your veins. The earth-tide…" He grimaced, as if he were about to be sick. "We have already discussed where you got that from. But it is your humanity that insulates your demon blood from the harmful effects of star-metal. That is what I would have you give me."

"My humanity? But how?"

"Perhaps you know of a better candidate for bestowing such immunity on me? One in whom the demon blood is less diluted, yet who can still wield star-metal? Perhaps your mother?"

"My mother is dead."

"But is she really dead, gone forever into the maw of oblivion? We both know her area of study, Anskar. I fiercely opposed it, but by then she wasn't listening to me. I tried to get through to her, but she was remarkably well defended, and her distrust of demons is legendary. But I have searched you inside and out. I know about the times the Necromancer Queen has visited you. I know about her plans for a return from the realm of the dead. All I am suggesting is that we get ahead of her and speed her return. Not to Wiraya, of course. Together, we could bring her here."

"For what purpose?"

"I've already told you: to gain the ability for myself to withstand star-metal."

"And if she won't give it?"

"I don't think for one minute she will. Which is why I plan to take it. Demons absorb other demons absolutely. We assimilate. There is no reason why the same process won't work on the lingering spirits of the dead. The concept has long been debated amongst the demon lords. As to whether or not it has been tried, I am not at liberty to say. But try it we shall, Anskar. Come, let us give my darling daughter a call, or rather, a summons. She is still half a demon, after all, living or dead."

"I don't know how to contact my mother, let alone summon her," Anskar said.

"Oh, come now, it's not that hard," Domatai said. "All you need to summon a demon is their full name and—"

"But I don't know her full name. Surely it's not just Talia."

"It is not, but I had not finished speaking. Interrupt me again and you will be punished."

The darkness inside Anskar seethed in rebellion, but he quelled it with a whipcrack of his will when he saw Domatai's eyes widen in a taunt.

"Even the name I gave your mother at her birth would not suffice. Under normal circumstances, I would not be able to summon her, which is, in large part, why she has evaded me all these years. But the second way of summoning a demon or, so I am told, a spirit of the dead is to possess a blood link. This I tried also, but in life she found a way to hide her demon blood from me, and in death she continues to elude me."

"But why?" Anskar asked. "Why would she hide?"

Domatai paused before he answered, and Anskar feared that he had once more interrupted the demon lord's train of thought. He braced himself for whatever punishment he had earned, but then Domatai said, "Why don't you ask her yourself? You see, she may have hidden herself from me, but she has clearly not hidden from you, her child—one who possesses the strongest of all blood links."

"I don't understand," Anskar said. "I was taught"—at the Abbey of the Hooded One—"that to summon a demon, you need a circle of summoning."

Domatai chuckled and indicated with his eyes the brass circle that Anskar had awoken within and was now standing inside.

"You knew all along who I was?"

"I suspected, and when a demon lord suspects something, it is but one slight step from a fact."

"And you planned from the start to use me to summon my mother?"

"You think in such small moves. It is to be expected, I suppose.

You are more beast than sentient being. I suspected who you were and saw how that could achieve my desire to once again see my daughter, while at the same time seeing how this might enable me to withstand star-metal, which, as I'm sure even you will appreciate, would give me yet one more advantage over those who plan to depose me, and a degree of leverage with my peers among the demon lords."

"And me?" Anskar said. "What about me? Am I nothing to you?"

"In a word," Domatai said, then hesitated. "On second thought, make that two words: not quite. I may have a use for you besides the summoning of my daughter. Several, even. But quiet now. First things first."

White fire flashed behind Anskar's eyes, swiftly replaced by symbols and sigils that swirled around inside his head. His entire gaze was turned inward to some sort of sorcerous sight. Letters of lightning dazzled him, revolving faster and faster around the center that he formed. But what center? He had no form here, no body at all. The center of his awareness? His essence? His spirit or soul?

Letters became words in a language he could not read. It resembled Skanuric at times, at others Nazgrese, then the two forms merged into one, and the words they formed, he realized, even if he didn't know how, were impossibly ancient. Words became phrases, and phrases concepts. The concepts revealed themselves to him, yet none of them could he grasp. The more he tried to understand, the more spikes of red-hot iron lanced through his mind. He screamed in pain, screamed in frustration. He screamed as his head seemed to turn inside out and his mind became a tattered sail ripped apart in a hurricane. He cried out, over and over, pleaded for help, begged for release.

With invisible hands, he clutched hold of something cold and not quite solid. A hand of mist tried to pull away from him, but he held on as if his life depended upon it.

"Let go!" the wind whispered in his head. "Idiot! You must let me go!"

"Please!" Anskar wailed. "Please!"

Domatai's laughter rolled like thunder above the roar of the wind. "Pull, human!" he commanded. "Give it all you've got!"

Anskar had no choice but to obey, so he pulled with hands that were not real in any physical sense. He tugged and strained with all his might.

The wind howled.

The wind screamed.

There was a faint pop, followed by the stench of forge-heated metal. Silver motes swarmed in the air; he could see them with his eyes—his real eyes. The bronze circle beneath his feet was ablaze with tongues of flame.

And there was a figure in the circle with him, her hand held tight in both of his: the shadow-woven figure of a woman, a crown of spikes upon her head, blacker than the shadows that formed her slender frame. Her features were defined by shades of darkness—the denser lines of lips, rivulets of shadow etching the lines of a hard face, calderas for eye sockets, and within them, the only splash of color: the golden eyes that had belonged to the crow that led him to Hallow Hill.

"Mother…" Anskar started, but the shadow woman wasn't looking at him. Her golden eyes were fixed on Domatai looming over her at his full height, the bone helm now covering his head.

Anskar's bones turned to jelly and he collapsed to his knees, whimpering.

"No…" Queen Talia said, her spectral voice quivering. "No,

you don't!"

"Abase yourself, daughter!" Domatai said in that gentle but thunderous tone.

Talia's ghostly form shivered. She dipped her head as if she could no longer bear to meet the demon lord's gaze.

He took a lumbering step toward her, chuckling from within the bone helm. "Long have I waited for this moment, dear child of mine."

Anskar prostrated himself fully now, trembling from head to toe. He feared for his mother—her, of all people! Queen Talia was the most powerful person he knew, but she was nothing to this lord of demons.

"I said no," Talia said, her voice frailer than before—the voice of a child frightened of the dark.

"You have no choice!"

"Carred…" Queen Talia muttered to herself. "Curses, Carred is here. Then who? Where? How can I…?"

"You can't," Domatai said. "There is no one for you to latch on to. You are mine once again. You have always been mine."

"Of course!" Talia cried, and Domatai flinched at the triumph in her tone. "The love of my love. Marith!"

And with that, the shadows that defined her spun into a vortex and drained away through the floor.

"Gah! Blood and fire!" the demon lord roared, swaying on his feet. "Blast that bloody woman! Damn her for all…"

A crushing silence pressed Anskar's face into the floor. He dared not look up; dared not even breathe.

Domatai chuckled. "She wants you, doesn't she? I saw as much in your puny mind. She *needs* you. Without you, she will indeed be damned, forever left to languish in the realm of the dead. Not at all to plan, I bet. Well, when I've finished with you, when

I've taken from you what I intended to take from her, there will be nothing left of her precious *Melesh-Eloni*." The inflection he gave that title was riddled with scorn.

Anskar began to shake violently as Domatai drew nearer and crouched down. Hands as big as shovels clasped the sides of Anskar's head and forced him to look into the excoriating light of the demon lord's eyes.

FORTY-EIGHT

MARITH CAUGHT HERSELF WHISTLING AS she drove her one-horse wagon back from Brittling Down, where she'd been to purchase supplies. It was a mild annoyance, whistling without knowing she was doing it. Such unconscious acts felt like a possession. And it wasn't as though she had anything to whistle about. Theltek hadn't answered her prayer. She still had no way of helping Carred.

But then she heard the chink of bottles as the wagon hit a rut, and she smiled. Along with the dried oats she'd bought for her horses, and the fresh fish and pickled eggs, she'd stocked up on wine. Lots of wine. Enough to make anyone whistle.

The first thing she'd do when she got home was pour herself a large glass of red and go speak with Theltek again. If she poured one for him, maybe he'd listen to her.

The real reason for the wine, though, was that she still wasn't sleeping at night. Drinking was the only thing that stopped the nocturnal voices.

And they had been loud last night, on account of her stripping her wine rack bare the night before. Conniving voices. She could tell that, though she understood barely one word in five of the Nan-Rhouric they spoke, with the odd Skanuric phrase thrown in. Educated voices. Sure of themselves. Manipulative. And they had let slip who—collectively—they were in a ferocious exchange that seemed to be about inciting war somewhere or other.

"The Consortium will benefit how?" a woman's voice had said. Those five words had stayed with Marith as she tossed and turned in bed. *The Consortium will benefit how?*

She'd awoken unrefreshed, with those words still echoing around her skull. A war where, though? Somewhere far off, she hoped. No doubt this Consortium would benefit from the supply of weapons. Somewhat cynically she wondered if they had a contract with the Order of Etern—

The horse pulling the wagon reared and screamed. The wagon jackknifed, and Marith was pitched from her bench, crying out as she fell. She hit the road hard, all the breath knocked out of her. White light flashed behind her eyes, and her head both stung and throbbed from where she'd banged it.

She rolled to her side, moaning as she made it to her knees. The horse continued to scream and pound the road with its hooves. Cold wind slammed into Marith, knocking her back down. Unnatural wind, but it was too late in the day for the dawn-tide and too early for the dusk.

She gasped as the wind skirled around her head and entered through her mouth. It sluiced through her veins. Tendrils of ice thrashed within her mind, clinging onto thoughts and memories, nesting down.

Theltek, a shade! Marith thought. *A dead spirit!*

She started to panic. She had no experience with such things, and no talent for the earth-tide. Blindly, she threw up wards of the dusk and the dawn. The tendrils slid around them or snuffed them out, but Marith dug deep and intensified her efforts.

"Hide me!"—a woman's voice. Niyandrian. "He's trying to get me!"

"Out!" Marith commanded, lashing the tendrils in her mind with the dusk-tide.

She could feel the spirit fighting ferociously, but Marith had it cornered now, pressed into a dark recess of her mind. Weaving the dusk together with the dawn, she formed a net around the writhing tendrils and forced it to contract.

The shade wailed as Marith compressed it into a tiny ball of hardness within the glittering mesh of her blended sorcery. She knew she had it when the ball popped, and all that was contained by her net was a wisp of shadow.

Retreating from her mind, Marith exhaled into her cupped hands. Ice brushed her palate, frosting her tongue as she breathed out a shadow-formed woman no larger than her thumb. She clasped her hands to contain it.

"Got you!" she said. "I'll send someone," she told the horse, and then she was running toward home, though she soon slowed to a brisk walk, and then a slightly less brisk one. Fear and excitement could only carry you so far, and Marith had never been one for running. Her mind she had trained, year in year out, but her body... About the only exercise it got was in bed.

She called out for help as she entered her land, and a workman came running.

"Gex, isn't it? I've had an accident with the wagon," Marith said breathlessly as she continued on past him. "Had to leave it on the road."

"I'll fetch some tools and bring it back, mistress," Gex said.

"You all right, mistress?" Gex's wife, Henza, asked, coming down the path of the cottage they rented from her.

"Fine!" Marith called over her shoulder. "Thank you, I'm fine."

Marith entered her workshop and dipped her head to the statue of Theltek, at the same time resentful that he hadn't answered her prayers. Or had he? It wasn't every day she captured a spirit from the realm of the dead, after all. And it was the first time one had tried to possess her.

She carried the shade to a workbench and coaxed it into one of the empty wine bottles she kept lying about in case they might come in handy—she'd never been good at throwing things away. She placed her thumb over the opening and watched as the shade grew to fill the bottle. Definitely a woman, though it was hard to discern her features, as she was entirely formed from shadow. Three prongs—a crown?—stood up from the top of her head.

"You must listen to me," the shade said, voice muffled by the glass. "I am... a friend of Carred's."

"Just a friend?" Marith said, shocked at the spitefulness in her tone.

This was no mere friend of Carred's. The spirit-woman had once been Carred's lover. The crown gave it away.

Sweet bloody Theltek, she had the shade of Queen Talia of Niyas in a bottle in her workshop—the greatest sorcerer Marith had ever heard of!

Yet she'd bested her, hadn't she? Stopped the shade from possessing her and forced her out of her mind.

"Queen Talia." Marith gave an awkward bow—more of a half-bow, really, a dip of her head. "What's this all about? Who's after you?" It made no sense, a dead spirit fleeing in terror.

"Never you mind. I am here now, and you must protect me."

"Of course, Majesty, but it would help if I knew from what."

"I doubt that," the Queen said, "unless you're an expert on demons."

"Ah…"

"One in particular. My father, the demon lord Domatai."

"Oh…" Marith said. How was she supposed to respond to that? The Queen of Niyas—the dead queen—was admitting to being the child of a demon lord. Well, that certainly helped explain her reputation and power. And Carred had slept with her!

"He has my son with him in the abyssal realms," Queen Talia said. "The *Melesh-Eloni*. You know what this means?"

Marith was hardly listening. All she could think of was red skies and a bronze sun beating down on circles of standing stones.

"Is that where Carred is?"

The shade didn't answer at once. At length it said, "I sent her there… for void-steel. It was necessary."

"Necessary?"

"For the completion of the Armor of Divinity."

"And Anskar? He went with her?"

"No! Anskar should not be there. This is not what was planned! You must go there, Marith. I command it. You must bring him back!"

"For Carred. I'll go for Carred."

"For both of them. You must. It is your duty as a Niyandrian, as one of the moontouched."

"For both of them," Marith agreed. "How do I get there?"

"We can't use the portal I sent Carred through," Queen Talia said. "My father will be alert to that. But there is another way— the way Anskar must have used, for I can conceive of no other.

Go to Dorinah, to the Ethereal Sorceress. Grant her whatever she demands in return."

"And you?"

"Take me with you to Dorinah. Find a safe place to hide me till you come back."

"And if the Ethereal Sorceress refuses to help?"

"Then retrieve me. Release me from this bottle. Together we will force her to comply."

FORTY-NINE

NO LONGER WITHIN THE CIRCLE of brass, Anskar was now lying upon a stone slab—a table of sorts—in a different room. He had no idea how he'd come to be here. The last he had seen was Domatai's violet eyes expanding to fill his skull.

With a start, he sat up… only he couldn't. His wrists and ankles were once more restrained, fastened to the stone slab. He could lift his head enough to see gray-skinned demons in blood-spattered tunics bustling around the chamber, fiddling with apparatus just visible on workbenches that lined the walls: glass bell jars, crucibles, retorts, and a bewildering array of interconnecting tubes through which viscous fluids pulsed.

One such tube had been inserted into Anskar's vein at the elbow. It pained his neck to get a good look at it. Sections of what looked like skin stitched together formed the tube, and the cannula inserted into his vein had the look of a long and slender fang.

Anskar strained to move his head a little more so that he could follow the course of the tube, and there, mere feet from him, reclining on a vast carved stone chair, was Domatai. The demon lord had removed his bone helm, which he held protectively in his lap. His eyes were closed and there was a contented expression on his face. In time with the demon lord's breathing, dark fluid pulsed through the tube connecting him with Anskar.

Blood.

Anskar's blood.

"Do you feel dizzy yet?" Domatai asked without opening his eyes. "Weak?"

Now that the demon lord mentioned it, Anskar felt tired beyond belief, his head so heavy he had to let it drop back to the slab. A wave of nausea rose from his guts, and he shivered. When had it grown so cold?

A female demon leaned over him and looked into his eyes one at a time. She touched two fingers to his carotid artery, waited a few seconds, then gave him a snaggletoothed smile.

Another demon came over to check the insertion of the fang into his vein, then gave the tube exiting Anskar's arm a quick squeeze.

"Why are you doing this?" Anskar asked, his voice coming out thready and weak. He could hear his own heartbeat now, pounding in his ears.

"You know what I asked of you. You were most uncooperative, so here we are. I am taking it."

Anskar couldn't see, for he couldn't raise his head, but he felt the demon lord's eyes on him now.

"You've grown pale," Domatai said. It sounded like a detached observation rather than concern. "Like a regular human rather than a half-blood Niyandrian. An improvement, I think."

"I am… I am…" Anskar said, but his head felt woozy, and the words wouldn't form.

"Part Niyandrian? But of course you are. Your mother was, too: part Niyandrian, part…" And now Domatai hesitated in his speech, as if what he had to say next was repugnant to him. At last he spat it out: "Part demon lord. I have only myself to blame. I should never have sated myself with a full-blood Niyandrian. Oh, she beguiled me, I have no doubt of that. The conniving woman was what they call moontouched, a sorcerer of rare ability. I suspect she was a necromancer. The fool of a woman tried to summon me from the abyssal realms. Summon me! I should have destroyed her for such an affront, but I toyed with her instead, and the longer I played with my food—"

"Your… food?" Anskar asked blearily.

"Oh, yes, I ate her eventually, but only after she had given birth to your mother. That was my second mistake."

"How was it…?" Anskar felt too weak to complete the question, and this time, Domatai didn't complete it for him.

"I really should be grateful to you for coming to see me. Immunity to star-metal will be an immeasurable advantage, both here and in my dealings with Wiraya—which are quite substantial these days. The shame for you is that I shall probably need all of your blood for the transfusion. Blame your mother for running from my summons like the timid, self-absorbed coward she is. If you ever thought she cared about you, I'm sure the scales have now fallen from your eyes."

"I didn't…" *Didn't think my mother cared about me,* Anskar completed the words in his mind.

"But the two of you have such a strong connection," Domatai said. "I felt it when I scoured your mind. "A bond that could only exist between mother and son. Ah, but you have felt abandoned by her... since birth. You feel you are no more than a tool to her, to achieve her ends. I almost pity you. More than that, I might even have an iota of... empathy. Don't let that surprise you: we demons are not at all as your Church describes us. Well, the lower orders are. Compared with us, your kind, all you races of Wiraya, are but stinking, rutting brutes.

"And so, yes, I empathize with you, Anskar. We demons are born alone, ripped from our mother's wombs and left in the wastes of Shimrax to live or die according to the whims of fate."

The demon lord's words took on a dreamlike quality as Anskar felt himself falling, drifting, drowning in a rising tide of night. It felt as though the dark-tide that inhabited his bones, his blood, rose up to devour him.

Something called him back from the chasm that engulfed him: a rushing, gurgling sound; coughing, choking, a roar. Fluids spattered the floor amid a long, groaning cry. Despite his weakness, Anskar raised his head and with blurry vision saw Domatai vomiting as the demons in tunics came to his aid. And then his head hit the slab and he gave himself over to the dark.

Anskar didn't expect to awaken, but when he did, lying upon the stone slab, Domatai was seated by his head. No restraints held his wrists and ankles now, but there was still a tube in his arm, the other end inserted into the throbbing vein at the demon lord's elbow crease. Anskar felt the steady pulse of blood in his veins—entering his veins, not leaving.

"My blood," Domatai said. "It already flows through your veins in diluted form. You were close to death, and we had no other way to restore you. My servants' blood is inferior."

Anskar became aware of the gray-skinned demons in tunics tidying up around them, coiling spare tubes, collapsing retort stands, wiping down beakers and jars with cloths.

"What happened?" Anskar asked. He meant, *Why am I not dead?*

"Menselas is what happened!" Domatai said. He sounded irritated, bordering on anger. "The taint of the Five. You carry the god's mark."

"But isn't that the same mark as for sorcery?" Anskar asked. The doubt had been introduced, and now he seldom differentiated between the two supposed marks. He'd come to believe they were one and the same, seen from different perspectives.

"It is not. The mark of sorcery is a gift granted with your blood. The mark of a god is akin to the branding of cattle on Wiraya. Apparently, it is also a poison to me; but, as with the star-metal, not to you."

"You were sick… because of my god's mark?"

"Because of the taint it leaves in your blood. Is that concern I hear in your tone? I didn't know you cared."

"I…" *I don't care.* But even with Domatai not wearing the bone helm, Anskar was frightened of what might happen if he gave voice to his true thoughts and feelings. "I'm sorry."

"Thank you," Domatai said in a tone of pure condescension. "I am touched. It seems I made the right decision."

"I don't understand," Anskar said.

"To revive you. You see, I've come up with a better idea than taking from you what I lack." His crescent eyes shone with what Anskar could only describe as malice. "I thought I might train you like a dog and have you wield the star-metal on my behalf. Your mind is weak—I don't even need my bone helm to cow you! What do you think? It could work. You might even prove to be the perfect tool!"

"You want me to be your slave?" Anskar tried to prop himself up on one elbow, but still he lacked the strength.

"We all have to start out somewhere," Domatai said. "But serve me well… please me… and I will grant you a longer leash. Who knows? One day, I may permit you to come into your inheritance. You are my grandson, Anskar, whether you like it or not. Diluted as it is, you still have the blood of a demon lord."

A demon bent over Anskar to check the tube in his arm. Satisfied, she pressed down hard on his elbow crease and pulled out the fang that was acting as a cannula. A second demon took the fang and the connected tubing as she covered the puncture mark in Anskar's arm with a wad of cloth and applied pressure. A third demon removed the fang from Domatai's arm and set about binding his wound.

"There, all done," Domatai said, dismissing the demons with a wave once they were done. "That wasn't so bad, was it? Now, lie still and try to recover. I'll do the same."

The demon lord looked frail despite his great size. Without the glamor of the helm, he had taken on a wizened appearance, and his movements seemed heavy and ponderous. As he settled back in his chair, his joints creaked, and his breaths came out ragged and labored.

"You are wondering how it is," Domatai said as he shut his eyes, "that a demon lord can age so terribly, how his impassible body could become riddled with arthritis, his feet aflame with gout. I might have misled you a little earlier. Infirmity is not natural to demons—even demons who have lived as long as I have. It's what happens when you *fuck* a moontouched Niyandrian necromancer.

"Talia's mother—your grandmother—cursed me, I tell you,

after I'd finished with her. The very next day I felt the decline in my strength, my movement, even my intellect. I suspect she underestimated the durability of demon lords, though. She probably hoped I would die before she gave birth to our child, but I didn't. I am stubborn like that. And in the long months as her belly swelled and I grew ever more infirm, I made a few inquiries among my contacts in Wiraya. You see, with sorcery, there is always a countermeasure, if you know where to look—and my contacts knew just where to look."

"They were sorcerers?"

"Friends among the Tainted Cabal."

"What did you do?" Anskar asked. When the demon lord, eyes still closed, smiled and said nothing, he repeated his question.

"I waited," Domatai said with a self-satisfied smile, "until she had given birth and was so terribly, pathetically weak. And then I ate her. Not the most appealing solution, I'll grant you. The lower demons would have devoured her with gusto, but I have a far more sensitive palate. Nevertheless, with a period of aging, the right seasoning and basting in her own juices, it was no worse than eating one of the giant lizards from the Plains of Shimrax. Tasted quite similar, in point of fact."

"And did it work?" Anskar said, doing his best not to think about it.

"It arrested the progress of my illness, but it did not reverse it. That, it must be said, caused me a good deal of trouble: challenges from lower demons who would not have dared trouble me had I been my old self. Hence the need for the bone helm."

"And the baby? My mother?"

"I raised the child myself—with help from lesser demons, of course. Raised her... until..."

"Until what?"

"She was old enough and powerful enough to flee. I sent demons to bring her back. They did not return. I could have gone myself, I suppose, but I was told she feared me."

The demon lord opened his eyes and looked at Anskar for a reaction. When there was none, he swallowed and carried on.

"They say she made preparations in case I went after her, that she trod dark paths and learned powers I am unfamiliar with, just in case. She used those powers to take control of Niyas. I never really understood why, but I suspect her fear of me bred paranoia, and that she felt she needed an army, an entire nation, an empire to protect her from me, her dear old father." Domatai gave the slightest of shrugs. "I never went after her. There are other ways to deal with an errant daughter."

"What ways?" Anskar asked.

"The invasion of Niyas, for one. The fall of Naphor."

"That was you?"

The demon lord smiled. "Oh, you give me too much credit. I was what you might describe as a fringe player. Others objected to my daughter's pretensions and invited me to participate in their plot to overthrow her and her burgeoning empire. How was it, do you suppose, that Queen Talia's prodigious sorcery was nullified to the extent that she had no other option than to destroy herself along with her capital city?"

"Demon sorcery?" Anskar said. "The mainland allies—led by the Order of Eternal Vigilance—used dark-tide sorcery against the Niyandrians?"

"Very few of them knew, and none of them asked why it was that the sorcery they had been led to fear was so ineffective, up until that last devastating, but suicidal, blast. There was no overt use of the dark-tide, no offensive strike, merely the power of negation, which you have so recently experienced at my hands.

The Niyandrians, and the great majority of the mainland allies, never even knew of my intervention at the behest of the Consortium."

"But you were there at Naphor? You crossed over the veil?"

"I was not. I could have been if I had wanted to. I have a method of passing from this realm to Wiraya, though I have not personally made use of it in years—not since my daughter used it to flee from me. But I did use this portal to send my contribution to the war effort once the Order of Eternal Vigilance seized it from your mother's forces. Mostly logistical support: aerial surveillance, coupled with the odd disappearance of key Niyandrian leaders, the sowing of dissent among the provinces. Our shapeshifters took many forms during the war and walked among Talia's allies, persuading them to abandon her: the Plains of Khisig-Ugtall, for one, and several other of Niyas's allies who remained mysteriously neutral in the war."

Anskar's head buzzed with the implications of what he was hearing. "The governments of the mainland nations formed an alliance with you... against Niyas?"

"I'm fairly certain the governments remained blissfully unaware of the part the demons of Vulthanor played in their victory. But the powers behind the governments of virtually every mainland state were quite appreciative."

"The Consortium?"

"It always amazes me," Domatai said, "the ignorance of the sheep. Most humans have no idea who really holds sway in their world. Gods have surprisingly little to do with the way things are run—they have too many issues of their own to contend with. Rather, it is the business acumen of a very few that determines policy shifts and decides who is in and who is out, in terms of the neighboring nations."

"That's not true," Anskar said. "Much of the mainland falls under the power of the Church. The Patriarch keeps the rulers of nations in check."

"Obliquely, perhaps, through his membership of the Consortium. But even the Patriarch of the Church of Menselas must bow to the will of the markets. He is a useful member of our exclusive club, but he is by no means preeminent. Nor is he unexpendable."

"So this Consortium is a secret organization like the Tainted Cabal?" asked Anskar.

"Most people have heard of the Tainted Cabal," Domatai said, "but very few have heard mention of the Consortium. I would say that makes it a far more shadowy organization."

"Yet *you* have heard of it," Anskar said.

"I am a member. I may not entirely approve of the Consortium's methods, but I find it advantageous to know the inner workings of every ally, every potential foe.

"The Consortium poisoned Queen Talia's trade deals, replacing them with generous offers of their own—the terms of which were later altered in their favor once Talia was out of the way. Dominance! That is how it is achieved on Wiraya: with treachery and wealth. Not at all like here, where we still believe in the right of might, direct and brute, and above all else, the power of the mind.

"Of course, I rule supreme these days, purely due to perceptions. Without the bone helm, I would be vulnerable, fodder to be absorbed like poor Sicth-Na'Jagalot, whom you so readily assimilated. But in a simple battle of sorcery, I feel quite secure behind the fortress of my mind. Go on, try it!"

"No," Anskar said. "I don't want to."

"Wants and needs are for animals, not the stock of demon

lords. Do it, I say. Send threads of your sorcery into my mind and see what harm you can do."

Anskar looked away from those violet eyes, as if doing so could break their hold over him. "I don't want to do you any harm."

"Really? Truthfully? Come on, Anskar, you bear the mark of Menselas, the god of truth! One little lie—even with the best of intentions—could cause you a loss of balance. The Five won't like that at all. Be honest: you would kill me if you possessed the power."

"I would..." Before he could say "not," Anskar caught his own lie. If he could kill this demon—his grandfather, who had eaten his own mate, who had caused such suffering for his daughter... would he do it? Without Domatai's evil—for how else could the demon lord's actions be described?—maybe Talia would have turned out differently. Perhaps she would never have become the Necromancer Queen. How different Anskar's life would have been then.

But then another thought occurred to him: with no Necromancer Queen expanding the borders of the Niyandrian Empire, there would have been no war. No war, and no need for Queen Talia to visit Vihtor that night. Anskar might never have been born.

So be it, he thought. Perhaps it would be better if he had never lived.

Domatai was watching him intently, hard-pressed to keep the smirk from his face.

"You're right," Anskar said. "I would kill you if I could."

"I know you would." Domatai's expression grew hard as stone. "Then do it! Everything you've got, now! Unleash your full power against me! Destroy my mind! Go on, do it!"

Tendrils of awareness peeled away from Anskar's core and

whiplashed into the demon lord's mind. Still more threads of sorcerous intent separated out from his veins, from the nerves all throughout his body. A forest of tendrils sprouted from within his skull, and all of them—all these conduits of the sorcery that flowed through his blood and marrow—converged on the demon lord. Within Domatai's skull, they intertwined, occluding, smothering, subverting every thought, every volition. A thousand tendrils took root amid the complex patterns of the demon lord's mind. New threads branched off them, weaving a canopy around all that defined Domatai, squeezing him out.

But when Anskar had entered the minds of others—Sareya's— he had glimpsed thoughts, memories, desires. Here, he saw only blackness. Emptiness. Nothing.

He glanced at Domatai's face. Saw only contempt in those violet eyes.

Anger swelled within Anskar. Black fire coursed through his veins, following the lines of his tendrils of awareness, saturating the canopy he had woven through the demon lord's mind. Then, with a cry of rage, Anskar emptied himself of the darkness that was now an essential part of him. He directed the blistering tide with an unmitigated command of his will, spent himself totally as he aimed to incinerate the demon lord from within.

And Domatai laughed as Anskar crumpled to the floor, ragged and panting. Hot sweat burned his skin. He shuddered and twitched. His fingers and toes grew numb. He lost sensation in his arms and legs. And he felt weak, so weak. Even the effort of keeping his eyes open was too much. His head flopped to one side, and he groaned.

"Interesting," Domatai said. "An impressive attack, but as you can see, what you intended for me was revisited upon yourself. It is only my merciful nature that warded you from incineration.

It is that same mercy now that restores to you what you just lost. I like you, Anskar, far more than I ever liked your mother. We should get to know one another."

FIFTY

"I WANT TO SHOW YOU something," Domatai said as he walked with Anskar along an endless corridor. The demon lord was carrying Anskar's sword by its scabbard, and he used it to gesture with as he talked. His bone helm was tucked beneath his other arm.

The floor was coated with powdered bone that crunched underfoot—a memento of the demon wars, allegedly. The ceiling and walls were curved, with rib-like struts of dark metal. There were no windows, no doors, just an interminable progression that seemed to lead nowhere.

"I assumed as much, Grandfather," Anskar said. "So where are you taking me?"

Domatai towered above him, and though his legs were twice or more the length of Anskar's, the demon lord had set a snail's pace.

"What I want to show you does not depend on a location, merely an impression. And as of this moment, I am not taking

458

you anywhere. I use this corridor to ponder, to plan, to be unhindered in my contemplation. You are the first ever to accompany me here. How does that make you feel?"

"Special," Anskar said. Actually, he felt afraid. He felt as though he had gotten into something far worse even than his contract with the Ethereal Sorceress.

"You do not feel special, Anskar," Domatai said. "You feel confused, frightened. You long to escape, and at the same time, you are curious. Admit it."

"I am curious," Anskar said.

"You wish to know me, grandson to grandfather. You wish to explore your ancestry."

"I have always wondered where I came from."

"Of course you have. It is only natural. A crime, is it not, that your mother kept everything from you?"

Anskar dutifully nodded. "What was it you wished to show me?"

"Grandfather," Domatai said. "I like it when you call me grandfather."

"What was it you wished to show me, Grandfather?"

"This."

Suddenly, Domatai stopped walking. His violet eyes flashed, and Anskar spun away into the void.

Misty streamers thrashed around him. Along their lengths were blurry images. There were sounds, too, garbled and high-pitched, too rapid to comprehend.

Anskar came to a juddering halt. The streamers wove about him, encasing him in a cocoon made up of moving images—thousands of them, too small for him to see what they were. Then patterns began to form out of the disparate images as they clumped together, shape overlaying shape as order grew out of the chaos. Then, with a ripple, all the pictures resolved into one: the scene in the Adjudicators' chamber before Anskar had awoken under Domatai's glare.

First he saw the hooded demon that had held him, then the seven judges, then his own unconscious body slumped on the floor. The Adjudicators were wide-eyed with terror. One or two tried to stand. The first disintegrated. As his body collapsed in a heap of dust, smoke separated out from it. Anskar felt, rather than saw, the Adjudicator's intellect, his memories, his spirit—if demons could be said to have such—drawn towards Domatai and absorbed.

The second Adjudicator to stand went the same way. Then, one after another, the other five crumpled into ash as their spirits were taken.

The demon in the hangman's hood turned to flee, but a strand of dark-tide essence snagged him and pulled him, screaming for mercy, back. Fractures spread throughout his body, and then he too crumbled into dust and was taken.

All of them—all eight—Anskar could feel, despairing, silently screaming, throwing up sorcerous defenses that were instantly smashed aside.

"There was nothing I needed from them," the Domatai said, no more than a disembodied voice, "but, like an overly indulgent meal, it felt good. Others will now vie to replace them. There will be a period of terror, of infighting, perhaps even of war, but such fights for status are good for our people."

Anskar could feel Domatai's intelligence—unconscious, the barest fragment of his full capacity—eating away at the memories, the aspirations, the powers of those poor demons, dissolving them like a vat of acid, and all without the slightest effort or volition.

What was this, then—a warning? The same could just as easily be done to him. He had the blood of demons—of this particular demon lord. How easy it would be for Domatai to simply absorb him.

"Don't feel sorry for them," Domatai's voice continued, and then his face came slowly into focus as the visionary cocoon surrounding Anskar dissolved and he was back in the endless corridor again. "The Adjudicators wanted you for themselves. I have always known of their ambitions, for those are the ambitions of all demons. But they should have played a more subtle game. To have you—my blood—and not hand you over... Tsk-tsk. A beginner's mistake. But my point was not to gloat over what I did to them. I simply wanted you to see how transferable memories are between demons, and I could think of no better, or fresher, example. In this most intimate manner, I can teach you all you will need to know if you are to flourish here—and you do want to flourish, don't you?"

Anskar nodded mutely.

Domatai added more sternly, "I will be the arbiter of how much you know of me. Too much too soon, and your mind may well fracture."

Anskar doubted that was the only reason. Domatai trusted him as much as he trusted the demon lord.

"Now, I will ask you once again: What were you and the woman doing here? Was it your intention to steal from my star-metal hoard?"

"We were sent," Anskar said. There was no point telling a lie. Domatai would know if he did.

"Go on," the demon lord said, a satisfied smile curling his lips.

"The Ethereal Sorceress sent us here. Blaice and I are both bound to her—under contract. I didn't want to come, but I had no choice."

"No choice?" Domatai asked. "None at all?"

"I didn't think so."

"There is always a choice, Anskar. Always the power to challenge once you know where to look. But you did as you were bidden. Perhaps I will forgive you that. So what was it you were after? Which of my star-metal pieces?"

"The entire hoard."

"And how were you planning to carry it?"

"I don't know."

"Of course you don't. There is something you are not telling me, Anskar. Perhaps you are unaware of it. Perhaps you have simply forgotten."

"I don't know what you—"

"You know I can take it from you—whatever you seek to conceal."

"I know."

"Tell me," Domatai said, "what is the purpose of the object in your pocket?"

Anskar's hand went to his pocket, where he felt the hard form of the miniature depot. "Why did you let me keep it? To test me?"

"I examined it while you were unconscious. I don't mind admitting, Sheelahn has abilities that I am not familiar with— one of the limitations of working solely with the dark-tide. It is a scale model of her depot, yes? It does not feel sorcerous to me. Perhaps it is just a model."

"I don't know," Anskar said.

"But you know more than I."

"I was told to keep it, that Blaice would know how and when to use it."

"Yes… Blaice. We should pay her a visit. Before we do, what

do you know about the other one?"

"What other one?"

"Your mind tells me you know nothing, but then it would, wouldn't it, if you were shielding your thoughts from me."

"I'm not. I mean, I don't think I could if I wanted to."

"And I believe you. But one can never be too careful. You have the potential to do such a thing, but alas, it has yet to be actualized. Who knows? Maybe one day, when a bond of trust has been built between us, I might even show you how to unpack that particular latency. Would you like that? Would you like to be able to keep secrets from me? Don't answer. I know that you would."

The corridor dissolved into soot, amid the smell of heated metal. Anskar's stomach lurched, and he tasted bile. He fell for the merest of moments, and when his feet connected with solid ground, it was with a teeth-rattling shudder.

Before his eyes could make sense of the still-forming surroundings, his nose picked up the smell of spices and roasting meat. Fat sizzled and spat, and his eyes were drawn to the flicker of red flames that danced atop of bed of orange crystals. Above them, suspended from meat hooks, were the skinned, crisp carcasses of several dog-sized lizards. A lesser demon, yellow-skinned and covered with spines, set one of the lizards spinning with a prod from a long pole. When it saw Domatai and Anskar, it dropped to its knees and sat on its heels, head bowed, body trembling. Domatai had put on the bone helm.

Anskar felt it then, though not as strong as before: the dread that something terrible was about to happen. He ground his teeth to stop them chattering, and made fists of his hands to combat the trembling.

"Sorry, I should have warned you," Domatai said, his voice

present in Anskar's mind. "I always like to wear the helm on the lower levels. Appearances are important here. One sniff of weakness and they'll pack together and rip me to shreds. Or at least try to."

Domatai led him to the far side of a vast chamber—some kind of kitchen? The walls were of brass, wet with condensation and shimmering with heat. A vent in the ceiling—shaped like a drakkon's fanged maw—acted as a flue for the smoke rising from the roasting lizards. There were different kinds of animals roasting in different sections of the room: huge insects, grubs, six-legged rodents, and snakes that still writhed with life as they cooked.

There was an alcove, large enough to be a room in its own right, away from the heat. Its walls were rimed with frost, and half a dozen meat hooks hung down from the ceiling. From one, upside down, bound to the hook by her ankles, her naked skin revealing her piercings and tattoos, was Blaice.

"Anskar?" she muttered, as if she wasn't sure he was real. Her face was drawn, and her eyes were ringed with black bruises. She glanced at the demon lord then squeezed her eyes shut, unable to stand the aura emanating from the bone helm. She began to thrash about on her rope, then she started to scream. "Help me! Anskar, please!"

Domatai inclined his head to look at Anskar through the eyeholes on the bone helm. "Well?" he asked. "What do you propose to do?"

"Anskar!" Blaice shrieked.

What could he do? It took every last vestige of strength to stop his knees knocking together from the effects of the bone helm. So he turned his back on Blaice and pretended not to hear.

Domatai seemed to enjoy that.

"She lied to me, Anskar," the demon lord said. "And I did

not have such easy access to her thoughts as I do yours—there was an Orgol ward tattooed on her neck, or did you already know that? I'm so glad you didn't lie too, and that you told me everything you know."

"Traitor!" Blaice cried. "You betrayed me."

Anskar shook from head to toe. Tears of frustration, of anger, of hopelessness burned his eyes. And still he couldn't look at Blaice.

"Even if that were true," Domatai said, "betrayal is so sweet. But really, my dear, you should have been more forthcoming. All this barbarity could have been avoided. The other woman, I'm sure she'll be the first to agree, suffered no such discomfort."

"What other woman?" Blaice whimpered.

Anskar turned as one of the walls shimmered, and then a demon stepped through as if the wall weren't there.

In one hand, it held the end of a glistening black leash.

The other end was fastened to the neck of Carred Selenas.

FIFTY-ONE

TOLAK URG MALIZ YANKED ON Carred's leash—which was an improvement on the rod and the metal collar. She followed him through yet another wall. Theltek only knew how, but with the demon present, she could pass through solid stone or bone or whatever it was; yet when she tried it by herself, she ran the risk of serious injury.

She stumbled as she emerged on the other side into a vast chamber redolent with the smell of roasting meat. She saw an ice-coated alcove and a woman hanging within, upside down, naked, her clothes in a pile beneath her, two daggers and a glinting metal compact on top of them.

Seemingly waiting for her was a demon twice her height—the demon lord who had interrogated her when she was captured, she was sure of it, though he now was wearing a monstrous bone helm. He was carrying a scabbarded sword—a sword she thought she recognized. And at the demon lord's side... the

Melesh-Eloni, Anskar DeVantte.

Before she could piece together what this all meant, a wave of terror rolled over her, some kind of sorcery that emanated from the demon's helm. She collapsed to her knees, trembling from head to foot, teeth rattling.

A cold sweat broke out all over Carred's skin. She felt like she had as a child again, afraid of her father, more afraid of her mother. But it was her body that was terrified, she realized. In her mind, she knew the fear was some kind of sorcerous glamor.

Almost at once, her teeth stopped chattering. She continued to sweat, and a fine tremor passed through her hands—she even exaggerated it so the demon lord would see and be convinced that he had her cowed.

But Carred was not so easy to frighten. She had faced a wraithe and held her ground. She had shared a bed with the Necromancer Queen. Theltek, she had even survived her very own demons—her parents. She was thankful for what they had done to her now. The contempt, the drunken rages, the callous indifference, the cruel abandonment in the woods had all hardened her, inured her to the worst effects of fear. Especially the illusory variety.

But Anskar... Why was he here? His mother had sent Carred to the abyssal realms, but there had been no mention of Anskar. Did Talia even know? Surely she wouldn't have sent her own son to the world of the demons. The Talia Carred had known in life had been terrified of the demons coming for her. Terrified of one demon in particular. One lord. This one?

"So," the demon lord said—he was speaking to Anskar— "which of them would you like to keep? The woman you came with or this red-skinned beauty? Perhaps both are a bit long in the tooth for you, what with you being so young and virile, but the red one has a certain mature charm, don't you think? And her scars speak volumes for her character. The other," he said, prodding the woman hanging upside down and making her twirl, "has disfigured herself with these vile inkings and piercings, as if her own flesh, her own shape, were distasteful to her."

And then Carred saw the serpent tattoo and the piercings; recognized the black hair and the odd, violet eyes.

"Blaice Rancey," she muttered under her breath, then quickly lowered her head in case she revealed that she was not as cowed by fear as she was supposed to be.

So Anskar had hooked up with that chancer, that stealer of relics from the ancient places. Carred should have killed the bitch when she'd had the chance back in the Plains of Khisig-Ugtall. It raised the question, though: what was Blaice Rancey looking for in the abyssal realms? And why had she brought Anskar with her?

"Can I choose both of them?" Anskar asked. He sounded like a dutiful son. There was no fire in him, no belligerence, and Carred despised him for that. Was Talia's son so weak?

"Just one," the demon said. "Your choice. The other we will feast on."

There! The slightest twitch of Anskar's jaw as Carred looked up, and a lump passed down his throat as he swallowed. He was appalled at what the demon had suggested. He met her eye for the barest second before looking away again, focusing on Blaice.

"This one," Anskar said, meaning Blaice, "we will eat."

"Fuck you!" Blaice swore as she spun at the end of her rope. "You traitorous little shit!"

"An excellent choice. And the other," the demon said. "What would you like to do with her?"

The demon lord's massive hand took hold of Anskar's head

and forced him to look at Carred, and this time she couldn't look away. Something passed from the demon lord into Anskar—Carred *saw* it as a ribbon of shadow. Anskar's eyes widened. His lips parted, showing his teeth. Drool trickled from the corner of his mouth. His chest rose and fell, faster and faster as he started to pant.

The demon holding Carred's leash sniggered even as it cowered. She glanced behind at it and noted with repulsion that the creature was erect, its yellow eyes glinting with anticipation.

"Watch, don't touch!" the demon lord commanded, and the lesser demon whined and let go of Carred's leash as it scraped and bowed.

Carred was distracted. She didn't see Anskar move towards her. The first she knew was when he pulled her hair and made her face him.

"Oh, how wonderful!" the demon lord exclaimed. "So much like the lesser demons. Such lusty sport. Do you know, there are higher demons who would pay to watch this."

Anskar's cat's eyes were frenzied, so bloodshot the sclera were completely red. He smothered her mouth with his, wet and drooling. His hand roughly grabbed her breast through her shirt, and without thinking, she punched him in the mouth.

Blood sprayed—more from her split knuckles than his teeth—and Anskar dropped on his backside.

"Exquisite!" the demon lord cried. "What will you do now, my Anskar?"

Anskar tried to rise, but Carred hit him again—a clubbing hammer-fist to the temple. He grunted and pitched to his side. Carred stepped over him, fist raised to strike again, but when he craned his neck to look at her, there was shock and bewilderment in his eyes—eyes that were no longer red.

And they flicked now to the sword clutched by its scabbard in the demon lord's hands—only briefly—and then they met Carred's gaze, and she gave the barest nod that she understood.

Rather than hitting Anskar, Carred spun around and punched the lesser demon still cowering on the ground behind her. The creature snarled, but she struck it again and again, not giving it time to recover, then she dragged it by the arm and flung it toward the demon lord.

As the lord stepped back in shock, Anskar lunged for the sword in his hands, snatched it by the hilt, and drew it from the scabbard. Ribbons of darkness streaked from the demon's fingers, but Anskar was too quick, and the blade bit deep in the demon lord's belly. He ripped out the sword amid a spray of purplish blood.

"Blood and fire!" the demon lord cried as he staggered away.

"Come on!" Carred said, grabbing his wrist and tugging him away toward an arched opening only just visible through the smoke of the kitchen.

"What about me?" Blaice cried from where she still hung upside down.

"Bloody, pissing star-metal!" the demon lord roared. Black fire surged from his fingertips, cauterizing his wound.

Anskar ran toward Blaice, but not to rescue her: he dipped down and scooped up the silver compact from atop her clothes and headed back.

Carred felt a weight pressing down on her mind. Her knees started to shake.

But Anskar showed no such weakness now. Now, it was he pulling her toward the archway, strong, purposeful, full of urgency.

A wall of rage slammed into Carred from behind, but Anskar

scooped her into his arms, somehow still managing to hold onto his sword, and then he was running for all he was worth, the voice of Blaice Rancey crying in their wake:

"What about me?"

FIFTY-TWO

PANIC DROVE ANSKAR ON, TERROR from within and from behind. The only reason he kept stumbling ahead with Carred in his arms was that he knew the fear was manufactured, an effect of Domatai's helm. It still made him want to throw himself to the ground and gibber, as it had done before. He had the blood of a demon lord, yet it wasn't clear if that protected him or rendered him more susceptible to the bone helm's power. Being Queen Talia's son was certainly no help: she had fled from her father in utter terror. Was it the god's mark that gave him strength, or the way he had been molded by the Order at Branil's Burg? Or was it something that came from himself—something as simple as grit and the refusal to give in?

He staggered along dank corridors where the walls sweated and water dripped from the ceiling, and every once in a while he shadow-stepped, pouring himself into the shadows far ahead to speed their escape. They were lower down in the mountain citadel now, he realized, back beneath the surface of the lake. He flipped open Blaice's compass and waited for the needle to settle.

Carred begin to wriggle in his grasp, and he set her down with relief, for his knees ached and his heart pounded in his chest.

"Why no pursuit?" she said.

Anskar snapped shut the compass. "Maybe I killed him," he said, though he was far from convinced.

"You wish," Carred said. "Didn't you see him heal himself? But your sword... How did you even wound him?"

"A secret of the Order of Eternal Vigilance," Anskar said.

"No doubt the reason their weapons fetch so much in overseas markets."

"What are you even doing here?" Anskar asked. The way his mind worked, it was too much of a coincidence. "Did Sheelahn send you as well?"

"Your mother sent me."

"My mother? Sent you how?"

"There's a portal on the grounds of a mansion that once belonged to her father..."

"You realize that's who I just cut open with my sword?"

"I might be slow, but I'm not that slow. I see now why your mother was so afraid of him. She used to have such nightmares."

"You'd know all about—"

"Grow up, *Melesh-Eloni.*"

Heat rose to Anskar's face. He knew he was in the wrong, but the dark-tide seethed in his veins.

"Domatai," he said through gritted teeth, "the demon lord, used me to summon my mother from the realm of the dead."

Carred's complexion changed from red to pink. "He has Talia?"

"Not anymore, and it wasn't for long—mere moments. But

473

she was terrified of him. She fled somewhere… not back to the realm of the dead. To the love of her love, she said. Something like that. Maybe you know something about that?"

"Love of…" Carred said. "Did she say who? A name?"

"It began with an 'M', I think. Meredith? Martha?"

"Marith." Warring emotions made their marks on Carred's face. For a moment, she resembled a little child, lost. "I don't understand. How could Talia know? I thought I was so… Noni! Of course. Noni knew."

"And my mother possessed Noni," Anskar said. "It makes sense. But why did she send you here?"

Carred was still distracted, shocked out of her wits. "For void-steel. To complete the Armor of Divinity."

"It'll take more than void-steel to complete it," Anskar said. "All we have is a vambrace, and the blacksmith we needed to work divine alloy is dead"—though not for long, if Talia had her way. "Even if I learned how to make it myself, it would take months, if not years." And that was if he wanted to go through with it, which for the most part he did not. "Are you listening?"

Carred nodded vaguely. "You may not have to make it. I have a full suit." She met his eyes. "I found an ancient Armor of Divinity."

"You what? Where is it?"

"Later. When we get out of here, I'll take you there if you like."

"If we get out!"

Anskar started to move on again, but Carred stopped him with a hand on the shoulder.

"Why did you choose me over Blaice?"

"Because." Anskar shrugged her off and strode ahead, Carred hurrying alongside him.

"Because what? You came here with her, didn't you?"

"Not exactly by choice. She's an adventurer, Carred, a raider of ruins. If anyone can get out of this alive, it's Blaice. She has a knack for surviving."

"We should go back!" Carred said. "Save her."

"I doubt she'd do the same for either of us. In fact, I know she wouldn't."

"When did you become so callous?"

"Ask my mother. I must have inherited it from her. I assume she was as callous in life as she is in death. You would know better than most, wouldn't you?"

Carred said nothing, only glared.

"Did you know my mother was half demon?"

"I just worked that out," Carred said. "I'm a little slow on the uptake, but you'll get used to it."

"I thought you might have noticed when you were sharing a bed."

"Stop!" Carred said, slamming him against the wall and thrusting her face in his. "You are not like this!"

"Oh, really?" Anskar's blood burned with anger, resentment, hatred. "You know nothing about me."

Carred recoiled from something she had seen in his eyes, and he pushed her away from him and strode ahead.

"I know what you were like in the Plains of Khisig-Ugtall," she said as she caught up. "Scared, confused, but a good—"

"Boy?" Anskar snarled. "Is that how you think of me? A boy who needs to grow up? I can assure you, I am no child." The glare he shot her was intended as a challenge: *Try me, and I'll prove it.* He'd already done so, in his dreams—in the flesh, in a way, when the Abbess had created the illusion that she was Carred.

And that bitter memory was like ice-cold water poured over

him. He stopped, hands on his thighs as he bent over, shuddering and gasping for breath.

"What is it?" Carred said. She went to touch him, but seemed wary of making contact. Her hand trembled. "Are you all right?"

Tears spilled down Anskar's cheeks, no matter how much he refused them. "I don't know... I don't know how I am—what I am. Carred, I'm sorry. Please forgive me. I chose you because... I don't know why I chose you. I went looking for you at your camp. Well, I needed to speak with Orix..."

"Did you see Vilintia? Was she all right?"

He nodded. He'd done more than see Vilintia. Sweet Menselas, what was he becoming? What had he already become?

"I think maybe I chose you because you're Niyandrian. I don't know. Maybe because you were close to my mother. Maybe because..." Because she represented hope... for himself in some hidden way that he nevertheless intuited. Or for Niyas. "I know," he said with gathering conviction. "I know which side I'm on."

"Ours? You accept your title?" Her chin quivered, and her eyes glistened.

He nodded grimly, then raised *Amalantril*, the blade gleaming even amid the gloom. "We're going back for Blaice," he said.

"Spoken like a true knight of the Order of Eternal Vigilance. Are you sure you're on our side?"

"I've never been more sure of anything." All the things Domatai had told him—about the war, about the Consortium who steered the fortunes of nations, about even the Patriarch of the Church of Menselas... All this time, he'd been taught Niyandrians were demons, but it was the mainlanders who'd been aided by demons, whether they knew it or not. He was willing to believe people like his father had not known, but that only meant they had been lied to, and duty had forced them to comply.

"You have a way out of here?" Carred asked.

Anskar nodded. He felt in his pocket for the miniature depot and relaxed when his fingers encountered it.

"Blaice first," he said, and together they started back the way they had come, then stopped abruptly.

At first it sounded like the distant buzzing of insects, but already it was growing louder, coming towards them. And in among the buzzing, a hissing started up, howls and gibbers.

Carred retreated a step, and Anskar backed away with her, eyes still locked on the passageway that led back to the kitchens and Domatai.

A shadow emerged at the limit of his vision. Then another, with dozens more shadows crowding behind. Yellow eyes flashed through the darkness, and the wall of noise—the buzzing, the hissing, and the gibbering cries merged together into a unified shriek of unmitigated hunger.

"Sorry, Blaice," Anskar said, then he turned around, grabbed Carred's hand, and ran.

Along corridors formed from black bone, past cell doors, they ran, and dozens, if not hundreds, of footfalls pounded the ground behind them. Ululating cries savaged Anskar's eardrums, guttural cries, Nazgrese curses.

They ran blindly at first, taking turns at random, and always the corridors were the same: brooding and dark and studded with doors onto storerooms or cells. His heart was pounding in his chest so hard he could hear it in his head. Beside him, gripping his hand tightly and urging him on, Carred had taken the lead. If she was scared, it was a fierce sort of fear, and her cat's eyes were narrowed in determination. Her red skin was coated in a sheen of sweat that caused it to glisten brighter than usual. It stood out like a flag to Anskar, a badge of allegiance.

They hesitated at a crossroads, frantically looking down each intersection.

"Which way?" Carred asked.

Anskar frowned as he tried to remember, then kicked himself for panicking and not using the lodestone. He drew it from his pocket, flipped open the lid, and checked the arrow. Carred's breath was hot on his neck as she tried to see what he was doing.

"This way," Anskar said, moving straight ahead and half-dragging Carred with him. They were near now, he could tell. The silver arrow of the compass didn't waver in the slightest.

Demons appeared at the far end of the corridor—lesser demons, snarling and aroused, as if they intended to defile their prey before ripping it apart with their needle-sharp teeth.

"Theltek's balls!" Carred cursed as she craned her neck to look behind, where the noise of pursuit was an avalanche rushing towards them.

Anskar kept his eyes ahead on the gathering tide of lesser demons swelling the end of the corridor and creeping rather than streaming towards them. They were waiting for something, he felt, and then he saw what it was as a monstrous demon entered the corridor behind them. It towered above the lesser demons, its bullish head grazing the roof. Its shoulders brushed either wall of the corridor, and its torso was a patchwork of bristling hair and striated muscle. It fixed Anskar and Carred with eyes of blazing emerald, pointed a taloned finger, and roared.

And that was the command the lesser demons had been waiting for to charge.

"Forward!" Anskar yelled, and Carred seemed to understand they had nowhere to retreat.

Drawing *Amalantril*, Anskar ran straight at the horde. He could hear Carred on his heels, panting, invoking Theltek with every title under the sun. Then, before that first concussive collision where sword would meet tooth and claw, Anskar swerved aside and shouldered his way through a door.

And it was the right one!

He pulled Carred inside and slammed the door behind her.

"No lock," she said. "Nothing to bar it with."

Anskar looked around and spotted a large chest, which he dragged toward the door. Carred lent him a hand, and when the chest was against the door, she turned back to the room. Her eyes gleamed in the reflected light from the stash in the center.

"Star-metal," she breathed. Her gaze flitted left and right. "And void-steel." She started toward the dark metal ingots.

"It's the star-metal I was sent to retrieve," Anskar said.

"Good luck carrying it," Carred said as she hefted a casket filled with void-steel ingots. "But my stuff's not that heavy. I could carry two boxes if we had a way out."

"The Ethereal Sorceress provided me with a way out," Anskar said, as a fierce pounding started at the door. "Though I've no idea how, or even if, it will work."

He rushed to the racks of weapons, sized up a scabbard and removed its sword so that he could sheathe *Amalantril*. He unfastened his belt and ran it through the scabbard's loops. Once he had secured the belt around his waist again, he reached for the miniature depot in his pocket.

"That's it?" Carred said, as she stacked a second casket of void-steel atop the first. "That's our way out?"

She didn't look as surprised as Anskar had expected, but then, why would she? Carred was a Niyandrian, used to all manner of sorcery beyond that employed by the Order of Eternal Vigilance.

"Stand here," he said, moving to the center of the star-metal stash, as Blaice had indicated they should do.

A massive blow splintered the door. Emerald light bled through the gaps between door and jamb.

"So, what does the Ethereal Sorceress want with all this star-metal? There's enough here to wage war on the abyssal realms."

"She didn't say," Anskar said. "Only that it was stolen from her and she wanted it back."

Green mist started seeping beneath the door.

"You know how to use that thing?" Carred said, a tremor in her voice.

Anskar frowned as he twisted the top of the depot, then the middle, then the base. It was in three sections, and each moved when he applied pressure. But nothing happened.

"Turn each the other way," Carred said.

Anskar did, and still nothing happened.

Casket set down her caskets of void-steel. "Give it to me!"

The green mist curled up the inside of the door. The emerald light bleeding through the cracks brightened, flashed like an exploding sun, and the door disintegrated.

Carred rapidly twisted the segments of the depot this way and that, muttering under her breath as she systematically ran through the combinations. There was an audible click, and shimmering mist spewed from the depot amid a shower of silvery motes.

Lesser demons swarmed into the room, drooling with hunger. Behind them, in the corridor, their bullish master appeared, and there were other, higher demons beside him now, figures in shadow-woven armor, with flaming swords and eyes like lightning.

The depot in Carred's hands began to expand at an alarming rate. She put it down at their feet, and backed away from it, dragging her caskets with her.

"Stay where you are," Anskar said as he saw what was happening: the depot was losing density as it expanded, becoming as ephemeral as the mist that plumed from it.

The lesser demons surged toward them, claws extended, teeth gnashing. The bullish higher demon stepped into the room, ribbons of blackness streaming from his outstretched hands.

Walls of misty stone grew up around Anskar and Carred, and the lesser demons bounced off the exterior as they collided… as if the walls were solid.

The black ribbons of sorcery frayed and at the same time wove into a billowing net of shadow that fell toward Anskar and Carred.

And vanished from sight.

The stone walls had solidified.

They were in a massive room now. A room Anskar recognized.

The checkerboard floor was partially obscured by the star-metal stash they stood upon. And they now faced the depot's double doors of iron-banded blackwood, which were barred against the outside.

A masked functionary stood waiting for them.

It was Blosius.

FIFTY-THREE

CARRED LOOKED ABOUT NUMBLY. SHE had never been here before, but she knew where she was. Kind of.

She'd known Niyandrian merchants who claimed to have been inside the Ethereal Sorceress's depot in Dorinah, and she'd heard tales of other, identical depots, all over the mainland, and at least one other in Atya. But she'd never thought to enter a depot herself, and especially not in the abyssal realms.

But there had been no depot until Anskar's model had grown up around them. Whatever sorcery had been employed was far in advance of any she'd known. Not even Marith could do such things. Not even Talia.

Was this how it always started—how the Ethereal Sorceress's business spread throughout the world? With a scale model, some kind of sorcerous seed for the full-sized building?

But how could you account for the functionary now standing here? How did he get in?

He was wearing a dark gray coat and a blackwood mask. He was of slight build with bandy legs, and his hair was almost golden.

The functionary snapped his fingers, and doors that had not been there moments before opened inwards. Not onto the storeroom, as she'd feared, but onto corridors that disappeared into the darkness. That meant... that meant the depot was larger than the room it had grown within.

Carred's head throbbed just thinking about what that meant. Either the room must have been destroyed by the expanding depot, or the depot both occupied that small space and did not. Like the place Luzius Landav had spirited her away to: when she'd stood before the shadowy members of the Consortium, it seemed to exist in some other realm.

People in tunics and pants of gray entered the chamber: dusky-skinned mainlanders, scarlet Niyandrians, even a few green-skinned Ilapa. All had fixed eyes, focused on one thing, and that something was not outside their heads. Mindless and mute, the only sound the shuffle of their feet on the checkerboard floor, they converged upon the piled-up star-metal and began to sort through it. Others arrived with hand-drawn carts of steel, into which the demon lord's stash was neatly packed.

Carred snatched up her caskets of void-steel, one stacked atop the other, and clutched them protectively to her chest.

Anskar looked on, taking it all in, studying what he saw, filing it away for some other day. That was the impression he gave Carred. There was a coldness about him that she'd not felt before, and when he turned his Niyandrian eyes on her, it was hard not to remember the lust the demon lord had instilled in him. He reached both hands toward her, and she flinched, but he only wanted to take one of the caskets from her. His eyes widened as he realized the casket's near weightlessness.

Carred felt an idiot then. Had she read too much into his demeanor? He'd been through a lot in the demon citadel. They both had. Not just whatever had been done to him, but the way they had left Blaice Rancey hanging from a meat hook, food for the demons. Carred could hardly care less, but Anskar... for Theltek's sake, he'd slept with the woman.

She found herself looking at the barred double doors, imagining what might now lie on the other side.

"Do not concern yourself," the functionary said. "The demons will never break through those doors. We are here now. The depot is here, embedded in the soil of the abyssal realms. And here it will remain for good. Either the rulers of this realm will come to an arrangement with my mistress, or they will not."

Carred breathed a sigh of relief. So, they had made it. They really had escaped. She had gotten off lightly. It could so easily have been her rather than Blaice. But why?

She turned to Anskar for answers. "Why would that demon lord treat me differently? You saw what they did to Blaice Rancey. Why wasn't that me?"

Anskar nodded toward the orderly—a warning not to be so open with information. "Just be thankful you made it out," he whispered.

The functionary strode across the room and opened another door Carred had failed to notice. At the same time, teams of gray-clad people began to wheel carts laden with star-metal away through their respective doors.

The masked orderly cocked his head as he waited by the open door. He seemed impatient. He also seemed to be trying to listen in.

Together they crossed the room to where the functionary was

standing in front of a rectangular cage. When Anskar entered, as if he'd done so before, Carred followed him. Finally, the functionary entered the cage and closed the door behind him. Then, with a whir and a click and a background thrum that came through the walls of the shaft beyond the bars, the cage rattled as it started to descend.

Carred's heart skipped about in her rib cage, and the hairs stood up on the back of her neck. She kept glancing at Anskar for reassurance, but he never once met her gaze. He was preoccupied with his own problems, and he seemed quite familiar with the cage, which took them into the bowels of the depot.

When the cage clattered to a stop, the functionary opened a blackwood door and led them along a green-carpeted corridor, at the far end of which stood a woman in an orichalcum mask and stiff black robes. The mask was featureless save for eyeholes of absolute blackness. She interlaced black-gloved hands over her belly and waited, empty eyes taking in Carred and lingering on her.

"No Blaice Rancey?" She turned the mask to take in the functionary. "She is a fugitive from us, her debts unpaid?"

The functionary deferred to Anskar.

"She was captured by Domatai," Anskar said.

"Ah, so you met the demon lord. And this Niyandrian woman with you…" She held up a finger, as if consulting with someone unseen. "Captain Carred Selenas of the Last Cohort. I am not unsympathetic to your cause."

"Nor are you helpful to it," Carred said.

The Ethereal Sorceress said nothing, merely waited. Giving Carred enough rope to hang herself, no doubt. Well, she'd never been much good at holding her tongue.

"Looks to me like you're expanding into the abyssal realms,"

Carred said. She'd long entertained suspicions that the Ethereal Sorceress was using her business to attain undue influence in the world. "Hardly the act of an ally of Niyas. You're with the Consortium, aren't you?"

"Blosius, you may leave," the Ethereal Sorceress said.

She held up a hand for silence until the functionary reached the cage and shut the door behind him. The thrum of whatever powered the cage reached Carred faintly, accompanied by a high-pitched whir. She judged that the cage was ascending this time.

"Are you going to tell us the Consortium doesn't exist?" Anskar asked when the Ethereal Sorceress lowered her hand.

"The Consortium," the Ethereal Sorceress said, "is comprised of an exclusive group of the extremely rich and powerful, who have their tentacles into every mainland government and beyond."

"Judging by the little I've seen," Carred said, "that includes your precious Church of the Five, Anskar, or at least certain prominent members of it." And it was becoming increasingly clear, these were the people behind the scenes who had brought Queen Talia down through a mainland alliance built on lies.

"My expansion here is not on behalf of the Consortium," the Ethereal Sorceress said. "Indeed, it is designed to fragment the Consortium. The demon lord Domatai's interests, for example, are not clearly aligned with the rest of the Consortium. Now that I have taken back what was rightfully mine, I intend to make overtures to him... from a position of strength."

"So you're opposed to the Consortium?" Anskar asked.

"Sometimes I am a rival. Sometimes I am not. The Consortium is not the only power in Wiraya. There are others who seek—"

The Ethereal Sorceress gasped, gloved hands going to her chest. She bent at the waist and took a single, stumbling step.

Carred couldn't help herself: it was an instinct to drop her casket and rush to the Ethereal Sorceress's aid. She took hold of an elbow for support. Anskar ditched his casket and did the same, supporting the Ethereal Sorceress from the other side. He glanced at Carred, eyes wide and fearful. When he looked away to the Ethereal Sorceress's hands, still clamped over her chest, Carred followed his gaze, and a chill crept up her spine. Viscous fluid, like golden blood, was seeping between the Ethereal Sorceress's fingers and blooming beneath her hands across the front of her robe.

Carred cast a look around for sign of who or what could have done this. There had been no flash of a dagger, no movement, no sound. And there was no one there with them in the corridor.

"What is it?" Anskar asked the Ethereal Sorceress as they lowered her gently to the carpet and laid her down. "What just happened?"

A single-word response, little more than a rasp from behind the orichalcum mask: "Death."

"I don't understand," Anskar said. "What should we do?"

"The *izindel...*" the Ethereal Sorceress said, her voice no longer lyrical, but thready and weak. Her breath started to rattle. "Dorinah... Go."

Her hands fell away from her chest. Golden blood spurted from a stab wound, soaking the front of her robe and spattering the carpet.

Carried covered the wound with her own hands, one on top of the other, then leaned into it to apply pressure. She had done the same a dozen times on the battlefield, and then, as now, it didn't work. Not on this kind of wound. All she got for her efforts was hands drenched with golden fluid, which was ice cold and prickled her skin. She felt a reactionary ripple in her neglected repositories, and bile rose in her throat.

Anskar might have sensed it too: the force of the sorcery dissipating from the dying woman's body; its utter alienness. He stood and started toward the door at the end of the corridor, behind where the Ethereal Sorceress had been standing.

"What did she mean: *izindel?*" Carred asked as she wiped her hands on the Ethereal Sorceress's robe and stood.

"If you're coming, follow me," he said.

"And what about the void-steel?" Carred reclaimed her casket, but Anskar's lay upturned on the carpet.

"What good is void-steel to me?"

And with that, he opened the door and slipped through.

Perhaps she shouldn't tell him. Perhaps she should let him make his Armor of Divinity without the void-steel; let him end up like the Necromancer Tain. Considering the changes that she'd seen in Anskar, it might be for the best.

But it would have bothered Talia, and Carred wasn't ready to risk angering her queen just yet.

"All right then," she muttered, balancing the second casket on top of the first and clutching them both to her chest. "I'll bring it myself."

FIFTY-FOUR

ANSKAR BARRELED INTO THE *IZINDEL* chamber with its polished granite floor and circular band of orichalcum set into the center, Skanuric runes inscribed around the circumference.

But how was it operated? Sheelahn had used a Skanuric cant before. He wracked his brains, trying to recall the words she had used and the cadence of the chant, but all he could hear was Carred's footfalls approaching down the corridor and her ragged breaths as she entered the room.

"What are you doing?" she asked.

"Trying to concentrate," he said. He sounded irascible, even to himself, but he was beyond caring. Something terrible had happened, something he couldn't begin to guess at.

Think, Anskar! he told himself. *Think!*

But all he could think of was how Carred was a distraction, even just standing there with both caskets clutched to her chest. He started to pace, pounding his forehead with the heel of his hand. What were the words he needed? What was the melody?

Then suddenly it was there: a musical voice in his head—Sheelahn's voice—chanting the Skanuric words. His lips moved as he mimicked her cant, his chant growing stronger as he gained confidence.

The light in the room dimmed and flickered.

"Get ready," he told Carred without even glancing at her.

"For what?"

And then he was falling through blackness.

Carred cried out, her voice skirling around him like the wind.

Silver sparks and golden motes raced past him. Thunder boomed. The smell of burning wood clogged his nostrils.

This time around, he gnashed his teeth, fighting the urge to scream as his flesh was blasted apart into millions of burning fragments that swiftly chilled and died.

Light bled through his closed eyelids.

He wavered on his feet as he felt once more the granite floor beneath him.

He opened his eyes to find Carred on her knees, hunched over the caskets of void-steel.

"Are you going to be sick?" he asked.

She shook her head and swallowed.

"Good. Then let me help you." He offered his hand, but she refused it. He stooped to pick up a casket, but she slapped him away.

"Don't bother."

What had he done to upset her? So many things, he admitted. Too many to remember. He should apologize, but there was no time, and his blood burned with urgency, irritation, the need to get a move on.

In the corridor outside the *izindel* chamber, men and women in gray tunics hurried past with bulging eyes and gaping mouths. None of them made a sound save for the muffled thump of their feet on the green carpet, but they were frantic. Something had driven them to panic. And there were so many—hundreds that they passed on the way to the cage, swarming like ants whose nest had been stepped on.

Anskar led Carred into the cage, closed the door behind them, and frowned. How was he going to make it go up?

Perhaps he didn't need to. Far above, metal groaned, and the cage shuddered and started to rise. It was as if the cage had been expecting them.

Carred watched him above the caskets she held. Compared with Anskar, she seemed calm, but at the same time alert, as if she expected danger but saw no point worrying about it. A soldier's instincts, he realized, shaped by a lifetime of training and action.

His gaze switched to her hips. "You have no sword," he said.

"The demons took it from me. You think I'll need one?"

He swallowed, his hand falling to the pommel of *Amalantril* to make sure his sword was still there.

When the cage came to a juddering stop, Anskar opened the door onto the entrance hall with the checkerboard floor. The double doors to the outside world were wide open. There were armed men and women everywhere, knights of the Order of Eternal Vigilance in white surcoats and full plate armor, not the ringed mail usually worn. They all wore full-faced great helms with only a narrow slit for the eyes.

"Anskar," Carred breathed, "what's going on?"

His mouth dropped open in shock. He couldn't answer that. Surprise turned his vision blurry. Either that or he was dreaming.

Carred nudged his arm. "They have Orix."

Anskar saw his old friend then, held between two of the knights. Orix looked in a bad way, his face even more of a jumbled mess than before, as if someone had tried using sorcery to fix it and had failed. His eyes had merged into one saucer-sized disk where his nose should have been. His mouth was a diagonal slit on one cheek, his ears were below his chin like some grisly beard, and he had two noses, one on either side of his head.

But his face wasn't the worst of it. He was naked save for his smallclothes, black and blue with bruises, and red in between from fresh welts. Dried blood striped his skin from where he had been beaten with sticks or flogged. Anskar had the impression that if not for the knights holding him upright, Orix would have lacked the strength to stand.

Carred nudged him again, and Anskar looked where she indicated.

The Ethereal Sorceress lay supine on the checkerboard floor, golden blood drenching the front of her robes. Blosius stood over her, a dagger dripping golden ichor clutched in one hand. Beside him on the floor was his blackwood mask. His face was pale, his cheeks gaunt, his eyes frenzied. He caught Anskar watching him and looked away.

"We were wondering when you'd show up," one of the knights said, her voice muffled by the great helm that covered her face. "We've been waiting. Who's this you've brought with you, *Anskar DeVantte*?" The way she emphasized his name, he could almost see her sneering. "Your mother?"

There was something about the muffled voice, the mocking tone… He knew he should have recognized it, but his thoughts were like slippery eels that he couldn't quite grasp. Dumbly, he glanced at Carred then back at the woman who had spoken.

"She is not my—"

"I know who she is! Her severed fingertips give her away. Captain Carred Selenas of the Last Cohort. The leader of the soon-to-be-crushed rebels."

"Who are you?" Anskar asked. "What is the Order doing here?"

The woman advanced until she was standing mere feet from Anskar and Carred. Several knights moved to her flanks, swords leveled. Several more got between Anskar and Carred and the cage.

The woman stared through the eye slit of the great helm. At first all Anskar could see was blackness, but then her eyes started to glow violet, backlit by sorcerous fire. Cat's eyes. The eyes of a Niyandrian.

She placed a hand on either side of her helm and lifted it from her head.

And Anskar gasped.

"Sareya!"

FIFTY-FIVE

CARRED'S FIRST THOUGHT WAS THAT Anskar had led her into a trap, but she rejected the idea instantly. It made no sense. But with all these Order knights overrunning the Ethereal Sorceress's depot, and the sorceress herself dead on the ground…

She tried not to let her expression betray that she was more confused than she'd ever been. Judging by his face, Anskar was clueless too, and he was doing an appalling job of disguising it. The Niyandrian traitor in the plate armor—Sareya—was enjoying the fact way too much. So much so that Carred was sorely tempted to fling caution to the wind and smack her in the mouth.

But that would have been rash. It would have been suicide, judging by the sorcerous energies rolling off the woman's repositories.

Of course! Sareya had been the name of the trainee knight Carred's agents had initially thought was the *Melesh-Eloni*.

Aelanthe had said she was moontouched.

Carred had felt such power before: first from Queen Talia; secondly from Marith that night the assassins had come. Before that, Marith had managed to keep her abilities hidden, and maybe Sareya had too at some point, although she was making no attempt to cloak them now. Her eyes glowed violet, and she was radiating enough force to bring the entire depot down, the way Talia had destroyed Naphor.

Without a doubt, Sareya was moontouched. And that only served to double her betrayal of Niyas.

Sareya's silky black hair was plastered to her scalp from where she'd sweated inside the helm. Now that she'd made her point, her eyes dimmed, fading from blazing violet to green-flecked brown.

"Is it true Queen Talia used you as a bed warmer?" Sareya asked Carred, watching Anskar for a reaction.

"Rumors abound," Carred said. "Don't believe everything you hear."

"You don't deny it, then?" Sareya reached out with manicured fingers to touch Anskar's face, her nails painted with the red star of Menselas on a white background. "It doesn't bother you? Don't tell me *you've* slept with Carred Selenas as well—I know what you're like. Good for you if you have. Perhaps that's as close to your mother as you'll ever get."

He grabbed her wrist, and there were instantly two swords at his throat, the helmed knights holding them looking at Sareya for permission.

She merely smiled, though her eyes turned cold. "Remember that time you slapped me?" she asked. "It was at the pre-trials dinner. Of course, now that we know who your father was, it's easy to see where you get your violent streak from."

"You lie," Anskar said. "Vihtor wasn't like that."

"Vihtor Ulnar was your father?" Carred said.

"Rapist," Sareya said, rubbing her wrist and nodding for the knights to stand down.

"I doubt that," Carred said. "I'd like to see the man who could have made Queen Talia do what he wanted. If Vihtor Ulnar is your father, it's only because your mother wanted him to be." *Without consulting me.*

Not that she'd had any right to expect Talia to ask her permission, just because she was sleeping with the Queen. But it still smarted, the more she found she'd been left in the dark. All those years she'd fought for Talia's cause, yet even this traitorous tart seemed to know more than she did. *Why, Talia? Why would you do this to me?* "Oh, and by the way: I would never presume to sleep with the *Melesh-Eloni*. That would be a betrayal of Niyas."

Sareya stiffened, and Carred suppressed a smirk. Little victories could sometimes add up—so she'd been told. She couldn't tell for sure, but Anskar might have flinched at her words. Was he disappointed she'd never lain with him, as she had his mother? Crestfallen? Angry? Good.

"So this is how it's to be under the new Seneschal?" Anskar said, gesturing around the entrance hall, his eyes lingering on the Ethereal Sorceress before coming to rest on Orix.

"Entirely in character for the Order of Eternal Vigilance," Carred said. "Storming into places, killing, taking what they want by force."

"Is that so?" Sareya said. "And what does the Order want here, I wonder?"

"That's easy," Carred said. "The Ethereal Sorceress's trade empire. With control of her depots, the Order would be the preeminent military force in the world. And the wealth her trading empire brought in would be enormous."

"Maybe," Sareya said. "But that's not why we're here. Believe it or not, belief in Menselas still stands for something, and no one here is going to believe your lies, old woman. Barbarians like you always demonize the enemy. It's how you get the idiot masses to flock to your cause."

"Except they don't," Anskar said. "Flock, that is."

Carred almost told him to shut up, then—told him not to divulge information—but what would be the point? The Order must have known the truth, the same as Carred knew it for herself.

"So what's Monash up to?" Anskar said. "And why kill the Sorceress?"

"Because she got in our way," Sareya said. "Of course we expected trouble; hence our man inside."

"Blosius," Anskar said.

The young man with the knife still wouldn't meet Anskar's eyes.

"I thought you left the Order," Anskar said.

"Who said we're on Order business?" Sareya said. "Our presence here is not officially sanctioned. Off the record, as they say."

"Then—"

"What possible interest do you think Seneschal Monash could have in Orix?" Sareya asked, and at mention of his name, the Traguh-raj lad slumped in his captors' arms, and they lowered him to the ground.

"Enough games!" Anskar said. Tremendous force swelled within him, causing Carred to take a step back. Nausea washed over her. Her temples throbbed and her repositories whipped and snapped like a sail in a strong wind. Anskar's eyes burned red, and the air around him started to ripple.

Knights backed away to the walls, silver ward spheres springing to life. Only Sareya stood her ground, her own eyes blazing and turning once more violet. The stench of forge-heated metal filled the air, and the pressure continued to swell until Carred found herself wincing in expectation of the imminent crack of thunder.

"You think you can best me?" Sareya said, taking a step toward Anskar. "Poor confused Anskar—the orphan everyone loved to mock."

Inky filaments of darkness burst from Anskar's skin, surrounding him like a mass of seething briars. They writhed and twisted, began to contract, then compacted into a kind of jagged second skin: plate armor wreathed from shadows.

Sareya stiffened. She lost her resolve… but only for an instant. Then her own tidal forces swelled until she was sheathed in an aura of gold. Violet lightning streaked from her eyes, stopping a hair's breadth from Anskar, fizzing and crackling.

He didn't bat an eyelid. Wings of shadow sprouted from his back, and he lifted into the air. Sareya rose from the ground to the same height, though she had no wings. Anskar drew his sword; Sareya did the same. All eyes were fixed upon them as the room grew dark and oppressive under the pressure of the sorcerous thunderhead.

"They want you," Orix cried, his voice thick and garbled. "All they want here is you. Blosius betrayed you, Anskar, then he betrayed the Ethereal Sorceress."

Anskar and Sareya stared into each other's eyes for a long moment, then they both drifted lightly to the floor. Anskar's wings retracted, and his shadow armor disappeared. Slowly, deliberately, he sheathed his sword.

Satisfied the immediate threat was over, Sareya dispelled her golden aura, and her eyes returned to green-flecked brown.

"We want you, too, Orix," Sareya said. "Surely you don't

think the beating you've taken will assuage our employer."

"What employer?" Anskar demanded. "You serve the Order."

"Indeed I do. We all do."

"And Monash condones this?"

"Whether she does or does not is beside the point," Sareya said. "But she certainly wouldn't want to upset such an important sponsor."

Anskar glanced at Carred, who just shrugged. She had no idea who or what Sareya was talking about.

"The Consortium?" Anskar asked.

Sareya's frown showed she'd never heard of that shady conglomerate.

"Archduke Peleus," Orix said, twisting his lopsided lips to get the words out. "You warned me about him, remember? The nobleman who put a price on our heads. The father of that bastard who tried to…"

Orix couldn't finish the thought, but Carred could read the shame and self-loathing even on his mangled face. She knew Orix, as well as she could in the short time they'd shared a bed. He was an immature simpleton, but his heart was in the right place. And some son of a noble had done him some harm. Her gut told her what manner of harm, but then Sareya went and confirmed it.

"You should have let him. Perhaps you'd have liked it."

Orix dipped his head in shame.

Sareya shrugged. "Has to be better than being hung spread-eagled and watching as they pull your intestines out with a hook, which is what the archduke has in store for you both."

"You're working for Archduke Peleus?" Anskar asked, the disbelief evident in his voice.

"Subcontracted," Sareya said. "Blosius was recruited first.

Peleus reached out to Blosius's father on the mainland. They share several business interests, apparently. What with Blosius leaving the Order but still inside Branil's Burg, he was the logical choice. A mountain of gold goes a long way to covering a multitude of failings."

"And I thought you were helping me," Anskar said.

"Why would I do that?" Blosius said, finally speaking up. "If you hadn't embarrassed me in the fight square and made me fail the first trial…"

"But you could have tried again!" Anskar said.

"Try explaining that to my father," Blosius said. "And besides, I never wanted to be a knight. I know what I am, and I'm not cut out for it."

"But this…" Anskar said. "The Blosius I knew would never have done something like this."

"Then you didn't know me as well as you thought."

"Well, now that's settled," Carred said, clutching her two caskets to her chest, "I'll be off."

"Stay where you are," Sareya said.

Three knights came away from the walls to stand around Carred, their swords drawn.

"What's in the caskets?" Sareya asked.

"Void-steel," Carred said, as if it were nothing unusual.

"Void…" Sareya looked from Carred to Anskar. "What have you two been up to?"

"I thought I'd already answered that," Carred said. "Nothing to write home about."

"Put the caskets down," Sareya said. "I'm sure the Seneschal will find a use for the contents."

Well, that would please Talia no end! Another bloody failure. Maybe this would be her last.

Carred dipped her knees to lower the caskets, cursing under her breath as the one on top fell and spilled dark metal fragments on the floor.

Several of the knights touched five fingers to their chests, as if they considered void-steel evil. And perhaps it was. Perhaps this entire scheme of Talia's was evil. But then again, what was the alternative? A world ruled by the Consortium and its puppets? The Tainted Cabal?

Carred started to scoop the void-steel back in the casket.

"Leave it," Sareya said, then to the knights: "Secure them."

Rough hands grabbed Carred's arms. Two more knights restrained Anskar.

Sareya took Anskar's sword from its scabbard herself. "I'll hold onto this. You named it for me, after all."

Carred shot Anskar a look. "What did you call it, *Bitch Blade*?"

"*Amalantril*," he said. "Her spirit name."

"Well, aren't you an original thinker?" Carred said. "Moontouched."

"Enough!" Sareya snapped. "You will be taken to Branil's Burg, Captain. I'm sure Seneschal Monash will appreciate your snide remarks. Or maybe she won't. You are the most wanted enemy of the Order on Niyas, after all. As for you, *Melesh-Eloni*," she said with a sneer, "a ship is waiting to take you back to the mainland, where you'll face trial for the murder of the archduke's son."

"But, Sareya…" Anskar started.

"What? You think I wouldn't do this to you because we slept together? I consider that a blemish on my soul, a defilement brought about by my immature rebellion against perceived oppression."

"Is that what Monash told you? She's changed you, Sareya.

You're not like this. And let's not forget, it wasn't just me you slept with, was it?"

"The same applies to Tion and all the others," she said. "That Sareya is dead, Anskar. But you... I've been inside your head, and I find there only filth! Oh, and before you think of using your depraved sorcery to escape, I have been restrained with you thus far, but I'll not hold back again. Bring them."

Sareya started toward the open doors, but Anskar called her back.

"What about the depot?"

"It's under Order control now."

"Sareya..." Blosius began, and she responded with a sigh.

"What is it now?"

Blosius was staring at his dagger and shaking. The golden blood on the blade had dried... and formed letters.

At his feet, the Ethereal Sorceress's mask lay atop her robes, nothing inside either of them. She had vanished.

"What does it say?" Sareya snapped. "You can read, can't you?"

"It's in Skanuric," Blosius said in an awed whisper.

"I'm waiting..."

Blosius licked his lips and struggled to mouth the syllables, clearly not understanding what it was he was reading.

"*Na-tia so vannenti?*" He looked at Sareya for confirmation.

"Don't look at me," she said. "Ask Anskar."

"You..." Anskar started uncertainly. "You did this."

"Did what?" Carred asked, but the answer came before her question was finished.

"No!" Blosius squealed as he reversed the dagger. His muscles bulged, and the veins stood out, as if he were fighting with himself. "I won't do it! I won't..."

He plunged the blade into his chest, gave a pathetic grunt,

then collapsed face-first on the floor.

While everyone just stood there and stared, Anskar slipped his guards and bowled into Carred, literally sweeping her off her feet. He called to the dark-tide, and wings of shadow sprouted from his back. He held on tight to Carred as, together, they flew through the open door.

FIFTY-SIX

"YOU'RE FAT AND LAZY," MARITH told her horse, Barnaf, as she reined him in amid the trees and climbed out of the saddle. She touched her nose to his muzzle. "You know I don't mean it. Good boy, bringing me so far."

Truth was, the stallion was tending towards ribby rather than fat, and she made a mental note to have the stable hands give him more hay and an extra helping of oats from now on. She rode so infrequently, it was no wonder Barnaf was a bit neglected.

She fitted his feedbag and left him to it.

Theltek, her thighs chafed from so long in the saddle, and her ass ached. She took a swig from her canteen, then removed Talia's wine bottle from one of Barnaf's saddlebags. The wax plug was still intact, as were the wards she had set about the bottle at Talia's request—to keep her safe from scrying. She was terrified of her father finding her.

The shade of the Niyandrian Queen within the bottle swirled

504

in agitation. "Why have we stopped? Are we there yet?"

Marith held the bottle up and turned a slow circle so Talia could see. They had been following the forest road through Rynmuntithe for hours. Slower than the straight, the paved road had been built by the Order of Eternal Vigilance over the past several years to grant them greater speed and mobility in their efforts to suppress the rebellion; but the trees gave shelter from the sun, and there was less chance of running into an Order patrol deep in the woods.

"You must let me out of the bottle," Talia said.

"You're not a prisoner, Majesty," Marith said. Not now that they had an understanding, and so long as Talia didn't try to possess her again.

"Then hurry. I need to make contact with my eyes and ears in Niyas."

"You're sure you want to do that?"

"I'll be quick. My father is not all-seeing, much as he might like others to think he is. I must take the chance. Something feels... not quite right."

Marith used her belt knife to remove the wax plug, and Talia left the bottle in a stream of inky vapor that dissolved into the air.

"Huh," Marith said, then slumped to the ground and sat with her back against a trunk. In her haste to leave, she hadn't brought a bedroll; otherwise she would have curled up and...

Her head lolled forward, jolting her awake. She had no idea how long she'd dozed—seconds, minutes, hours? Not long, she decided as she checked the position of the sun. Her stomach felt as though someone had slit it open and let the contents drain out. Something else she'd forgotten: food for the journey. At least she'd brought her canteen—filled with mistberry wine, of course.

She passed the time waiting for Talia to return scouring the vicinity for berries, leaves, anything at all to eat. The maggot-infested carcass of a pink wood pigeon cured her hunger in an instant, until amid some deadfall beyond, she glimpsed some kind of trumpet-shaped fungi growing on a decomposing branch. The mushrooms, if that was what they were, were gilled and mostly brown, but she couldn't for the life of her remember how to identify them as safe to eat. Carred would know. All the rebels knew. They had to, in order to survive for long periods hiding out in the woods. Well, surely one bite couldn't hurt...

A hand of black mist enclosed her wrist, not solid at all, but it was so cold it almost burned.

"Not a good idea," Queen Talia said. She was as tall as Marith now, though little more than a shadow.

"I wasn't going to—"

"Of course you weren't."

"So, did you hear or see anything?" Marith asked.

"I did, and the news is disturbing. The rebels have come together, before time. They're marching on Dorinah. Curse that girl Noni! I should possess her again and rip her tiny mind to shreds!"

"Noni?"

"An idiot," Talia said, drifting through the forest toward the horse. Marith followed. "Moontouched, but a fool. Her lover was taken, so she lied. And Vilintia—Carred's deputy—is a bigger fool for believing her. Noni claimed that I was speaking through her, as I used to. She said I'd commanded Vilintia to gather together all the rebels for a decisive strike on Dorinah."

"Sweet Theltek!" Marith said. "That's suicide."

"More reason for you to hurry. With your power, you could help them. We must not let Niyas die!"

Marith removed Barnaf's feedbag and stroked his mane.

"The horse is too slow," Talia said. "Permit me to enter you, and I will speed us there through the shadows."

"Dark-tide?" Marith said. "I think not. I have a few tricks of my own."

She unbuckled one of the smaller saddlebags and slung it over her shoulder, then whispered a cant in Barnaf's ear. A trickle of dawn-tide bled from her repository, which was all she could spare. She'd need a whole lot more for what she had in mind.

"Home, boy," she said, slapping Barnaf on the rump and watching as he cantered down the woodland road the way they had come.

"You staying like this?" Marith asked.

"It would not be safe." Talia poured herself back into the wine bottle.

The wax plug wasn't exactly reusable, but Marith figured they were beyond the need for one. Talia didn't need containing; she needed a place to hide. And so, after checking her wards on the bottle were intact, she put it in the saddlebag.

"Ready?" she asked.

"Impatiently so," came Talia's muffled reply.

Marith sighed. She'd not done this since she was a little girl, and she'd almost ended up rupturing her dawn-tide repository then. Add a twist of the dusk, though, her grandma had told her, and you could travel twice as fast.

And so she wound threads of dusk around the dawn, encouraging the energies to surge within their disparate wells. She made the calculations in her head and spoke Skanuric cants of shaping. She focused on the road ahead, and already the trees and undergrowth were starting to blur. White light streaked past the edges of her vision. The sounds of the forest coalesced into an accelerating, high-pitched whine.

She took her first step.

And in a streak of motion, the forest road seemed to shift beneath her feet.

One mile.

If she'd planned ahead and consulted a map before she left, she might have had some idea how many more there were to go.

She collapsed in the shade of Dorinah's walls.

"Thirty-two," she muttered. Thirty-two bursts of the blended tides. Thirty-two miles in a matter of minutes. Nan was right: the addition of the dusk made it so much faster. But her head throbbed and her legs had turned to jelly, as if she'd really covered all that distance... at a sprint.

Niyandrians were everywhere, drawn up in ragged battle lines. Some fired arrows enhanced with dusk-tide sorcery over the battlements. Dozens of men carried a felled trunk with which they presumably intended to batter down the city gate. Well, that would never work. Who in Theltek's name was in charge here?

A huge wolf-like thing on a leash turned and hissed at her. It had the head of a cat and scaled legs—six of them. The old woman holding its leash called out a name: "Vilintia! Over here!"

Vilintia. Carred had spoken of her. A calm head in a crisis. A bit of a bore, but good to have on your team.

Marith gritted her teeth and pushed herself to her knees. She wavered there for a moment, then stood. Interesting. She was already starting to recover. As a child, the sorcerously enhanced trip would have killed her. But she was no longer a child. She'd come a long way since those days.

A tall woman strode toward her. Her red skin had lost some

of its sheen, as it did with age. It was hard to determine how old she was, though: her gray hair was cut severely short, and her exposed arms were knotted with muscle. She wore a mail hauberk and a broadsword scabbarded at her hip.

The old woman who had first spotted Marith followed at a distance. Sizable repositories, but unrefined. And there was some other sorcery about her—an *odor* that might have been the earth-tide.

"Vilintia Yoenth," the tall woman said. "And this is Eadgith." The old woman looked wary, as if she sensed what Marith was— what she'd finally embraced. Moontouched. "Explain your presence here."

"Explain yours," Marith countered. "Who gave the command to assemble the rebels?"

"I did."

"Does Carred know?"

Vilintia narrowed her eyes. "Who are you?"

"My name is Marith Pelhur." She waited to see if her name meant anything to them.

Apparently it did.

"Carred's Marith?" Vilintia said.

"I wouldn't put it quite like that, but we are friends, yes."

Vilintia's lips curled at one side. "Carred's not here."

"I know. And she left you in charge, I suppose? You think she'd approve of mobilizing all her people for the sake of... who was it that was taken?"

"Orix," Vilintia said. "Another *friend* of Carred's."

If that was intended as a barb to hurt her, Vilintia obviously had no idea how open Carred was about her relationships. She was used to hearing about them all—though the name Orix was new to her.

"Isn't he also a *friend* of someone called Noni?" she asked.

"How do you know all this?" Vilintia asked. She cast an uneasy look at Eadgith.

Tell her I sent you—Talia's voice at the edge of her mind. Marith smiled at the partial intrusion. *This far, Majesty,* she thought back at her, *and no further. Agreed?*

Agreed.

"I was sent by Queen Talia."

Vilintia merely nodded—not the reaction Marith was expecting.

"It was Queen Talia who sent us here too."

It most certainly was not! Talia said.

"Noni lied to you," Marith said. "She pretended Queen Talia was speaking through her, so that you would do as she asked."

Vilintia ground her jaw. At her sides, her hands bunched into fists. "And the Queen doesn't approve?" She looked horrified. "But if this isn't the right time..." She swallowed and cast a look around at her ragtag army, as if she realized they were about to be slaughtered, and it would all be her fault.

"Bit late to worry about that now," Eadgith said. "Do you think they'll just let us walk away? They'll run us down with horses."

Archers appeared atop the parapet, and dozens of arrows shot down into the massed rebels. Most missed the mark, but someone screamed.

Storm the city! Talia said in Marith's mind. *Anskar... he's inside. I feel him.*

"Back from the abyssal realms?" Marith hadn't realized she was speaking aloud until Vilintia shot her a startled look. "And Carred?"

With him!

"We have to get through those gates," Marith said, striding

toward them. She spoke a cant and sheathed herself in a shield of emerald light. Another volley of arrows flew from the battlements, this time converging on her.

They all fell smoldering to the ground.

FIFTY-SEVEN

ANSKAR LAUNCHED HIMSELF OUT OF the depot and into the air. Carred twisted in his grip and threw her arms around his waist, clinging on. The warmth of her body contradicted the chill of the wind that buffeted his face and made his hair stream out behind him. But the feel of her so close, after what she'd said, served only to fuel his anger. *I would never presume to sleep with the Melesh-Eloni.* As much as he tried to deny it, as much as he'd hidden his desire behind a mask of aloofness or even contempt, he'd thought about little else since the Abbess, since he'd been filled with a compulsive longing for Carred. *That would be a betrayal of Niyas.* But he was the *Melesh-Eloni*! He *was* Niyas.

His wings of shadow snapped and flapped, catching more wind than he could control. He flipped onto his back, and now he felt Carred's weight dragging him down. With a fierce flutter he righted himself—righted them both. Dark-tide essence poured into his wings, but way too much. He felt as though he

512

were losing mass, that he had a million tiny ruptures in his veins, bleeding tidal force.

He started to drop back towards the depot a hundred feet below. Carred craned her neck to look down and cried a warning.

A bolt of violet lightning streaked toward them from the ground. Anskar veered aside at the last possible instant, and the sorcerous projectile sizzled as it shot past this face.

There, below: Sareya, a second bolt of lightning already leaving her hand.

Turning his back on it to protect Carred, Anskar wreathed his body in shadow plate armor. He grunted as the lightning struck his back, but it fizzled away to nothing as the dark-tide protecting him dissipated its arcane energy.

Wheeling in midair, he left Carred clinging to him by her own strength as he jabbed an arm toward the knights pouring from the entrance to the depot and toward Sareya.

His guts lurched, turned inside out, as a ball of black fire burst from his hand and hit the ground. The concussive blast threw Anskar spinning through the air. Carred screamed as she fell, but Anskar's hand lashed out and he caught her wrist. Together they spiraled down, the streets of Dorinah spinning up to meet them.

A huge cloud like a smoke-formed toadstool billowed up from the front of the depot. Pieces of armor-plated bodies were strewn all over the ground—all that was left of the knights. At the heart of the cloud, the precise center of his target, gold light backlit the smoke.

As Anskar's feet hit the ground and his knees buckled, Carred leaped clear and rolled. She came up lithely and caught his elbow before he collapsed. His heart was a feeble patter in his chest. Cold sweat dripped into his eyes. He was weak, so weak. All he could do was stare at the clearing smoke as a golden ward sphere emerged from the carnage, Sareya within, her eyes blazing suns of violet.

"Run!" Carred said, dragging him by the arm.

Anskar stumbled, still looking back at Sareya, whose ward sphere rose into the air and drifted toward them.

They ducked into an alley, but Anskar had gone no more than twenty feet when his legs gave out. Carred caught him and lowered him to the ground.

"Anskar!"

His head fell back against the cobbles that paved the alley. His body was drained of energy, his mind clouded as if he'd drank too much. He couldn't go on.

He felt her lift his torso from behind and slide her arms beneath his. And then she was dragging him along the alley. With a curse, Carred kicked open a door and bundled Anskar inside, closing the door behind them.

It was dark within, and it smelled of fish. He could hear the scratch and patter of mice or rats. A few feet above the level of the floor, a chink of dirty light showed—it could have been coming beneath a door at the top of a short flight of steps.

He tried to rise, but Carred clamped a hand over his mouth.

"Quiet," she whispered urgently. "Not a sound."

Golden light bled through the cracks in the door they had entered by, lingered for a few moments, and then moved off.

Carred waited what felt like an age before she removed her hand from his mouth.

"What happened to you?" she asked.

"Too much…" Anskar said, every word a torture.

"Too much dark-tide?" Carred said. "Any amount is too much, if you ask me."

"Without it…"

"Without it we wouldn't have escaped?"

"If there'd been any other way…" His hand went to his chest, and his fingers traced the puckered scar where his catalyst had been removed. His braided repository of the dawn- and the dusk-tides was a flaccid sack within his mind, useless to him now. All he had was the dark, yet he'd lost so much of its essence. He felt as though he'd bled to death and now lingered as empty, as immaterial as a wraithe.

But then he felt it: the putrid touch of the earth-tide seeping into him through the floor, laying claim to him, wanting to possess him.

He shut it out with a thought like a whiplash, then turned his head and vomited. A stream of vileness poured from his mouth, and he saw Carred cover her mouth and nose. Rankness. Rot. Every inch of him felt diseased, but when he had finished, he felt, if not better, then purged.

But the earth-tide did something else do him. He felt first the warmth of the rodents scurrying around in the dark. Felt the frantic patter of tiny hearts. A tickle passed through his veins, then they began to throb. He could still hear the rodent heartbeats, fainter now, and slowing down. Then with an almost audible snap in his mind, the earth-tide released its hold.

And the room went terribly quiet.

No more mice or rats scratching in the dark.

Only Carred's breathing now, and his own, fuller than it had been moments ago and less ragged. The rodents' life force had been sucked into him, giving him strength.

Anskar pushed himself upright on his elbows, and then he managed to stand.

"We can't stay here," he said.

"Agreed. But we can't just walk out of the city. That's what they'll be expecting. I have people in the Niyandrian quarter…"

"People like Dargul? I know. I've met them. Sareya's not stupid. She'll expect us to flee there."

"Then what?" Carred said. "What do you suggest?"

"I don't know!" Anskar said, and then a tendril of awareness lashed his mind, its touch burning like acid. He clutched his head.

"What is it?" Carred asked.

"Sareya…" he gasped. "She's hunting me with her senses."

"Then we can't just wait here and do nothing," Carred said.

Anskar's eyes were adjusting to the dark, more so now that the earth-tide had restored him. Dead mice littered the floor, their tiny corpses wasted away to little more than bones. He swallowed. Told himself he'd committed no sin, that the earth-tide had acted without his consent. Told himself he didn't care, in any case. He'd come too far now to worry about what Menselas thought—an impotent, five-faced god!

He saw Carred at the top of three short steps, and he followed her as she opened a door and stepped through.

He winced at another stab inside his mind as they entered the rear of a fishmonger's store.

"What in the bloody hells do you think you're…?" a fat-bellied man started, then stopped as Carred pushed over a tray of fish and ran from the store with Anskar in tow.

He followed her across the street and down a narrow lane. At the other end, they emerged into a major street and wove in and out of the crowds milling in the road. Not shopping: people were just standing about in the street, muttering and gawping. Armor glinted from one end of the street, and he picked up the sound of hoofbeats and marching feet heading toward the city limits. Anskar glanced behind and up at the towering walls of

Branil's Burg, where for the first time he could remember, there stood a knight between every merlon.

"Is this all for us?" Carred asked.

"It can't be. I've never seen the Burg mobilize its forces like this. Something's happening. Something bigger than the archduke's bounty on me and Orix."

"You surprised me," Carred said.

"I surprised myself," he said, thinking she was talking about his demonstration of power. "I never knew I could fly, or cause such destru—"

"Not that," Carred said. "Orix. I never thought you'd just leave him behind."

"I didn't think!" Anskar protested. "There was no time."

"Then we go back for him," Carred said. "It's the last thing Sareya will expect, and the Order are focused elsewhere—the city walls, it would seem. Let's just hope Orix wasn't caught in the blast of your sorcery."

Quickly, they made their way back to the depot and climbed the steps to the open doors. Limbs, heads, and torsos in charred armor littered the approach, from where Anskar's sorcery had wreaked carnage. There was no blood: the body parts had been cauterized by the dark fire. Somehow, that made it seem worse.

Anskar stood brooding over his work, a single thought echoing through his mind as it embedded itself there: *You couldn't even let them bleed.* His perceptions all closed in on that one point of self-chastisement. He saw nothing but armor-encased limbs and helms that obscured heads. Was that why he had so readily killed them? Because, armored head to toe, they didn't resemble people? Or was it him? Was he the one that no longer knew what it was like to be a person—a human person? His time in the abyssal realm… What Domatai had done to him… the awakening of latencies in his blood…

"Anskar!"

Carred's hand on his shoulder snapped him out of his head. "Do you think you had a choice?" she asked. "You didn't."

She meant well. All's fair in war, and all that. But she was wrong. He'd had a choice. He'd just made the wrong one.

And he'd do it again in an instant.

Carred tugged him towards the threshold, but Anskar pulled free from her grip and clutched his head as burning threads thrashed about inside his skull.

Sareya!

"What is it?" Carred asked.

"She's in my head again."

"What can I do?"

"Get Orix." Anskar hunched over in agony. *Where are you?* Sareya was whispering like the wind in his head. *Show me where you are.*

He was only dimly aware of Carred entering the depot as he battered Sareya's feelers with shadows and scorched them with dark fire. She laughed in response, so he tried again, this time sending thorny vines of dark-tide to coil around her probing tendrils. He intended to smother her presence within him. Crush it. But her feelers flared golden, and he cried out as his dark-tide sorcery dissolved into sparking motes that burned his mind.

From within the depot, he heard the rasp of a sword, and he remembered that Carred was unarmed. His hand went to the sword at his hip, but it wasn't there. Sareya had taken it.

Where are you? A demand, not a question. *Show me where you are!*

He tried dark-tide again, but she seemed to read his every move, as if she learned from every contact with his mind. And so he tried something new. Throwing his senses into the stone of the steps, he drove them downwards, deep into the earth, all the way to the pooling corruption at the core of the world. And then he flooded his mind with vileness and rot. Pure earth-tide.

Sareya gasped. She might even have gagged. But instantly, she was gone from his head.

Before he could enter the depot, Carred came out, supporting Orix by the arm. Orix's face was so grotesquely deformed, Anskar couldn't tell whether his old friend was looking at him or not.

"Here," Carred said, passing him the scabbarded *Amalantril*. "I found *Bitch Blade* on the floor. Sareya must have dropped it when she followed us outside." She wrinkled her nose and wiped her hand on her pants, as if the sword were coated in oil or slime.

It wasn't, but it throbbed in Anskar's grasp. Dark-tide flowed from *Amalantril's* hilt into his fingers, filling his veins, leaving the sword… empty? Hungry!

He secured the scabbard to his belt. As he did, he noticed that Carred had a sword hanging at her hip now. Then he remembered the rasp of the sword he'd heard from inside.

Carred must have read his mind. She shrugged as if it were nothing. "Not as old and washed up as I look," she said. She was shaking—the aftermath of fighting. Anskar knew the feeling well.

"You're not old," he said. "But you weren't armed."

"I fight dirty."

"Filthy," Orix said, his voice thick, the words malformed. "In so many ways." His attempted joke fell flat. There was no humor in his tone, only pain bordering on despair. "But at least your Nan-Rhouric's improving."

"You noticed? I'll have to rinse my mouth out. Theltek's tongues, I'm even starting to think in Nan-Rhouric."

"I think I can heal your face," Anskar told Orix. And given

time, perhaps he could.

"That's what Noni said," Orix replied. "She only made it worse."

Anskar's nostrils flared and he grew suddenly alert.

"What is it?" Carred asked.

"Sareya."

"You can smell her? That's... disturbing."

But it was no natural smell. It was her taint, drawing nearer. She'd invaded his mind, and now he could scent her approach. It was the dark-tide, he was certain, that Domatai had fully awakened within him. Senses he hadn't even known he had were working beneath his conscious awareness. Demon senses. Sareya must have realized they had doubled back, that they would go after Orix.

"We shouldn't just stand here," Anskar said.

Together, they helped Orix to his feet and half-carried him down the steps. When they reached the street, they moved as quickly as they could, glancing down side streets before taking them. There were disgruntled cries from somewhere behind them and the tramp of booted feet. As they ducked into an alley, Anskar caught sight of a flash of silver and white in pursuit—Order knights.

"I'm slowing you down," Orix said. "Leave me."

"Be quiet, please," Carred said.

At the end of the alley they came onto the main street that wound through the heart of the district all the way to the city gates. It was deserted.

"The gates will be closed, no doubt," Carred said. "And there will be guards."

"Back the way we came?" Anskar asked, but no sooner had he said it than more knights appeared at the far end of the alley.

"This way," Carred said.

They wheeled Orix around and crossed the road, but there were knights there too, coming from the intersection. And behind them on the main street, more knights funneled onto the road; and at their head was Sareya.

"The gates it is, then," Carred said. "I'm sure we can handle a couple of guards."

Virtually lifting Orix between them, they ran.

They followed the wend of the road past stores, the courthouse, a bank. People stared out of windows. A dog yipped from the mouth of an alley. Boots stomped behind.

Anskar sensed sorcery hurled at his back, and his black ward sprang up around the three of them. Something struck. He grunted. They all fell as the sphere of dark-tide juddered from the impact. Anskar's legs were jelly. He couldn't stand. Carred was sprawled on top of Orix. Breathing. Both still breathing.

Up the street, through the sphere, he could see Sareya streaking ahead of a large group of knights, lightning arcing between her hands.

With a panicked thought, Anskar set the dark sphere rolling, slowly at first, then faster as it built momentum and hurtled toward the city gates. With the same ability that had allowed him to scale the walls of the Scriptorium in Wintotashum like a spider, Anskar made the three of them adhere to the insides of the sphere, so that as it rolled, they rolled with it, over and over in a giddying tumble.

Lightning struck, and the sphere bounced. A hairline crack split its black surface.

If he could keep the sphere moving, accelerate its pace…

The city walls loomed high above them, the barred gates growing at an alarming rate as the sphere raced towards them.

There were knights manning the walls, which was far from usual: Niyas was at peace.

With enough dark-tide power, the sphere might crash through...

Lightning struck again. Cracks webbed the surface of the sphere, and daylight streamed in. After a third blast, the sphere disintegrated, pitching Anskar, Orix, and Carred to the ground.

Anskar tumbled over and over, collapsed as he tried to stand, and pitched to his face. He heard Orix moan in his ear. Saw Carred roll to her feet like a cat and draw her sword.

The tramp of boots was deafening. He craned his neck to see Sareya striding toward them at the head of a force of at least fifty knights. She grinned in triumph, and he followed her gaze back toward the gates, where dozens more knights were stepping from the streets on either side to block the road ahead. And with them, shining in full plate armor, was Seneschal Monash.

FIFTY-EIGHT

BETWEEN A BITCH AND A bastard. That was Carred's frank assessment of their situation. Anskar was down, unmoving save for the sporadic twitching of one arm. Orix was a groaning lump beside him on the ground. Funny, that: he'd been a groaning lump in bed, too. Up ahead, the gates were barred, the walls above them manned, and now knights were pouring out of the side streets and forming up in ranks.

And their leader… Carred could tell she was someone who fancied herself important from the ermine-trimmed white cloak, the mirror-bright breastplate, and the hilt of the long sword sheathed at her hip, wrapped with gold wire and studded with gems. She was too skinny to be called lean, but had too much ropey muscle to be emaciated. She had a face like a skull and a nose sharp enough to cut a steak with. Her hair was cut severely and the color of iron, but Carred had the sense she wasn't as old as she looked. Bad living would do that to you. Or stress. Or cruelty. Perhaps too much resentment. After all, she only had the one eye, the other covered by a white leather patch, with one end of a scar above, the other below. Scars had a way of twisting you up inside, a visible mark of your failures. She of all people knew that. She glanced over her shoulder.

"Nowhere left to run, Captain," Sareya said from behind as dozens of silver ward spheres sprang to life around her, overlapping and forming a wall of light within which Carred could see the silhouettes of the knights.

In front, the old woman in the ermine stood with her arms folded across her chest. Knights flanked her both sides, and one by one, their ward spheres burst into existence.

"To be perfectly honest," Carred said in Niyandrian, "I'm done with running. It's my age, see. Although I lasted longer than these two younglings."

Sareya didn't even do her the courtesy of smiling. Instead she was all seriousness, and when she spoke—sticking to her polished Nan-Rhouric—she sounded a condescending, pious little prig.

"I used to revere you as a hero of Niyas, Captain Carred Selenas of the Last Cohort. All of us Niyandrians at Branil's Burg did."

Carred continued speaking Niyandrian. She could be a stubborn cow when she wanted. "The stolen children. I can understand why you needed a hero, a hope to cling on to. The dream of someone who might one day come to bring you home."

"Only you didn't." Sareya had spoken in Niyandrian, apparently without thinking—something that seemed to irritate her.

"There are a lot of things I didn't achieve," Carred said, emphasizing each Niyandrian word. "I lost a lot of skirmishes, one or two major battles. I failed to keep Niyas united in defiance of their mainland oppressors. Failed to stop the destruction of our culture. And yes, I failed to find all the stolen children and return them to their families. But I never once forgot who I was, where I came from, which side I'm on." Let the little bitch chew on that.

"Perhaps that's because you've been deluded all these years," Sareya said. "Queen Talia's never coming back, and even if she were, why would that be a good thing? Face it, Captain, after so many losses, and now this… yet another failure… how can you still believe?"

Carred chose that moment to switch to Nan-Rhouric. She glanced at Lady Ermine in front of the city gates, then back at Sareya. "How can you not, betrayer of Niyas?"

Violet embers smoldered in Sareya's eyes, but she was distracted as Orix, naked save for his smallclothes, bruised all over, groaned and rolled to his knees. He angled his distorted face so that he could see Sareya, and as he stared, the light went out of her eyes. She swallowed and seemed to flinch.

"Iron fist, Sareya," the older woman barked. "Iron fist."

"Seneschal," Sareya said, her back straightened, her resolve swiftly restored. She glanced left and right at her knights. "Take them!"

As one unit, the knights within their silver spheres took a step forward but then stopped. Sareya's nose wrinkled and she started to retch.

At first Carred had no idea what was happening, but then she picked up the stench of rot rising from the ground.

Anskar!

He was lying prone, arms outstretched above his head, palms pressed against the surface of the road.

"What's he doing?" Sareya asked, wiping her mouth with her gloved hand. "Make him stop, or I'll…"

"You'll what?" Anskar said, voice a rasp, less than a whisper, yet somehow carrying as if he'd shouted.

"Is that supposed to impress me?" Sareya said, her own voice a concussive boom. "The only wonder is that you can perform such a simple party trick without a catalyst."

The smell of rot grew overpowering. Knights bent double and vomited, their ward spheres flickering erratically.

Anskar rolled to his knees and made it to his feet on shaky legs. All the red had gone from his skin, leaving him pale and bloodless. His eyes were bloodshot, sunken in dark cavities, and his lips were tinged blue. Pallid fingers curled around the hilt of his sword, and he drew it from the scabbard.

"Idiot!" Lady Ermine said. "You really think you can fight us? All of us?"

"Seneschal Monash," Anskar replied, sword extended toward her. "You look old."

"I look a damned sight better than you. We've coddled you enough. Archduke Peleus will understand if we have to take you to him in a box. Sareya…"

"Seneschal?"

"Kill him. Kill them all."

"No!" Orix said. He raised his fists as he backed away, but his knees buckled and Carred had to catch his elbow before he fell.

Anskar raised some kind of ward sphere around the three of them, only it was blotchy with blues and purples and reminded Carred of bruises.

"It's going to take more than that," Sareya said. She shouted a cant and flung out her hands, and tendrils of mist streamed from her fingers, weaving into a web that settled over Anskar's sphere. Where the misty strands touched, the ward smoldered, until Anskar dissolved it and readied his sword to fight. Carred drew her own blade.

Monash made a fist of her gloved hand. "Do I have to give the command twice?"

Sareya appeared to waver with uncertainty, but then she screamed cants and threw her arms skywards, and purplish flames erupted from her hands. Her knights started forward again as Sareya brought her hands down, the flames between them swelling into a churning ball of fire.

But before she could fling it, Sareya staggered back, blood coming from her nose. The air in the street thrummed, and Carred felt a twinge in her dusk-tide repository. But it hadn't been her—as if! And Anskar could no longer use the dusk-tide…

"Attack!" Monash shouted, and the knights in front and behind charged.

Get down, my love! a voice commanded in Carred's head. Marith?

Instantly, Carred grabbed Anskar and Orix and dragged them with her to the ground.

Just as a colossal blast blew the gates apart.

Blood mist sprayed the air as knights fell in a hail of wood and iron. Bodies twitched amid the carnage, one with a splinter like a spear jutting from her chest, another with half a face, many with limbs missing. There was blood and rubble and burning wood everywhere. Smoke plumed skywards, backlit by a brilliant emerald glow.

A woman stood silhouetted in the opening, hands extended, sparks of viridian arcing between her fingertips. Hundreds of armed men and women surged around her and into the city, screaming battle cries… in Niyandrian.

In a dreamlike daze, her ears ringing from the explosion, Carred registered the redness of their skin, black hair, eyes with slitted pupils. Dimly, she knew these were her rebels, but not only from her own camp—there were far too many. Some of the neighboring groups, then? All of them? She'd only ever dreamed of this moment, when the rebels of Niyas would come together for a decisive strike, but that moment wasn't meant to be now. She'd given no order.

Her mind a confusion of warring thoughts and feelings, Carred could do nothing but stare at the woman in the dissipating smoke, eyes on fire with the same emerald light that sparked from her fingers. And before she could decide if this was for real or if she was only dreaming, she ran toward her.

"Marith! Theltek's hairy asses! Marith!"

Marith stepped forward, hand outstretched in warning. "Carred! Look—!"

Silver flashed in her peripheral vision, and on instinct, Carred ducked and spun, swinging her sword in a wild arc. A blade whistled above her head. Her own struck a golden ward sphere, sending up sparking motes, glancing off without inflicting so much as a scratch. Lady Ermine—Monash, Sareya had called her. Her golden ward was the only thing that had saved her from the blast that had destroyed the gates.

Carred tried to back away, make some space, but knights and rebels seethed around her amid the deafening clangor of steel. Silver wards flickered and sparked as weapons slammed into them. The odd fizzing crack of Niyandrian sorcery flashed by Carred's eyes.

Monash thrust for Carred's unprotected belly, but Carred sidestepped and parried. Her sword was unfamiliar—unfamiliar good, not bad. The knight she had taken it from had probably made it himself. Its balance was good, and it was surprisingly light, with not a nick on its keen edge. Easily the best blade she had owned.

Monash's pretentious sword came down hard, and Carred blocked. Steel met steel, and sparks flew. And her blade snapped halfway up. Broken steel clanged to the ground, and she stared at the useless hilt in her hand. *Shit.*

Monash smiled from within her golden sphere. "The blade of a novice, as compared with this: the blade of a knight-superior. There really is no comparison."

"Carred!" Marith cried.

She dared not look behind, with Monash poised for the killing blow. Space had opened to Carred's left. She backed away into it, but Monash came after her, swift and sure of her movements. As the gaudy sword came up, Carred heard Marith scream in frustration and fear: "You're too close together. I'll catch you in the blast!"

Monash gave an apologetic smile and then swung her sword.

Carred threw her arms up and shut her eyes, but the impact never came.

In one timeless instant: the pad and scratch of taloned feet, hot breath rushing past her cheek, a throaty growl.

Carred's eyes shot open as Monash gasped. A massive gray-furred wolf slammed into her ward sphere, bowling her over. Only it wasn't a wolf. Through a flurry of rending and biting, Carred saw six reptilian legs and the head of a gigantic black cat.

Bala!

Eadgith's pet hybrid monster.

Claw after claw pounded and raked at the golden ward, which grew thready and started to fail. Monash somehow retained her grip on her sword and thrust at Bala's underbelly. The wolf-cat-thing twisted aside and snapped her jaws at the ward sphere. And the ward sphere buckled.

A knight slammed into Bala, using his silver ward as a weapon, but Bala smacked him aside with a paw. Another knight checked his charge as the cat-thing roared. The knight's ward sphere flickered and went out, and Bala pounced. Blood sprayed amid gurgling screams. More knights moved in to shield Monash, who even now got to her feet and retreated through the ranks. A second silver sphere winked out. Bala slashed her claws across the woman's belly, ripping through the protecting mail. Blood sprayed, and the knight's guts spilled.

Carred was forced to look away as a knight ran straight at her. He was young—as young as Anskar. His ward sphere wavered as he drew back his sword—too much tell, and the poor fool realized too late as the jagged tip of Carred's broken blade pierced his feeble ward and plunged into his throat.

Dozens of knights swarmed towards where Bala was growling and hissing, but Carred was again distracted—this time seeing Orix dragged out of the fray by two rebels. One of them was Vilintia.

"They came!" Vilintia called to her. "They all came."

"Except Fult Wreave, I'll bet," Carred said.

"Except him."

"But why? How did you know I'd be here?" She wanted to ask, "Was this your doing?" Because it was downright foolhardy. Crazy, even.

"Not for you," Vilintia said. "For Orix… and something else. We'll talk later."

If we survive!

Rebels closed around Vilintia, taking her from Carred's sight.

Leaving her staring down at Anskar lying on the ground, unscathed by the first clash of forces. And she could see why. Overlapping scales of shadow, not quite solid, covered his back and legs, and a helm of shadow protected his head. As she looked, his fingers splayed, and he groaned.

A shrill scream made her turn. Bala! Run through with a sword. The cat-thing twisted and thrashed, but another sword came down, half severing her head, and the hybrid beast fell. She heard Eadgith shrieking curses, but couldn't see the old woman amid the rebels behind, hundreds of them, pouring through the gates.

The knights around Bala retreated as the rebels pressed in on them, and Carred found herself in an ever-widening space between the two sides.

Anskar grunted as he pushed down with his hands and got to his knees.

"Let me…" Carred started, but he shrugged off her hand.

He wavered on his feet, turned toward the gate, and stumbled away from her, wreathed head to toe in shadowy armor. Rebels parted around him. Some touched their eyes in the sign of Theltek. A roar went up from the knights, who had re-formed into disciplined lines. They started to advance, a scintillant wall of silver wards.

As the rebels braced to meet them, Carred went after Anskar. He was the *Melesh-Eloni*, and he was not right. Someone had to watch his back.

Mere feet from the shattered gates, he was crouching beside the body of a knight who'd been impaled by flying wood. Carred faltered and then covered her mouth as Anskar's shadow armor faded away, and he plunged his hand into the woman's gushing wound.

Carred looked away before she gagged. Behind her, the front ranks of the knights and the rebels collided, and the ward spheres held. They had fielded more seasoned knights for the second wave, and several rebels went down.

The stench of rotting meat drew her gaze back to Anskar. Movement to her right startled her, but it was Marith striding toward her.

"Is that him? The *Melesh-Eloni*?" Marith looked repulsed by the idea.

Carred swallowed as she nodded. "I'll deal with him. Go help the others."

"You've taken control back from Vilintia, I assume?"

"Not yet."

Marith blew her a kiss, then rose into the air and drifted toward the battle. Lightning streaked from her fingers, detonating in the middle of the Order's ranks. In response, slender lines of violet shot towards her—Sareya! The young woman was standing beside Monash in her golden ward sphere toward the back. Marith deflected the attack with a shield of emerald light, but a second volley hit her and sent her spinning into the side of a building.

Carred started toward her, heart pounding. She couldn't afford another loss. Couldn't bear it.

But before she'd taken half a dozen steps, the knights' wall of silver wards surged forward, and the rebel line buckled.

And behind... more knights raced down the steps from the walls to come at the rebels from behind.

FIFTY-NINE

ANSKAR'S FINGERS SUCKED ON THE dead knight's essence. They drank it up, filling his veins. Only the flaccid sacks of his dawn- and dusk-tide repositories remained empty. The rest of him grew sated on the seething earth-tide in the still-hot blood.

He pulled his hand from the now gaping wound in the woman's chest, accompanied by a slurping pop. His muscles felt swollen, his skin taut and ready to burst. He raised his hands to his eyes: one dripping with blood, the other pallid, the veins prominent and blue. Vileness filled his nostrils, of bad meat and sulfur. And it wasn't just the earth-tide that swilled through his veins and clouded his mind with putrescence: the dark-tide was back, even stronger than before, caressing, intermingling, merging with the earth-tide. For a moment, his senses turned inward, and he heard the seethe of the dark amid the gurgling slop of the earth. He smelled disease and sulfur, saw in his mind's eye bruises and dead flesh, shadow and decay.

And then he remembered.

Remembered where he was, if not quite who.

He grew once more aware of the shouting, the screams, the clash of steel on steel. He could feel the ripple of repositories, some puny, others a match for his own. Two of them. He recognized Sareya's. The other: the woman who had blasted apart the gate. Carred had known her. *Marith?*

The stomp of booted feet came from behind. Yelled curses— no, invocations of Menselas.

Against him!

Rising on wings of shadow, he twisted in midair and threw out his hands, sending shards of shadow ripping into the knights charging from the walls. Blood misted the air from dozens of wounds. Screams, slaughter, bodies hitting the ground.

He turned to face the main fighting, hundreds of Niyandrians, massively outnumbering the knights. But the knights had superior weapons, and their ward spheres made each knight easily a match for five rebels.

There: a golden ward sphere beside a silver one. Sareya! Lines of violet sorcery lanced from her fingertips, razing the ranks of the rebels and dicing them into offal.

"I see you," he whispered, shadow armor forming around him with barely a conscious thought. With the languid beat of shadow wings, he propelled himself above the fray towards her.

Knights encased in silver ward spheres closed around Sareya, forming a wall of protection, but he slammed right through them, bowling them over amid sparks and fizzing motes. Sareya's eyes widened, and the violet rays sputtered on her fingertips. Out of the corner of his eye, he saw a flash of gold, and he turned just as a fist of golden light smashed him out of the sky—Seneschal Monash, slumped to her knees, her golden ward petering out.

Anskar fell into the massed rebel lines, knocking several from their feet as he hit the ground. Air rushed from his lungs. His head smacked into the road. His shadow wings and armor were snuffed out instantly, and the dark-tide tendrils that formed them retreated into his mind.

A Niyandrian man lay on the road beside him, his neck twisted at a gruesome angle. Another screamed as he nursed a broken leg. All around him, rebels stared with wide eyes. A red-skinned woman started toward him, trembling with fear. *"Melesh... Melesh-Eloni?"*

"Stay back," Anskar growled as he shook his head to clear it. Then the earth-tide poured into him through the ground, coming unbidden now. It knew him. Knew him for its own.

He rose to his feet without bending a limb, as if invisible hands were lifting him, raising him up.

The battle still raged in front of him.

Iridescent lines of violet streaked overhead, then struck a spinning disk of emerald flame in a booming impact that shook the street.

A shadow fell over him—Marith, hovering high above the battle, her eyes burning with emerald light and flames wreathing her fists.

Ahead, the rebel line buckled. Silver ward spheres began to make headway. A Niyandrian shrieked as a sword ran her through. The man beside her slipped in her blood. Orix—near-naked—snatched up her axe and filled the gap, blocking a chopping blow from a sword intended to finish a man on the ground. A second block, and Orix stumbled back. Anskar saw Carred forcing her way through the ragged ranks, then pulling Orix back. Sparks flew from her blade as she parried and thrust low with her counter, but her sword bounced off the knight's ward sphere.

Stiff and numb—though not from his fall—Anskar strode through the rebel ranks. The earth-tide sluiced through his veins, oozed in his guts. He felt strong, powerful beyond imagining.

With a crushing blow from *Amalantril*, he smashed a knight down, blood spattering the inside of the ward sphere as it winked out. And she drank. The sword sucked in the essence contained in the knight's blood, wholesome and pure—Anskar felt it passing from *Amalantril* to him. Not the dark-tide she'd fed him earlier; not any tide he could differentiate. All of them and none… It was as if the separate tides were considered one.

A wall of silver spheres converged on him as the rebels pulled back, retching and gagging. He didn't care. He didn't need them!

He heard Carred yelling, screeching at the rebels to re-form, to stand their ground. A sword came at his face, and he almost let it hit, certain it wouldn't harm him. But instinct brought *Amalantril* up to parry. With a twist of his torso, he elbowed the knight's ward sphere, then kicked it and hammered his sword into it, and the ward sphere split and went out. The knight dropped his sword and threw up his hands, but he had no space to back away. Anskar ran him through, then ripped his blade out and swung for the ward sphere on his right. And *Amalantril* howled in his mind as she sated her appetite… and his.

"Hold, you miserable cowards!" Carred yelled.

He could see her now, side by side with Orix, one hand holding him up as she hacked into a ward sphere over and over. The knight within seemed stunned by the impacts, and then he turned to flee as the ward sphere collapsed.

Carred cut him down from behind, her sword slicing into his back.

The rebel line surged forward then, slamming into the Order's front ranks. *Let them fight,* Anskar thought as he held back, relishing the fizz of stolen essence in his blood. *Let them prove themselves worthy.*

Letting his shadow armor drain away, he weaved through the Niyandrians pouring back to the fray, making his way to Carred. When he reached her, he helped her drag Orix back. The Traguh-raj lad was beyond exhausted, his jumbled-up face gray, and his chest rising and falling rapidly as he gasped for breath through his misplaced mouth.

Blood from a dozen cuts trickled over Carred's red skin, making it glisten. Sweat drenched her shirt. Anskar was transfixed by her wiry muscles, her curves, the lines of her scars.

"What?" she snarled. "What are you staring... Oh, sweet Theltek, no!"

A hunched-over woman shambled out from an alley behind the enemy lines. She looked old, impossibly old, but there was something about her...

"Noni," Carred breathed. "What have you done?"

Her hair was like lank seaweed and her face long and drooping, as if the chin had melted into her neck. And her eyes! She only had the one, right in the center of her face, nose above, mouth below.

Anskar knew at once what must have happened. She'd tried to help Orix, to fix his face. Only the forces she'd unleashed had somehow rebounded and made a mess of her own, as well as making Orix's worse.

She was yelling something, but it was lost amid the din of battle. Order knights turned toward her as the fighting ceased, and both sides stood and stared.

"Orix!" Noni wailed. "Orix, I'm coming!"

Anskar glanced at Orix, who tried pushing himself away from

the wall they'd left him leaning against. His legs buckled, but he continued on his hands and knees. There were ranks of rebels in his way, but Noni had seen him.

She hobbled forward. A wall of silver wards advanced to meet her, then pulled up sharp as Noni thrust her hands outward and down, fingers splayed, her voice rising in a deep, rumbling chant that couldn't possibly have come from her vocal cords.

Noni's cant ceased. Silence hung over the street. Silver wards shimmered. The air was thick with the sulfur from the sorcerous clash of Marith and Sareya. The atmosphere grew heavy. A putrid odor rose from the earth, manifesting as a billowing cloud of filth.

And then Noni shrieked, "Orix!"

The road cracked. Dust plumed. Fractures raced through the flagged surface toward the Order's lines. Men and women cried out and tried to flee, but it all happened so quickly. A rent opened in the ground beneath them, widening to a fissure, a crevasse. Dozens of knights tumbled into the widening abyss, their wards winking out as they screamed.

The old woman, Eadgith, appeared behind Noni, her face a mask of horror. "Stop, girl!" she cried. "You've no idea what you're…"

Eadgith pitched to her knees as the ground shook. Masonry cascaded from buildings on either side of the street. Knights scattered, fleeing back toward Branil's Burg. Sareya was supporting Monash by the arm, protecting her within her expanded ward sphere.

The rebel lines dissolved into a mass of individuals pulling back to the sides of the street, keeping their distance as the ravine that had opened in the ground snapped shut like monstrous jaws.

Orix found his feet and stumbled toward Noni, crying out as she collapsed to the road. Injured and weak as he was, Orix somehow managed to reach her and lift her into his arms. He turned and struggled back towards Anskar. Blood trickled from Noni's misplaced nose, her mouth, her ears.

"She's dead," Orix moaned. It sounded like an accusation. "You can fix her! Bring her back!"

"No," Anskar said.

"Bring her back!"

Anskar shook his head.

"You can't?" Orix said, stopping in front of him, tears spilling from his unnaturally placed eyes. He looked down at Noni, cradled in his arms, as he sobbed.

"I didn't say that," Anskar said.

Orix continued sobbing as Anskar walked past him, watching the knights flee, looking up at the walls of Branil's Burg, knowing this was where he belonged: outside. But not for long.

"I'm coming for you," he muttered. Images of fire and blood swamped his mind. He indulged them, reveled in them. In his grasp, *Amalantril* twitched.

Behind him, he could hear Orix weeping. Carred was arguing with someone. Was that...? He turned to see Vilintia.

She glanced his way, almost scowling.

"What have you done?" Carred yelled. "Why did you come? Noni, I understand: she came for Orix. But an attack on Dorinah? Are you mad?"

"It's not her fault," Marith said, striding towards them. "If you must blame someone..."

A column of putrid gas rose from the ground beneath Anskar's feet, carrying him into the air, higher and higher, till he stood atop a pillar of murk. Had he willed it? Had the earth-tide come at his bidding?

He faced Branil's Burg once more as the knights reached the

gates and scurried inside.

Diseased mist plumed from his every pore. They had come too far to let the Order knights go. To win the battle and let them live to fight another day… to summon reinforcements from the strongholds on Niyas, from the mainland…

He wouldn't permit it.

His head throbbed. A red curtain dropped behind his eyes. Shadow armor once more wreathed his flesh, and the dark helm formed around his head. Wings like black smoke unfurled from his back. He drew *Amalantril* and she sighed—she *sighed* in his mind. He could feel her urgent need, as if it were his own. She hungered. And he hungered with her.

"Anskar!" Carred's voice was enhanced by sorcery.

He looked down and saw her hand in hand with Marith. His anger roared into rage.

"Anskar, stop!" She commanded him in Niyandrian, as if he were one of her rebels. "You have to stop!"

"Why would I stop now?" His voice sounded dead to his ears, muffled by the shadow helm.

"You're not like this. You are not your mother!"

"My…"

The shadow helm dissolved as Anskar glared down at Carred, down at Marith standing protectively beside her, eyes burning with emerald fire.

His eyes stung; his head pounded; he struggled to breathe. Coldness sloshed through his veins. He started to shiver. His wings retracted, his armor dispersed, and the column of smoke sank slowly back down.

Anskar stumbled as his feet touched the ground. He felt suddenly weak.

"Cold," he said through chattering teeth. "So cold."

"That'll be the earth-tide turning on you," Eadgith said. The old woman stood on the opposite side of him from Carred and Marith. Anskar bunched his fists. He felt trapped.

"Do you no longer serve my mother?" he asked Carred.

He glared at Marith, then behind at Eadgith. Orix closed in too, leaving Noni unmoving on the road.

Anskar's guts clenched. He spun to one knee and vomited, a gushing stream of vileness.

No one spoke. They just waited for him to finish. Waited to see what he would do.

As he stood, he swayed with dizziness, but no one tried to steady him.

He looked afresh at Carred and saw how worn out, how cut up she was. Saw Marith's hand in hers, eyes a burning warning. Marith had a saddlebag slung over one shoulder. Something inside it pricked at Anskar's senses, but when he tried to *see*, powerful wards repulsed him. Marith cocked her head and narrowed her eyes.

"I'm... I'm sorry," he told Carred. "I didn't mean to scare you." Both the dark-tide and the earth-tide had taken a hold of him, and he'd been powerless to resist. And the truth was, he'd savored the feel of unbridled power.

Vilintia stood with Marith and Carred. "Noni came to save you, Orix," she said. "We followed. Eadgith tried to stop her."

Orix dipped his chin to his chest, nodding that he understood.

"And Carred?" Anskar asked Vilintia. "You came for her too?"

"If only," Carred said. "And even then, I'd have disapproved."

"But they're here now," Anskar said, wiping vileness from his chin. "We're all here. Together. We've crossed a line, and there's no going back."

"No, there's no going back," Carred said. "For any of us."

Anskar turned to take in the hundreds of faces around them, their eyes locked on Carred.

"They believe in you, Carred," Marith said, the emerald fire abating from her eyes. "They believe in Queen Talia's return."

"Is that what you want?" Carred asked the crowd. "What you really want?" She sounded uncertain, and Anskar could understand why.

"Niyas for Niyandrians!" a woman shouted, and others took up the chant.

"With Talia as our queen!" Marith cried.

Carred gave her a sharp look, but whatever objections she might have had seemed to melt under Marith's gaze.

"So what do we do?" Anskar asked. But he knew. In his bones he knew the only way forward.

Carred was still staring into Marith's eyes as she answered, "We see this through."

"My mother's plan," Anskar said firmly. One more millstone for his overburdened soul.

Marith gave an almost imperceptible nod, and Carred broke eye contact, turning instead to Anskar, and kneeling.

"*Melesh-Eloni*," she said, her voice loud enough to carry.

At first a murmur rippled through the assembled Niyandrians. Exclamations and mutters of "*Melesh-Eloni*" and disbelieving stares and shakes of heads.

Then silence fell over the road. There was a grim determination in their eyes, as if Carred's show of submission, her allegiance, wasn't enough to convince them.

Anskar nodded his head to Carred, acknowledging her loyalty. He scanned the crowd, all too aware that his fate and the fate of Niyas depended on what he did next. He knew in his soul that Niyas would never relinquish him.

Without a word to Carred or Marith, he turned his back to them and faced the crowd.

Again he drew upon the dark-tide, and shadow armor coalesced and wreathed his flesh, and wings like black smoke unfolded behind him.

But it wasn't enough. He could see it in the Niyandrians' faces: hope warring with despair.

What did they know of sorcery? Anskar realized. To them, he could be a knight of the Order with powers they'd never seen before. They needed a sign he was Queen Talia's child.

And so he drove his senses downward, deep into the earth's crust and beyond, until he found the earth-tide. He drew on its power, and corruption and vileness flooded through him.

The buzz of utter exhaustion hammered at Anskar, but he couldn't give in to it now.

He wouldn't.

And then came an itch, something sharp prodding his awareness. Guilt. Contrition at what he was about to do. But Anskar ignored it. It was no small thing he'd done, no small thing what he was: the grandchild of a demon lord, the child of a necromancer queen, gifted control of both the earth- and the dark-tides, having escaped the abyssal realms and risen to this very peak, where these men and women were now looking to him for answers that would determine their fate. And the fate of Niyas.

There were no forks in the road before him.

Anskar sent the earth-tide outward, and it hungered. Invisible, corrupt tendrils slithered into the corpses of the slain. Order knights, Niyandrians—none of the dead were immune to its touch. He felt hooks of the tendrils bite, felt the cold rush of earth-tide sluicing through his insides.

And one by one, the dead rose until scores of corpses stood

among the survivors.

Then with a single thought, Anskar cut the earth-tide ties to the undead, and they crumpled to the ground.

At last the Niyandrians understood the abyssal gap that existed between them and their rulers. And were reminded of the promises made: eternal life for those who believed.

Hundreds of Niyandrian voices echoed Carred, chanting, "*Melesh-Eloni*," and all the Niyandrians bent a knee to Anskar.

END OF BOOK FOUR

TO MY READERS

As always, if you enjoyed the read, leaving a review supports the books and helps keep me writing! You can return to where you purchased the novel to review it or simply visit my website and follow the links: WWW.MITCHELLHOGAN.COM

There are also websites such as Goodreads where members discuss the books they've read or want to read or suggest books others might read: WWW.GOODREADS.COM/AUTHOR/SHOW/7189594.MITCHELL_HOGAN

If you never want to miss the latest book sign up here for my newsletter. I send one every few months, so I won't clutter your inbox. MITCHELLHOGAN.COM/NEW-RELEASE-ALERTS/

Having readers eager for the next installment of a series, or anticipating a new series, is the best motivation for a writer to create new stories. Thank you for your support and be sure to check out my other novels!

ABOUT THE AUTHOR

Photo copyright © 2018

When he was eleven, Mitchell Hogan received *The Hobbit* and the Lord of the Rings trilogy, and a love of fantasy novels was born. He spent the next ten years reading, rolling dice, and playing computer games, with some school and university thrown in. Along the way, he accumulated numerous bookcases' worth of fantasy and sci-fi novels and doesn't look to stop any time soon. For ten years he put off his dream of writing; then he quit his job and wrote *A Crucible of Souls*. He now writes full-time and is eternally grateful to the readers who took a chance on an unknown self-published author. He lives in Sydney, Australia, with his wife, Angela, and his daughters, Isabelle and Charlotte.

Printed in Great Britain
by Amazon